# REUNION

# BY ALAN DEAN FOSTER

## *Published by The Ballantine Publishing Group*

# REUNION

## A Pip & Flinx novel

## ALAN DEAN FOSTER

THE BALLANTINE PUBLISHING GROUP ■ NEW YORK

A Del Rey® Book
Published by The Ballantine Publishing Group

Copyright © 2001 by Thranx, Inc.

ISBN 0-345-41867-0

Manufactured in the United States of America

For my niece, Lauren Elizabeth Hedish
With love from Uncle Alan . . .

# CHAPTER

# 1

When bad people are chasing you, life is dangerous. When good people are chasing you, life is awkward. But when you are chasing yourself, the most simple facts of existence become disturbing, destabilizing, and a source of unending waking confusion.

So it was with Flinx, who in searching for the history of himself, found that he was once again treading upon the hallowed, mystic soil of the spherical blue-white womb among the stars that had given birth to his whole species. Only, the soil he was treading presently was being treated by those around him with something other than veneration, and a means of sourcing the information he hoped to uncover was still to be found.

Tacrica was a beautiful place in which to be discouraged. Sensitive to his frustration, Pip had been acting fidgety for days. An iridescent flutter of pleated pink-and-blue wings and lethal, diamond-backed body, she would rise from his shoulder to dart aimlessly about his head and neck before settling restlessly back down into her customary position of repose. As active as she was colorful, the mature female minidrag was the only thing he was presently wearing.

His nudity did not excite comment because every one of the other sun and water worshipers strolling or lying about on the seashore was similarly unclothed. In the human beach culture of 554 A.A., the superfluity of wearing clothing into the sea or along its edge had long been recognized. Protective sprays blocked harmful UV rays without damaging the skin, and frivolous, transitory painted highlights decorated bodies both attractive and past their prime. It was these often elaborate anatomical decorations that were the focus of admiring attention, and not the commonplace nakedness that framed them.

Flinx flaunted no such artificial enhancements, unless one counted the Alaspinian minidrag coiled around his neck and left shoulder. Such contemporary cultural accoutrements were as alien to him as the primeval grains of sand beneath his feet. Culturally as well as historically, he was an utter and complete stranger here. Nor was he comfortable among the throngs of people. With its still un-settled steppes and unexplored reaches, Moth, where he had grown up, was far more familiar to him. He was more at home in the jungles of Alaspin, or among the blind Sumacrea of Longtunnel, or even in the aggressive world-girdling rain forest of Midworld. Any-place but here. Anywhere but Earth.

Yet it was to Earth he had finally come for a second time, in search of himself. All roads led to Terra, it was said, and it was as true for him as for anyone else. Beyond Earth, the United Church had placed a moral imperative lock, an elaborate Edict, on all infor-mation about the Meliorares, the society of renegade eugenicists re-sponsible for whatever bastard mutation he had become. Travels and adventures elsewhere had left him with hints as to their doings, with fragmentary bits and pieces of knowledge that tantalized without satisfying. If he was ever going to unravel the ultimate secrets of his heritage, it was here.

Even so, he had been reluctant to come. Not because he was fearful of what he might find: He had long since matured beyond such fears. But because it was dangerous. Not only did *he* want to learn all the details of his origins: so did others. Because of contacts he had been compelled to make, the United Church was now aware of him as an individual instead of merely as an overlooked statistic in the scientific record. As high-ranking an official as thranx Counselor Second Druvenmaquez had taken a personal interest in the red-haired, bright-eyed young man Flinx had become. The novice beachgoer smiled to himself. He had left the irascible, elderly thranx on Midworld, slipping away quietly when the science counselor had been occupied elsewhere. When he eventually discovered that the singular young human had taken surreptitious flight, the venerable thranx would be irked. He would have to be satisfied with what little he had already learned, because neither his people nor anyone else would be able to track Flinx's ship, the *Teacher*, through space-plus.

Ever cautious, Flinx had decided for the moment to hew to the hoary principle that the best place to hide was in plain sight. What better place to do that than on one of the Commonwealth's twin world centers of government and religion, where he had come looking for information years ago? It was where he needed to be anyway, if he was ever going to find out the truth about himself. In addition to his burgeoning curiosity, there had come upon him in the past year a new sense of urgency. With the onset of full adulthood looming over him, he could feel himself changing, in slow and sometimes not-so-subtle ways. Each month, it seemed, brought a new revelation. He could not define all the changes, could not quarantine and assess every one of them, but their periodic nebulosity rendered them no less real. Something was happening to him, inside him. The self he had known since infancy was becoming something else.

He was scared. With no one to talk to, no one to confide in save a highly empathetic but nonsapient flying snake, he could look only to himself for answers—answers he had always wished for but had never been able to acquire. It was for those reasons he had taken the risk of coming back to Earth. If he was going to find what he needed to know, it lay buried somewhere deep within the immense volume of sheer accumulated knowledge that was one of the homeworld's greatest treasures.

But if he was *home*, as every human who came to Earth was supposed to be, then why did he feel so much like an alien? It bothered him now even more than it had when last he had visited here some five years ago.

He tried to wean himself from the troubling chain of thought. Belaboring the accumulated neuroses of twenty years would solve nothing. He was here on a fact-finding mission; nothing more, nothing less. It was important to focus his attention and efforts, not only in hopes of securing the information he sought, but in order to avoid the attention of the authorities. With the exception of the thranx Druvenmaquez and his underlings, who were specifically looking for him, what other agencies and individuals might also be interested in one Philip Lynx he did not know. It did not matter. Until he left the homeworld, a little healthy paranoia would help to preserve him— but not if he allowed his thoughts to float aimlessly, adrift in a distraught sea of incomplete memories and internal conflicts.

Of course, he might well secure answers to all the questions that tormented him by the simple expedient of turning himself in. Druvenmaquez or a specialist in some other relevant bureau would gladly take the plunge into the secrets of him. But once committed to such research, he would not be allowed to leave whenever it might please him. Guinea pigs had no bill of rights. Revealing himself might also expose him to the scrutiny of those he wished to avoid—the great trading houses, other private concerns, the possible remnants of certain heretical and outlawed societies, and others. Becoming a potentially profitable lab subject carried with it dangers of its own—a long, healthy, and happy future not necessarily being among them.

Somehow he had to discover himself *by* himself, without alerting to his presence the very authorities who might help alleviate his seemingly illimitable anxieties. And he had to do it quickly, before the changes he was experiencing threatened to overwhelm him.

For one thing, the unpredictable, skull-pounding headaches he had suffered from since childhood—the ones that caused blinding flashes of light behind his eyes—were growing worse, in intensity if not frequency. When and if it occurred, would he be able to tell the difference between a common headache and a cerebral hemorrhage? Would he be able to deal with the physical as well as the mental consequences of the changes he was undergoing? He needed answers to all the old questions about himself, as well as to the new ones, and he needed them soon.

Of all the billions of humans on all the settled worlds scattered across the vast length and breadth of the Commonwealth, no one could claim that "nobody understands me" with the depth of veracity of a tall young redhead named Philip Lynx, who was called Flinx.

Before setting his small transfer craft down at the Nazca shuttleport north of Tacrica, he had spent much time in free space planning his approach to the grand library that was Earth. First he had tried accessing the Shell, the free and omnipresent information network that spanned the globe, from one of the numerous orbiting stations that circled the planet. Unsurprisingly, the small segment he was

able to access from orbit had been devoid of all but the most fundamental, freely available birth information on the subject of himself—
save for one small historical reference to the destruction of the
outlawed Meliorare Society in 530, three years before his birth. That
information was already known to him. For what he wanted, for data
that was no doubt restricted, banned, or even under Church Edict, he
would have to probe much deeper.

That meant accessing in person one of the intelligence hubs that
sustained the Shell. The Commonwealth Church and Science hub
on Bali would have been ideal, but presenting himself at a highly
visible and tightly secured site that offered only restricted access to
the general public would have been asking for trouble—especially
since he had entered its corridors once before, seeking information
then only on the specifics of his birth. Ignorant of how widely and
well his current physical description might have been disseminated
to local authorities, it behooved him while conducting his research
on Terra to keep as low a profile as possible. That meant avoiding
the most famous and closely monitored centers of research.

Names and faces from his past congealed in the mirror that was
his memory. Did a padre named Namoto still roam the depths of Ge-
nealogy Sector on Bali? Was Counselor Second Joshua Jiwe still in
charge of security there? And where might a certain lissome thranx
named Sylzenzuzex be working these days? On the other side of the
vast ocean that lapped against his feet, which humans called the Pacific, remembrances lay like driftwood on a beach, waiting to be re-
examined. He forced all such thoughts from his mind. He could not
afford to present himself at the entrance to Church science headquarters for a second time in five years. Like it or not, whatever
research he chose to conduct would have to be done from afar.

Roaming the Shell from the comparative anonymity of the orbiting station, he had reduced the number of suitable hubs he might

safely visit to three. From centers in the Terran provinces of Kalahari, Kandy, and Cuzco, he chose the Shell hub at Surire, on the western slope of the mountain range called Andes. On-site access to the physical core was naturally off-limits to all but qualified personnel. But as with many such impressive, meaningful facilities, tours of its outer, less sensitive areas were offered to the public. They were deemed educational.

Wanting ardently to be educated, Flinx had taken one such tour. As expected, internal security, to which the tour guide casually alluded, was conspicuous. To penetrate both the facility and the knowledge it hopefully contained, he would need help. In order to secure it, he for one of the few times in his life prepared to use his talent not simply to receive, but to project. To perceive, and to then act upon those perceptions. Previously, he had done so only to defend himself against those intending to do him harm.

This time it made him feel, well, dirty.

It was why he was presently strolling along the beach at Point Argolla, well south of the highly developed mouth of the Garza River, with its amusement park and dedicated hotels that occupied choice sites both above and below the water. Though he was surrounded by hundreds of fellow sun worshipers, he did not feel comforted, or at home. The sooner he left this world of origins for the far reaches of Commonwealth space, the happier he would be. He did not like being here, and he liked what he was having to do even less.

Off shore, children frolicked in the gentle surf. The chilly waters of the northward sweeping Humboldt Current were warmed by excess heat outflow from the massive desalination plant to the south, but the transitory warmth extended only to a depth of four to five meters. Below this artificial thermocline, the life of the Pacific ebbed and flowed normally. Behind the beach, the fruit and vegetable gardens of the Atacama Desert rapidly gave way to the foothills of the high Andes. Known as Tacrica, the elongated beach resort was one of the least crowded on the continent. It well suited the multitudes that thronged to its shores in search of sun, fun, and sea. Like the rest of Earth, it did not suit Flinx. He had felt no sense of homecoming when he had set foot on its soil. No tears of upwelling, deep-seated feeling had been forthcoming from the redheaded, olive-skinned off-worlder. To him the Earth was nothing but a spherical clump of history circling a third-rate sun. From it he wanted answers, not spurious emotion. That much he had learned in the course of his previous, awkward visit.

Elena had told him where he could expect to find her. He perceived her before he saw her. The carefully memorized nodule of individual feminine emotions was as recognizable to his talent as the odor of day-old meat to a dog: tincture of mildly infatuated young woman. She had become interested in him not because he represented the partner she had been looking for all her life, not because he was some peerless paragon of manly virtues, but because he had projected those feelings onto her, mixing and applying them as precisely as an artist would lay paint on canvas.

Flinx was an empathetic telepath. When his inconsistent abilities were functioning, he had always been able to read the emotions of others. Within the past year he had discovered that his ever-mutating, apparently blossoming talent, while still only hardly less erratic than ever, could occasionally also be projected onto others. Using equipment on board his ship *Teacher*, he had even managed to measure the minuscule electrical discharges that were generated by specific moieties of his mind when he undertook such efforts. Understanding the actual neurophysical mechanism would require a great deal more study, as well as expertise he did not possess. One thing was not in dispute: It took considerable effort of will, of mental strain, for him to accomplish the feat.

At first it had been nothing more than a diversion, a game, a way to play with his disorienting intellect. Until recently, when he had been forced to use it to defend himself, it had not occurred to him that it might prove useful in other ways. And there was, as ever with his peculiar and still-undefined abilities, a good chance it would not work when he wanted it to. His talent had a wicked way of abandoning him just when he needed it most.

Such concerns had consumed him in the course of the tour of the Shell hub at Surire. In addition to viewing various aspects of the facility, the contented knot of tourists to which he had attached himself had been introduced to individual personnel at various stops along the tour. Maintenance, engineering, cryonics design, communications, cygenics—representatives of each department had paused in their daily duties to speak briefly to the members of the tour on the nature of their respective specialties.

Security had not been omitted.

In her spotless black-and-yellow uniform, Elena Carolles had methodically and without revealing sensitive detail explained the basics of the installation's security system to her attentive, transient guests. When she had finished, the visitors were allowed several moments to inspect for themselves a sealed room located beyond the nearest transparent immunity wall. Flinx did not avail himself of the opportunity. Instead, with deliberation and a sense of purpose that were as alien to his personality as he was to his present surroundings, he had wandered away from the chattering tour guide and over to their host for that domain. To her credit, she had not flinched away from the pet minidrag dozing on his shoulder. Instead, she had eyed them both with polite indifference. Her mind had been elsewhere, and it had been closed to him.

But her emotions had not been.

She was only a few years older than he and was vulnerable,

mildly insecure, and like many women her age, searching. Not for her inner self as much as for someone to complement her existence. He'd been able to feel it. Whether there already was someone in her life he did not know and had not been able to tell. He hoped not. It would complicate matters. Soaking up her feelings, he had categorized them each and every one, sorting them like cards. When he had felt he knew as much as there was to know about her emotional makeup, when he had been reasonably certain he knew where the buttons were and how to push them, he had extended himself in an effort of empathy to a degree he had never attempted before. It had made his head hurt, but he had persisted.

On his shoulder, Pip had suddenly looked up. The lethal little iridescent green head had begun to weave imperceptibly back and forth. Responding to the effort being put forth by her friend and companion, the minidrag's own mind had opened. Having few and simple emotions of its own, the unique and uncomplicated organ acted as a lens for Flinx's talent. She could enhance his ability to perceive. He had learned then that she could also heighten his capacity to project something less blatant than fear.

The security officer had blinked. A look of uncertainty tinged with surprise had palpated her face. Her expression had noticeably altered; she had stood as if struck by a sudden thought—or something else. A moment had passed before she turned to find a slim, green-eyed young man staring back at her. Flinx had smiled with just the proper degree of hesitancy. Though he had never enjoyed anything like a long-term relationship with any female except his adoptive parent Mother Mastiff, he *had* spent time in close contact with women—and other aliens. Lauren Walder, for example. Atha Moon, Isili Hasboga, Clarity Held—he dragged his thoughts back to the moment and away from entangling, fuzzy reminiscences. The officer's expression creased with invitation.

As the tour moved on, he had held back. Though his dawdling violated accepted procedure, the woman had not objected to his lingering presence. Her name, he had learned, was Elena Carolles. Each time he had spoken, his words had been accompanied by a subtle emotional push, conveyed through a carefully calculated mental pulse. Each time she had responded, a part of him had absorbed what she was feeling much as his ears took in what she was saying. It was an awkward seduction made harder by the dispatch with which it had to be carried out and by the fact that he had hated what he was doing. Not long ago, he had been compelled to project overwhelming terror in order to secure his freedom. What he had attempted with the security officer required greater subtlety applied with moderating force, lest he overwhelm his subject.

He had not tried to persuade her right then and there to allow him access to sensitive, security-controlled sections of the facility. The queries he needed to make were not yet thought out, and such haste would have caused the mentally swooning woman to react with dangerous instability. Besides, the guide for his tour would certainly have missed him the next time the man conducted a head count of his charges. It was enough that a relationship had been established and that she had agreed to meet him elsewhere and elsewhen. He had made careful note of the directions she gave him.

Now he fought to recall every potentially useful detail of their initial meeting as he swerved away from the water and walked toward the artfully orchestrated pile of boulders she had described to him in the course of their first contact. He experienced a moment or two of unease as he searched among the beach crowd without locating her face. Then he saw her, seated beneath a polarizing sunshade. He had not recognized her right away with her clothes off. Annoyingly, she was not alone.

The other woman appeared to be approximately the same age,

perhaps a year or two older. Neither was unpleasant to look upon, but Flinx had not extended himself on her behalf in search of sex. What he wanted from her was an entrée to information.

"Philip!" Espying him, Carolles sat up and smiled. "Arlette, this is my new friend, Philip Lynx."

The other woman regarded the unclothed young man standing before her with a critical eye. Sensing hostility beneath her neutral expression, Flinx summoned up feelings of inoffensiveness, safety, and goodwill, and strained to project them onto her. For a worrisome moment he feared his wandering talent had taken the morning off. Then the woman smiled. It was a confused smile, as if its owner was uncertain of its origins, but it would do.

Taking a seat beside them, he let Carolles chatter on, making small-talk while striving to convince the woman who was apparently her best friend of this new-won male's virtues. Though these were more imagined than factual, he did nothing to dissuade her from accepting them whole and entire. Pip stirred infrequently on his shoulder, luxuriating in the heat. Beyond the surf, all manner of recreational watercraft hummed silently as their owners raced them in intricate patterns.

Occasionally he would inject a few words into the conversation. These were always pleasant and innocuous, just enough to feign interest in what was being said and indicate that he was paying attention. Inside, he chafed at the need to muddle through such preliminaries. They were necessary, he knew, if only to persuade the security officer's friend of his benign intentions. Over the course of several hours this was accomplished through a combination of reassuring words from Carolles and a subtle empathetic push or two from the young man seated by her side. When the friend inquired as to his profession, he responded that he was a student living on a comfortable inheritance.

They went for a swim. They bought food from a passing, hovering robotic vendor. They discussed Commonwealth politics, about which Flinx cared little, and Church ethics, which interested him a little more. There was mention of travel, all of it Earth-bound, and he had to smile when they complained about the time and distances involved in getting from one place to another. His own voyaging he was used to measuring in parsecs, not kilometers.

It was a pleasant enough way to waste away a day, but his impatience prevented him from really enjoying the company of the two attractive young women. When Carolles's friend Arlette decided to go for a solar sail up the beach, Flinx was left alone with the security officer. It was time to make his move—one different from that which would in similar circumstances have been contemplated by any other male on the long, curving stretch of sand.

Idly, he picked at the grains, letting stars of mica and quartz trickle away between his fingers. "You must really like your job, Elena."

Lying on her back, she adjusted the sunscreen to let in more light and sky while continuing to filter out damaging rays. "It's a job. It's okay, I guess."

"A lot of responsibility." Slithering down his arm, Pip sampled the sand with her pointed tongue and flinched back sharply from its inedibility.

"Not so much," she disagreed. "We've never had any trouble at the facility. It's too out of the way. Anyway, sabotage and rebellion hasn't been in fashion for quite a while." Rolling over, she smiled affectionately up at him. Knowing that the source of the emotion she was projecting was involuntary, he felt the sudden need of absolution.

Grimly, he pressed on, a forced smile dominating his expression. "Well, I found it very interesting. The only problem is, I'd really like to see more. The public tour only hints at what lies beyond." Glancing up the beach, he was pleased to see that there was no sign of her friend.

"You're that interested in the mechanics of Shell administration?"

"I'm interested in everything," he told her truthfully. "It would mean a lot to me to be able to go inside, even if just for an hour or so."

Her smile flickered unsteadily. Sensing conflict boiling up within her, he exerted himself to suppress it. Pip twitched slightly. Elena's smile returned, though there were some signs of strain in her expression.

"I can't do that. You know I can't do that, Philip. It could mean my job."

His smile widened. "Aw, c'mon, Elena. I just want to have a little look around, see what you see. Access the Shell directly instead of from a remote for a few minutes. I'd be able to tell my grandkids about it. I won't touch anything sensitive," he lied flagrantly. He made himself edge nearer to her, bringing his face down toward hers. The dark eyes, the small mouth beneath him were close, vulnerable. Hating himself, he kissed her. Simultaneously, reading her like an open diary, he projected into her that which she most wanted to feel. What emotional defenses she still maintained collapsed beneath his effort. The back of his head throbbed mercilessly. He wanted to leave then, to stagger off to someplace private and dark, and retch.

Still smiling, he drew back from her. She was adrift in the throes of feelings she did not understand. That made sense, since they were not entirely hers.

"You can do it, Elena," he whispered tenderly. "It's such a little thing, and I promise I'll never ask it of you again." That much, at least, was true. "You can do it—for me."

Panting, her eyes half closed in false reverie, lids fluttering, she considered his request. "It might be possible—won't be easy." Her eyes flicked open. "I know! No one is allowed to wear security gear home, or even off hub grounds. We change in a locker room on site. If I can slip you in there, we can find you a uniform. There are always personnel changes, and transfers within the complex. It's much too big a place for every employee to know everyone else, even within individual departments. Over a period of days you'd be found out, but for a couple of hours—" She choked abruptly, one hand going to her bare throat.

Alarmed, he reached for her. "Elena! Are you all right?"

She swallowed hard several times in succession. "I think so. I guess so." Uncertainty returned to her smile, pulling at it like a bend in a high-speed thrill ride. "I just had the strangest feeling." The smile widened. "It's gone now."

It wasn't, Flinx knew, but it had been curbed. "I'd like to do it as soon as possible."

"Why the rush?" She gazed up at him out of limpid, dazed eyes.

"I don't want to give you time to change your mind." Reaching up, he stroked Pip's muscular length, and the minidrag all but purred. "Who knows? Next week you might not like me as much."

"Philip, you're different from anyone I've ever met." Wandering toward him, her fingers twined in his. "I can't imagine ever not liking you."

That's funny, he thought silently. I can.

# CHAPTER

# 2

She found room for him on an afternoon tour, but did not include him in the official count. Near the end, before the usual group of attentive seniors and noisy families and the occasional solo visitor were to be discharged, there came a moment when everyone's attention was diverted. Waiting impatiently while a door scanner read her retinas, she hurriedly slipped him through the resultant opening. No alarms sounded. As long as an on-duty officer accompanied them, guests from specialist repair technicians to visiting politicians regularly made use of such portals.

While Elena made her concluding presentation and individual farewells to the other members of the tour group, Flinx found himself in the empty locker room, checking idents on each individual cubicle until he found the one she had specified. Entering the unsecured module, he found himself surrounded by items that identified it as hers. Electrostatically suspended in a corner was a tenantless security officer's uniform. As he slipped into the one-piece garment he found himself wondering how she had acquired it. Borrowed it without asking, she had whispered naughtily to him, without going into details.

These did not really matter. He was *inside*. Idly examining the other items within the cubicle, he tried not to watch the time as he waited for her. Beneath the upper part of the uniform, Pip stirred against his shoulder. She sensed his nervousness, and he had to repeatedly murmur soothing whispers to quiet her.

After what seemed like an interminable wait but in reality was no more than a few minutes, Elena reappeared and beckoned for him to follow. Exiting the locker room via a different portal, he soon found himself within the heart of the Surire hub.

"Remember," she whispered to him, "if anyone challenges us, leave the talking to me. If someone addresses you directly, tell them that you're a transfer from Fourth Sector. There've been a lot of personnel changes there recently."

He nodded, only half hearing her. The greater part of his attention was devoted to the facilities they were passing, from small privacy-screened offices to larger chambers occupied by busy, silent technicians wearing identical absorbed expressions. Occasionally they would encounter another security officer. Elena would invariably smile at them, or wave in their direction. Once, she saluted. But no one challenged them.

They were now deep inside the ring of bone-dry, barren, ash-brown peaks that surrounded the flamingo-infested, alpaca-browsed salt lake that gave its name to the installation they were roaming. Outside, the sky was a painfully bright blue. Located five thousand meters above the not-very-distant, crowded beaches below, the Surire hub might as well have been on the moon. No towns congested its borders, no major transport venues meandered close to its high valley. It flaunted the exceptional isolation that was the hallmark of every one of its sibling facilities scattered around the planet.

Scanning their surroundings, she directed him quickly into an unoccupied office. In response to her softly murmured code string, the cubicle promptly erected a privacy screen, cutting them off both visually and aurally from the rest of the installation. Gathering unease showed in her face and he hastened to calm her.

"There you go." She indicated an empty chair. "Hurry up. I checked the work schedule last night, and this office is supposed to be unoccupied for another week. The tech who uses it is on vacation. No one has registered to use it in her absence, but you never can tell."

"I won't be long." He sounded hopeful as he settled himself into the chair. Slipping the induction band over his red hair, he glanced back at her. "I'm ready."

She nodded, the curtness of the gesture surprising her, and recited a string of verbal commands. Flinx felt the familiar slight warmth at the top and back of his head as the band read his E-pattern and established the requisite neural connection between himself and the station. On board the *Teacher*, he preferred to speak directly to the resident AI instead of using a wave band because he enjoyed hearing the sound of another voice besides his own. Here, verbal commands could be bypassed in favor of more direct neurological connections. In addition, he wanted to keep the exact nature of his inquiries concealed from his companion.

At his request, the planetwide citizens' Shell opened up before him. At the same time, he was well aware that the unit he was utilizing, while personally secure, was not coded exclusively to one user. If that were the case, others would not be able to make use of the office. The station was, after all, only a small component of a much greater machine. He did not expect to be able to peruse actual spools with the same degree of ease.

Behind him, Elena Carolles was struggling to suppress a growing alarm—and uncertainty.

"Hurry up, Philip."

He replied without looking back at her, concentrating on burrowing deeper into the Shell. "I thought you said this office wasn't scheduled for use."

"I know, I did." He could sense her undergoing the mental equivalent of a wringing of hands. "But you never know when someone might come along to run a service check, or just call in." She was looking around nervously. "This is crazy, Philip. The penalties for unauthorized use of restricted hub facilities are severe. How did I ever let you talk me into this? What do you want here, anyway? Come to think of it, I don't really know you, do I? It's only been a couple of days since we even met, and I . . . ."

Alerted to her companion's rising concern, Pip poked her head out from beneath the collar of his borrowed uniform. Turning in the chair, a compassionate Flinx regarded his suddenly apprehensive hostess. Tired. It had been a strenuous morning, a wearisome week. She was *so* tired. Or so he persuaded her, projecting an irresistible lassitude that overrode anything and everything else she might be feeling. When she leaned back against the wall of the office, and then slid down its unyielding length, and finally slumped over onto her side, he rose from the operator's chair to gently place a couple of seat pads beneath her head. Her emotional exhaustion reinforced through his exertions, she would sleep soundly for a while. By that time he hoped to be done with his search. Afterward, he need only maintain his empathic hold on her until they were safely out of the facility and back down among the swirling vacation crowds of Tacrica. Leaving her on a familiar street corner dazed and bewildered but otherwise unhurt, he would quietly vanish from her life forever.

That was for tonight. Presently, he had work to do.

She had already entered the necessary keywords. Entry had been parsed. Nothing more was required of him. Given the amount of security outside the cubicle, that was not surprising. Relevant authority had chosen to put its energies into screening out the unwanted and unauthorized before they could ever reach the interior of the hub. Having done so, it had been decided that there was no need to lavish on excessive redundancy within. Still, he was wary of overconfidence. So far he had only accessed hardware. The real test would come when he attempted to probe beyond levels that were open and accessible to the general public.

Automatically adjusting to the appropriate thought impulses from the human seated before it, the terminal imaged a flat page in the weft space above the desk projector. As required, this device could wrap space to produce any three-dimensional object required, from simple spheres and squares to complex maps and elaborate engineering diagrams. No such exotics were required by Flinx. In reply to his thoughts he hoped only for responsive words.

A glance backward showed that Elena Carolles was snoring softly. Directing the unit to respond verbally to specific commands, he double-checked the office's privacy curtain to make certain it was intact. With a flip of a mental switch, he could see out whenever he wished, but none of those striding past the cubicle could see in. Finding the unceasing procession of others a distraction, he directed the unit to opaque the curtain from within as well as without. Not a sound would escape the confines of the cubicle until he ordered it dropped.

Thus comfortably cocooned, he settled back in the chair, the induction band resting easily on his head, and started digging.

He began with a casual search of global news for 533: the year of his birth. Needless to say, his coming into the world had not been front-page news. A narrowing of focus to the Indian subcontinent yielded little except what he already knew from previous inquiries. Most of the headlines for the week when he had been born were full of news about the legendary Joao Acorizal winning the surfing competition on Dis. Having not expected to encounter anything startling, he was not prematurely disappointed. What he was trying to do was back into the information he sought without coming upon it directly, just in case any alarms were attached to specific files. A rambling, semirandom search was much less likely to attract unwanted attention.

The basic birth records for Allahabad were there, just as they had been when he had accessed them years earlier on Bali. But he was after other data this time, information dealing with a far more sensitive subject. From 533 he skipped unobtrusively backward to 530, spiraling in on his subject like a raven dropping down on road-kill. And there they were: several small articles on the discovery and subsequent exposure of the Meliorare Society and its illegal, outrageous work in eugenics. As he devoured the details of the Society's unmasking, the arrest of its members, and the removal of their unwitting "experiments" to an assortment of homes, hospitals, and medical laboratories, he felt as if he were sitting in witness to his own creation.

Some of the information was known to him. Some was new. During his previous visit to Earth he had researched only his birth history, knowing nothing then about the Meliorare Society, its experiments and misshapen aims, and how they related to him. When he came across the uncensored details of the euthanasia that the authorities had been compelled to carry out on the Society's least successful "procedures," his spine went cold and Pip stirred uneasily. In addition to the cool, detached prose of the report there were accompanying visuals: disturbing images, of twisted bodies housing tormented minds. Forcing himself, he deliberately enlarged the most grotesque. Out of eyes overflowing with anguished innocence, fear and terror and uncomprehending madness spilled forth in profusion unbounded. He forced himself to look at them, to not turn away. Any one of them, he knew, might be relations; distant genetic cousins hideously deformed through no fault of their own.

For the most severe cases there was no future save a quick and mercifully painless death. For those deemed sufficiently undamaged, the government provided new identities and lives. These nominally healthy survivors were scattered across the Commonwealth so that any lingering, undetected genetic time bombs implanted in their DNA by the Society would be dispersed among the species as widely as possible. Even those considered normal would be subject to scrutiny by the authorities for the rest of their natural lives.

Eventually, it was solemnly intoned in one article, all would die out, and the potentially injurious effects of the Meliorares' nefarious gengineering would pass harmlessly into history.

Except—at least one participant in the Meliorares' work had escaped the attention of the pursuing authorities long enough to give birth. Her history and that of her offspring had thus far escaped the notice of the otherwise relentlessly efficient monitors. Somehow evading their attention, raised on the backward colony world of Moth by a kindly old woman with no children of her own, he had matured unobserved by Commonwealth science. Now he stood on the brink of adulthood, gazing back at what little scraps he could scrape together of his personal history. Conceived in a laboratory he might have been, but he still had parents. The egg had belonged to a live woman named Ruud Anasage, the sperm to an unknown man, even if the ingredients had subsequently been stirred and shaken and diced and spliced by the well-meaning but wildly eclectic Meliorares. He wanted to know everything about them, especially the still unknown sperm donor—his father. And he wanted to know the specifics, insofar as they might be possible to know, of his own individual case and what the Meliorares had hoped to achieve by manipulating the innermost secrets of his fetal DNA. Possessing only hints, he sought certainty.

He probed further, combining keywords from the reports with what he already knew. This was dangerous. If there were alarms posted on such information, cross-correlating might well trigger them.

Tunneling deeper into the most detailed of the correspondence, he found himself searching actual original source material. That led him from the media siever that had compiled the report to central Commonwealth science repositories on Bali and in Mexico City. Newly emergent warnings were followed by implacable lockouts. Utilizing skills sharpened from months of working with the sophisticated system on board the *Teacher*, he bypassed them all. Disappointingly, much of the material he ultimately scanned was useless, or repetitive. So far, he was tempting grave danger for very little reward.

One file was disarmingly demarcated "Meliorares, Eugenics, History." It appeared to contain material already perused, but it remained sealed under the by now familiar heavy security. He fiddled, and tweaked, and wormed his way in. As expected, he found himself scanning well-known information, dry and indifferently transcribed. Public sybfiles and footnotes of equal content mentioning his birth mother's name—nothing new, nothing revelatory. Among his hopes, boredom proposed to frustration: a terminal matrimony. Perhaps he really had seen everything there was to see about his personal history during his previous visit to Earth and to the science center on Bali.

He drifted into a sybfile labeled "Relationships, Crossovers,

Charts." Cruising effortlessly, he gave a mental push. Nothing happened. The syb stayed shut even though its security overlay seemed unexceptional. But he could not get in. Then something very interesting happened.

It went away.

Sitting up straighter in the chair, he gaped at the screen. All the rest of the relevant information was there—unchanged, unaltered, freely available for his perusal. But the last sybfile had vanished. In its place, not unlike a masticating ruminant, it had left a pile of something behind, and moved on. To the inexperienced or unsophisticated, the new object looked just like the syb it had replaced. Flinx, however, knew exactly what it was: an alarm.

A whole bunch of alarms.

Very, very carefully, operating with the utmost delicacy of which he was capable, he directed the search unit to back off. The alarms remained in place, subtle in stature, undisturbed, their true nature artfully disguised. He had trod on something sensitive, and it had responded with a quiet growl. As he maneuvered around the lambent little land mine, playing the Shell like a finely tuned instrument, he examined the intricate knot of toxic tocsins with every scanning tool at his disposal. The appearance of the camouflaged alarms did not unsettle him half so much as the disappearance of the syb. Only when he felt more comfortable with what he was seeing, and in control, did he take the risk of querying the Shell AI directly as to what had happened. Its reply was instructive.

"What sybfile?"

The Shell's memory was infallible. Therefore it was deliberately ignoring his query, or following instructions to avoid making a direct reply to the question, or an independent component of itself was overriding the nuclear command structure. He had stumbled onto something that somebody thought important enough to pretend did not exist.

Settling himself, Flinx ran through a series of thought commands designed to restore the syb while avoiding the elegant subset of alarms that had taken its place. When that failed, he exited the system, reentered, and repeated his search, replicating the tunneling sequence precisely. It made no difference. The sybfile never reappeared, and the camouflaged alarms reasserted themselves in its place. Bringing up the subject had shut down access to the information it contained, for how long he did not know. It might reappear in a matter of hours, or days, or not for months. It didn't matter. He had none of those time periods to spare. His operational time frame was being ticked off by the soft snores of the woman sleeping on the floor behind him. If he was ever going to have the opportunity to access that particular sybfile again, it was now.

But how? No matter what route he plumbed, no matter how artful his probing, every attempt led only to the cloaked clump of alarms that he dared not make contact with directly. And the AI continued to insist that the information he sought did not exist. Or at least, the relevant Shell search module so insisted. Could he appeal to the central AI itself? Would that set off any alerts, or would he simply be denied access? Behind him, Elena Carolles shifted in her sleep. Whatever he did, it would have to be done quickly.

Over the past half dozen centuries, artificial intelligences had grown remarkably sophisticated. Like any other intelligence, they varied considerably in capacity, from tiny devices that monitored domestic needs to immense networks of intricately modulated electronic pulses that came close to mimicking the function of the human or thranx brain. Of necessity, a global shell ranked near the top of the intelligence pyramid in depth and functionality. Approaching it with logic and engineering skill had produced only frustration. Might there be another way?

A truly advanced AI, like the Shell, was built to comprehend and cope with human emotions as a natural and expected consequence of the billions of queries it had to deal with daily. Like thoughts, these feelings were conveyed via the transducer circuitry packed into the headband resting on Flinx's skull. When his talent was functioning optimally, he could read the emotions of others from a goodly distance.

There had been a time in his recent past when he had "communicated" on an unknown level with another incredibly complex machine. That device had been of alien manufacture. He remembered very little of the encounter and still less of the inscrutable neuronic interchange that had taken place. However it had been accomplished, the mental reciprocation had saved his life and those of his companions of the moment. Whether an advanced human-fabricated AI was capable of similar cerebral intercourse or of generating anything akin to "emotions" was a question that had been much debated, particularly in light of thranx-aided design advances that had been made in the last hundred years. Some cyberneticists said yes, others were vehement in their denial, and still others were not certain one way or the other.

One way to find out was to ask, and try to read behind the verbalizations that responded to his inquiry.

"I really need that particular sybfile," he murmured lucidly as he provided the relevant loci of the object in question.

The Shell responded with a polite verbalization. "The informational object to which you refer does not exist."

He repeated the query several dozen times. By the thirtieth, he thought he might be sensing something beyond the rote response. What *was* that there, elusive among the sounds? Something in his mind. His thoughts were sharp, his talent svelte and penetrating as a blade. Resolutely, he ignored the pounding that had begun at the back of his head and the occasional flash of bright light that obscured his vision.

"I know the syb exists. I saw it, briefly, unopened. I know it's there, somewhere beyond the alarm cluster that has taken its place. You *have* to help me. I know that you can. You just have to want to."

"The sybfile to which you refer . . ." The artificial voice halted prior to conclusion. Flinx held his breath. "The sybfile to which . . ." the voice in the shielded office began again, only to once more terminate prematurely.

*"Please,"* Flinx pleaded. "You *know* the syb I want is there. There's no reason not to show it to me. You can't pretend it doesn't exist when I've already seen it. Bring it back. I won't keep it long. I promise. No harm will come to the system. It's only one little, tiny, harmless syb. Comply. Do what you were designed to do. I'm a citizen, desperately seeking. *Help me.*"

"The sybfile . . ." the voice of the Shell began again. Suddenly, Flinx felt something in his head that was not a preverbalization. Thoughts could roil, and so could emotions. Staring at the floating screen, he strained to project, straining harder with his ability than he ever had with Elena Carolles. The pounding advanced from the rear of his skull to the median. Pain shot through him, and he winced. Alarmed, Pip stuck her head out from beneath his shirt and searched for a danger that existed only within her rangy companion. Her small, bright eyes were twitching.

"This is an unauthorized override of system procedure." Within the chair, Flinx hardly dared move. "I am required to generate a record, citizen. The sybfile in question is restricted. Anything beyond its name lies under Church Edict."

Flinx exhaled. It was a warning sufficient to frighten away most, but not him. He had violated Church Edict before, and successfully. What was more important was that he had wormed a first, critical byte of knowledge out of the Shell.

"Then you concede the existence of the sybfile. This contradicts your previous—" He checked a marker. "—thirty-two statements delivered in response to the same question."

"I am required to generate a record." The AI paused, neither volunteering any additional information nor denying its interrogator's conclusion.

When would that record draw the attention of those responsible for supervising the accuracy and operational functionality of the Shell? Flinx wondered. His circumscribed time was growing shorter.

"Show me the syb in question. The original, not the alarmic. Show it to me *now*. Please," he added after a moment's thought.

"I cannot. The sybfile requested is under Edict. You do not show appropriate clearance for access."

Quickly, Flinx composed a response. "But you *know* that I have to view it. You're sensitive enough to tell that, aren't you?" Once again, fighting back tears that the pain in his head squeezed from his eyes, he fought to make the AI understand the depth of his request. To see his need. To *empathize*.

"I will have to generate a report," the voice of the Shell declared uncertainly.

"That's fine. Generate all the reports you want. Let someone in authority read and rule on its contents. But *I need to see the contents of that file*, and I need to see them *right now*, here, this minute. Please, *please,* bring it up. I *know* that you understand."

Something flowed through Flinx that he did not comprehend. This was understandable, because it was highly probable that no one else had ever felt anything quite like it before. If it was whatever passed for cybernetic empathy, he could not have identified it as such. It came and went in a twinkling, and then was gone.

In its place was one more syb identifier among hundreds, alive within the depths of the floating screen. There was no mistaking its identity. As near as he could tell, no twitchy alarms parasitized its boundaries. It was exactly as he had seen it originally, unaugmented and unchanged. Supporting his pounding head with one hand while wiping tears from his eyes with the back of the other, a quietly triumphant Flinx tersely directed his thoughts at the bright green tiara of an induction band that crowned his head.

"Open it."

The tiny image brightened; a minuscule flare of activation. The hovering screen flickered infinitesimally. And went blank. Part of Flinx sagged while the rest of him surged with anger. So *close*.

"What's this? What happened? I told you to open the sybfile."

The reply of the Shell AI was as prompt as it was incomprehensible. "As you requested, the Edicted informational object in question has been opened."

A bewildered Flinx tried to make sense of this response. Easy . . . careful, he told himself. The AI was not being obstinate, nor had it hesitated. Could it lie so serenely and effectively? But why bother to do so, when it could simply have continued to deny the existence of the sybfile, or at the last, refused to open it?

"The syb is open?"

"That is correct. I am required to generate a report." Evincing neither hostility nor reluctance, the Shell waited patiently for further instruction.

Perhaps there was nothing insidious going on here, Flinx decided. Maybe the AI was being straightforward as well as truthful.

"The syb appears to contain no information," Flinx remarked.

"That is not true. Do you wish me to conduct a search of contents?"

Flinx knew the AI would not look at the interior of the file unless instructed to do so. It was not interested. Its task was to search and find, not waste time perusing. "I do."

"Here is the information."

Flinx leaned forward eagerly. The pain in his head was receding slightly. He read:

CONTENTS REMOVED—OUTDATED MATERIAL

He took a deep breath. Something here was very, very wrong. First the Shell had found and brought forth the sybfile. When Flinx tried to access its contents, it vanished, to be replaced by a sophisticated alarm manifold and a stinging warning to avoid the site altogether. Now that he had succeeded in accessing it, he found it contained nothing more than a simple declaration of truancy.

Why maintain such an elaborate system of dissimulation, threat, and protection to guard material that was no longer worth maintaining? It made no sense. Given the virtually unlimited storage capacity of the global Shell, why delete *any* potentially useful material from anywhere? And Flinx had no doubt the recalcitrant syb contained potentially interesting material.

"Full fragment search," he ordered.

The AI complied. "The sybfile contains no more information."

"But it once did!"

"That is so. The additional material has been deleted."

Though he thought it bound to trigger an alarm, Flinx pressed ahead. There was no point in trying to sustain the illusion of discretion any longer. "When, and on whose authority?"

"You do not possess sufficient clearance to have access to that information."

As he persisted, Flinx wondered what would happen first: Would he finally get some answers, or would his head explode from the effort of the exertion? Once more, he implored the AI. The pause that ensued was too long, and he debated whether it was, at last, time to flee the facility.

"Something is not right. There are errors within the fragmentary operational matrix of this sybfile."

Flinx sat up a little straighter. "Pursue and investigate. What sort of errors?"

"I am processing." In order to better communicate with humans and thranx, the Shell AI was designed to mimic as well as comprehend emotions. It managed to give a good impersonation of confusion. Or perhaps, Flinx thought, mimicry had nothing to do with it.

"There are a number of alarms functioning as placeholders. I am disarming them." Another pause, then, "This is most distressing."

"What? What's distressing?" Behind Flinx, the somnolent security officer snuffled in her sleep. "The alarms?"

"No. I have progressed several levels beyond their sensitivity. As previously stated, the sybfile in question has been deleted—but the echo of the procedure strongly suggests that the transfer string that was employed is counterfeit."

Eyes half shut, Flinx frowned at the screen. "I don't understand."

"The removal was not carried out by an authorized government agency. Residue within the syb ghost suggests the utilization of a renegade probe."

Flinx's heart sank. "Then the information was destroyed."

"No. Transferred. The syb was removed, leaving only an echo behind. This is highly illegal. I must generate a report."

"Yes, yes," Flinx commented hurriedly, "but first—can you trace the transfer? Can you find out where the information originally contained in the syb was sent?"

"The echo has been very skillfully fabricated. Anyone attempting to access the sybfile would be fooled into believing that a legal transfer had taken place, or would activate the replacement alarms."

"But not you," Flinx observed.

"I am the Monitor. I am the Terran Shell. Counterfeits do not escape me. I shall examine the residue."

Flinx was left to ponder furiously. Who would want access to the kind of information the syb under investigation was likely to contain? And if these persons unknown had succeeded in accessing it successfully, why go to the trouble of removing it from the Shell? The fact that it was under Edict should be enough to discourage anyone else from tampering with the structure of the sybfile itself. Yet someone had gone to the trouble not only of circumventing the powerful prohibitions against accessing, but of removing the information and leaving alarms in its stead. Who would do such a thing? Who had the need, the desire, and the resources?

The Meliorares? But the last of them had been selectively mindwiped long ago. Their disgraced organization was but a memory, their intentions dishonored, their members scattered. Had the authorities missed unregistered disciples who were even now wandering about the Commonwealth, intent on resurrecting that long quiescent, notorious research? Who else would go to such trouble?

"There is a trail. It is very faint," the AI declared.

"Can you trace it?" Flinx felt his hopes evaporating in the intangibility of cyberspace.

"Not only faint," the Shell AI continued as if it had not heard, "but cleverly disguised. There are many false echoes. However," it added briskly, "while these have been fashioned with skill, they employ known commercial technology. I am reviewing options. This will take a few seconds."

Words appeared on the floating screen. *LARNACA NUTRITION.* Flinx stared at them. They were not supplemented.

"This restricted sybfile that supposedly doesn't exist, that was placed under Edict and was subsequently illegally lifted and replaced by sophisticated alarms, it was done by a *food company*?"

"Do you wish me to examine the totality of the commercial concern identified as the transfer site?"

"Yes, dammit!"

"This will take a few nanoseconds. Yes—Larnaca Nutrition is a specialty foods concern with multiworld interests. Rated moderate to moderate-small within its industry. Makers of Caszin Chips, Havelock Power Bars, Poten . . ."

An impatient, frustrated Flinx interrupted. *"What happened to the syb?"*

"The illegally removed information under discussion was transferred to the headquarters offices of the company in question and absorbed by its confidential industrial shell."

It was difficult for Flinx to imagine outlawed Meliorares working in the commercial food business. He decided to hypothesize motives later. "Where in the company shell is the file now? Can you access it?"

"Processing." After a pause that lasted longer than the customary few seconds, the AI replied. "The stipulated sybfile is not there. It was, but was almost immediately retransferred out."

Was there ever to be an end to this road? Flinx wondered tiredly. How much longer did he have before someone at the Surire installation decided to check on who was using the office, or before Elena Carolles woke up?

"Can you track it to its present location?"

"There is residue." A pause, then, "I can track it to its last known location, but cannot access it."

"Why not?" Still agitated, Pip stirred beneath his shirt.

"Because it has been shifted off-world, and I can only access files within this stellar system."

A ship! The AI confirmed Flinx's suspicions. That was the end of it, then. Not even a system as powerful as the Terran Shell could access another AI beyond the orbit of Neptune. Not without a special space-minus hookup, and that would only put it in touch with a Shell on another inhabited world. The ship that held the precious syb was truly beyond reach.

But not, perhaps, beyond identification. He made the request.

"The terminus of my search string indicates that the ship shell aboard the commercial KK-drive freighter *Crotase* was the last to hold the illegally transferred sybfile."

The trail was cold, then, but not dead, Flinx decided stoically. "Where is the vessel in question at this time?" he inquired sternly. "Can you locate its position by accessing company files?"

The AI's reply was not encouraging. "That would constitute an illegal intrusion into the records of a private commercial concern."

Once again Flinx strained to make the AI feel, to make it understand. "I *have* to know. You are only following up on an already documented violation of the law." He brightened at a sudden thought. "These details will be necessary in order for you to generate a proper report."

"Yes, that is so. This will take several seconds. There are the usual commercial-industrial safeguards. I can bypass them."

"This *Crotase*, it's in orbit?" Flinx inquired hopefully. The AI's reply was not encouraging.

"According to the information I have accessed, it is outbound from Earth and should presently be in space-plus."

One last hope, one last chance. "Destination?"

"A moment. The safeguards on such information are particularly strong. There. The commercial freighter *Crotase* is on course via the Hivehom vector for the Analava system, Goldin IV, Largess, and Pyrassis."

"I recognize most of those worlds." Flinx's knowledge of galographics had improved considerably in the course of his past several years' wanderings. "But not Pyrassis. That name is unfamiliar to me."

"That is not surprising. The entire itinerary is rigidly coded and coated to provide the maximum security of which its generator is capable. The name itself is not given. I have deduced it from the scrambled coordinates that originated within the ship *Crotase*'s own AI."

"Can you show me the itinerary?"

"Processing." Within seconds the flat screen floating before Flinx was replaced by a three-dimensional spherical map of the portion of the outer galactic arm that contained the Commonwealth. Tiny lights brightened within and names floated benignly beneath them. There was the well-known Analava system and there the colony world of Goldin IV. Farther still from Earth, the outpost world of Largess. And beyond—much beyond—a world identified as Pyrassis. Flinx leaned forward, his hands gripping the arms of the chair whose malleable material fluxed to accommodate his tightening grasp. No wonder he had never heard of Pyrassis.

The final destination of the Larnaca Nutrition company ship *Crotase* lay within the borders of the AAnn Empire.

# CHAPTER

# 3

Slowly, Flinx settled back into the chair. It relaxed, but he did not. What in the name of all the topologic inversions of space-minus was going on here? Commonwealth vessels intruded on Empire space on pain of instant obliteration. Military craft in the spatial vicinity traveled with caution, and usually in pairs. Even the neutral Torsee Provinces were dangerous to visit without special permission from both governments. A vanilla-plain commercial craft like the *Crotase* simply did not go to such places.

Was it under the control of the Meliorares, or some as-yet-unidentified philosophical progeny of theirs? Were they, or someone else within innocent-appearing Larnaca Nutrition, cooperating with the AAnn? A sardonic smile curved his mouth. Had the remorseless reptilian AAnn suddenly developed an insatiable craving for cheap human snack food? None of it made any sense.

It was too much to try and comprehend. The lengthening thread was too knotted to unravel. He needed to focus on the contents of the stolen syb. All the rest was incidental, and could be sorted out later.

Removing a chyp from a pocket, he inserted it into the appropriate receptacle on the desk. The tiny slip of activated nanostorage would hold all the information he might need. Idly, he wondered what a "chyp" had originally been. Like much else, the derivation of the colloquial name for any form of portable storage was lost in the mists of technological antiquity.

"Transfer ship *Crotase* itinerary and plotting."

"That would be stealing." The voice of the AI was maddeningly calm. "There could be adverse consequences. I have no authority, and neither do you."

"A crime has already been committed here." Flinx was running out of patience, and out of time. "And not by me. You have reports to generate. To ensure confirmation of factual material it would be useful for the authorities, when they have been properly alerted, to have access to witnesses. That would be me."

"I do not require witnesses. My storage is inviolate."

"You don't, but live human judges like to have them around during judicial proceedings. My memory does not begin to approach yours. To refresh it for the benefit of the authorities, I should have my own access to all relevant material. Please initiate copy."

The AI seemed to hesitate. "You argue persuasively. Remember that I will retain a record of this conversation, and that together with all other relevant material it will, when requested, be reported to the authorities."

"I acknowledge," Flinx responded with a wave of one hand. He felt free to agree to anything since he had no intention of sticking around to suffer the consequences of his actions.

"Very well. Initiating transfer."

Half a world away, in a sizable commercial complex located on the eastern edge of the Bangalore Economic Ring Number Three, the dominant information AI on the planet sucked a minuscule, seemingly insignificant syb out of the depths of a Ranglou Level Eight industrial AI server. Within seconds, self-activating switches buried deep in the matrix of the Ranglou unit reacted. Only the fact that the much more powerful Shell AI operated in terms of nanoseconds prevented a catastrophe of scandalous proportions. As it was, the retort expressed by the Ranglou manifested far faster than could have been expected. It responded with a speed and to a degree more appropriate to the military than to an elemental commercial facility.

Destruction raced through cyberspace, searing dozens of pathways and obliterating routings as the incendiary reaction bundled within the incognizant Ranglou tried to track the intruding thief to its source. The application was absolutely fearless, smashing through safeguards and shields as if they did not exist. Humble distance was all that prevented further damage.

At first, nothing appeared amiss to Flinx. The floating screen and galactic map continued to hover before him, the Shell AI's presence awaiting further commands. Reaching forward, he removed the nanostorage device from its holder. A quick perusal showed that, as requested, material had indeed been transferred. Placed in the proper slot back on his ship, it would deliver the same information to the *Teacher*'s own AI, would insert the *Crotase*'s coordinates and itinerary into his vessel's navigation system.

An instant after he had removed the chyp, the receptacle crackled. Several actinic yellow flames shot from the orifice, making him jump. Bursting from beneath his shirt, Pip hovered in midair above his shoulder, searching for the source of the disturbance.

"Easy, girl," Flinx murmured. To the AI he inquired, "What was that?"

"A moment. I am processing. There is some unforeseen difficulty with concluding the connection recently established on your behalf. I must terminate the link now in order to—"

The floating screen vanished. So did the spherical map. In their place, a small sphere of refulgent yellow appeared. No bigger at first than Flinx's nose, it ballooned rapidly. A rising hiss filled the cubicle. Behind him, a groggy Carolles had begun to stir.

Eyes wide, Flinx rushed to her side, knelt, lifted her up, and placed her in a safety carry across his shoulders. Hastily deactivating the privacy screen, he stepped out of the cubicle into the nearest corridor. An approaching clerk saw him and frowned at the tall young man's softly moaning burden.

"Hey, what's going on here? What's wrong with—?" Catching sight of the rapidly bloating ball of yellow light that filled the now laid open office, he broke off his questioning as his lower jaw fell. Legs pumping, Pip darting to and fro above his head like a berserk component broken loose from a holoed advertisement for a nearby zoo, Flinx brushed past him.

"Run!"

Confused, the clerk turned to shout at the younger man's retreating back and the comatose security officer bouncing on his shoulders. "Why? Hey, who are you? What is that thing, anyw—?"

Whatever it was, the murderous application that had been bundled within the bowels of the commercial Ranglou shell managed to generate a reaction half a world away. The ball of yellow light suddenly expanded exponentially and blew up with stunning violence.

Despite his limp, now periodically moaning burden, Flinx had already traversed the main portion of the complex and was heading for the nearest clearly marked exit when the bloated clandestine energile that filled the now vacant cubicle detonated. Within an important facility like the Surire hub, he reassured himself, there ought to be enough self-activating defense mechanisms to prevent any significant loss of life or serious damage. As he strained under his increasingly heavy feminine encumbrance, he found himself hoping fervently that it was so. In his quest to learn more about himself he willingly accepted the need to lie, dissemble, invent, and conceal. The thought that he might be responsible for one or more innocent deaths did not appeal to him.

Sirens, whistles, and all manner of aural and visual alarms generated a phantasmagoria of aroused sight and sound around him. Occasionally he encountered other security officers, racing to secure the infracted sector. They ignored him. And why not? he mused as he ran. He was dressed as one of their own, carrying an apparently injured comrade to safety. It was beginning to look as if he would make good his escape, provided he was not first stopped and forced to accept an award for bravery.

The further he fled from the theater of havoc, the fewer security personnel he encountered. Grim-faced officers gave way to bewildered technicians and stunned administrators. Praying that Pip would remain hidden beneath his shirt where she had finally settled, he rounded a corner and found himself slowing to wait for an automatic door to open before him. While the highly evolved systems that restricted entry to the complex were exacting, there was little impediment to departure. Within moments he found himself in a covered transport garage, surrounded by individual vehicles of all descriptions, from the expensive and elaborate to the simple and prosaic.

Crouching, he eased Carolles off his shoulders and onto the rubbery floor of the chamber, sitting her up against a parked and locked vehicle. She was coming around quickly, and he decided that it would be safe to leave her. His energetic persuasion of her feelings should leave her none the worse for the experience. Not physically, anyway.

Half a world away, a passing clerk frowned uncertainly at the luminous glow that was emerging from beneath the door of an executive office. The light was intensely yellow, far brighter than elementary room illumination demanded. Pausing, he put a tentative hand on the door plate, not really expecting it to respond. But it was unlocked, and the barrier slid efficiently aside at his touch.

Within the room, there was only the yellow glow, fierce as a newborn sun and cool as glass made of gold. The clerk had only seconds in which to appreciate the rapidly dilating phenomenon before it erupted in his face. He vanished, annihilated instantly together with the yellow-fluxed office, the floor on which it resided, and a significant portion of the regional executive headquarters of Larnaca Nutrition. The resulting conflagration closed a good-sized portion of the commercial estate on which the enterprise was located, and kept numerous units of the Bangalore fire department busy for the rest of that day and well on into the early hours of the night as they fought to put out the yellowish-tinted inferno that stubbornly refused to be extinguished. When they finally succeeded, there was very little left of the central core of the main administration building, and certainly nothing for exceedingly curious forensics experts to trace.

Within the capacious garage, Flinx was waiting for Carolles to revive to the point where he would feel safe in abandoning her to whomever might follow in his footsteps. He decided that time had come when she opened her eyes, gaped disconcertedly at him, and started screaming for help.

"Elena, it's me, Philip!" Startled by the unexpected violence of her reaction, he moved back out of her reach. She continued to claw in his direction, trying to rise from her seated position, using the vehicle against which she had been leaning to push against. She did not immediately succeed. Command of her neuromuscular system was not quite back to normal, and her legs refused to obey.

"You bastard! What did you do to me?" Her face reflected anger, fear, and a profound sense of disorientation. "Where are we? What are you doing here?" Looking past him, she exclaimed, "Why are we at the hub? And what are you doing in the uniform of a security officer?"

"You agreed to help me. Don't you remember?" As he spoke, Flinx continued to enlarge the space between them.

"No, I—wait, yes. I do remember something." Reaching up, she clutched at her head. She was swaying slightly, balancing against the vehicle. "I—I was in love with you. Or thought I was." Looking up, she blinked bewilderedly. "The question is—why?" She shook her head slowly from side to side. "You're a pleasant enough guy, but all of a sudden I can't remember why I thought you were anything special."

"Just think back, Elena. It will come to you." Smiling reassuringly, Flinx strove to once more project feelings of unbridled warmth and affection onto the security officer, to again induce within her that sense of fondness and respect he had inculcated in her for the past several days.

With a cry, and in spite of her unsteady condition, she launched herself at him.

As it had so many times before, his eccentric, unpredictable talent had chosen not to function just when he needed it the most.

Sensing the attack, Pip was up and out of concealment before Carolles could reach her master. At the sight of the flying snake, hovering like a gigantic, iridescent, deep-throated hummingbird before her, the security officer slewed to a halt.

"That thing—is it poisonous?"

"You could say that." Flinx replied softly, gravely understating his winged companion's lethal capabilities.

Cautiously, Carolles edged around man and minidrag. Both

turned to track her progress, Pip pivoting gracefully in midair. The pointed tongue flicked in and out repeatedly, sampling the emotion-filled atmosphere.

He needed to stop her, Flinx knew. As more untailored emotions regained ascendancy over those he had imprinted on her, the readier she would be to report everything she could recall to her superiors. Fortunately, those worthies were presently occupied in dealing with an egregious breach of hub security. With luck, she might not gain a hearing for her fears and suspicions for several days. By then he would be gone—not only from Surire and Tacrica, but from the overcrowded, claustrophobic, superannuated world that had given birth to his species.

Whirling, she turned and ran, racing back in the direction of the violated hub. So much for love at first sight, he thought compla-cently as he turned his attention to the vehicle against which she had been leaning. Time and circumstance never failed to mute his won-der at the use to which he was invariably able to put his youthful skills as a thief. Within the space of two minutes he was safely in-side the private vehicle and speeding out of the garage.

The compact air-suspension transport was preprogrammed to travel to an unknown destination. Anyone who attempted to tamper with the secured navigation system risked pinpointing the stolen vehi-cle for local authorities. Better to accept a trip to whatever destination it was now accelerating toward than run the risk of attracting addi-tional, unwanted attention, he decided. With luck, it would soon com-mence the steep but safe descent from Surire, heading for the bustling resort community on the coast below. Or perhaps it would turn inland, toward Lapaz. He would be content with either destination.

It chose neither. Instead, he found himself traveling almost due west, toward the edge of the Andes. Unfamiliar with any part of the region save that he had already traversed, he had no idea where he was headed. His concerns were only partly alleviated by the fact that his ride in ignorance was not interrupted, and was unexpectedly brief.

"Welcome to Surire Park," the vehicle announced as it began to slow.

Peering cautiously out the polarizing dome, Flinx saw that they were pulling into another garage. Unlike the quiet repository at the Shell hub, this one was frantic with families and couples, mostly young. Free-floating holos proclaimed the virtues of products he had never heard of, while subdued but insistently cheerful music filled the air. Wherever he was, it seemed to be a happy place. That would last only as long as he succeeded in avoiding the attentions of the authorities.

When the transport parked itself, deactivated, and refused to respond to his insistent requests to move on, he had no choice but to exit. It took him only a holo or two and an agitated stroll through several insistent and exceedingly raucous sound cones to discover where the vehicle had taken him. Surire Park was not the nature preserve of the woolly vicuñas and viscachas he had read about. That blissfully unspoiled wilderness lay farther north. This Surire Park was entirely artificial, as were its amusements.

Given his state of mind, it was not a bad place to be. While uncrowded in the middle of the weekday, there were still enough people present—jostling and laughing, vacationers and locals alike—to lose himself among. Trying not to make contact with the eyes of any of the discreetly identified park security staff, he ambled freely amidst the animated throng, absently cataloging the attractions, ignoring the multitude of clever advertisements, and treating himself to specialty sweets whose sticky composition was beyond the capabilities of the autochef aboard the *Teacher*. Automatic readers accepted his carefully coded credcard without comment.

One ride promised a swift but sizzling run through the heart of one of the active volcanoes that dotted this sweep of the Andes. Another shouted the exhilaration to be had from spiraling at high speed down the slopes of smoking Mount Isulga. There were electrostatic sleds that could be raced across the frozen snowfields, and opportunities to participate in bloodless but noisy holoed recreations of the ancient battles that had scarred this part of the planet. One could choose to wear either the weapons and armor of the conquistadors, or of the Incas. Families partaking in the elaborate historical recreations were invited to purchase recordings of themselves giving advice to or fighting alongside Pizarro or Atahuallpa.

Recreated tombs gave children the chance to play amateur archeologist, while their parents could compete for reproductions of Inca, Moche, Lambayeque, and Chimu artifacts. An observation platform tethered at eight thousand meters provided spectacular views of the mountains, the Pacific, and the sprawling Amazon Reserva to the east. Flinx was almost enjoying himself and Pip was wholly occupied in consuming fragments of the pretzel protruding from one of her companion's shirt pockets, when he spotted the uniforms working their way through the crowd. The attitudes of the wearers were intent, their demeanor grim, and he did not think they were looking for a pickpocket or a drug abuser.

As always, his time of ease and relaxation was brief. He needed to leave, and fast. Burrowing deep within the densest portions of the crowd, he made his way back toward the entrance—only to find it conspicuous with uniforms. They were manually checking everyone coming into the park, and everyone going out.

How much did they know? he found himself wondering anxiously. Had he been reported running from the building with the unconscious Carolles on his back? Or had she recovered sufficiently from her induced slumber and emotional manipulation to give a good description of the young man she had so fleetingly believed she might have loved? Either way, he could not chance donning an air of indifference and trying to slip past the uniforms. In the event of a confrontation, there were too many of them. If he was challenged, Pip would strike out instinctively, and he would not be able to prevent her from killing.

How to avoid an encounter or being taken into custody? Backing unobtrusively into the crowd, avoiding children upset at being denied the chance to go on one more ride, he searched with increasing anxiety for another way out. There seemed to be only the one entrance/exit. As he explored the park's farthest reaches, the percentage of persistent, relentlessly pursuing uniformed security personnel and police steadily increased.

The ride entrance he eventually found himself standing alongside presented itself to the public as the *"Highest, Fastest, Most Exhilarating, Adrenaline-Pumping Exercise in Tandem Racing This Side of the Himalayan Chute!!!"* After all the imperious capitals, the tacked-on multiple exclamation struck him as brazen. A quick check of the ride's entrance showed that it was devoid of guards or other armed hunters looking for a certain redhead. Approaching an information booth, he queried the fixed-position humaniform robot as to the nature of the ride. It was no less effusive in its sales pitch than any biological tout.

Within the ride's core, participants boarded individual maglev boards that adjusted to their height and weight. Each board was encased in a transparent, unbreakable capsule that was automatically pressurized to prevent injury in the unlikely event of a crash. Since each capsule was monitored by the ride's automatic overlord, it was impossible to run over a capsule descending in front of you, or to be overtaken by one from behind.

Beneath the launch ledge, riders plunged into one of two dozen intersecting channels. Powered by precisely spaced electromagnetic rings that encircled each open conduit, board riders could choose to descend by gravity alone, or to accelerate even faster than nature provided. Each board could also use the maglev system for braking, to slow its one or two passengers to a more sedate velocity. Sitting on the board within the protective transparent capsule, feet extended, body riding less than a meter above the ground, the electronic tout promised Flinx that one could rocket down the western slope of the Andes at over 300 kilometers an hour. Because of the board's proximity to the surface and its diminutive size, the sensation of sheer speed, the recorded spiel promised, was unparalleled. He would plunge from an altitude of five thousand meters to sea level in less than a hundred kilometers linear distance.

It was just what he needed.

A glance behind showed a trio of police making their way toward the ride, their eyes doggedly searching the crowd as they approached. Choosing a skill level and paying for passage, Flinx purchased admission for one.

The controls on the board were simple enough for an eight-year-old to handle, which was the intent of the ride's designers. Waiting his turn, he watched as shrieking children, grinning adults, and intimate couples were boosted forward until they dropped out of sight. The slow, the timid, or the simply fearful would automatically be shunted into specific channels reserved for their kind. Daredevils and speed demons shared other routes. Three to four trajectories were saved for the truly mad. Knowing where he had to go and how he needed to proceed, Flinx made certain Pip was secure within his shirt. He was not overly concerned. Her diminutive but powerful coils would allow the minidrag to hold onto him tighter than he could grip the board's controls.

A slight lurch sent his board forward. They were moving. He

felt the air harness contract against him, but not uncomfortably, as it molded itself to his lanky form. Though he was now cinched in too securely to turn, he could hear shouts behind him. Had he waited too long? Could the ride still be locked, freezing him helplessly in place before he could fall free of the landing?

Another jolt and he felt himself accelerating a little faster. Ahead of him a board occupied by a dark couple suddenly vanished as if it had dropped off the face of the Earth. Which, to a certain degree, it had. In its wake it left delighted screams. The board he was riding slowed. To left and right he could see other boards, other riders, disappearing. The shouts behind him had faded, but he could clearly sense rising as well as conflicting emotions somewhere nearby. Lips set, he waited for another boost.

Then, without warning, he was careening downward, the angle of descent not yet acute but the board beginning to pick up speed nonetheless. The perfect transparency of the capsule created the illusion that there was nothing around him. Air pressure pressed against his sides and face like a big, comforting pillow. Outside the tube, undisturbed Andean countryside raced past on both sides, an unpolluted dark blue sky stark overhead. He shot through a large metal ring, the first of his chosen channel's magnetic accelerators. Taking a deep breath, he pushed down hard on the board's accelerator.

The digits on the speedometer floating in front of his eyes climbed as he dropped. Next to it was a heads-up three-dimensional diagram that charted the various available intersecting channels while describing their individual attractions. Ignoring ruins, waterfalls, canyons filled with alpine and then subtropical wildlife, he opted straightforwardly for the shortest and fastest. As the board continued to accelerate, it began to vibrate slightly. The vibration never grew uncomfortable, but it served to remind him that he was now rocketing downslope at over 275 kilometers per hour.

The scenery might well have been spectacular, but it went past too fast for him to notice. Even a police vehicle traveling a cleared commercial conduit would have been hard-pressed to match his speed. How had they traced him to the park from Carolles's remembrances? Most likely, she had provided a description of the private transport he had temporarily appropriated. It would take them some time to decide that he was not anywhere within the park. From the start, the ride had been run wholly by automatics. Probably at least one component was equipped to record visuals of every rider, if only for insurance purposes. With luck, it would be a little while at least before the authorities got around to checking the park's security files for the day. Once that had been done, however, a police chyp could match him out in a matter of seconds—assuming a security recorder had caught a clear glimpse of him.

Used to functioning in situations in which he never knew how much time remained to him before something unpleasant happened, he remained calm, concentrating on running the ride. Beneath his shirt, Pip rested peacefully, the mellow minidrag contentedly digesting recently ingested carbos and salt. Capable as she was of remarkably rapid flight on her own, the speed at which they were presently traveling did not excite her.

Other board riders in proximate channels were momentary blurs in his vision. The trajectory grew steeper still, the encircling magnets continuing to accelerate his board until the speedometer would read no higher. If a magnet failed, he could potentially lose the channel. In that event the board would fly off track, soar briefly into unrestricted air, and slam into the ground at sufficient speed to reduce both it and any passengers to scattered fragments of unconnected tissue. Having faced death in far less resolutely insured forms, Flinx was not worried. It was a good thing, however, that his stomach did not have a mind of its own.

In a very short space of time indeed, the ride's automatic safety features took control of his board. Air pressure and harness restraining him, he began to slow. The broad blue plain of the Pacific lay just ahead. As a final, unannounced fillip, the last half kilometer of the ride shot him into the water, through an underwater tube, past a school of startled jacks and a brace of pouting barracuda, and back around in a tight curve to end at the ride's terminus. He did not linger there long enough to respond to the human monitor's smiling query of "How was it?"

Passing through the innocuous medical scanner that pronounced him and everyone else who finished the ride physically and mentally unscathed by the experience, he hurried as inconspicuously as possible out into the nearest street. Busy Tacrica bustled with tourists and townsfolk alike, a contented, milling throng not unlike that inhabiting any other resort anywhere else on Earth—or for that matter, off it. Two minutes after he vanished into the gaily outfitted crowd, a squad of four police accompanied by a pair of grim-faced hub security personnel disembarked from three commandeered maglev boards, pushed past the bemused employees assigned to monitor their respective arrival channels, and fanned out into the surging multitude. But the wiry, tall redhead they sought was nowhere to be seen.

Frustrated as they were, they had not even been able to enjoy the ride.

# CHAPTER

# 4

Wandering the slightly sloping, carefully preserved colonial quarter of the city that night, Flinx paused to watch the local news stream on a free-ranging public channel. Receding into the background without disappearing, the announcer systematically reported that a major industrial accident whose nature remained as yet undetermined by the relevant authorities had seriously damaged the Surire Shell hub, knocking out all but emergency information services from Arequipa to Iquique for an extended period of time. Some services, the announcer declared with a proper sense of outrage, were not expected to be restored for several weeks. The cause of the incident was under investigation.

Turning away from the display and keeping his head down, Flinx tightened his lips. Somewhere, he knew dourly, the Terran Shell AI was generating a report.

The lights were kept atmospherically dim in the preserved colonial quarter and at this time of night the main street was comparatively tranquil. Those tourists who were out and about were interested in atmosphere, not their fellow promenaders. Eiffel's fountain sparkled in the balmy night air, a monument to the skills and vision of long-dead engineers who thought iron the ultimate building material. Using modern materials and techniques, skillful restorers had preserved much of the seventeenth- and eighteenth-century architecture. Even up close, the reinforcing nanotube sheets were invisible to the curious eye.

He had to get to the port at Nazca and to his shuttle. There was no reason to suppose the authorities would connect its ownership to their wanted fugitive and put a watch on it. Even if they somehow managed to identify him, there was nothing to link him to a specific KK-drive craft. The Counselor Second for Science Druvenmaquez had seen it, the senior thranx's own ship's personnel and instrumentation had doubtless imaged it. But while very different internally from any other vessel, from the outside the *Teacher* looked like any other small commercial interstellar craft. And Flinx was careful to see to it that his vessel's maintenance ware altered its identifying external patterns on a regular basis.

Still, he would not be able to relax until he was back within its familiar confines. That meant safely boarding the shuttle at Nazca's commercial port, obtaining clearance to lift, and making it through the atmosphere without being challenged.

His talent was functioning again. Around him, the air was charged with fleeting, or persistent, or hysterical, or affectionate emotion. As always on a populated world, the sheer volume of sentiment threatened to overcome him. It was better in uninhabited space, where his mind could float free of unwanted, unsought empathetic intrusion. He was tired, unfamiliar with his surroundings, and unsure of how best to make his way to Nazca while avoiding the attentions of the authorities. Of one thing he was reasonably sure: No convenient amusement ride would take him there.

A pair of local police wearing subdued uniforms were coming up the avenue toward him. Though they were conversing animatedly between themselves and not looking in his direction, Flinx turned quickly down a side street. There was no need to expose himself to unnecessary scrutiny. Having spent an entire childhood on Moth darting through damp air and dark surroundings, he felt almost at home in the alleyways of the coastal community.

The backstreet was old and blissfully deserted. It was remarkable how much truly ancient construction had survived the centuries. The crumbling brick wall on his right had to date from no later than the twenty-first century, at least. A pile of primitive nondegradable containers formed a small talus slope to his left, overflowing their collection bin.

From the vicinity of the bin, something moved. He sensed the threat before he saw its owner—a small, stocky bundle of inimical energy whose black eyes glittered in the faltering light. The man's skin was as brown as Flinx's, and in his right hand he held a weapon of indeterminate parentage.

Two more armed individuals emerged from a dark doorway, a lean whip of a woman from behind the container bin, and another from the shadows up ahead. Turning to leave, Flinx found the way back to the main street blocked by a trio of stimstick-smoking youths whose thin smiles did nothing to illuminate the darkness or their sour personalities. The police he had turned into the alley to avoid might still be within shouting distance, but calling for help would mean having to answer their questions. If they ran a check on him, they would identify him as the individual wanted in this morning's incident at the Surire hub.

"My-o, he's a glimmer one." The woman with the whipcord body, much of which was on unapologetic display, eyed him approvingly. Her torso was maybe twenty, her eyes ten years older.

"Your cred, visitor." The stocky man who had stepped out from behind the bin motioned nervously in Flinx's direction. His sedate squirming was a consequence not of unease but of the drugs in his system. "Clothes, ident, everything. Right now." He gestured sharply at the ground.

"Hait." Another, even younger woman was grinning. "Let's see wot you got, boy-o." Her emotions and those of her companions stank of predation.

Traveling with weapons was a good way to attract the immediate attention of the authorities. They inevitably marked the bearer as worthy of closer attention. So Flinx disdained guns and vibraknives and similar mechanisms of extermination. That did not mean he was unarmed. There were a lot of them, though, and the alley was narrow.

He started backing up the way he had come. The police whose attentions he needed to avoid should be elsewhere by now. "I'm going to leave. I need what little I have, and you don't. Please, don't try to stop me."

"Hi-o, he's polite as well as pretty." Stepping forward, supple muscles visible within the webwork of her outfit, the tall young woman produced a sharply finned dart. She juggled it easily in one hand, flipping it in casual circles. "After I waft him out, can I play with what's left?"

Her stocky companion grunted. "Just get it over with." Peering past Flinx and the three mougs behind him, he tried to scrutinize the distant street. "I hate it when they don' cooperate."

The woman's grin widened. "I like it." The dart paused in her hand, held casually in throwing position. Flinx wondered what chemical cocktail it contained.

"Don't throw that." His voice was composed, unruffled.

The woman's smile faded slightly. She wanted him to be afraid, and though tense, he clearly was not frightened. It unnerved her more than she cared to show. Maybe Marvilla was right. Time to get it over with. Business first, play-o later.

Reading her rising emotions, Flinx knew that despite her indifferent attitude and the fact that she was looking at her male companion and not in his direction, she was preparing to throw the dart. As the synchronous emotional outbreak began to rise within her, he threw himself to one side, into the pile of discarded plasticine containers. Cool from lying in the dark alley, their accumulated bulk masked his body signature. Seeking human heat, the flung dart whizzed through the space where he had been standing. He heard the startled oath from one of the three mougs who blocked the outlet as the dart struck home. There was a brief, crude flare of panic from the youth, then nothing as the illicit pharmaceuticals shut down his system. Paralyzed, he crumpled to the ground.

As Flinx had hurled himself sideways, something small, winged, superfast, and angry exploded from within the folds of his shirt. Brightly hued and reptilian of aspect, it was in the woman's face before she could draw a second dart from its holder. Emitting a startled scream, she stumbled backward, tripped, and fell on the half-exposed dart she was holding. With a moan, she reached down to pull it free of her left buttock, only to crumple onto her side as the soporific cocktail of enhanced animal tranquilizers it contained took effect.

Raising his pistol, the leader of the pack took aim at his girlfriend's assailant. Or tried to. In the dimly lit alley it was difficult to focus on anything so small, particularly when it seemed to be moving in every direction at once. The shot misfired. The minidrag's response did not. A few droplets of incredibly caustic venom struck the man in his right eye. Dropping his weapon he staggered backward, slammed into the brick, and sat down, clawing at the eye from which a thin stream of corrosive smoke was rising.

Rolling to his feet, Flinx assumed a defensive posture with the bin at his back. The two mougs who were still conscious had drawn weapons of their own, as had the man and his companions who had been loping toward him from the other end of the alley. Pip sped back to hover protectively above her master, slitted eyes alert, still full of piss and poison.

Glancing backward, one of the mougs suddenly paused and muttered something to her mate. Holstering her weapon, she broke into a run. Flinx watched as they passed right by him. Joining the surviving pack members, they fled up the alley.

He lowered his hands. Pip descended toward him but remained airborne and alert. A lone figure was coming up the alley toward them, advancing at a leisurely pace. Flinx searched for the sheen of a police uniform.

The old man was solidly built but not tall. White stubble covered his squarish face, indifferent to depilatory and fashion. His lower jaw protruded as if he suffered from some incurable orthodontic contraction. Like the facial stubble, his hair was entirely white and combed back over his high head, to pause at the collar of his rough, natural cotton shirt. A small communicator was visible hanging from his waist, and he wore a finger-sized reader/probe above one ear. His back was only slightly bent. He might have been 70, or 170.

Halting a safe distance from Flinx, he flourished a grandfatherly smile and surprisingly good teeth. One thick, callused finger jabbed at the air above the younger man's head.

"Call off thy winged devil, sonny. The street slime have all run away." He nodded in the direction of the dead pack leader and his twitching, silent girlfriend. "Them that could, anyways."

Flinx searched for the glint of a weapon. "They ran from you, but you're not armed."

"Only with my reputation." The old man chuckled with amusement. "Afraid old Cayacu would hex 'em. I would, too. Eight against one—not righteous." He shook his head disapprovingly. "What's thy name?"

The subject of the old man's query almost started to say Philip, but hastily corrected himself. "I'm Flinx. The one with the wings is Pip." As he spoke, the flying snake settled back onto his shoulder, remaining vigilant and visible. In this new arrival she sensed no threat.

"She be a one, too." The oldster chortled a second time, then beckoned with a broad gesture. "Thou'rt the one hub security's looking for, aren't thou? Come with me."

Straining, Flinx tried to appraise the elder without speaking. Like Pip, he perceived no threat. "Why should I go with you? So you can turn me in for the citizen's reward?"

"I don't need the government's credit. Thou'rt a strange one. I like strange things." He indicated the far reaches of the alley into which the surviving pack members had fled. "They knew that. That's why they ran." Aged but still bright brown eyes met those of the younger man. "You know what a shaman be, sonny?"

Flinx frowned. "Some kind of witch doctor?" He stared. "In this day and age?"

"What day and age be that?" The deeply lined, weathered

face overflowed with wisdom and good humor. "Shamanism never goes out of style, sonny. No matter how advanced the technology, no matter how grand the accomplishments of hard science, there'll always be them for whom mysticism and magic transcend knowledge. Never forget that for many folk, it's always easier to believe than to think."

"Then you're a self-confessed fraud." Flinx had always been too forthright for his own good.

"Didn't say that." The old man chuckled. "Come on, sonny. Let's get thee out of here." He turned to leave.

Flinx continued to hesitate. "You still haven't given me a compelling reason for going with you." On his shoulder, Pip was finally relaxing, her tiny but powerful heart pounding like a miniature impulse drive.

Cayacu looked back. "Because I can get thee to wherever it be thou wantst to go. Assuming, that is, that thou hast someplace thou wantst to go. Or perhaps thou wouldst prefer to stay here?"

The younger man eyed the constricting walls of the alley, the dead and unconscious bodies that littered the ground. "I do have a destination, and this isn't it."

"Didn't think so." The oldster beckoned again. "Come and chat with a jaded old man. The authorities tolerate individuals like myself, but they disapprove of what I do. It gives me pleasure to thwart them." He shook his head. "Eight against one," he muttered softly. "Best get thy pet out of sight."

It was not the oldest skimmer Flinx had ever seen, but it was close. Cayacu drove it out of the city center and into the suburbs, heading for the sea. As soon as they reached the beach, they turned north, the vehicle wheezing and rattling in the darkness, the half moon hanging motionless over the Pacific, giving the water the sheen of rubbed steel. Soon they were out of the city altogether and leaving the highly developed resort area behind. Since they were traveling north, the direction he needed to go, Flinx saw no reason to comment on the route his host was taking.

Occasionally the ancient, battered vehicle lost power so severely that it bounced off the ground, dimpling the grassy track that was the main road leading north. Eventually, the shaman parted with the avenue altogether and turned seaward once more, following a narrow path that snaked through rock and sand. In the absence of irrigation, the terrain had reverted to its natural amalgam of gravel, sand, and gritty soil. It would remain so for hundreds of undisturbed kilometers up the coast.

A few lights appeared in the distance. Simple, carefully maintained homes hugged the south bank of a small river. Where it emptied into the sea, snowy egrets patrolled the water's edge, far outshining the shore birds one would expect to encounter in such a place. The birds were sleeping now. A few heads glanced up, a few sets of wings fluttered, as the grinding, coughing skimmer faltered past their resting place.

Cayacu brought it to a halt in a covered port that was attached to an unprepossessing single-story structure of self-adhering tile and faux stone. North of the village, a high promontory thrust out into the sea. Bathed in the light of the half moon, the beige-colored sandstone was tinted gold. Small waves caroused perpetually on the nearby beach.

Gesturing for his guest to follow, the shaman hauled himself out of the malodorous skimmer and unlocked the front door of the house. Stepping across the covered porch, Flinx followed his host inside. Pip had been asleep for some time, and there was no sign of pursuit or police. Making an effort, he tried to approximate his minidrag's state of mind. No threats radiated from the compact, cozy structure he was being asked to enter.

The lighting within was suppressed, but sufficient for him to descry his surroundings. It occurred to him that he was very tired. Nevertheless, the decor was sufficiently interesting to spark both interest and wakefulness. From the preserved caimans grinning toothily at him atop rustic shelves to the bottles of unidentifiable solutions that glistened beneath, the outer room was a cornucopia of traditional folk medicine ingredients and occult appurtenances. Eyes plucked from an assortment of animals gazed dully from a wide-bottomed glassine cylinder while amputated birds' feet bound like a sheaf of scaly wheat protruded from a canister like so many customized antique umbrella shafts.

"Mouth dry?" Cayacu inquired. When Flinx nodded the affirmative, the oldster murmured to a wall. Grime and peeling projection paper slid aside to reveal a gleaming, thoroughly modern food storage unit. At Flinx's request, it dispensed a tall, chilled glass of passionfruit-orange-guava juice. He drank thirstily.

The shaman was sweeping selected objects from his extraordinary collection into a sack. When he was through, he lit a stimstick and beckoned for his guest to follow. Exiting the house, they strode down a street sealed with transparent paving material that allowed the sand, rock, and crushed seashells underneath to show through. Most of the buildings they passed were silent and dark. From a few seeped the lights and the sounds of tridee entertainment.

Leaving the tiny community behind, they followed the course of the small river before effecting a crossing on a string of inconspicuously linked stones. Disturbed, a pair of sleeping egrets eyed them owlishly, irritated at the nocturnal interruption. Overhead, the half moon continued to lavish its light on the nearby beach, giving the incoming waves an ethereal touch of fluorescence.

Reaching the sandy promontory, they entered a narrow cleft in the stone and began to climb. It was a short, easy ascent, and Flinx soon found himself standing atop the peninsula. Behind them flickered the few lights of the town. Hidden behind a bend in the coast, the extensive resort strip of Tacrica lay far enough away not to be visible, though the glow of its lights lightened a portion of the southern sky.

The top of the promontory was absolutely barren of life, as were the small hillocks that dotted the otherwise flat surface. When Flinx remarked idly on the apparent regularity of the protrusions, the old shaman chuckled.

"That's not surprising, sonny. They be mud pyramids, heavily eroded by many centuries of rain and wind." He gestured grandly, as if they had just stepped into an ornate parlor. "This site be called Pacyatambu. You be standing on the ruins of a sixth-century Moche city that was once home to some fifty thousand people."

A surprised Flinx examined his surroundings anew. Now that he had been enlightened, the outlines of the pyramids became more defined, their sides increasingly vertical. His imagination filled in the silent emptiness with a vision of a busy marketplace, meandering nobles, farmers bringing in food from the fields, fishermen hawking their catch. Brooding priests invoked from a high balcony, and brightly painted frescoes suffused the city with a riot of color.

Sixth century—A.D., not A.A. With one foot, he stirred the sands beneath him. So very long ago. Had ancestors of his once lived here, content in their ignorance, happy in their subsistence existence? In all likelihood, he would never know—just as he still did not know his true parentage. But these sands and the secrets they contained, they too were a part of him, whether he liked it or not.

In that wild and windswept place he felt for the first time the hoary history of humankind in a way he never had previously. Not on Moth, not here, not on any of the worlds settled and otherwise that he had trod upon in his short life. For the first time he sensed fully what it meant to be a human being, *all* of whose ancestors had come from the third planet circling the unremarkable star called Sol. Despite the disdain he had shown for it all his life, he understood now what others meant when they spoke of Earth as home, even those several generations removed who had been born on other worlds.

In front of him, Cayacu had spread an antique homespun cotton blanket out on the ground. Atop this he was arranging the contents of his sack; tiny vials and plasticine containers, an old dagger, ancient bits of broken pottery, bones animal and human, dried plant material, archaic electronic components, a pair of burned-out storage chyps, and more. When he was finished, he sat down cross-legged next to the blanket, facing the sea. Wind snapped the tips of his wavy white hair as he closed his eyes and began to chant.

Uninstructed, not knowing what else to do, a hushed Flinx sat down nearby and watched. Occasionally the shaman would emerge from his self-induced trance to reach out and touch this or that object on the blanket. Once, he leaned forward to rearrange a pair of ancient computer chyps and a preserved salamander. A lone gull cried, its voice breaking. Beneath Flinx's shirt, Pip slept contentedly.

Picking up a container and opening the top, the chanting Cayacu dipped his fingers into the contents and flicked them in his guest's direction. Charged water splattered the younger man's face, and he flinched slightly. The shaman repeated the gesture, then resealed the container. Moments later the ceremony came to an abrupt end.

Beaming, Cayacu uncrossed his legs and rose, reaching down to rub feeling back into patriarchal muscles. "You will be all right from now on. I have consulted the spirits, and they have assured me of thy safety." He tapped a shirt pocket. "Also, the tracer alarm I set on thy broadcast image has remained silent. That tells me that the police still have no idea where thou be."

Flinx had to grin. "So you rely on technology and not magic after all."

Cayacu shrugged as he gestured toward the cleft through which they had accessed the entombed city. "Let's just say that I prefer me eclipses total, sonny. I thought, though I have known thee only briefly, that thou would find this place of interest."

"Very much so." Flinx was not ashamed to admit that he had been moved by the experience. "Thank you for bringing me here. I think I may have made a kind of personal connection that had previously been denied to me." As they walked out of the ancient city, he indicated the looming mounds. "Why hasn't this place been excavated?"

"There be innumerable ruins in this part of the world," the shaman explained. "Far more than there is money to explore them. There be work here for hundreds of archeologists for thousands of years. Using the very latest and best equipment, they prefer to hunt for the most spectacular sites, those that are burdensome with unlooted gold and silver and gemstone artifacts. Places where people merely lived, like Pacyatambu, be very low on the list of localities to be explored."

Reaching the base of the bluff, they turned back toward the slumbering community and the shaman's house. "You can sleep in my home tonight, sonny. Late tomorrow I will try to take thee wherever it is thou wishest to go."

Flinx eyed him curiously. "Why? I'm a stranger to you, and to this place. Why should you want to help me?"

Cayacu chuckled. "It pleases me to confound the authorities. Officially, what I do they classify as simplistic entertainment. Though I am no unrepentant regressive preaching the virtues of a vanished age, I take these ancient ways more seriously than they do. Too many of them wear their air of technological superiority like a too-tight pair of pants. Every now and then, when circumstances permit, it suits me to shower in the waters of their discomfort."

The moon laid a silver road on the surface of the sea: the waters from which all life on this world, and subsequently the human intelligence that was now spreading throughout this arm of the galaxy, had sprung. Flinx felt a peace that had heretofore been denied him. But it remained a troubled peace, and would remain so until he at last secured the information he sought. His questions were basic enough. It was only the answers that seemed complex beyond reason.

"I have to leave Earth in a hurry. In order to do that, I must get to Nazca. My shuttlecraft is berthed there."

Old Cayacu nodded. "Dost thou think the authorities can trace it to thee? If so, then thy chances of departing without confrontation are much diminished."

"I don't know." Flinx considered. "They may still think they have me bottled up in Tacrica. So far I think they have just the visual description you alluded to a moment ago, and that only from witnesses' remembrances."

"Are they likely to be good remembrances?" The shaman stepped lightly, avoiding a scavenging crab.

"In one instance, I'm afraid so." Flinx's deliberate deception of the innocent, unaware Elena Carolles continued to weigh heavily on him. But it had been necessary. How well had she described him to the authorities, and how accurate was the resultant rendition churned out by the police compositor? "But I'm pretty good at disguising my identity where official channels are concerned, and my ship's AI is used to misleading any inquiries."

Wise eyes regarded him as they hiked together along the beach in the moonlight. "You're an interesting young man, sonny. How come thou to have thy own shuttlecraft?"

Flinx tried to make light of the query. "I've found that interesting people generally have interesting friends. For some reason, others have taken an interest in me. Some of it's benign, some inimical, and the rest just inquisitive. I don't know why. I'm just one citizen among billions."

"Are thou, now? I wonder. Why, exactly, are the authorities so anxious to question thee?" As Flinx prepared to deliver a carefully deceptive reply, the old man suddenly waved both hands at him. "No, no—don't tell me! I don't want to know." In the darkness, his teeth were resplendently white. "If I'm brought in for questioning later, I want to be able to take nullity along as my companion. Ignorance makes the best lawyer. It's enough that thou are a thorn in the side of those who govern." He gestured. "Almost home, sonny. I hope thou be not a city lad, used to its noise and roar. In this little village, we sleep in silence."

Flinx thought of the vast empty spaces between the stars that had been his refuge for much of the past several years. "I'll sleep just fine, shaman. Believe me, I know what quiet is."

As they rattled up the coast the following evening, Flinx found himself wondering more than once if his host's ancient rattletrap of a skimmer would make it all the way to the Nazca parallel, much less inland to the high plateau where the shuttleport was situated. Cayacu did nothing to improve their chances by keeping to the lesser-known, more bumptious routes, away from the main commercial and tourist thoroughfares.

Flinx regarded their safe arrival at the port's outskirts as something of a minor triumph. The sun had long since set, the only illumination coming from the powerful landing lights of the port and the streak of cold flame from a cargo shuttle straining to lift itself beyond the heavens. They had arrived after dark by design: The less help provided to anyone searching for someone of Flinx's description, the better his chances of departing unchallenged.

Certainly the automatic scanner at the Chungillo gate was not impressed by the pair of dirty, cowled figures who occupied the front of the antique skimmer. It passed them through with an almost audible synthesized whisper of disgust. Huddling beneath his cotton hood, old Cayacu tried not to grin too hard.

"They pride themselves on the sophistication of their contrivances, but it is amazing how easily some of them can be fooled by such simple baggage as dirt and grease. Especially when applied in thick but not overly conspicuous layers."

Reaching up, Flinx ran the tips of his fingers down his bare cheek, slick with the aromatic lubricant that had been thoughtfully supplied by his host. The disposable colored lenses that distorted his eyes itched, and during the past several hours of driving he had received every indication that there was something besides himself living in the filthy cotton hooded shawl Cayacu had insisted he wear. His discomfort was mitigated more than a little by the fact that they had been passed through the main gate without comment.

The success was cheering, but hardly a wondrous accomplishment. It was entirely possible that the gate had not yet been programmed with a copy of his likeness, which in any event was not taken from life but from an artist's rendition provided by the police. That was no reason to relax, he knew. On more than one occasion he owed his life not to precautions taken but to paranoia presumed.

The skimmer trundled past the imposing reproduction of the Chimu-era Huaca of the Moon that served as the passenger reception area, past the cargo receiving terminal, and finally slowed as it approached the more heavily safeguarded barrier that prevented

casual sightseers from wandering out among the parked shuttles
and aircraft. Here Flinx would have to identify himself in order
for them to gain entrance. It was the most likely checkpoint for a
confrontation.

Instead of attempting to pass scrutiny by the automatic sentry,
they parked the skimmer and headed straight for the security office.
It was a bold move, designed to catch any forewarned personnel off
guard. Whether it was a foolhardy one remained to be seen. The decision would be judged by its outcome.

If the automatics recognized him, Flinx knew, anxious dialog
and emotional manipulation was unlikely to sway them. Though it
was in some ways riskier, he preferred to take his chances with sentinels of flesh and blood.

There were three of them, seated at their positions behind a
shieldscreen. It buzzed slightly as Cayacu made contact, a warning
to stay back. Anyone trying to force the screen would receive a
strong enough shock to lay them out flat—outside the portal. Bored,
one of the guards looked up from his battery of security monitors
and eyed the two men reluctantly.

"Yar? What is it?"

The old man spoke while Flinx hovered in the background, try-
ing to conceal his face without appearing to do so. "I be Cayacu of
Pacyatambu, a shaman of much experience and great knowledge."
He indicated Flinx. "This is Gallito, my assistant."

The sentry was somewhat less than impressed. "So?"

"I have been asked by friends of the owner to bless a vessel
stored here." Reaching into the sack secured at his waist, he pulled
out a feathered rattle from which issued an especially noxious smell
and shook it lightly in the guard's direction. "I have everything with
me that I need."

Another sentry glanced up from his bank of monitors. "Process 'em, Avro, and let 'em in." Ignoring the silent Flinx, the senior sentry focused on the weathered shaman. "Better make it a short ceremony. You've got ten minutes."

"Thank thee, sir." Cayacu bowed gracefully and shuffled to his left, to stand within the confines of the security scanner. Flinx edged into the circular space alongside the old man.

There was a brief hum as the security device was activated. Other than a slight tingling of the scalp, there was nothing to indicate that anything had happened. The hum ceased, the warning lights went out, and the two visitors stepped clear.

"Just a minute." Frowning at one of his monitors, the second guard gestured to the third. "What's this here?"

"Hold it, you two." The first sentry remained seated, but his right hand had slipped downward to shade the butt of the weapon holstered at his waist. He waited for further details from his companions.

The middle sentinel spoke up. "You, 'assistant.' Come over here." Flinx sensed wariness, uncertainty, challenge within the woman. Not a promising combination.

Estimating the height of the fence that enclosed the shuttle service area, Flinx gauged his chances of making it up and over before port security personnel could run him down. The *Teacher*'s shuttle was located about halfway across the crowded tarmac. He decided his chances were slight, even if the fence was not electrified or otherwise charged to keep out the unauthorized. He took a couple of hesitant steps forward.

The woman who had called out to him was eyeing him intently. After a moment of silence, she addressed the younger man for a second time. "What's that coiled up under your outfit? On the shoulder? It shows here as organic." She indicated one of her monitors.

Flinx replied deferentially. "It's a minidrag—a flying snake." Should he say something else, he wondered?

Cayacu stepped in. "We use many serpents in our ceremonies. Some live, some dead, some pickled."

The woman made a face. "Spare me the details. Save it for those tourists with more money than sense." Turning back to her monitor, she muttered to her companion. "That gibes with what I see here. Let 'em through."

Heart pounding, Flinx followed a buoyant Cayacu as they passed through the deactivated section of fence. With a slight cracking sound it sprang back to life behind them. Ten minutes, the sentry had told them. He tried not to look back. At any moment he expected to hear the whine of security sirens and the shouts of eager police closing on them. Catching up to the shaman, he urged the old man to walk faster.

Flinx had been privy to many spectacular sights in his time, but none were as stirring as the silhouette of the *Teacher*'s shuttle, parked where he had left it many days ago. It did not appear to have been touched. Verbal contact activated its AI, which promptly assured him that its integrity had not been violated and that no unauthorized individuals had recently come snooping around. The shuttle could use force to prevent any such from boarding, Flinx knew, but denial of access could in itself be enough to set off alarms among the authorities. If anyone had linked him to this particular shuttle, they had not yet managed to pass the information along to those in a position to make use of it. He had no intention of giving them any more time to make the connection.

A few coded commands delivered verbally, a concise security check performed by the ship's AI, and the ventral loading elevator stood open awaiting his next move. Turning, he bade farewell to the old shaman, taking both deeply creased hands in his own.

"I owe you a lot, Cayacu. How can I repay you?" A quick glance southward showed that all was still quiet in the vicinity of the security post. Its denizens needed to remain bored for another few minutes, and then he would be beyond their reach.

The old man smiled encouragingly. "Continue to confound authority, sonny. Always do the unexpected." Chuckling, he stepped back and began fumbling in his sack. "I have a feeling thou hast a talent for it."

Smiling gratefully, Flinx turned to go, then hesitated. "What are you doing?"

A battered rattle heavy with colorful tropical feathers emerged from the sack. "Preparing to properly anoint thy craft, of course. Thou don't think I'd let thee get off without receiving the blessings of the ancients, do thou?" Half closing his eyes, he launched into a chant not unlike the one Flinx had heard him sing in the buried city.

"My thanks." Flinx started toward the elevator, speaking back over his shoulder. "Just don't linger too long, or you'll find yourself anointed by shuttle backdraft."


Cayacu finished and walked away as the powerful engines of the shuttle sprang to hollow-voiced life. A word into a pickup, and he was passed out of the parking sector and back into the port proper. As he cajoled his superannuated skimmer out the main exit and back into the coastal night, a flurry of activity could be seen off to his left, where the main entrance to the port accessed the main north-south Lima conurbation track. An unusual amount of excitement for this time of night, he mused. What could possibly be the cause?

Far overhead, a very small but efficient shuttlecraft was already streaking through the stratosphere. Turning south toward home, the shaman had no one to smile to but himself. It was enough. Not all magicians were old, he knew, and not every magic familiar. Some magicks were small, some great, and some inexplicable even to other shamans. It did not matter. He was neither resentful nor envious.

It was good to have been able to help a brother in trouble.

# CHAPTER

# 5

The clean, clear emptiness of space as the shuttle emerged from Terran atmosphere filled Flinx with relief. Not that he was safely on his way yet. In addition to the commercial stations that ringed the homeworld there were a number of orbiting military depots and other government facilities to which the public was not granted access. No one could simply approach as sensitive a place as Earth and set down in a shuttle. The identities of decelerating vessels and those individuals they carried had to be processed; quarantine procedures had to be acknowledged and followed; clearances had to be granted.

Leaving, however, was a far less complicated business. No one particularly cared if a contaminated crew or cargo set out to infect the void.

Even so, and even though he was not challenged as his shuttle's engines powered down from escape velocity to maneuvering mode, he paid close attention to every monitor within the cockpit. His presence was not necessary: The shuttle would warn him if they were challenged. But he was too nervous to stay stuck in transport harness while the craft worked its way through orbital traffic toward the drifting *Teacher*. He floated loosely in the command chair, held in place only by his grip on the arms.

Within the cabin, Pip tumbled free, twisting and turning contentedly. She had adapted to weightlessness years ago and thoroughly enjoyed the occasional release from gravity. Freed from the constraints of Earthpull, she coiled and contorted in the air, pleated wings fluttering gaily, looking more like a free-swimming nudibranch than an Alaspinian minidrag. Once back on board the *Teacher*, the overdrift from its posigravity drive would force her once again to beat air to stay airborne.

Like all ships waiting to depart outsystem, the *Teacher* was parked well away from the overcrowded equatorial belt. The farther the shuttle traveled from that glittering planetary necklace of stations large and small, automated and inhabited, the more Flinx relaxed. When at last the *Teacher* loomed large enough in the port to see with the naked eye, he would have jumped for joy had not the danger of doing so in zero g restrained him.

There was nothing for him to do now but loosen up, watch, and wait. Automatons handled nearly all modern navigation, with greater speed, efficiency, and accuracy than any human pilots could manage. In ancient times, he knew, machines had been built to serve as backups to people. Now the humans functioned as backups for their superbly crafted machines. Shuttle and mother ship communicated in high-speed bursts of compressed information while their master and his serpentine companion awaited their conjoined cybernetic permission to change ships.

A telltale lit up on the console and a voice, clear and crisp, filled the cockpit. "Shuttle ident one-one-four-six, this is peaceforcer station *Chagos*. The favor of a reply is requested."

Cursing silently, Flinx hesitated for as long as he thought tolerable before responding. By that time the shuttle's engines had shut down completely and the atmospheric transport was drifting with regulated precision into the open, expectant hold on the *Teacher*'s port side.

"*Chagos* station, this is one-one-four-six. How's the weather where you are?" Outside, the terminator line cut a black swath across the sapphire splendor of the Indian Ocean.

"Depends what side of the station you're sunbathing on, one-one-four-six. We are in receipt of a general query from western South America to hold all, repeat all, departures for half an orbital period. This is a general caution for all vessels that have applied to depart outsystem and is not specific to you. Can you comply?"

Muted clanking sounds reverberated through the shuttle's hull as it coupled with and was locked down in its holding bay. Pushing off gently, Flinx floated effortlessly out of the command chair. Gathering up Pip, he then kicked toward the main exit. Proper gravity would not return to his surroundings until the underpinnings of the *Teacher*'s KK-drive were reactivated.

"No problem." He responded promptly, knowing that the shuttle's omnidirectional pick-up would find and amplify his voice. "Hey, drifter, tell me—what's going on?"

"We don't know yet." The voice from the station was devoid of duplicity. "We're promised details within half an hour. But something has a lot of important bureaucratic types stirred up downstairs. Whatever it is, it's significant enough to kick orbital as well as dirt-grubber backsides into action. Drift easy, and you'll get the word as soon as we do."

"Must be serious." With a soft hiss, air from the recently drowsing and now revived *Teacher* blended with that of the shuttle. By his presence, Flinx announced his return. In corresponding silence, the ship acknowledged his arrival, identified him, and began to rouse itself. It would take only a little while for all systems to be up and online, Flinx knew. That was a good thing, since he now had less than thirty minutes in which to leave the Solar System and still avoid a confrontation.

Of course, he did not know if the general orbital alert even had anything to do with him and his flight from Nazca. It might involve some other matter entirely. He knew only that he could not take the chance of finding out, much less risk the arrival of a heavily armed peaceforcer sent to take him into custody.

As he drifted out of the shuttle, gently tugging a fluttering Pip along by her tail, gravity began to return. He made sure that he was perpendicular to the deck so that when the field reached full strength, he would land on his feet and not on his head. Without pausing to check on the status of the rest of the vessel, he made his way quickly to the bridge. The ship greeted him informally, in accordance with its programming.

"Set course outsystem," he told it as he settled into the lounge that fronted the main console. He could have given the same directions from anywhere on the vessel, including his bedroom, but would not have had access to the same number of reciprocal functions that he did here.

"Destination?" Today the ship spoke in the voice of a kindly old thranx.

"Manual transfer. Acknowledge receipt of coordinates." Reaching into a pocket, he removed the nanostorage chyp and inserted it into an appropriate receptacle. The ship responded in less than sixty seconds.

"Coordinates received. I am obliged to give warning. The intended destination lies outside Commonwealth boundaries, away from all safe sectors, and beyond the neutral zone. Do you really wish to penetrate the spatial parameters of the AAnn Empire?"

"I am aware of the loci indicated by these coordinates. Proceed at speed."

"It shall be as you command, O master."

"And no sarcasm!" Flinx snapped at the ship's AI, even though he was the one who had precountenanced such a possible response.

Out in front of the *Teacher*, beyond the vast generating fan that was the resonator of the KK-drive, a tiny pinpoint of light appeared as the Caplis generator was activated. Slowly at first, then gathering speed, the ship began to move. Flinx chafed at the pace. Changeover, the shift from space-normal to space-plus where interstellar travel became possible, could not take place within the Solar System. The *Teacher*'s own safety system would not permit it. Until he reached changeover, he could be followed. Whether he could be run down once under way was another matter.

The *Teacher*'s course took it out of the Sun's system well below the plane of the ecliptic. Consequently, it was unlikely that interception from one of the many military or commercial bases located at outsystem sites such as Europa or Triton would be possible. The more distance he put between himself and Earth, the greater the likelihood of a successful escape.

A voice crackled in the cool, pleasant air of the room. "Commercial deepspace vessel *Delarion Maucker*," it demanded, using the false identification Flinx had provided to orbital authority upon arrival, "there is a general hold on all departures from orbit. We show you cutting moonsphere in two minutes and continuing to accelerate. You have not received clearance for departure."

"Sorry." Once again, an omnidirectional pickup juggled his response. "We've got a schedule to keep. Important cargo for Rhyinpine. Guess someone mishandled the notice. Do you wish us to shut down departure program and return? Repeat, do you wish us to eventuate program and return?"

There was a pause, which Flinx had counted on. No one wanted to be responsible for forcing a commercial vessel that was already outbound to terminate its route. His immediate response to the query and indicated willingness to comply with its attendant directive would hopefully serve to diminish any incipient suspicion. It had better, he thought. Now that the ship's KK-drive was fully active, he could not make use of the *Teacher*'s formidable masking and screening capabilities.

"*Delarion Maucker,*" the enjoining voice finally replied, "did you embrace docking with shuttlecraft one-one-four-six?"

"What's that?" Numerals pregnant with meaning drifted above the console like stoned fireflies. Heading outsystem, the *Teacher* continued to accelerate rapidly. "You're breaking up. There's some trouble with clarification. Check your transmitter field, and we'll run an amplified throughput on our receivers."

There was, of course, nothing wrong with the communications at either end of the conversation. Flinx had heard every word sent in his direction with perfect lucidity. But by the time that fact had been established to everyone's satisfaction, the *Teacher* was cutting the orbital sphere of Uranus, the impossibly bright glow from the dilating KK-drive field too bright to look at directly. The synthetic gravitational distortion had begun to warp into a teardrop shape, the shaft of the drop flowing backward to distort space immediately behind the bulge of the field—space occupied by the *Teacher*.

"*Delarion Maucker.*" The original voice had been replaced by another that was both irritated and insistent. "You are instructed to terminate passage to Rhyinpine and return immediately to Earth orbit. This directive is ship specific. Repeat, you are directed to—"

Around the *Teacher*, the imposing strength of the KK-drive field shunted itself and everything contained within it from ordinary space into that strange region of compacted reality known colloquially as space-plus. Velocity, as it was understood in the normal universe, increased explosively. The domineering phonation that belonged to Earth vanished, cut off by suddenly achieved distances best described as absurd. Having been summoned from Triton, two peaceforcer patrol craft proceeding at speed arrived at the intended rendezvous coordinates five minutes after nothing was there. On distant Earth itself, rankled authorities fumed impotently.

Within the unceremonious, homey confines of the *Teacher*, Flinx relaxed. One ship could not follow or confront another while in space-plus. The *Teacher*'s navigation kept it on course, proceeding not to Rhyinpine, but to an unknown world lying within the outer boundaries of the AAnn Empire.

No, not unknown, he reminded himself. Someone connected with an innocuous-seeming food manufacturer was going there. *He* was going there. By the very act of their going, the world in question removed itself from the index of the unknown. Who was preceding him, and why, he had yet to find out.

Commonwealth vessels did not stray beyond the neutral zone known as the Torsee Provinces. It was not a sensible thing to do. Cultural aspects and attitudes of the AAnn were well known. Playing the role of forgiving hosts was not among them. He would have to tread very quietly. In this he had, to the best of his knowledge, several advantages that were denied those preceding him. Thanks to the singular skills of its Ulru-Ujurrian builders, the *Teacher* was capable of several tricks no other KK-drive craft could replicate. To enter and leave AAnn space without incident, he might well need to make use of all of them.

His thoughts were not only of the enigmatic quest that lay

before him, but of the unpretentious white-and-blue sphere that was now an invisible speck among the firmament aft. So—that was Earth. He had not thought much of it prior to his arrival, had not expected a second visit to do anything to change his opinion. Not until the old shaman Cayacu had put him in touch with its true past, one cool night on an isolated ocean shore in the presence of an entombed city, had anything been altered. Now he knew that, truly, it was his homeworld as well, in a way that Moth, the world of his youth, was not and never could be. Interesting, he mused. It appeared that one did not have to grow up in a place to recognize it as home.

His gaze rose to contemplate the sweep of distorted space outside the chamber port. Moth might be his childhood abode, and Earth his ancestral haven, but this ship was home to him now. Within his head, all was quiet for the first time in weeks. No tempestuous emotions flailed at him, no overwrought feelings instigated the familiar painful pounding at the back of his skull. His vision was clear. In void there was peace.

With a sigh, he settled back into the seat and bid the ship manufacture him something tall, cool, and sweet to drink. Such were the privileges of ownership and command. He would have traded them one and all for an ordinary life, for freedom from what he was and what he had seen. In lieu of that, ice, sugar, and flavoring would have to do.

Within the hour he was reclining, drink at his side, in the ship's main lounge. A refuge from overwrought thought as well as the peaceful cold deadness outside the hull, the spacious chamber had recently been redecorated and embellished to suit his unassuming preferences.

Instead of copies of great art, or synthesized enviros, or expensive holos, the lounge environment was presently composed entirely of natural materials. In this desire to keep something of the physical world close around him, Flinx was not exceptional among deep-space travelers. Hence the seeming incongruity of firms that special-ized in placing reassembled boulders and beaches, trees and flowers deep within the wholly artificial confines of space-traversing ves-sels. In this the Ulru-Ujurrians had complied admirably with their young friend's wishes. The *Teacher* contained mechanisms that al-lowed him to alter the decor as his mood demanded.

The log on which he was presently supine was composed of woody material, but it was not nor had it ever been in any sense alive. It was capable of motion, however, as it flexed to perfectly fit the curve of his spine. On the far side of the bathing pond, whose waters were held in place by the overflow of the KK-drive when the ship was traveling and by a transparent restraining membrane when it was not, a small waterfall tumbled and splashed into the clear water. Fish Flinx had added subsequent to the ship's construction swam lazily in its depths while frogs that had hatched from imported tadpoles and willowy grunps from Moth hunted for food in the shallows.

Programmed breezes stroked the water and the landscaping that surrounded it. At present the light was evening post-rain, subject to luminary adjustment at Flinx's whim. With a word, he could conjure up a cloudburst that would soak everything but him, a balmy tropi-cal evening, a soft shower, brilliant sunrise or easygoing sunset, or a cloudless evening in which the stars put in their appearance with carefully preprogrammed deliberation. *Any* stars, as seen from any one of a hundred different worlds. If he wanted meteors, he could call for meteors. Or comets, or a visitation from a perambulating nebula. Decorative simulacra of anything in the universe were avail-able for the asking.

Disdaining technology designed to fool the senses, he much preferred the waterfall, the pond, and the surrounding plants that the ship's automatics looked after and groomed as attentively as any human gardener.

The plants themselves were an interesting hodgepodge, garnered from half a dozen worlds. Many had their origins in Terran species. Others did not. Among the latter was an enchanting assortment from his last port of call before Earth, an almost forgotten colony its inhabitants had named Midworld. When taking his leave of the place, he had left behind not only the frustrated thranx science Counselor Second Druvenmaquez, but friends among the original human inhabitants. Notable among them were the hunter Enoch and a comely young widow named Teal. Sorry they were to see him go, and would not hear of sending him off without gifts.

Expecting carvings or necklaces of local woods and seeds, he was a little surprised to find himself the new owner of several dozen carefully transplanted growths ranging in size from mosslike clusters of low-growing greenery to budding saplings. Unable to find a diplomatic way of refusing the offerings, he had seen to it that all were transferred onto his shuttle prior to his secretive departure. From its cargo hold, the *Teacher*'s automatics were then able to transport them safely to the lounge, where they were quickly and efficiently placed in available soils deemed most likely to facilitate their survival.

Looking back, the presentation that had taken him by surprise at the time seemed perfectly natural in retrospect. What more appropriate gift to bestow on a visitor by way of send-off and remembrance from a world entirely overlaid with forest than a carefully chosen assortment of houseplants? Or ship plants, in his case. Uncertain at first about the unusual gift, he had quickly come to appreciate their presence. They added color and fragrance to the lounge.

One shrub boasted long, broad flowers of deep vermilion speckled with bright blue. Another put forth stubby purple cones whose single seeds, when cracked and ground to powder, made the best bread flavoring he had ever tasted. A small sapling that he had been assured would not outgrow his ship sang like a flute every time an artificially generated breeze passed over its hollow branches. Two others filled the lounge with the heady scent of pomegranate and clove, while another smelled abundantly of vanilla.

The new plants contributed ambrosial smells, interesting foods, and quirky sounds, just as did the vast forest that engulfed all of Midworld. The chief difference lay in the fact that none of them, Teal had reassured him, were capable of the often murderous behavior common to a host of Midworldian growths. They had been carefully chosen by her and her friends. He need not worry about brushing up against his new green companions, or relieving them of their fruits or seeds. Having observed close at hand and all too often the singular means by which the aggressive vegetation of that world had evolved to defend itself, he was glad of the guarantee.

Despite the assurances of his friends, for the first few weeks he had moved cautiously in the presence of the most recent additions to the lounge's decor. By the time he was preparing to drop out of space-plus and enter the Terran system, the last of his fears had fled. He wandered among the new plants as freely and easily as he did among the old. Save for the profusion of vivacious fragrances, there was not all that much to differentiate the new transplants from New Riviera roses or Alaspinian palmettes.

Actually, there was. And the difference was considerable: more so than he could have imagined. It was just that he could not see it.

His own state of mind might have provided a clue, had he been perceptive enough to notice the change. But someone who is generally healthy, relaxed, eating and sleeping well while at peace with the universe rarely stops to contemplate the causes of his contentment. An older, wiser individual might have thought to remark on the unusual degree of inner calm he was experiencing, but Flinx was too young to be anything other than abstractedly grateful. He went about his business without bothering to analyze the source of his serenity. Much of it was his own, a consequence of successfully departing Midworld while evading the professedly benign attentions of the visiting thranx. A good deal of the rest was due to outside influences.

Specifically, his newly acquired verdure.

The remarkable flora of Midworld, unmatched in profusion or diversity anywhere else in the galaxy, had over the eons developed a kind of massively diffuse planetary group-mind that participated in the ongoing evolution of something that was less than consciousness but more than thought. Forced to deal with the arrival of mobile consciousnesses containered within individual, highly mobile bodies, it had responded by trying both to understand these new mentalities and to selectively modify them. Drawing upon the intruders' own thoughts and feelings, it had provided them with companions both Midworldian and familiar, in the form of the six-legged, wandering furcots.

Then a new mobile intelligence had come into the world, slightly but significantly different from those of its fellows. These latter might not recognize the discrepancies inherent in the new arrival, but the world-girdling greenness did. Setting out to learn, it was stunned and appalled by some of what it found. Clearly, there existed threats to existence, to the expansion and health of the forest that was the world, that the expansive greenness had never before been able to perceive. This it was now able to do, thanks to the unsuspecting lens that was the new arrival.

After some time spent in observation and study, of one thing the greenness was certain: It must not lose contact with the singular individual under scrutiny. What it knew had proven to be shocking. What it might be capable of doing might turn out to provide salvation for all.

Or nothing might come of it. But the collective subliminal greenness had not come to dominate an entire planet by ignoring possibilities. The individual had to be monitored. At all costs, contact must be maintained.

So when Flinx departed Midworld, he did so in the company of some inoffensive decorative flora provided by his friends. Why they had chosen the particular growths that they had he did not know. He would have been intrigued to learn that Enoch, Teal, and the others of their tribe did not know why they had selected those certain plants, either. In actuality, the plants had chosen themselves.

Since the plants spawned no emotions he could sense, Flinx was unaware of the collective consciousness they possessed. Whether this constant flow of cognizance functioned in space-plus or space-minus depended on whether one considered it a product of sentience, or of something else not yet defined. It was enough that the awareness could exist simultaneously in two places at the same time, across distances that were vast only in human terms. Quantum thinking it was, different parts of the same discernment inseparable across distances measurable only in primitive and inadequate physical terms. Through a small portion of its own self, the greenness, the world-mind that was Midworld, was present on the *Teacher* as surely as it was on its far larger world of origin.

It would continue to be so, observing and perceiving, in its own undetectable, inexplicable fashion, unless deprived of light and water. It wanted, needed, to know all that Flinx knew, so that it might set about devising in its own uncommon manner a means for combating the overweening terror it sensed stored within him. While doing so, it would continue to provide the sentience it was studying with agreeable smells, pleasant tastes, and soothing sights.

None of the flora aboard the *Teacher*, transplanted from Midworld or elsewhere, bore acorns—but on that one small ship speeding through the lonely otherness that was space-plus, the seed of something exalted had nonetheless begun to germinate.

# CHAPTER

# 6

Pyrassis was the fourth planet out from its star. For company, it could boast the usual brace of uninhabitable rocky globes, a couple of unspectacular gas giants, a trio of diaphanous asteroid belts, a single methane dwarf, and the usual assortment of icy comets, meteors metallic and stony, and assorted drifting junk: stellar breccia. It was not a memorable system, and Pyrassis itself a less than awe-inspiring planet. Typical of the type of worlds favored by the AAnn, its primary colors when seen from space were not blue and brown, but yellow and red, though there were significant and sizable streaks and splotches of bright blue and green. The atmosphere was nitrox in familiar proportions, the gravity familiar, and the ambient temperature everywhere except at the polar extremes, hot. Just the way the reptiloids liked it, only more so.

Approaching from outsystem with extreme caution, Flinx had the *Teacher*'s preceptors make a thorough examination of the immediate spatial vicinity. A pair of lifeless, unprepossessing moons circled their parent world. Both were drab, heavily cratered, and insofar as his ship could determine, devoid of anything indicative of intelligent visitation beyond a couple of insignificant and probably long-dormant scientific monitoring terminals.

As for Pyrassis itself, the single network of artificial satellites locked in equatorial and circumpolar orbits was as elementary as Flinx had ever encountered, designed to facilitate nothing more complicated than rudimentary ground-based and low-orbital communications. By positioning itself within the umbra of the nearest moon, the *Teacher* would render itself invisible to detection from the ground. Analysis of surface-based signals suggested the presence of only a single deepspace carrying beam, and nothing in the realm of sensitive military detectors. Surface-to-surface signals were low-gain and infrequent, hinting at a trifling and widely scattered AAnn presence. Not one of the battered satellites circling in languid low orbit was large enough to pose a threat to an arriving vessel.

The lack of security did not surprise him. Clearly, the AAnn presence on Pyrassis was limited. There were no cities, most likely a single shuttleport, little in the way of surface infrastructure, and certainly nothing beyond minimal military facilities. With so little to defend, there was no reason for the Empire to waste precious equipage, resources that could be better employed elsewhere, in fortifying it. By every measurable criterion, here was an out-of-the-way, strategically unimportant world just barely worthy of the notice of the Empire that claimed it. Sheltered by its location within Empire boundaries, it required nothing else in the way of protection. There was not much here for the AAnn to watch over, and less for raiders to seize.

The last thing any AAnn based on the surface would expect to have to deal with was an illicit intrusion from the Commonwealth. They would be shocked to discover that an unauthorized ship was settling in behind the nearer moon, the better to keep clear of any roving sensors. Had they bothered to look closer, they would have been utterly stunned to discover not one but two unsanctioned craft occupying the same obscure location.

The *Crotase* did not react to his arrival. No hailing frequency activated the *Teacher*'s communications module. No salutation image materialized above the command console in front of Flinx. As he directed the *Teacher* to tuck in close beside the other Commonwealth vessel, Flinx examined the *Crotase* for visible indications that it was engaged on a mission fraught with extraordinary possibilities. Nothing he saw suggested that this was the case. The Larnaca Nutrition transport sported a standard light-freight configuration, with two passenger/cargo modules comprising the stern of the elongated KK-drive craft. Other than appearing to be in unusually good condition, there was nothing exceptional about the vessel.

Well, if they were going to ignore him, he decided, then it was incumbent upon him to open communication. Maybe they were waiting to make sure the recently arrived craft was crewed by humans or thranx, and was not a captured vessel being operated by the cunning AAnn to lead them into exposing themselves.

No one responded to his queries. Close enough to exchange personnel via suits, the two ships drifted in the shadow of the nearer moon, the *Teacher* calling, the *Crotase* not answering. What its presence here had to do with Edicted information on the Meliorare Society Flinx still could not imagine. As his ship's AI patiently continued trying to evoke a response from the other Commonwealth craft, he contemplated how best to proceed.

Like him, those aboard the *Crotase* had placed their ship in the shadow of this moon to avoid detection by the AAnn residing on the Pyrassisian surface. There was no other reason for their ship to be where it was. It therefore seemed sensible to conclude that whatever they were doing here, they were not cooperating with the lizards.

The elimination of this one possibility failed to elicit enlightenment, since it still did not explain what they were doing in such a dangerous and seemingly unpromising locale in the first place.

Pyrassis might be a world of inconceivable natural riches, though that struck Flinx as an unlikely reason for a Commonwealth vessel to pay it a visit. First, because its location rendered it impractical for any human agency to subsequently exploit, and second because the AAnn themselves had not done so. Or if they had, their diminutive presence on the planet suggested an enormous effort to conceal any kind of extensive development. There was no reason for them to make the effort to do so on a world they fully controlled.

Curioser and curioser, he decided. AAnn intentions aside, the best way to find out what the crew of the *Crotase* was doing here was to confront them in person with the questions they were reluctant to answer via intership contact. Making plain via open broadcast that he planned to pay them a visit, and directing the *Teacher* to repeatedly state his intentions, he left the command chamber and made his way to one of the ship's locks. Sensing that his master's excitement was conflicted with other emotions, Pip alternated humming along the corridor in front of him with landing repeatedly on his shoulder.

If they would not react to verbal or coded inquiries, Flinx decided as he entered the outer lock, perhaps they would respond to a knock on their front door.

Taking no chances, he donned a full survival suit before entering the *Teacher*'s shuttle bay. While the suit was awkward to wear, it would provide a degree of protection in the event of trouble. Its internal pickup automatically adjusted volume and modulation so that he could effortlessly deliver verbal orders to the shuttle's command nexus. Coiled tightly against his shoulder, Pip made a noticeable but not restrictive bulge within the suit.

He could have directed the *Teacher* to ease right up alongside the drifting freighter, but in the event unforeseen difficulty reared its Hydralike head, he wanted his ship out of easy attack range. Programmed to react in specific ways to explicit assaults, he had no qualms about leaving it to maneuver on its own. He had spent a good deal of time preparing the AI to cope with difficulties in his absence. Feeling confident that the vessel could take care of itself, he directed the shuttle to move out and head toward the elongated bulk of the silent *Crotase*.

If anything ought to have brought a response from the freighter, it should have been the approach of another large metallic object advancing on a collision course. But though he kept all hailing frequencies open, Flinx heard nothing from the ship he was approaching. It was a good deal more massive than the *Teacher*, with a bulbous cargo bay appended to the crew and passenger quarters. Light flaring from ports and telltales indicated that power was on throughout the KK-drive craft's entire attenuated length.

There was nothing remarkable about the ship. In detail as well as silhouette it fit the standard schematic for its type: a purely commercial vessel bearing no surprises. Shuttle bays were located where he expected to find them. Maneuvering cautiously around the cargo carrier's bulk, he discovered one bay open and empty. Designed to accommodate a much larger cargo shuttle, it offered easy ingress to the heart of the mother ship.

Once more he attempted direct verbal contact, and once again was rebuffed with silence. Shrugging, he directed the shuttle to dock in the most expedient manner possible. The automatics on the *Crotase* responded to his intrusion with alacrity. In less than two minutes his craft was tightly snugged in the bay. He barely had time to push free of the command chair before the shuttle felt the effects of the freighter's powered-down KK-drive field. Gravity once more took hold of his body.

Exiting in his self-contained survival suit, breathing canned air, he examined the outer lock controls. As with the rest of the *Crotase*, everything was stock and familiar. As a fully qualified, experienced thief, he was used from childhood to breaking into homes and businesses. Breaking into a quiescent starship required a greater command of existing technology, but many of the same techniques. Using the equipment on his suit's tool belt, which was in turn linked to the shuttle's AI, he was able to break manually into the freighter's living quarters. Within minutes he had accessed the autochthonous AI. In less than half an hour it had accepted him as a valid user.

Responding to his commands, it proceeded to secure the bay. He did not order it to close the outer hatch. No sensible thief locks doors behind him.

If Mother Mastiff could see me now, he found himself musing. It was a long way from pilfering bread to stealing a starship. He had no use for the *Crotase* itself, however. He had come to loot only information.

The inner lock doors opened as readily as the outer, responding briskly to his directives. Nothing emerged to impede his advance. Though his sensors indicated the presence of fully pressurized, uncontaminated, temperature-controlled atmosphere throughout the corridor he was traversing, he did not unseal his suit. There was no need to take chances. He felt confident he could get what he had come for without taking unnecessary risks.

Around him, the ship hummed efficiently while continuing to manifest only mechanical life. Corridors and rooms were brightly lit. In a prosaically decorated crew lounge he found dishes piled high with snack foods in addition to indications of at least two meals abandoned unfinished. No trays lay mute on the deck, however, and no food or drink had been scattered violently about. There was nothing to indicate that the diners had abandoned their fare in haste.

The entire ship lay open to him. His progress was restricted only by privacy codes that barred entrance to individual living quarters. Since several of these stood open to inspection, he had no reason to assume that the others contained anything of especial note, and he made no effort to bypass their personal security. He was not here to spy on an unknowing crew.

What crew? Where was everyone? Had they been surprised by the AAnn and taken down to the surface for interrogation? That particular experience was one that, fortunately, had so far been denied to him. From everything he had heard, a discomfiting gallimaufry of fact and fiction, it was one he would gladly continue to avoid. Had the crew committed mass suicide by blowing themselves out a lock into space? There was nothing on board to indicate anything so excessive had taken place. There were no signs of violence, of struggle, or even of internal dissention.

Based on what he found, or more properly, what he did not find, everything suggested that they had voluntarily transported themselves down to the surface on the freighter's other shuttlecraft. He could not imagine what for. What off Earth did a company that manufactured processed foods want with a desert world like Pyrassis? He stood outside the bridge, uncomprehendingly shaking his head. For that matter, he had yet to figure out what they wanted with Edicted records of Meliorare doings.

Like everything else aboard the *Crotase*, the command-and-control blister was considerably larger than its counterpart on the *Teacher*. Unmonitored glowing consoles beckoned, efficient instrumentation silently declaimed reams of unperused information, and chairs reposed unoccupied. Anyone else thrust abruptly into such hushed surroundings could easily and quickly have become spooked. Not Flinx. In his short life he had seen and been forced to deal with far more intimidating surroundings than a deserted ship. Avoiding the empty command chair, he settled himself into one of the secondary seats.

The freighter's AI was no less responsive in the control center than it had been in the outer lock. It replied to his queries promptly and without hesitation as he prodded it to divulge the information he had come so far to recover. Unfortunately, the admirably expeditious response did not take the form Flinx desired.

"The information you request is contained in an Edicted sybfile."

"I know that." Flinx had trouble controlling his impatience. Sensing it, Pip stirred beneath the fabric of the survival suit. "I don't seek disclosure. Transfer of the physical file to a blank storage chyp will suffice." He emphasized the request by running a finger over the Activate proximity control set in the arm of his chair.

"Transfer cannot be accomplished." The voice of the *Crotase* was serenely implacable.

"Why not?" Flinx inquired sharply. "Is there a command string lacking? Define the nature of the problem."

"It is straightforward," the AI responded by way of explanation. "The sybfile in question no longer resides within my cortex. It has been removed, and there is no copy."

Flinx slowly took a deep breath. He had not traveled an unconscionable number of parsecs to hear what he had already heard once before, on Earth. "Where is it now? Trace all echoes and ghosts."

"That will not be necessary." The AI's assurance was calming. Finally, something positive! "The sybfile you request has been transferred to and at last check resides within the storage mode of personal recorder DNP-466EX."

Hope and confidence returning, Flinx resumed his pursuit. "Where is the indicated recorder now? What is its present location?" Clearly, if he wanted the syb, he was going to have to confront the crewmember in whose possession it presently resided. As he contemplated his next query, he wondered if the individual was even aware of the sensitive nature of the information he or she was toting around.

For a change, the AI's reply did not surprise him. "Following recent disembarkation, all crew departed on shuttle drop for the surface of the world called Pyrassis, presently located—"

"I know where Pyrassis is," Flinx interrupted briskly. "I can see it out the nearest port. I need specifics. Touchdown coordinates." He tensed slightly. "Was disembarkation voluntary, or coerced?"

"Voluntary," the *Crotase* replied without hesitation.

Some of the tenseness flowed out of him. Whatever the crew of the freighter was up to, or involved in, or dealing with on the surface of the dry, remote world below, they had not been captured by the AAnn. That greatly enhanced his chance of recovering, by whatever means, the information he sought. But it still begged the question of what humans were doing here.

Time for one more highly sensitive question. Whoever they were and whatever their intentions, the one thing the landing party would not dare to do would be to lose contact with their ship. Which meant that if they were in regular contact with the *Crotase*, then the freighter would also be in contact with them.

"You have the present coordinates of all absent crew, including the individual in possession of the personal recorder containing the sybfile in question?"

"I am continuously monitoring the location of the landing party," the ship responded readily. "However, I do not supervise electronics on the personal level. There is no guarantee that the individual transporting the particular recorder under discussion is still in possession of it. In its absence from my presence, it may have been manually transferred to any other individual."

That was reasonable enough, Flinx concluded. No matter. He would locate the recorder when he located and confronted the crew. They might share several dozen such devices among them, but the freighter's AI had thoughtfully provided him with its identifying code.

Adopting his most assured tone, he once more addressed the *Crotase*'s AI. "Request that you transfer last known coordinates of landing party to navigation submodule of . . ." and he provided the necessary coding and security-pass information to the AI of his own shuttle, presently resting in the freighter's bay.

He breathed a small sigh of relief when the voice of the *Crotase* replied, "Complying," and seconds later, "Requested information transferred."

Rising from the seat, Flinx took a last look around the deserted command chamber. Strange that whoever was in charge of this eccentric mission had not chosen to leave even a skeleton crew aboard. It suggested that everyone might be needed to fulfill whatever purpose was intended. Or that whoever was in charge did not trust their own crew sufficiently to leave even one member of the company behind in charge of the ship. The absence of any evidence for discord prior to disembarking hinted at another possibility. Whoever Larnaca Nutrition had sent here might be cooperating with the AAnn.

Even this remote prospect still did not answer the question, Why Pyrassis? Though percolating natural curiosity demanded an answer, it was one he was willing to forgo if he could just obtain the information locked in the appropriated syb. Some kind of confrontation with the absent crew appeared inevitable. He smiled to himself. It might be direct, or accomplished by stealth. If the latter, then he would be on familiar territory. He was something of a master at concealing his presence from others.

Just as there had been when he had come aboard, there was nothing to stop him, either verbally or physically, from leaving the freighter. Safely back aboard his shuttle, he checked to make certain the *Crotase*'s AI had actually provided his craft with the requested landing coordinates. They were there, forthright and conspicuous, in the shuttle's data bank. Reaching down to unseal and slip out of the survival suit's confines, he decided to hold off doing so until he was clear of the hulking freighter.

Agreeable as before, the *Crotase* obediently acknowledged his request to disengage. The shuttle was gently released and allowed to drift clear of the bay. Addressing his own craft's onboard AI, he directed it to program in the newly received set of coordinates and set down within three kilometers of the identified locality, leaving it to the shuttle's nav system to choose the best site.

He could have returned to the *Teacher* and ridden his own ship to the surface. Thanks to several unprecedented and carefully concealed modifications built into her by the Ulru-Ujurrians, his vessel was, to the best of his knowledge, the only one in the Arm capable of advancing to within five planetary diameters of a target world—much less actually landing upon it utilizing its KK-drive. Commonwealth engineers would have been confounded by the revelation. It was only one of many secrets he had resolved to safeguard. In order to do so he was compelled to utilize, like everyone else, a shuttle for traveling between ship and surface. Thus far no observers had deduced this unique ability of the *Teacher*, and he was determined to keep it that way.

Noting that it was nighttime in the projected landing zone, he added the additional instructions that the forthcoming touchdown was to be carried out without external lights or power. Automatically trimming and adjusting the little vessel's delta wings to account for local climatic conditions, the shuttle would glide to a landing in virtual silence. With luck, its arrival would not be noticed by those on the surface. Obviously, this would greatly enhance his chances of approaching their camp unnoticed and on foot. It was and had always been his favored means of approaching the unfamiliar.

Should it prove possible to do so, he would much prefer to steal what he had come for.

The shuttle's engines fired, attitude control rotated the craft eighty-five degrees, and as steady acceleration pushed him back into the command chair, it began to move out from behind the shadow of Pyrassis's nearer moon. Very quickly, the familiar bulges and lines of both the *Crotase* and the *Teacher* fell behind. Ahead loomed a lambent beige and rust-red world against which white streaks and tufts of cloud appeared even starker than they did against the blue-brown backdrops of planets like Earth and Moth and Alaspin.

As soon as the shuttle's AI assured him they were on course for arrival, he reached down to release the increasingly uncomfortable survival suit's seals. Conducted to his ears by the suit's pickups, a faint hissing stopped him in midreach. Frowning, he glanced down to where his lower body lay secured in the seat's harness.

The hissing sound was not coming from his suit.

"I'm hearing what sounds like an atmospheric precipitance." His fingers moved away from the suit's seals. "Confirm and identify."

There was a pause. It was brief, and might not have been noticed by others less sensitive than Flinx. But he did notice it, and the hackles went up on his neck. Instantly, Pip poked her head out from within her brightly colored coils. The small, bright-eyed, triangular green shape rose up into his headpiece, obscuring a small portion of his vision. He was too busy and too anxious to admonish her. This was not a problem in which, however well-meaning, she could assist.

"I sense no disturbance," the shuttle's AI responded. "There is nothing to identify."

The hiss continued. He was not imagining it. "There is a barometric anomaly present. Confirm and identify."

The voice of the shuttle did not change. "I sense no disturbance."

Reaching out and over, Flinx activated a heads-up display. It appeared in front of him, frozen in midair. A few taps on manual controls brought forth the information he sought. It was chilling in its contradiction of the AI's declaration. Very plainly, with numbers as well as words, it indicated that atmospheric pressure within the shuttle was down to less than 0.5 PSI—and continuing to fall steadily.

The leak would have to be located later. Right now he was far more concerned with the AI's seeming incognizance. "Instrumentation indicates we are bleeding air. Confirm, and if possible, identify the source of the leakage."

"I sense no seepage of the kind you imply. Hull integrity is sound. All systems are operating normally."

It did not take long for the hissing sound to cease. According to the manual sensors, this did not come about because corrective measures had been applied to recalcitrant instrumentation. It occurred because there was no longer any breathable air within the shuttle. He could quickly confirm this by unsealing and removing any part of his survival suit. He elected not to do so because if the instrumentation was right and the AI wrong, he would perish quickly and unpleasantly.

Which is exactly what would have happened to him if, as was normally the case, he had been sitting confidently in the shuttle's command chair clad in nothing but his daily coveralls.

Something had caused the supposedly fail-safe shuttle to inexplicably vent its internal atmosphere. A check revealed that the AI's response had been at least partially correct: hull integrity had not been violated. Which meant that something had directed the ship's systems themselves to void the air. Only a command delivered directly to the AI could induce that kind of reaction. He had given no such command. It was inconceivable that it could have come from the now distant *Teacher*. Where could it possibly have originated? The shuttle had received only two recent external directives. One from him, ordering it to program in a touchdown proximate to recently acquired planetary coordinates. The second from the AI of the *Crotase*, providing those coordinates.

And just possibly, he realized with a sudden chill, supplying something else along with them.

No wonder he had been allowed free and easy access to the freighter. No wonder nothing had been denied to him, including access to the vessel's main AI. No wonder no door had been programmed to seal itself behind him, no explosive device to go off beneath his booted feet or at his approach. There was no need. Whoever had programmed the freighter's response to intrusion had done so with exquisite subtlety. The booby trap it had been trained to plant was designed to go off only *after* an intruder departed. While he had been tunneling into the *Crotase*'s AI, it had silently been doing the same thing to the controlling intelligence of his shuttle.

He ought to have anticipated something of the sort. The Shell blowback at Surire should have habituated him to the mind-set of the kind of people he was dealing with.

Lamenting the oversight now would do him no good at all, and would only waste time. "You are experiencing a malfunction," he announced solemnly. "Your cortex has been invaded. I direct you to execute all emergency clear, cleanse, and nullification programs and restore your system to health. If required, temporary shutdown of all functions may be permitted." A risky command, but no less so than allowing whatever had burrowed deep within the AI to continue to do damage with impunity.

The shuttle's reply was not encouraging. "All systems are functioning normally. There is no need for shutdown, or to perform cleansing procedures." Thoughtfully, it advanced a time frame for touchdown.

Safe within the self-contained environment of the survival suit, he and Pip could ignore the insidious evacuation of air from the shuttle's living quarters. The trouble was, given the blithe, blissful, persistent ignorance of the craft's AI, he had no way of knowing if that was the only problem he could anticipate having to deal with. Sure enough, within a couple of minutes, others began to make themselves known with unnerving regularity.

Most disconcerting of all was the unsettling realization that as it entered Pyrassisian atmosphere, the shuttle was making no attempt to moderate its velocity. Well after deceleration ought to have begun, the little craft was doing nothing to brake itself preparatory to landing.

"*Teacher*! Priority override!" Silence shouted back at him from the suit's speakers. "*Teacher,* acknowledge! Shuttlecraft emergency failure, all systems unresponsive. *Acknowledge!*"

Uttering an uncommon epithet, he found himself admiring the skill with which the pathocybergen had been implanted in the shuttle's shell, even as he fought to identify and disarm it. A major complication manifested itself when he realized that trouble was spreading through the system as fast as he could isolate individual components. Working furiously with manual directives, he managed to segregate and fix the command string that had caused the internal atmosphere to be evacuated from the shuttle. That proved easier than his frantic attempts to reestablish communication with the *Teacher*. If he could just make contact, he could direct its far more advanced AI to correct the problems the shuttle's shell continued to insist did not exist. All such attempts, however, came to naught.

Meanwhile, one onboard system after another continued to shut down, or fold into cross-purposes, or otherwise defeat every attempt by him to disentangle it from whatever treacherous pathogen the *Crotase* had cunningly inserted into supposedly safeguarded depths. And all the while, the shuttle continued to plunge surfaceward at an acceptable angle but at a decidedly inappropriate velocity on a vector designated for death. During which frenzied time the onboard AI continued to cheerfully insist that nothing was wrong, all systems were functioning normally, and that touchdown would occur within the specified time. That was not what troubled Flinx. What concerned him was the specific celerity with which the scheduled landing would take place. An efficacious touchdown was one in which everything involved, both animate and otherwise, retained its individual integrity. The long-sought-after sybfile would not do scattered shreds of him any good.

It struck him with brutal, indifferent force that if he could not effect some significant changes to his present situation within the next couple of minutes, he most assuredly was going to die.

# CHAPTER

# 7

The shuttle's AI stayed as calm as Flinx was frantic, blissfully ignoring all evidence of an increasingly desperate reality. When Flinx pleaded for it to reestablish communications with the master AI on the *Teacher*, the shuttle confidently assured him that such communications were active. When he tried everything to persuade it to increase deceleration, it insisted that all touchdown modes were operating on optimal, refusing to be dissuaded by the increasingly dense, increasingly heated atmosphere outside. When ordered to perform a thorough internal check-and-clean of its command systems, it promptly agreed to do so—only to conclude that everything was fine, nothing was the matter, and that they would be landing gently in a matter of minutes.

Meanwhile, the venting of critical fluids commenced, monitors began to fail, screens grew dark, and the shuttle gave every indication of shutting down section by section around its single human occupant. Fighting one system collapse after another as the unstoppable pathogen propagated throughout the shuttle, Flinx realized he had to set down quickly, while he still retained some semblance of control over the rapidly descending craft. Despite the desperation of his circumstances, the irony of it did not escape him. How fast would be too fast? How exacting an impact could he tolerate and still survive?

At least, if his remaining instruments could be believed, the shuttle was still on course for the chosen landing site. And why not? There was no reason for the crippling intruder to alter the path of descent. It could crash the ship as thoroughly on target as anywhere else.

Manual controls existed, but were a novelty to Flinx. Lacking time for a leisurely perusal of the relevant manuals, he set about fighting to disengage control of the vessel from its supervising AI. He had played with and practiced manual landings only a few times. Now he was going to find out what, if anything, he remembered.

He could not argue directly with the addled AI, but he could disconnect it. When he initiated the suspension sequence, there was some resistance, but nothing that drive and desperation could not overcome. Now in complete control of what remained of the craft's operating systems, he began by bypassing the host of monitors that governed the engines. He celebrated a small accomplishment when he succeeded in shutting down the main drive. A larger triumph was achieved when the braking drive sprang to life. Descent velocity proceeded to degrade precipitously.

Would it be enough, and in time? He would know all too soon. Bursting forth from the underside of the inert cloud cover, Flinx set the shuttle's delta wings to deploy to maximum. Screaming surfaceward, the trim little craft scattered a host of indigenous flying creatures from its path. The ill-defined blurring of beige and brown, blue and green that comprised the surface began to resolve itself into individual features. Flinx shot over canyons and badlands, defunct river deltas and eroded mountains. Somewhere in the jumble of anguished geology, he importuned, there had to be a suitable place to land.

Minutes later, it loomed in front of him: a broad, sandy plain bordered by dunes whose height he was too busy to estimate. Entering by way of the open seals, scalding hot air shrieked unimpeded through the cockpit. The survival suit he had so providentially donned prior to exiting the *Teacher* kept him from boiling in his own body fluids.

Landing skids deployed, nose up, braking drive blasting deafeningly, he continued to surrender altitude and hope for the best. A cliff riven with the intense blue and green of luxuriant copper mineralization materialized unexpectedly in front of him, forcing him to skew the shuttle sharply to the right. The hard surface leaped abruptly into view, an unforgiving, tawny terminus. Then it turned black, accompanied by a single overpowering, echoless banging in his ears . . .

Something was tickling his eyelids. Blinking, he found himself staring into slitted reptiloid eyes. Fearing dissecting AAnn, he jumped. Then Pip drew back, her head and upper coils blocking her master's view of much of what lay beyond.

Wincing, he struggled to sit up. It required several attempts before his damaged harness reluctantly released him from the command chair. His neck throbbed, and his chest felt as if it had recently served as a temporary resting place for a tired elephant. Intense, buttery yellow sunlight made him blink. Pieces of the polarizing port that ought to have minimized the glare lay strewn throughout the cockpit, fragmented by the force of impact. Something gripped his feet.

Glancing down, he pulled them free of the grasping sand that now filled much of the shuttle's forepart. Experiencing a sudden, uncharacteristic attack of claustrophobia, he hurried to remove the survival suit's headpiece. As the shuttle's instrumentation had originally confirmed when it had been functioning properly, the atmosphere of Pyrassis was safe to breathe. It was hot, incredibly dry, and smelled faintly of desiccated myrtle. Freed from the confines of the suit, Pip unfurled her pleated pink-and-blue wings and soared through the shattered foreport, out into the alien sky. He made no attempt to restrain her. She would not stray far, and he envied her the freedom. Should he feel threatened, she would come back to him in an instant.

Struggling to move in the clinging sand, which like the cliff he had barely managed to avoid was electric with blue and green ores, he took stock of his situation. Reflecting the confusion that had afflicted its AI, the interior of the shuttle was a useless mess. The fact that he had survived with little more than a few bruises was a tribute to the sturdiness and design of the Ulru-Ujurrian–installed harness. As bad as the shuttle's unflyability was the destruction of all internal communications facilities. Those built into his survival suit would also allow him to exchange basic commands with the *Teacher*, to let it track him, perhaps even to let him instruct it to send out a second shuttle to pick him up—except that his ship was concealed behind the planet's near moon to forestall just that kind of interactive communication with the Pyrassisian surface.

Eventually, the *Teacher*'s highly sophisticated AI might wonder at his continued absence, deduce that something was amiss, and initiate a search without having to be prompted. That would take time, and would require a decision on the part of the AI to countermand Flinx's instructions to remain where it could not be observed from the world below. Presently then, his best hope lay in that portion of the *Teacher*'s programming that allowed for cybernetic initiative. He was not sanguine.

What he was, not to put too fine a technological point on it, was stuck. On an alien world he knew next to nothing about. He did know, however, the approximate last location of the landing party from the *Crotase*. Several options were open to him. One was to try and contact his fellow humans—openly, now—while using the time prior to making such contact to invent a plausible excuse for being in the improbable place where he was. Another was to wait for the AAnn to find him, in which case he was unlikely ever to see a humanx world ever again. A third was to do his best to stay alive until the *Teacher*'s AI decided it was incumbent upon it to disobey directives and contact its owner, if only to seek clarification of those same prohibitions.

Eventually, he decided his best chance lay in combining the first and third of his alternatives. He would commence a search for the *Crotase* landing party. When contact was made, he would keep his distance until he could no longer survive on his own, in the hope that the *Teacher* would come for him before his endurance was exhausted and he was forced to throw himself on whatever mercies his fellow humans might deign to visit upon him. Meanwhile he could try to locate and appropriate the personal recorder containing the long-sought-after sybfile.

It sounded like a workable course of action. Provided, of course, that the crew of the *Crotase* were not already preparing to depart, having carried out and completed whatever plan they had come to fulfill. Provided that the local AAnn, sparse and scattered though they might be, did not first discover the humans who were prowling illicitly in their midst and irately obliterate them. Provided he could survive the harsh climate, difficult terrain, and unknown inimical life-forms that might inhabit this underpopulated, out-of-the-way speck of grit.

Yes, it was a workable plan—if one disregarded all the *pro-*

*vided*s he had not provided for. The survival suit would help. Having come through the crash landing with all its functions apparently intact, it could distill water from air even as low in humidity as that presently surrounding him. Its integrated storage compartments contained food bars and supplements that could keep him alive, if not sated, for a while. The tools that filled the sturdy service belt that formed an integral part of the suit's waistband were marvels of miniaturization. One leg pouch held a potent endural pistol that fired small but satisfyingly explosive pellets, on the theory that where caliber might prove inadequate, a loud enough noise might be sufficiently disconcerting to the unsophisticated to discourage attack.

And of course, he had Pip.

Taking time to apply salve from the suit's medikit to the worst of his bruises, he scavenged the ruined shuttle for anything else that might prove useful. Designed to convey travelers safely between localities, it was ill equipped for his present needs. He did manage to cobble together a crude backpack into which he loaded an improvised water bottle, in the event his suit's distiller either broke down or proved unable to suck enough moisture out of the air, and some plasticine sheeting from which to extemporize a shelter. Making certain that the shuttle's integrated, shielded emergency beacon was active so that the *Teacher*, if and when it grew so inclined, would not have to search half the planet to find him, he exited the downed craft by climbing out the shattered foreport. The main hatch was jammed beyond repair.

For someone so young, he had experience of a number of different ecosystems, from the rain forests of Alaspin and Midworld, to the urban centers and high mountains of Earth, to the underground world of Longtunnel and its wind-scoured surface. There were also the years he had spent growing up on Moth, a colony world that boasted a rich variety of environments. But only once before had he spent any significant time in a desertlike climate, and that was in the company of a hoary old prospector named Knigta Yakus.

He tried to remember all that he knew of such conditions as he set off, striding strongly away from the downed shuttle as he let the suit's tracker lead him eastward. Somewhere over the dune-dominated horizon the crew of the Commonwealth freighter *Crotase* was engaged in dangerous, illegal, and scandalous activity the likes of which Flinx could not imagine. It was sobering to realize that un-less his circumstances changed drastically, and soon, those interlop-ers represented his best hope for survival.

While the heat would not bother her, he knew that eventually Pip would begin to suffer from the lack of ambient humidity. He would have to take care to keep her properly hydrated. With its headpiece restored but faceplate retracted, the suit kept him reason-ably comfortable. Designed to allow its wearer to survive in free space for a period of up to ten days, its internal power source would last a good deal longer in the comparatively benign environment of a habitable world. It would keep him cool during the day and warm at night, and if he so felt the need, he could conserve its resources even longer by shutting the suit's eco-functions down when they were not required.

He let them run now, however, because otherwise he would not have been able to make nearly as much progress in the strength-sapping heat of the day. It was imperative that he locate and over-take the landing party from the *Crotase* before they concluded their work. Keeping his distance, monitoring their activities, and trying to find out what they were doing here would not only serve to take his mind off his present awkward situation, but perhaps also answer some of the questions that had brought him here as well. Unaware they were being stalked by one of their own kind, there was no reason for them to keep moving around. Presumably, they had set down and subsequently established themselves right where they wanted to be.

Try as he might, he still could not contrive a connection between the barren world across which he was presently striding and the disreputable eugenics work of the Meliorare Society. Above and ahead of him, Pip soared appreciatively on the warm air, elated to be free of the confines of the survival suit. With luck, they would steal up upon the *Crotase* encampment within a few days or so.

Had anyone from that ship descried and tracked the shuttle's descent, and if so, would it unsettle them enough to abandon their plans? He doubted the latter. They had come too far, at too great an expense, and risked too much to pull out at the first sign of the unexpected. The shuttle's touchdown had been rough and crippling, but nonexplosive. If they had followed the shuttle's descent, the crew of the *Crotase* had at their disposal any number of ways to rationalize what they had beheld. That was assuming they had seen anything. The shuttle had come in from the west, describing a very low angle of approach. Even in this clear desert air its distant touchdown might not have been noticed.

Lengthening his stride, he stepped confidently over the sand, Pip darting to left or right to check out an unusual formation, a plant, or something unseen that might be stirring in shadow. Activating the survival suit's distiller by sucking on the internal dispenser tube, he luxuriated in the cool moisture it provided. He was not worried about stumbling into the *Crotase*'s encampment, or even into an outlying sentry. This was because for the moment, at least, his sometimes erratic talent was active and alert. In this otherwise uninhabited alien desolation, he would be able to pick up even sedate human or AAnn emotions long before he sighted those to whom they belonged. He felt confident that before long, despite the temporary setback, he would finally be able to obtain answers to the flush of bewildering questions that had carried him beyond the farthest limits of the Commonwealth.

His emboldened convictions were not matched by certain growths he had left behind on board the *Teacher*. In ways that could not be explained by contemporary biology, physics, or any other branch of the familiar sciences, they sensed that something had gone seriously wrong with the warm-blooded vertebrate in whose charge they had been placed. When his absence persisted, they grew quietly frantic. Leaves twitched imperceptibly in the windless confines of the *Teacher*'s lounge. Petals dipped under the influence of forces far more subtle and less obvious than falling water. Unseen roots curled in response to wave patterns that had nothing to do with the subtle movements of soil and grit.

The situation was analyzed in the absence of anything Flinx or any other chordate would recognize as a brain. It involved a manifold process of cogitation far more alien than any propounded by AAnn or thranx, Otoid or Quillp. Among the known sentients, only the cetacea of Cachalot or the Sumacrea of Longtunnel might, upon exerting a supreme effort, have glimpsed an intimation of the process, but no more than that. It was not possible for compartmentalized organic brains deliberating by means of sequential electric impulses to fathom what was taking place among the plants of Midworld.

Contemplation occurred with consequences resulting. Meditation existed on a plane remote from the familiar. By virtue of reflection, resolution simply was. No human, equipped with the latest and most relevant tools, would have recognized the process for what it was. And yet—there were fine points of tangency.

In silence broken only by the whisper of air being recycled through the hull, envisionings sprang lucent and undiminished among the alien flora. What inhered among them inhered among every other growing thing on the world from which they had come. It was not a discussion in the sense that subjects were put forth for disputation and debate. Did clouds moot before resolving to rain? Did atmosphere argue prior to sending a breeze northward, or to the east? When a whirling magnetar blew off overwhelming quantities of gamma rays, was the direction and moment of eruption a consequence of cognizant confutation?

Among the incredibly diffuse but nonetheless vast aggregate worldmind of which the verdure on board the *Teacher* were an inseparable part, what *Was* became what *Is*. Call it thought if it aids in comprehension. The plants themselves did not think of it as such. They did not think of it at all. They could not, since what transpired among them was not thought that could in any sense be defined as such.

That did not mean that what came to pass among them was devoid of consequence. It was determined that, for the moment, at least, nothing could be done to affect what had transpired. Patience would have to be exercised. The disturbing situation might yet resolve itself in particulars agreeable to those whose awareness of it was salient. Their perception of the physical state of existence humans defined as time was different from that of those who inhabited the other, more-remarked-upon biological kingdom.

It seemed that nothing could be done until the situation on the surface of the planet below resolved itself. Except—the dominating flora of a certain singular green world had progressed beyond the first sight to which their rooted brethren on other worlds were still restricted. Their equivalent of thought was capable of generating aftereffects. Normally, these took prodigious quantities of time to manifest themselves. But since humans had come among them hundreds of years earlier, circumstances attributable to consequent interactions had resulted in the celerity of these distinctive ruminations accelerating. Happenings took place within expedited time frames that could not even have been imagined millions of years earlier, when the worldmind had first begun to become aware of itself as a disparate but solvent entity.

Tentatively, with none but the uncritical electronic oculi of the *Teacher*'s AI to see what they were about, tendrils began to emerge from the cores of several growths, slowly but perceptibly extending themselves outward from the planters in which they had been rooted.

# CHAPTER

# 8

Seen from orbit through high, swirling white clouds, Pyrassis was a globe dominated by Earth tones but highlighted with unexpected streaks of brighter hues. The origin of the multiple shades of blue and green was not ocean, while that for many of the yellows and oranges, reds and purples, was not sand—though there was plenty of that. The sources were more solid, more inflexible, less mutable. They also provided a rationale for the existence of at least a small AAnn presence.

On Pyrassis, the process of cupric precipitation had run riot.

Everywhere within the streaked and banded rocks past which Flinx traipsed, pockets of crystals sparkled in the diffuse light of the alien sun. In the depths of punctured vugs, needlelike clusters of fragile silicates and bladed arsenates sparkled with the promise of new combinations of elements. He marveled at them in passing, intent on reaching the site where the visitants from the *Crotase* had established their illicit camp. Despite his resolution, it was impossible to completely ignore the fantastic diversity of shapes and colors.

Pausing by one open vug, he pointed his suit's interpreter at the dazzling interior and requested a chemical analysis. "Gebhardite, Leitite, Ludlockite, Reinerite, Schneiderhöhnite, and at least three compounds unknown to science. All arsenites or arsenic oxides."

Flinx didn't even try to pronounce them. "Never heard of any of them."

"It is debatable which is rarer than the next," the interpreter observed. "To find them all together is quite remarkable."

Seeing no need to comment further, since the interpreter's ability to sustain a conversation was limited to the information in its straightforward knowledge kernel, Flinx leaned forward as he began to ascend a series of stairlike ridges. The rock underfoot was composed of yellowish orange silicates, sprinkled in protected cracks and rills with druzy calcite and quartz. Pyrassis was a mineralogist's paradise, but he was not interested in collecting specimens: only information. At least, he mused, his unexpected trek would not lack for visual stimulation.

Taking another sip from the suit's distiller while scratching a resting Pip on the back of her head, he paused at the top of the last ridge. Spread out before him was a gleaming panorama of spectacular colors and twisted formations set against a sky that was a hazy mixture of turquoise and chalk. Nothing in his line of vision looked to be too high to ascend or too difficult to traverse. In the distance, he thought he saw several dark shapes undulating lazily among the low-lying clouds, but he could not be certain. They might have been nothing more than a trick of the light, reflections, or mirages. When he looked again, from halfway down the far side of the ridge, they were gone.

His boots crushing a fortune in collector's specimens with every other step, he paused frequently to check his bearings. Knowing that the visitors from the *Crotase* would utilize only low-level communications to keep in touch with one another, lest they alert any AAnn monitoring devices located on the ground or in the sky, he had instructed the interpreter to home in on only the slightest electronic emanations coming from the specified area where the other humans had set down. In the spectacular alien wilderness of rock and crystal, it was reassuring to have the device confirm that he was in line and on track for his intended destination every time he checked it.

Nightfall brought with it a smothering silence that was broken only by the moan of an occasional breeze, and an unidentifiable but nonthreatening chirping. The wind, he decided, sounded as lonely and isolated in this place as he was. More out of boredom than interest, he played the interpreter's scanner over a glittering cluster of gemmy needles huddling together beneath an overturned, slab-sided boulder.

"Molybdofornacite, Thometsekite, and ferrilotharmeyerite," the device deduced.

"Never mind." Gazing up at the unfamiliar stars, he chuckled softly to himself. Responding to his mood, Pip shifted her position on his stomach to blink sleepily up at him. "No iron?" That, at least, he could pronounce without severely spraining his larynx.

"There is some, but the base element here is copper. Would you like a rundown of all the derivatives in the immediate vicinity?" the device inquired hopefully.

"No thanks." Flinx was only indifferently interested in the mineralogical wonders surrounding him. They were emotionless.

Beautiful, though. Take the undulating cluster of tiny brownish crystals that filled the gap between two yellowish gray boulders a few meters from where he had chosen to spend the night. In the glow from his suit's integrated illumination, they shimmered like a

pool of shattered glass. Locking his fingers across his chest and trying not to think about the familiar, comfortable bed that waited for
him back in his cabin on board the *Teacher*, he let silence and fatigue steal through him, heralding the onset of sleep. His eyelids
fluttered, closed—and fluttered anew.

Were those unpronounceable mineralogical intangibles all that
was creeping up on him as he watched, or was there something more?

Blinking, he gazed evenly at the bed of crystals and frowned.
On his belly, Pip stirred slightly. Light brown highlighted with
splotches of darker maroon, the crystalline configuration appeared
no different from hundreds of similar formations he had noted and
forgotten about during the day. Like their similarly striking geological brethren, they caught the light and threw it back at him in dazzling patterns, even with the limited illumination that was available.
Most certainly, they did not sway. Even a stiff gale would be insuffi-
cient to bestir them.

Shifting his backside against the unyielding stone, he struggled
to find a more comfortable position, as if by continually adjusting
his spine he might somehow happen upon a softer rock. He closed
his eyes—but not quite all the way. Through the slim slit of vision
he retained, he thought he saw the twinkling accumulation of small
crystals stir again, albeit ever so slightly.

This is ridiculous, he told himself. Until he satisfied himself as
to the reality of the rocks before him, he was not going to be able to
relax. Pulling his legs up under him, he rose to his feet. As he stood,
an irritated Pip slithered from his stomach up to her familiar resting
place on his shoulder. In the distance, something exotic and unknown continued to chirp systematically.

Walking deliberately up to the mat of crystals, he removed the
suit glove from his right hand and ran the exposed palm lightly
across the pointed brown tips. The siliceous material was hard and

unyielding, reminding him of similar material he had encountered before, like the crystals from which Janus jewels were cut. The material he was caressing was manifestly inorganic. Slipping the glove back over his fingers, he started to turn back to his chosen resting place. Giving the shimmering formation a last admiring glance, he kicked out gently with one foot, intending to test the sturdiness of the glittering, individual siliceous depositions.

A cluster of larger crystals located near the base of the formation promptly split apart, allowing a mucus-coated bronze-colored tube to emerge. Its annular terminus was lined with what looked like more crystals but which were, in fact, teeth. Or more properly, a startled Flinx decided as he jumped backward, fangs. Interestingly, they did not snap, but rotated rapidly around a central esophageal axis. He marveled at the biological mechanism that permitted the novel range of motion.

At least, he did until the boulder-sized lump of brown crystal rose up on a quartet of stumpy, muscular legs and started toward him.

Sensing his alarm, Pip was instantly awake, a blur of pink and blue hovering above him and slightly to his left. Pleated wings beating too fast to see, she positioned herself to deal with the ponderous, slow-moving threat, preparing to direct her expectorated poison at the exquisitely camouflaged predator's eyes. Only one difficulty, only one problem held her back.

It had no eyes.

By what method it sensed his presence, Flinx did not know— only that as he retreated, slowly but with a care for where he placed his feet, it followed. It might only be curious about him—though the presence of those rotating, scythelike fangs within the circular mouth implied that their owner fed on something other than leaves and blossoms. While its mouth might be overtly threatening, its mass, body design, and movement did not suggest a carnivore capable of rapid movement. When it did give indications of accelerating, he simply took another step backward. All the while, its lethal mouthparts continued to rotate expectantly.

An ambusher, a silent stalker supreme, Flinx decided as he monitored its approach while continuing his slow, steady retreat. It was fortunate he had reacted to his suspicions instead of ignoring them in favor of incautious sleep. His forceful contact, in the form of an experimental kick, had induced the creature to abandon its facade and accelerate in his direction. Fortunately, though its intent seemed clear enough, it was handicapped in its eagerness to sample this new type of potential prey by a range of motion only slightly swifter than that of an adolescent sloth.

Pip was more agitated by the creature's behavior than her companion, who stayed close enough to examine the blanket of crystals that grew from the alien's back. They were indisputable crystalline formations, not biological pseudomorphs like glassine hairs. Some marvel of internal chemistry allowed the animal to sprout cupric silicates from its skin. Flinx pondered what other biological wonders barren but colorful Pyrassis might contain.

The trunklike mouth extended another half meter toward him, rotating teeth straining to reach the soft flesh that remained just out of reach. He scrambled effortlessly over a recumbent boulder and waited to see what the creature would do. The stout, cumbersome legs looked no more adapted for climbing than did the rest of the beast. As it advanced, it continued to probe the air with its fang-lined proboscis.

Her rapidly beating wings filling the air with a hum like the mother of all bumblebees, the increasingly aggrieved minidrag darted down at the sluggishly advancing predator, striking repeatedly at its back and the place where a head ought to be. Her own much smaller teeth were, of course, unable to penetrate the glistening sheath of crystals that covered its bulk. Flinx made an effort to reassure her.

"It's all right, Pip. See how slow it is? I could walk, much less run, circles around it." He stepped out from behind the rock, his eyes already looking for another resting place. "If its presence bothers you that much we'll go find another spot to sleep right now." With a wave, he bid farewell to the probing carnivore and turned to go.

Whether it was the act of turning his back on the creature, or ignoring it with his eyes, or some other factor that triggered the unexpected reaction, he did not and probably would never know. Regardless of the cause, the consequences were as immediate as they were unanticipated.

The mass of crystal-coated stone directly in front of him erupted, rising to a height of seven meters or so, and thrust a sawlined snout the size of an escape hatch directly at his face. Several things flashed through a startled Flinx's mind at once: No wonder the small creature at his back had been curious about him. It was normal for the infants of most species to be curious about all new phenomena. The adult that now towered before him was less inquisitorial. It intended to macerate him first and evaluate his nutritional potential later.

The massive buzz saw of a snout struck at him. As it did so, something bright of hue and swift of wing darted down to spit a stream of toxic venom at the creature. Striking just above the proboscis and its fine coating of brown crystals, the corrosive liquid hissed as it dissolved mineralogical camouflage and underlying flesh alike. The hulking brute flinched, the fanged snout retracting slightly, as smoke rose from the site of the strike. Then it lumbered forward once more, advancing sluggishly but on monumental legs each of which was taller than Flinx. Not speed but stride rendered it far more dangerous than its inquisitive, smaller spawn.

Still, having now been alerted to its presence, Flinx felt he could outrun it despite the restraining bulk of the survival suit. Turning, he vaulted an eroded layer of stone and was preparing to break into a run when a sharp, hot pain raced up his right leg. Jerking his head around sharply to look down, he saw that a flexible, moist tube had penetrated the survival suit and was gnawing methodically into his calf. For the first time since he had risen from his place of intended rest, fear overtook his initial curiosity.

In his haste to escape the adult, he had forgotten about the infant.

Rotating teeth tore at his skin. Behind him, a sonorous rumbling heralded the approach of the laggard but long-legged parent. Its much larger proboscis could snap off his head as neatly as he would twist and pluck an apple from a tree. He wrenched forward with his right leg, putting all his weight into the effort. The silent infant came away with a large chunk of tough fabric in its snout that it promptly chewed up, inhaled, and regurgitated. This alimentary rejection did nothing to lessen its interest, nor that of its hulking genitor.

Trailing blood from his injured leg, Flinx broke into a harried limp. In a long leg pocket lay the small firearm that might have stopped the infant but that he knew would only irritate something as massive as the adult. With each stride, his injured leg responded more favorably. The wound he had suffered was messy, but shallow.

Unexpectedly elongating its proboscis to twice its apparent length, the adult struck him squarely in the back, knocking the breath out of him and sending him crashing to the ground. He could hear as well as feel the rotating teeth tearing into the back of the survival suit. Idly, the ever-speculative part of him wondered how long it would take for those spinning fangs to cut through the durable material and begin slicing into his spine. Knowing it would probably be futile but refusing to go down without a fight, he fumbled for the pocket that held the compact survival weapon. He had trouble getting a hand on it because as the creature was working to consume him, the muscular snout was also dragging him backward across the rocks.

The minidrag dove again. In the absence of eyes, she struck at the only orifice that presented itself. Caustic venom entered the upper, exposed portion of the tooth-laden snout. A puff of noisome smoke accompanied an audible hissing sound. Emitting a throbbing, almost subaural vibration, the alien proboscis gave a sharp jerk and released its intended prey.

Scrambling to his feet, Flinx staggered momentarily and stared as the limber appendage thrust upward, exploring the air for the tiny winged thing that had been responsible for the hurt. Pip could have avoided the clumsy probe on one wing. Without waiting to see how long his winged companion could maintain the diversion, Flinx turned and stumbled up the nearest slope. He was battered and bruised, but the flow of blood from his leg had slowed. Within minutes he had put reassuring distance between himself and the remarkably camouflaged local predators. Pip joined him shortly, fluttering anxiously about his face, examining him out of slitted, reptilian eyes. Able to read his emotions and therefore sense that he was hurt but otherwise all right, he knew that she would soon relax and settle down.

Which was more than he could say for himself. He was angry. He ought to know better by now than to be beguiled by exotic beauty or the alien bizarre. Had he learned nothing on places like Longtunnel and Midworld? The fact that this biosphere appeared deficient in life-forms did not mean that it was. Heretofore he would be more careful, would respect anything and everything as implicitly biotic and therefore potentially hazardous no matter how inert or inactive it might initially appear to be. On a new, unfamiliar world, one should not trust even the clouds.

He counted himself lucky, having escaped with only a slightly injured calf and a torn pants leg. The latter would greatly reduce the ability of the suit to keep him cool and comfortable unless he could figure out a way to seal off the damage below the knee. But the tear hardly constituted an environmental crisis. At worst, he could solve the problem by the simple low-tech expedient of binding the torn material up in a simple knot.

By the time he had put the deceptively inviting hillside and its voracious but sluggish denizens far behind, he was feeling much better. He resolved to find a place to sleep that was not already occupied. With his lips, he took a sip of cold water from the suit's distiller.

A tiny, almost apologetic red telltale materialized before his eyes, warning him of an occurrence he would greatly have preferred to ignore. Feeling the effects of the long day, he could not keep the irritation out of his voice. Not that it would matter to the suit.

"Yes, what is it now?"

The synthesized reply was spasmodic and full of dropped vowels. In the electronic background, underlying the response, reverberated a series of intermittent twitters, as of a metallic mouse gnawing on steel cheese. Worrying sounds.

Worrying words, as well. "Suit integrity has been infringed."

Glancing down at his right leg while maintaining his forward stride, Flinx smiled ruefully. At least the bleeding had stopped. "I can see that. Anything else?"

"Unfortunately, yes. The Parc Nine-Oh electrostatic distiller has been damaged."

Flinx pulled up sharply, and Pip had to tighten her grip to keep from sliding off his shoulder. A torn suit he could deal with. A broken distiller . . .

"Can it be repaired?"

"Yes," the suit informed him encouragingly. "A new outer coil and condenser unit will restore the unit to full functionality. There are two of each required replacement component in aft supply bay four."

"On board the *Teacher*." Flinx's tone was flat.

"On board the *Teacher*," the suit confirmed.

Looking down, Flinx scuffed idly with one booted foot at a patch of delicate dark blue azurite crystals. "That's not very helpful, since I have no way of contacting the ship."

"It does present a problem," the suit agreed.

"Have you any suggestions as to how to compensate for this difficulty?"

Advanced cogitation was not the suit's forte. It was, after all, nothing more than a tool. "Drink less."

Nodding to himself, Flinx chose not to reply. Sarcasm would be lost on the unit. It required an advanced AI to appreciate irony. Examining his surroundings as exhaustively as he could, he chose the inner curve of a dry wash for his new bed. The underside of the slight overhang where he lay down was ablaze with enormous red-orange crystals of vanadinite. He noted the fiery display without appreciating it. He was not in the mood.

Carefully disrobing, he laid the survival suit aside. Now that it was off, he could see the true extent of the damage it had suffered. Not only was the distiller ruined, several other built-in components lay exposed to the elements or had otherwise been damaged. The spatial sensors were still operational, which would allow him to continue to monitor the location of the landing party from the *Crotase* by sensing the faint emanations of their electronics. He no longer calculated the distance to the site in kilometers, but in swallows of water. The suit's tank was full, but in the heat of the day its contents would not last long: a few days at most, provided trekking conditions remained amenable and he could avoid any more ticklish encounters with the local wildlife. What he would do for something to drink when he reached the encampment he did not know.

He had to repeat the order three times before the damaged suit complied with his request to shut down its internal cooling system. If he ran it at maximum while leaving the faceplate open and the torn leg flapping as he walked, thus admitting air, some water ought to condense on the cooled interior. He would make certain to gather those precious droplets as best he could, saving the water in the suit's insulated tank until he had no choice but to drink from it.

Walking at night would be cooler, but not easier. The suit's internal illumination was limited. Unable to see very far ahead, he could easily step into a dark crevasse—or onto a relative of the slow but exceedingly well-disguised predators he had left frustrated in his wake. Better to wait until sunup, when he could at least see and identify any potential obstacles.

Also, he was exhausted. In the morning he might need water. Right now, what he needed more than anything else was sleep. He would deal with rocks, however fantastic their formations, and their protoplasmic mimics tomorrow. Stretching out beneath the unfamiliar sky on smooth, flat stone that took no pity on his bruised self, he wrestled with his worries until sleep overcame them. As it turned out, he need not have concerned himself with rock and crystal at all.

Ahead of him lay nothing but sand.

With the faceplate locked in the up position to admit moisture-bearing air to the now near-frigid interior of the suit, whose cooling unit he had manually set on maximum, he stood shielding his eyes from the morning sun. As he had hoped, dampness condensed on the now exposed inner lining. Lowering his head, he licked tasteless condensation from the material. It did not kill his thirst, but it slaked it. Enough, he decided, so that if things went well and his resolve held, he could put off until midday taking a real drink from the suit's tank. Pip slithered down his chest, her tongue gathering moisture from lower down before she emerged from the hole in the suit's leg and took to the air.

He had never seen dunes of such color. He wondered if anyone had. Scraped and worn by the wind from the spectacular copper cliffs and valleys of Pyrassis, dunes a hundred meters high marched eastward in banded tones of dark green and purplish blue, fervid orange and pink and red. It was wonderful to see. If only death by thirst was not following a few paces behind him, he might have been able to properly appreciate their beauty.

Striding down from the last of the solid stone, he felt his boots sink a centimeter or so into the soft green sand. He made better progress than he expected. The sand had packed down over the centuries, providing unexpectedly solid footing. It was slower going than walking on bare rock, but neither did he sink up to his knees in the multicolored grains as he initially feared he might.

The homing signal within the suit remained a constant and comforting companion. Provided he could maintain his present pace, he should reach the *Crotase*'s encampment in four or five days. He did not linger over what his options might be should the landing party from that vessel decide to depart before then. At this point, making contact with them was his only option. Perhaps by then the sophisticated AI that was the heart and mind of the *Teacher* would wonder at the lack of communication from its master and come looking for him.

He could not worry about that now. His thoughts were centered solely on surmounting the next dune. Not for the first time, he found himself envying Pip's wings. Hard flat stone or soft undulating sand, it was all the same to the soaring minidrag.

Climbing the dunes was akin to ascending waves of rainbow. Like the colors he had encountered in the rocks, the hues were manifold and fantastic. Reflecting the prevalence of copper in the planet's crust, every imaginable shade of green and blue was present, streaked with startlingly bright bursts of yellow and red, or more somber purple. The first night he spent on the dunes, in the blissful absence of wind to stir the sands, was a complete contrast to the near-fatal encounter he had suffered among the crystal-bearing rocks. The sand was soft and warm. Nothing emerged to disturb his rest. By the time he awoke the following morning, refreshed from an unexpectedly sound sleep, Pyrassis's sun was already high in the sky.

The morning after that brought visitors.

Something was crawling up his exposed right leg, making its way past the shreds of torn material in an attempt to reach the interior of his suit. Most of his life had been spent in awakening quickly for fear that something, or someone, might be after him. But so comfortable was he on the tepid sand that his reflexes were slower than usual, and he failed to react in his normal prompt fashion. The tickling sensations that now afflicted his skin brought him to an upright position quick enough, however.

There were three of the visitors. The largest was as big around as his thumb and twice as long. Tiny dark protrusions near the front were elementary eyes. Mouths were wide, flat, and protruded slightly from the region that might be considered a head. Boldly tinted forest green with alternating stripes of dark blue and lavender, the trio of alien trespassers inched their way forward on dozens of minuscule, barely visible legs.

His initial reaction was to scramble backward while reaching down to slap them off. He had not survived an adventurous and difficult life, however, by slavishly conceding to initial reactions. Tickle the trio of advancing creatures might, but other than waking him from a sound sleep they had so far exhibited nothing in the way of inimical behavior. Hand poised to strike, he eyed them speculatively.

There was a flash of pink-and-blue wings as Pip glided across his leg. When she settled to the sand, it was with one of the pseudoworms in her mouth. Dividing his attention between the two crawlers still ascending his leg and the one that had become prey for the minidrag, he watched as she devoured it headfirst. Other than by strenuous wriggling, the striped alien made no move to defend itself, and was soon consumed.

Exhibiting no ill effects from her meal, Pip rose, dive-bombed his leg a second time, and settled down to devour a second pseudoworm in less urgent fashion. Reaching down with tentative fingers, Flinx plucked the surviving caller from his leg. The flattened, protruding mouth made tiny sucking noises while multiple legs churned furiously. He wondered if he would find the writhing, thick-bodied creature as nutritious as Pip apparently did. Making a face, he decided such drastic experimentation could wait awhile yet.

Placing the pseudoworm back down on the sand, he waited for it to start toward him again. Instead, taking no chances with its newfound freedom, it immediately burrowed into the sand, throwing up a spray of granules in its wake. Watching it work, he wondered uneasily what other invertebrates might be living within the dunes, meandering sinuously beneath his vulnerable backside even as he sat there contemplating the astonishingly swift disappearance of the many-legged worm. The images thus conjured induced him to stand, a posture that would expose less of him to the sand.

As he straightened, he felt something slide down his right leg.

Their cylindrical green bodies swollen with fluid, two more of the sand burrowers fell out of his suit. Mouth agape, he watched as they imitated their less successful predecessor in tunneling expeditiously into the dune slope.

He felt no pain, but that did not keep him from scrambling out of the suit. Many parasites and predators secreted substances that numbed the area where they chose to feed. Clearly, the pair that had fallen from his upper regions had engorged themselves on *something*. Horrific thoughts raced through his mind as he feared what that might be, and what he might find.

But no wounds, circular or flattened, showed on his body. Standing naked in the hot sun, wishing for a mirror, he examined every square centimeter of himself that he could reach or see. All of his skin and flesh appeared to be intact. Relieved but bemused, he climbed slowly back into his clothes and the damaged suit. It took him a moment to realize that something had changed.

The suit's cooling unit was chugging silently away on maximum, but the interior of the suit, instead of being lined with cold damp, was bone dry. The pseudoworms had not been after his blood. They had come looking for, and had found, more easily accessed moisture. The condensation on which he had been relying to supplement the remaining water in the suit's tank had been stripped from the suit's inner lining. What would the three ascending his leg have done, having penetrated the interior of the suit only to find that those that had preceded them had vacuumed it dry? Would they have started on his blood? It was just as well he had awakened when he had.

Conversely, the lethargic invasion had provided a solid meal for Pip. Give up a little moisture, take a little back, he mused. Gathering himself, he started toward the crest of the next dune.

# REUNION

Sand dunes gave way to salt flats later that afternoon. The fact that they were bright green and blue instead of white did not mitigate the hazard they posed. If his calculations were accurate, the encampment established by the *Crotase* ought to lie not far on the other side. The uninterrupted panorama presented bothersome complications: How could he approach the camp undetected across perfectly flat terrain?

Cross first, worry later, he told himself. Taking a sip from the precious remnant in the suit's tank, he started across, malachite sand clinging to his boots. Overhead, the sun basted him for his temerity in attempting to traverse such blatantly wicked topography.

It was midafternoon when he allowed himself another sip from the tank. The flow of cool water slowed much too soon. Frowning, he sucked harder. A few drops emerged from the tube to enter his mouth. Then they ceased altogether.

For the second time that day he stripped off the suit. Turning it over, he unsealed the protective fabric above the ruined distiller's storage tank. Everything looked normal—until he saw the hole near the bottom. It was shallow and curved. Hard to believe something so insignificant, so slight, might have sealed his impending demise. It was, in fact, exactly the sort of opening that might have been made by a small, flattened, slightly extruded mouth. Despite the heat, a shiver raced through him. Fortunate indeed that he had awakened before the second wave of pseudoworms had entered his suit, where they would have found themselves disappointed by the absence of readily available moisture and in need of locating another source. Straightening, he shielded his eyes as he looked back the way he had come. Somewhere, hidden deep beneath the sheltering colored sands, was an especially waterlogged worm.

There was some liquid left in the bottom of the tank. He would have to find moisture of some kind to supplement what remained. Turning again, he surveyed the barren, kaleidoscopically pigmented wasteland that lay before him. There was no sign of vegetation, canyons, or anything else that might hint at the presence of water. Overhead, dark shapes rode obliging thermals. He had the uncomfortable feeling that he might be in line for a closer look at the alien scavengers sooner than he otherwise would wish.

# CHAPTER

# 9

By the following sunrise there was little water left, even though Flinx had been exceedingly careful with the pitiful remnant. Pip continued to ride his shoulder, shifting her position uneasily in response to her companion's dispirited mood. There was nothing she could do for him, he knew, unless she could somehow put herself emotionally in touch with a nearby lake. On the other hand, her lithe, limber, snakelike body was itself full of moisture. He quickly banished such unholy thoughts from his mind. The flying snake had been his friend and protector since childhood. No matter how desperate the circumstances he would never, could never, harm her.

But he was no longer strong enough to keep his drifting, increasingly moisture-starved mind from at least contemplating the unthinkable.

The sun had no sympathy for the lone trekker trolling the blasted cupric landscape. Its heat fell on him as if it had real weight, and only the sputtering but still functioning cooling system built into the suit kept him alive. If not for the moisture it condensed on the interior fabric, his pace would long since have slowed to a stagger. It kept him going, but for how long? The entire volume of condensate did not amount to a quarter liter of fluid a day. That was not enough, he knew. And if the overstressed unit froze up, or otherwise ceased to function . . .

Something glinted not far ahead, catching his eye: an apparition that resided somewhere between his retinas and the green-washed horizon. Above it, the unfiltered sunlight danced and tempted. Even as his brain urged caution his pace began to quicken, his legs carrying him forward seemingly of their own volition.

Water. Or free-standing liquid, in any event. The reality of the pool that grew steadily larger in his sweat-stung eyes could not be denied, nor could the half dozen or so similar ponds that dotted the dazzling green-and-blue flats. Their rippling surfaces shone like silver in the sun, mirroring its rays and the dense growths of yellow, pink, and blue crystals that lined their shores. Assailed by so many piercing reflections, Flinx had to shield his eyes as he approached.

No two ponds were the same size or shape—not that he cared. At the moment, Pyrassisian geology was far from his mind. Stunted and straining but otherwise apparently healthy native vegetation lined the lips of each pool, luxuriating in the presence of so much water in the otherwise parched terrain. There was more than enough water in even the smallest of the ponds to fill his tank to overflowing, to fill him to overflowing, even to permit the luxury of a bath. The presence of the green and brown growths that fringed each pond suggested that the pools were a permanent feature of the landscape. Searching for the diminutive fauna that could reasonably be expected to dwell and thrive in such a place, he was somewhat puzzled to find nothing. Perhaps the local inhabitants were sensibly nocturnal, he mused, and denned up during the heat of the day.

As he drew nearer, he slowed. Merely because the ponds appeared to be filled with water did not mean that it was safe to drink. Thirsty and tired he might be, but he was not about to go diving into the nearest puddle with jaws wide and throat agape. Surrounded by plains exuberant with copper ores, he could at the very least expect the water to have a sharp tang. Then too, it was entirely possible that the presence in the vicinity of magnificently crystallized arsenates might have imbued the pools with something much worse than bad taste. Before drinking, he knew, must come the testing.

Even if the water proved unpalatable, he could still enjoy a refreshing soak. As he approached the nearest pond he methodically began to undo the seals of the survival suit. He was half undressed when Pip, who had been circling overhead, suddenly appeared in front of him. When he tried to step around her, the minidrag promptly darted sideways to block his path.

"Get out of my way, Pip." Advancing, he waved a hand at her. In the face of his determined approach, the flying snake reluctantly gave ground.

He was almost to the water's edge when he saw what had caused her to try and slow his advance. Quickly taking cover behind one of the few sizable boulders sitting on the open plain, he watched the desert dweller approach. The impressive beast walked on three legs, advancing at a steady tripodal pace. Occasionally it would totter sideways, as if unexpectedly unbalanced, but it always recovered its equilibrium.

Maybe it's as thirsty as I am, Flinx decided as he licked cracked lips. It had come trotting across the coppery flats and not from among the sand dunes. How long it had been since it had last had anything to drink, the solitary human observing from his hiding place could not have said.

Without a doubt, it accelerated noticeably as it sensed the

presence of water. Increasing its pace to a fluid willowy lope, it neared one of the larger ponds. Given the new arrival's imposing size and speed, Flinx expected at least one or two small bush denizens to flee from its path. But the vegetation that lined the ponds remained devoid of movement save for the quickening approach of the trilegged visitor. The absence of any wildlife whatsoever at the alien oasis struck him as decidedly odd, if not inexplicable.

Slowing as it neared the edge of the pool, the creature tentatively tested the waters with its middle leg. Satisfied with the brief inspection, it followed with the other pair. It had an irregular body, black with white spots, and a head that hung long and low in front. Large, alert yellow eyes scrutinized the shallow water in which it was standing. Like the crystal camouflagers, a kind of trunk-siphon dominated the front of its face. Lowering and extending this useful organ, it began to drink. From his place of concealment, Flinx could not only watch the activity but could also hear the systematic, slow slurping sounds the engagingly cumbersome alien uttered as it took on water.

The pool exploded as if a bomb had detonated beneath it. Startled, Flinx lost his grip on the boulder he was hiding behind and fell backward. The vegetation fringing the pond erupted skyward. Soil did not spill from its roots, however, because the growths were not rooted in soil. Instead they lined the lips of a mammoth maw: one that snapped shut with a thunderous echoing *boom* around pond and contents alike. The mighty jaws to which they were attached were smooth and slick, as if permanently oiled.

As abruptly as they had burst forth, colossal mouth and fringed jaws sank back beneath the surface of the ground. Hardly daring to breathe, wondering now at the solidity of the rock and soil beneath his own feet, Flinx rose to his full height. Within minutes a concavity appeared in the ground where the pond had been. As a shaky

Flinx looked on, bushlike "vegetation" slowly unfurled from its bare edges, once more thrusting skyward in perverse imitation of real foliage. From a dark, mephitic hole in the bottom of the exact center of the depression, water began to seep forth, until the pond was once again filled to its brim. Sullying the greenish-blue terrain nearby, other pools sat motionless, undisturbed—and waiting.

Treading as softly as possible, Flinx emerged from behind the boulder, resealing his survival suit as he walked. Unhesitatingly, he described a wide arc around the pool that had awakened just long enough to consume the hapless, unsuspecting trilegged walker. At the same time, he was careful not to come too close to the edges of any of the other ponds. They might be natural, brimming with cool, fresh spring water. Or they might be buried cousins to the monstrosity that had just erupted upward.

Catching sight of a dimple in the stone where several droplets of water had been hurled as a consequence of the skirmish, he bent to examine the fluid. Cupping some in his hand, he saw that while it had the perfect appearance of water, it was denser and slightly viscous. Dripping some onto the appropriate receptacle in the sleeve of his left arm, he resumed walking while the suit proceeded to analyze the solution. He had been right to hesitate prior to approaching the deceitful ponds, but for the wrong reasons. The thick liquid did indeed contain salts, but they were neither arsenates nor other poisonous derivatives of the minerals over which he was walking. The pools were not filled with water.

According to his suit, the liquid he had recovered was saliva.

He had spent time, often against his will, on other worlds where the native predators were well camouflaged, but none that surpassed what he had already encountered on Pyrassis. As he put the gaping, waiting mouths he had believed to be ponds farther behind him, he tried to envision what filled the unseen burrows beneath them.

Given the size of the saliva-filled apertures that were all that showed above ground, the bodies of the carefully concealed predators must be truly prodigious. Did they lie patiently in wait vertically, or horizontally? If the latter, he might be striding over their backs even now.

What better bait to employ to lure prey in a desiccated desert environment than the promise of desperately needed water? The vegetationlike fringe that grew from the jaws only completed the deception.

With one hand, he reached up and back to caress Pip, who once more lay coiled atop his shoulder. She had not been trying to warn him of the approach of the thirst-driven three-legged strider, but of what lay in wait beneath the sorely needed yet deceptive water they both sought. He would have to find drink elsewhere. Preferably something that would not try to drink *him*.

Thinking pools or streams might occupy basins in the rock, he was repeatedly disappointed. The copper-rich, heavily mineralized surface was permeable enough to allow water to penetrate, but not to accumulate. He spent the next night in a small dry cavern lined with sparkling malachite and dozens of beautiful, exotic minerals he did not recognize and did not trouble to have the suit identify for him. He was too tired to bother with the analyzer. Focusing on the dark green stalactites that formed a fascinating coppery curtain before his tired gaze, he fell asleep dreaming of water.

Two days later the last of the water in the reserve tank was gone, leaving him and Pip to try and survive on the wholly inadequate condensate generated by his suit's cooling system. Ahead, he thought (though he wasn't sure) he could make out a long, straight ridge of dark rock stretching from north to south. A ridge meant low places, shaded places, where he could rest and where, with luck, water might collect in small seeps. Even a glassful would be welcome now.

Whether he could reach the ridge was another matter. It was at least a full day's hike from where he was standing and staring at the distant, dusky streak that separated sand and sky. There would have to be water *somewhere*, he reasoned. He was still several days' march from the site of the *Crotase* encampment. Swallowing, his throat uncomfortably dry, he forced his legs into motion. It seemed as if a fresh command from his brain was required each time he wanted to do something as simple as place one foot in advance of the other.

It was at that moment of contemplation, with the sun high and relentless, that the suit's overworked cooling unit sputtered, gasped out one final mechanical exhalation of chilled air, and expired.

He spent ten minutes trying to restart the apparatus, only to come to the conclusion that it could only be done with access to the full resources of a microtech repair facility. Unable any longer to cool him or to provide moisture in the form of condensate, the suit was quickly transformed from benefactor to burden. Slipping out of its confining folds, he found himself fully exposed to the air of Pyrassis for the first time since his shuttle had slammed into its unsympathetic surface. More importantly, he was now entirely exposed to the sun. His olive-hued epidermis would not be as sensitive to those alien rays as that of more fair-skinned humans, but he was still going to have to monitor and moderate his exposure. With a rapidly accumulating inventory of troubles, sunburn was an extra he could do without.

Salvaging what he could from the suit in the way of food concentrates and equipment, he resumed his trek eastward. Behind him, the discarded, ravaged survival suit lay in a shapeless pile atop a cluster of exquisite ferrotic crystals, looking altogether too much like the shed exoskeleton of an emerging desert insect. Deprived now of even the little bit of internal condensate the suit had been producing, finding palatable water within the next forty-eight hours became a matter of dire necessity. With luck, Pip might last a little longer.

That wasn't luck, he told himself. It was resignation. He had survived too many crises, been through too much on behalf of others and in search of his origins, to perish on an alien world of something as simple and undramatic as thirst.

Unimpressed by his determination, the Pyrassisian sun beat down heartlessly as ever, systematically robbing his body of its remaining moisture. By evening, the black ridgeline that might, that had to, shelter water beneath its cooling ramparts, was noticeably closer. And he was notably weaker, he realized. His breathing alarmingly shallow, he slumped in the shade of a quartet of slim, rectangular gray growths that rose without protruding branches or variance from the vertical to a height of some five meters. They had solid cores and woody flanks interrupted only by hard, knobby protrusions: fewer surfaces from which to lose moisture, he knew. They kept their narrow faces to the sun. A few hints of green streaked their planklike sides. Any water they drew from the parched psychedelic ground was surely too deep for him to reach.

A coiled Pip lay hot and heavy on his shoulder, but he did not brush her off. Her familiar presence was the only comfort that remained to him. At the base of one of the near-featureless growths, a trio of small black blobs was busily gnawing at an exposed root. Like miniature earthmovers, they cut into and consumed bits of the exposed woody material. When he found himself contemplating how much moisture the unpretentious little grotesqueries might contain, he turned away in disgust. He was not yet desperate enough to resort to swallowing alien bugs.

Tomorrow, he knew as he sat panting in the heat, he might be.

Turning around brought a different vista into view. As he stared, something rose from the heat-rippled blue-green surface, moved toward him, and sank back to the ground. It was not a cloud. Despite his weariness, he stood up to get a better view. There it was again— only this time there were three of them. What they were he could not yet say, but of one thing he could be certain in spite of his exhaustion: They were moving in his direction.

Looking to his left, he weighed once more the distance to the shadowy ridgeline. How far could he run before dehydration and fatigue overcame him and brought him to his knees one last, final time? How fast were the stealthily approaching creatures? For such he had decided they must be. His hasty, heat-singed calculations were not favorable.

Maybe they were only curious plant eaters, he told himself. Or soil filters, or scavengers of small dead things. As opposed to, say, large live things, like himself. Maybe it was only coincidence that they were advancing in his direction, and would pass to left or right without taking notice of the strange biped in their midst.

When the count reached nine and he saw that they were still coming straight for the cluster of treelike growths, he instinctively pressed his back up against the nearest bole. The trunk behind him seemed solid enough to serve as a barrier. By now the advancing organisms were close enough for him to make out details of their physiognomy. The first particular that impressed itself upon him was that they had no limbs.

This was not surprising. In the case of the flat ground-skimmers, or flimmers, legs would have been superfluous. Indeed, they would have been in the way. Two meters long and nearly as broad, but only half a meter thick, the flimmers traveled on a cushion of air. Several large, membranous sacs on their backs expanded to startling dimensions, filling and emptying repeatedly. Each time one voided, the air it had contained was pumped out through small jets in the underside of the creature, propelling it off the ground and forward. A pair of large, black, pupilless eyes were set in the front of the animal, above and to either side of a wide mouth filled with dozens of small, sharp teeth. Another native that had neither the aspect nor demeanor of an herbivore, Flinx determined ruefully. Irregular, seaweedlike growths fringed the bizarre creature all the way around its flattened periphery, with those in front being by far the most attenuated and prominent. Perhaps they functioned as feelers to educate the animal as to the nature of its surroundings. Perhaps they worked to inform it of the proximity and palatability of potential food.

His characteristic unquenchable curiosity aside, he did not think he wanted them investigating him.

Pip was already safely airborne and out of their reach. As they continued their approach, he could hear the soft *whoosh* and thump as multiple air sacs repetitively discharged their gaseous contents. Up close, the tiny teeth that filled the narrow jaws looked at once larger and more menacing. The absence of visible arms, claws, tentacles, extrudable proboscises, or other gripping appendages was encouraging, but despite this he doubted he could fight off all nine of them should they choose to attack as a pack. Standing alone and exposed on the glistening emerald-and-azure plain, he had exactly one option left open to him. Despite his exhaustion, he did his best to take it.

Turning, he briefly contemplated the challenge before him. Then he wrapped his legs tightly around the sturdiest of the four alien growths, extended his arms above his head, and began to climb.

Without the knoblike tumescences that lined the trunk, the task would have been impossible. As it was, in his weakened condition the ascent proved arduous enough. The wheezing, eerily sibilant emissions of the flimmers did much to inspire his efforts.

Somewhat to his surprise, he succeeded in making it all the way to the crown of the distinctive growth. It was an uncomfortable, precarious perch. But it was better than being caught below, where the pack of flimmers clustered around the base of the four growths, their air sacs expanding and contracting mightily as they strove to reach the bipedal food that had moved out of their reach. Despite their most strenuous efforts, none managed to rise more than halfway up the treelike growth. Pip hovered nearby, uncertain whether to attack or wait for some further indication of distress from her companion.

Adjusting his uncomfortable position in search of a more accommodating one, and not finding it, Flinx was relieved when the brownish stalk of the growth he was clinging to did not shift beneath him. Unpleasant and awkward his roost might be, but at least it was well rooted. It did not sway beneath his weight, nor tremble when several of the eager flimmers threw themselves against it. Before too long, he hoped, perhaps with the onset of evening, they would grow bored or give up and whistle away, allowing him to slide back down to the ground and resume his trek.

A new sound reached his ears. Curious, he turned as sharply to the right as his perch would permit. Three of the flimmers had clustered at the base of the quasi-tree, their foreparts jammed tightly together. Since he could not see what they were doing, it took him a minute to connect the noises he was hearing with references from his own memory. The instant he made the connection, his heart began to beat a little faster. Those multitudes of small, sharp teeth could rend other things besides flesh.

They were eating away at the base of his tree.

More than a little concerned, he contemplated his choices should they succeed in chewing their way through the tough material. Unfortunately, plunging helplessly to the ground was the first alternative that occurred to him, and it was less than promising. He still had the endural pistol he had salvaged from the survival suit, but he had no idea how effective it would be on the flimmers. If he had to use it, a lot would depend on whether they approached their potential prey cautiously, or swarmed him all at once. If the latter . . .

Pip would help, but the poison sacs in her cheeks were of finite dimensions, and took time to replenish. The stout treelike growth that was his refuge began to quiver ominously. Reaching into a pocket while his perilous perch communicated a conspicuous quiver to his backside, he carefully drew out the survival gun and sighted the muzzle on the largest of the flattened predators gnawing at the base of the growth. Better to use the weapon to try and drive them away, or at least to diminish the pack's numbers, before they cut completely through the base of the quasi-tree and sent him crashing to the ground.

The trunk shuddered afresh, but remained upright. Looking down as he took aim with the tiny endural, he paused as an entirely new kind of vibration shuddered through the trunk. Beneath him, near the base of the growth, the protruding nodules that had provided precarious footing for his ascent were inflating alarmingly, like so many infected pustules on the skin of a dermatically challenged giant. The voracious flimmers paid no attention to the development. As the protuberances continued to swell, their dull gray integuments became almost translucent. Flinx thought he could detect movement within, but could not identify the cause.

With a hundred subdued plopping noises, the swollen tubercles finally burst. A cascade of clear, cool liquid gushed forth to drench the attacking carnivores. Reacting as one, they immediately abandoned their assault on the tough, stubborn trunk to imbibe as much of the precious deluge as they could before it vanished into the parched earth. Flinx would have risked an attack and rushed to join them, save for one recent memory that made him hesitate.

He had already had one enlightening encounter with water that had turned out to be something else.

Nothing sprang at the eager flimmers from within the liquid that was already beginning to form rapidly shrinking puddles on the blue-green ground. The soft tissues of the thirsty predators did not hiss and blister from contact with artfully disguised acids. They continued to drink, the diligent pack swarming around the base of the growth, smaller individuals fighting for their share of the unexpected liquid bounty, until the last priceless drop had been swallowed or lost to the dry earth beneath them. They then returned their attention to their isolated, treed quarry who, despite his wishes, had not been forgotten. The same ravenous trio resumed chewing at the base of the bole while the rest waited in a hungry circle, bouncing up and down with excitement and anticipation on their individual cushions of air.

If the Pyrassisian growth's intention had been to divert the attackers at its base from continuing their onslaught, the ploy had failed. If anything, the liquid they had just ingested seemed to give the industrious gnawers renewed energy and determination. Trying to focus on the largest of those doing the damage to his perch, Flinx once again took aim with the endural.

Before he could fire, the big flimmer he had fixed in his sights jerked spasmodically and fluttered away from the trunk. It was followed in rapid succession by its two companions. The entire pack, in fact, had suddenly begun to exhibit symptoms of unmistakable distress. As Flinx looked on, they engaged in a brief group paroxysm of twitching and tremors. Then, one by one, they convulsed, shuddered, and sank to the ground.

Only when the last of them had stopped quivering did Flinx dare to descend from his discomfiting refuge. Walking over to the nearest of the motionless creatures, he kicked hesitantly at its flattened body. It did not move. If it was paralyzed, the paralysis was total. Kneeling tentatively, he examined the motionless predator at close range. It was not paralyzed, he concluded: It was dead.

That was when he noticed the fine spray of transparent crystals protruding from the creature's broad mouth and stilled lips. Picking up a rock, he used it to gingerly snap off several of the centimeter-long formations. Save for several green liquid inclusions that might have been embedded alien blood, they were perfectly pellucid. This time, he realized somberly as he rose and tossed the rock aside, one of the local life-forms had used specialized liquid masquerading as water to defend itself instead of to capture prey.

The fluid that had spewed from the quasi-tree's bloated nodules had looked like water, flowed like water, had even, from his unsteady perch at its crest, smelled like water. But instead of that life-giving liquid, it consisted of complex organic polymers that, when exposed to air, congealed rapidly into a solid, crystalline form. In ingesting it, the flimmers had committed a particularly gruesome form of group suicide. The fluid had crystallized and expanded *inside* their bodies, piercing vital organs and suffocating them from the inside out. Were he to dissect one, he suspected he would find the organs of the dead flimmer's digestive system filled to bursting with enchanting, jewel-like, and utterly deadly crystalline formations.

Turning away from the deceased predator, he eyed the four silent brown growths still standing tall and straight behind him with new respect. The quasi-tree had defended itself most successfully.

First the hulking saliva-baiter, now this. He wondered if he would be able to trust real water when he found it.

Momentarily overwhelmed by the effects of the quasi-tree's cunning defense, he knew he was being disingenuous. When he finally found something that looked like water, he knew he would rush to it with little regard for the consequences. He had no options left. If it chose to drink him before he could drink it, well, at least he would die hydrated.

As he stood over the inert bodies he contemplated slitting several of the dead flimmers and sampling their blood. Reckoning that their green, copper-infused life fluid was as likely to poison as revivify his system, he reluctantly decided to pass on the opportunity. He wasn't that desperate, he decided. Not yet. Maybe he was well down the road to that unenviable destination, but he still had a ways to go before he got there.

Shouldering his shrinking sack of supplies, he resumed his march eastward. The dark ridgeline loomed in front of him, a highly attenuated but nonetheless promising grail. If it sheltered no water beneath its dusky brow, then the question of what he would do when he reached the *Crotase* encampment would be rendered moot. If it did . . . He tried not to think about what he would do after enjoying a long, long drink and an invigorating rest. He tried not to think about drinking at all.

As he advanced, he viewed every rock with suspicion, dodged the homeliest plants with care, and tried to avoid anything that moved. It was a secure way to travel, but not a very nourishing one. For one tantalizing, brief moment, clouds seemed to gather, only to dissipate beneath the brutal heat of the merciless sun. He found himself wondering if during a flash flood on this spectacularly tinted world, the riverbeds would run bright with dissolved azurite and other vividly colored copper minerals. The images thus evoked served to occupy his mind while doing nothing for his throat or belly.

Offered a choice, he would rather have been tramping through dense jungle. Not only was he more familiar with such an environment from his travels, at least there, despite the unavoidable endemic dangers, he could have found water easily. He tried not to think too much about what he did not have: about the cool, soothing rush of liquid down his throat, about the lubricious bloating sensation that resulted from too much drink accumulating too rapidly at the bottom of his belly, about . . . Unable to stop himself, he meditated on how different things might be if the battered and torn survival suit were still intact. And as long as he was wishing, he decided wryly, he might as well wish for an intact shuttlecraft to be waiting for him, door ajar, on the other side of the ridge.

He stumbled onward across the brilliant blue-and-green copper salts with their intermittent eruptions of incredibly rare crystallized minerals, no longer appreciative of the striking tints and hues, seeing in them only exceptionally vivacious harbingers of doom. Despite her small size, a weakened Pip was rapidly becoming a debilitating weight on his shoulder. She took to the air less and less frequently, rising only when irresistibly prompted by some exceptionally intriguing sight or movement. The rest of the time she preferred to rest in the bouncing, very limited shade provided by his head and neck. Though he looked forward to her occasional flights for the momentary cooling her rapidly beating wings brought to his face, he was not about to chivvy her airborne just to provide him with a few seconds of heightened comfort.

He had fashioned an improvised patch for the worm-punctured water tank. Now if only he had something to put in it, and the empty bottle he had salvaged from the wrecked shuttlecraft. The larger container was beginning to chafe against his back, threatening to raise a painful welt. At least he had something to take his mind off the raging thirst that otherwise occupied his every waking moment. They were almost out of food, too. In that regard, Pip was a little better off. At least she could hunt, though in her weakened condition she did so less and less often. Her elevated metabolic level demanded that she eat frequently. Despite the increasing desperation of his situation, he still refused to consider sacrificing her to save himself.

From overhead, from beneath cracks and holes in the chromatically hued salts, from behind the cover of strange flora, hungry eyes watched and waited. Flinx doubted his off-world origins would prevent their owners from closing in when they thought the moment propitious. Meat was meat, protein was protein, and in the truly barren expanses of any world, scavengers would always eat first and suffer any bellyaching consequences later. He had to keep alert and on the move. When his intermittently active talent was functioning, he could sometimes sense their primitive presence nearby, out of sight but not out of perception. Unfamiliar though their emotive projections might be, he had no trouble interpreting them. They were menacing, and expectant.

The sun of Pyrassis was as merciless as its counterparts on other worlds. Repeatedly, clouds would gather, only to break apart. Hesitant and fluffy, their sole purpose seemed to be to tempt and then frustrate him. They shuffled and re-formed in the clear indigo sky as if uncertain what was expected of them, only to eventually disperse as thoroughly as his hopes.

This was no place to die, he resolved. Not here, so far from Moth, from Alaspin, from the comforting confines of the Commonwealth itself. His determination, however, did nothing to alleviate the thirst that dominated his thoughts or the growling in his belly.

A pointed tongue caressed his neck. Breathing slow and steadily, he halted in the semishade of a rocky outcropping, a cracked green surface beneath his feet. Fumbling in a pocket, he removed half a food bar. Breaking off a chunk and setting it carefully on his shoulder, he waited while Pip gratefully consumed the nutritious segment. He considered trying to collect some condensate, but held off. They would drink tonight, he told himself firmly. After the blazing orb had dipped behind the horizon and both moons were high in the sky.

Squinting, he looked upward. Despite the deterioration of their condition, there was no sign of the *Teacher*. It must still be hovering behind the nearer of the two moons, its functions on hold, patiently awaiting the next communication from its owner. Sophisticated as its AI was, the means for including theoretical speculation in its cybernetic cortex remained more an art than a science among designers. Besides, he had foolishly, perhaps overconfidently, not specified a time frame for his return. In the absence of one, the ship was unlikely to assume that anything had gone amiss and act, or not act, accordingly.

Within its duralloy depths was a sufficiency of foods both synthesized and natural, a perfectly maintained atmosphere, various diversions and entertainments, and cool, freshly processed water. Enough water to swim in. Enough water to . . .

Pip had finished eating. For an instant, her slitted eyes flashed more brightly than they had in a while before she once more settled her triangular, iridescent green head back down on his shoulder. Stretching painfully, he resumed his eastward march. By now he would have been grateful for any sign of civilization, AAnn or human. At least before they interrogated him, the reptiloids would give him food and water. He was beginning to fear that he had reached the point where that was as much as he could hope for.

Then the dark ridgeline loomed before him, transformed from distant goal to impending obstacle. At the sight of it, the muscles in his legs protested. Halting at its base, he surveyed the barrier that he had made his immediate destination. It was steeper than it had appeared from a distance, but climbable, and thankfully not too high. Interestingly, the crest was of uniform height. Taking final stock of his surroundings before beginning the ascent, he saw that it ran away to north and south as far as he could see. Certainly, there was no going around it.

Moving slowly but with deliberation, his perception dangerously fogged and his reflexes slowed, he approached the base and began to climb. The otherwise slick-surfaced formation was ribbed with knobs and projections that provided excellent foot- and hand-holds. He was halfway to the top when he slipped, scrambled to regain his footing, and in doing so noticed something that would have greatly excited his interest had he been capable of feeling anything so peripheral to his continued survival as scientific curiosity.

From the time he had begun his long march, he had believed the ridge to be a natural formation made of dark stone. Slathered as it was in sand and grit and gravel, there was no reason to suspect otherwise. Now he saw that where his scrabbling feet had kicked away the adhering granules and accumulated cupric silicates, something black and shiny lay underneath.

Bracing himself against the inward-sloping wall, he used one hand to hold on and the other to brush at the coarse grains. More of the curious ebony slickness appeared beneath his fingers. Running his dirty nails along the now exposed surface, he found that he was unable to scratch it. His survival knife did no better. With only such crude devices at his disposal, he was unable to tell if the slope was metal, ceramic, plastic, some kind of welded fiber, or something even more exotic. Of one thing he was certain: It was unquestionably artificial.

Straightening slightly, leaning away from the wall, he looked along its interminable length first to the north and then to the south. If it was all composed of the same dark, reflective material, it suggested a unified assembly of considerable magnitude. From the air it doubtless resembled the natural scenic ridge he had previously imagined it to be. Who or what had raised it up in this desolate place, and to what purpose, he could not imagine. He was too tired to expend time and energy on lofty speculation. Had this world once been home to a people in need of such structures as long, high walls? Had at one time in its history, ancient wars raged across the surface of a greener but not kinder Pyrassis? As he struggled upward, slipping and grasping, he had time to weigh only the most insignificant of conjectures.

Even from the higher vantage point provided by the top of the wall, which he finally gained fifteen minutes later, the rampart showed no signs of abating or tapering off. In the clear, unpolluted air, he could see for quite a distance. Shielding his eyes with one hand, he thought he could detect a slight curving of the structure off to the southwest, but he couldn't be sure. Ahead, the by now familiar green dunes and dry washes and bluish hillocks gave way to an unexpected, unprecedented jumble of broken rock and bizarre protrusions. From the air, the terrain might well have appeared impassable. But from his much more intimate location he could see winding pathways penetrating the formations. Gratefully, he realized there would be shade. That would make a nice change from walking beneath direct sunlight, and he would be able to make much better progress during the day—provided he could find water. Gathering himself, he started down the inner slope of the artificial ridge.

The wall had long since been lost to sight behind him when he happened to stumble against one of the eccentric structures among which he was walking. Somewhat to his surprise, he discovered that it was composed not of native stone but of the same singular dark material as the barrier he had just crossed. So was the utterly different shape next to it, and the one behind. Pausing in the convenient shade provided by the curious contours he was examining, he knelt to scoop sand from its base. He soon saw that the construction did not emerge from ground, but from a slightly ribbed, lightly warped surface of similar but distinctively different material. When a stray shaft of sunlight struck the glossy seam he had exposed, it seemed to absorb the light and respond by throwing back half a rainbow composed of artistically subdued hues.

For the first time since he had abandoned the ruined shuttlecraft, he found himself walking on and through a wholly artificial environment. What its purpose might be he did not know. If it was an ancient alien city lost to time and buried in sand and adhesive grit, then where were the houses, the workshops, the meeting places and temples? Entombed beneath him? What were the functions of the thousands of strikingly misshapen structures among which he was meandering? Their vermicular shapes and convoluted outlines failed to convey their function. He could only continue to stagger onward, and wonder.

# CHAPTER

# 10

Another wall.

It wasn't much of a wall, no more than a couple of meters high, but it was enough to stop him. He stood swaying slightly, sweat streaming down his face, looking older than his years and staring at the new obstruction as if it were Mount Takeleis back on Moth. He was nearing the end of his strength.

He still possessed enough sense to reflect on the irony of it all. Considering what he had been through, taking into account everything he had experienced in his short but intense life, for him to perish ultimately of thirst, of a simple lack of water, could be seen as almost a blessing. In death he would finally achieve the homely humanness he had sought for so long. He was sorry only for Pip, whose devotion to him would result in her unsought and near-simultaneous demise. On the whole, however, he would prefer not to die.

Struggling to summon hidden sources of strength, he made a tentative run at the wall. His hands scrabbled for the crest, found no purchase, and slipped. As his weakened body fell back, he lost his balance and found himself sitting instead of standing on the sandy surface. Where he struck, the grains had been shoved aside to reveal more of the enigmatic ribbed black material beneath. Not for the first time since he had descended into the jumbled maze he felt there was something almost familiar, indeed well-nigh identifiable, about his surroundings. Unfortunately, at the moment his brain was not functioning any more efficiently than the rest of him.

An attempt to stand failed. He remained sitting, Pip fluttering apprehensively in front of him as he struggled to recall the taste and tactility of plain water. The memory did nothing to comfort his desiccated system. Aside from the fact that the top of the wall now seemed out of reach, if he did not find liquid by the end of the day he knew he was not likely to see another dawn. It *had* to be here somewhere, he felt. Collected in a hollow beneath one of the gray-black contours, or running just beneath the surface of the porous sand. It was only a matter of finding it.

That, however, meant rising, walking, and searching—all activities that all of a sudden seemed beyond him. Without him having to open his mouth, Pip could sense and appreciate his distress. But he could not tell her to find water. Not that he had to. She was as in need of the life-giving fluid as he, and would go straight to it if a source was encountered.

Glancing up, he sighed heavily. If he could not go over this latest obstacle, he would have to go around it. Cursing gravity, he struggled to his feet. It took him a moment to be certain he was standing upright and to secure his balance. Then he resumed walking, this time to his right. The slightly pitted ebony wall curved away from him, and he followed the ribbon of unknown material as if it were a trail beneath his feet. Around him, other shapes and contours contorted against a cloudless blue sky while alien scavengers swooped low, checking on their impending two-legged meal as they avidly monitored its increasingly laggard progress. His vision was beginning to blur.

A dip appeared in the crest of the unbroken rampart. Breathing shallowly, he tensed himself and leaped, arms outstretched. Hooking his fingers over the top of the smooth rim, he somehow pulled himself up and over. The far side of the wall proved to be as slick and smooth as the one he had just surmounted. Unable to slow his momentum, he lost his balance and felt himself falling, falling. The wind-swirled sand rose to meet him.

Nightmare shapes pursued him through the unending maze of black monoliths and colonnades, enigmatic obelisks and waves of liquid soot frozen in time. They twitched threateningly, extending ebon pseudopods to try and trip him as he fled from something monstrous that was darker than dark. Like black pudding, the maze threatened to congeal around him, suffocating his debilitated form from pore to nostril. It coagulated around his feet, holding him back, sucking at him with a vacuous evil the likes of which he had never encountered before. Had he possessed the strength, he would have whimpered in his stupor.

He did not know whether he awoke from a deep sleep or had been knocked unconscious by his fall. Regardless, it was the sound of voices that roused him from insensibility. They were sibilated, inquisitive, and convicted. They were also not human. He retained just enough presence of mind to lie still, eyes closed, unmoving, as he listened to the querulous conversation that was taking place above and nearby his prostrate form. Pip's coils formed a tense weight on his spine, between his shoulders. Inhuman emotions impinged on his feebly perceptive consciousness.

Fortunately, he understood as well as spoke reasonably fluent AAnn.

". . . *ssfwach nez pamaressess leu ciezess* we sshould let it die," the slightly deeper of the two voices was insisting.

"Agreement. Iss nothing to be gained by keeping it alive," the other responded all too readily.

"Do you think it knowss about the transsmitter?"

Hesitation, then the second voice replying, "I do not ssee how it could. But then, I cannot imagine what the creature iss doing here anyway. The quesstion will be obviated by itss passing."

"That iss sso."

The sound of footsteps turning away shushed in Flinx's ears. He fought to rouse his weakened, moisture-starved body. AAnn or no, they represented his only, perhaps his last, chance at survival. True, he might only be postponing death from thirst for a more painful, lingering demise under interrogation at some unknowable future date. But as Mother Mastiff had always taught him, survival even under unpropitious circumstances offered far more choices than death under the best of circumstances. Managing to partially prop himself up on one elbow, he waved feebly and opened his eyes.

They focused on the dorsal sides of two AAnn in the process of striding away from where he was lying. Each was clad in a light, buff-toned jumpsuit festooned with pockets, some of which bulged with unknown contents while others lay flat against the gracile, muscular bodies. Dark brown tails streaked with yellow and flecked with golden highlights protruded from holes in the back of the jumpsuits. Both figures traveled burdened with multihued equipment packs diverse in size, shape, and composition. Accustomed to and evolved for life on desert worlds, they wore neither hats for shade from Pyrassis's powerful sun nor artificial lenses to reduce the glare. Though they had no external ears, their hearing was excellent, as was demonstrated by the sharpness with which they turned at the sound of his voice.

Curled up on Flinx's back, an enfeebled Pip nonetheless stirred, preparing to defend her companion so long as she could spit. He whispered to her, trying to keep her calm, hoping his commands made sense. He perceived no overt maliciousness in the AAnn. Only the usual muted enmity, and a general indifference to whether he lived or died.

"I . . . need water. You . . . you can't let me die." The whispery AAnn phrases emerged with difficulty. Someone had coated his throat with a tacky varnish to which half a kilo of dust seemed to have adhered.

From their slightly stooped posture and the muted color of their scales, he judged that both the male and female AAnn gazing down at him were mature specimens. Quite mature. In fact, he decided through dry, throbbing eyes, they were downright elderly. What were they doing out here, in the middle of nowhere, amidst the in-scrutable ebony maze? Though both wore highly visible sidearms, they had neither the aspect nor the attitude of soldiers of the Empire. His erratic talent chose that inopportune moment to quit on him. As abruptly as if someone had turned off a switch, he found that he could no longer sense their feelings.

He could still hear their voices well enough, however. As he squinted at the male, Flinx noticed that the service belt containing his salvaged tools and endural pistol lay draped loosely over one sharply raked alien shoulder. Without his gun, he stood no chance of extorting water from the two aliens. Instead, he would have to rely on a contradiction in terms—AAnn mercy.

Its tone more academic than curious, the male responded impas-sively to Flinx's desiccated, raspy-voiced entreaty. "Why sshould we not? Why sshould we waste preciouss liquid on a dying human?"

Sharp teeth flashed in the wide, reptilian mouth as eyes that were scimitars of chalcedony regarded the prone biped without emotion. "Even on an educated one who understandss the language of Empire."

His hastily concocted rationale had better be accepted, Flinx knew. Mostly because he did not have the strength to prepare another one. He tried to sit up, managed to make it halfway. Showing the alarming extent of her dissipation, Pip did not take to the air. Instead, she slid off him and lay nearby, coiling weakly on the sand beside him but still ready to strike.

"Because if it becomes known to the military that you allowed an intruding human to die before they had the opportunity to question him, it will go hard on you."

The female gestured third-degree inquisitiveness. "How do you know there iss any military on thiss world? It iss an empty place."

"Very empty," he agreed. It was hard to hold a conversation and participate in a discussion of differences, he reflected, while barely lingering on the borders of consciousness. He had to keep going. If he fell back into insensibility, he knew they would turn once again and walk away from him for good. "But Pyrassis is an AAnn world, and no world the AAnn claim is ever ungarrisoned."

The male hissed grudging assent. "That doess not mean any hypothetical military iss any more aware of our pressence than it iss of yourss."

"Are you willing to take that risk?" Flinx prayed the argument would not last much longer, because he couldn't.

In the silence that ensued, he dreaded their abrupt departure. Though he fought to keep his eyes open, even the reduced glare within the maze was almost too painful for his enervated system to stand. He was certain he had closed them for only seconds when something struck him full in the face with shocking force. Something cool, unexpected, and magnificently damp.

Water.

It hit his cracked lips with the force of liquid stone, simultaneously outraging and soothing his parched throat. Slim, muscular coils writhed about his face and neck as Pip rushed to partake of the grudgingly proffered bounty.

"More!" he gasped as he tried to keep his mouth directly beneath the spout of the AAnn waterpak.

"Dissgussting." The male indicated second-degree revulsion as he continued to pour water into the human's open mouth. "Look how much it takess."

The elderly female clicked her teeth. "Mammalss. It iss a wonder they can ssurvive at all in a decent climate. And they pride themsselvess on their adaptability."

Eventually the flow ceased. Evidently water was not a problem for the two AAnn. Had that been the case, despite their lesser personal requirements they would not have been so lavish in their dispensation of the precious liquid to a traditional foe. They must have ample supplies with them, a rapidly reviving Flinx decided. Even better, they might have a distiller. With Pip once more coiled securely about his shoulder, he rose and wiped at his mouth and face. Able to perceive clearly again, he was struck anew by the comparatively advanced age of his reluctant saviors. What were they doing here, in the middle of emptiness, on the nowhere world of Pyrassis, so far from the centers of AAnn culture and civilization? Not that the desert-loving endotherms would be uncomfortable in such surroundings. The heat and lack of humidity would be entirely to their liking.

The male continued to hold the waterpak. His companion held something smaller and more lethal, its muzzle focused on the now erect Flinx. "How did you find out about the transsmitter? It iss an archeological disscovery of the utmosst importance."

"Ssuch wise, it is to us." The male's accompanying gestures suggested first-degree importance tinged with excitement. "There are thosse in the Department who will believe otherwisse."

The female's tail switched like a metronome as she talked, the steady side-to-side movement quietly mesmerizing. "It iss interessting, if not particularly flattering, to have our convictionss confirmed, if only by an intruding human."

Flinx offered no comment, letting them ramble. As they chattered away, the two AAnn were doing an excellent job of carrying on the conversation without the need for any uninformed input from him. Every time they opened their scale-lined, tooth-filled jaws, they were unwittingly providing him with the basis for sustaining future conversation. Furthermore, their ongoing physical proximity combined with certain subtle hand gesturings suggested a relationship that went beyond the bounds of the merely professional.

He felt his initial supposition confirmed: They were not military operatives. Had that been the case, they would have said as little as possible. Their manifest lack of martial sophistication allowed him to believe he might even have a chance, however slim, to slip away to continue his search.

Any such possibility lay in the future, because the female continued to keep her small but contemporary-looking weapon trained on his midsection. That they were unaware of the minidrag's lethal capabilities was evident by the lack of attention they paid to Flinx's coiled, revivified companion. It was potential he decided to hold in reserve, unless and until they gave him no choice but to reveal it.

"Naturally," he said when they finally finished, "I also believe in its importance."

He addressed them matter-of-factly in his fluent AAnn, wondering as he did so what the hell he was supposed to be talking about. They had alluded to the existence of some kind of transmitter. True, his powers of observation had been weakened by his recent ordeal, but up until yesterday he had felt himself still capable of recognizing any type of device that even vaguely resembled a transmitter.

The elderly reptiloids exchanged whispered, hissing comments. "We had believed that recent confirmation of the field'ss exisstence wass known only to oursselvess and a few otherss in the Department. How did the Commonwealth learn of itss exisstence?"

"Oh, you know," he murmured confidentially. "Information travels in mysterious ways. In these days of modern long-range communications, secrets are difficult to keep."

"Truly," the female admitted. The muzzle of the gun did not waver from his belly. "Sso you came to carry out field sstudiess for yoursself."

"Truly." Stepping into deeper shade, Flinx took a seat on a frozen rope of black ceramic-like material. Still weak, he tried to recall which AAnn foods were suitable for human consumption. "Isn't that what you're doing?"

The male gestured absently, a fifth-degree gesticulation at best. He seemed reluctant to believe that their secret was out. He would have been most unhappy to learn that it was he and his mate who had revealed its existence, and that very recently indeed.

"Of coursse. As you can imagine, our ressourcess are limited by the sskepticissm with which our reportss have been greeted." This time his gesture was much broader, encompassing a wide area in multiple directions. "It iss difficult for our ssuperiorss in the Department to accept the exisstence of a transsmitter of unknown dessign that iss more than one hundred qaditss in extent."

Keeping his expression carefully neutral in case either of the AAnn was skilled in the interpretation of human facial contortions, Flinx did some hasty calculations. A hundred AAnn qadits was . . . They were talking about a "transmitter" nearly two thousand square kilometers in area. His heart raced. No wonder he hadn't seen any transmitter.

He had been walking on it.

The continuous high wall he had scaled upon leaving the salt flats was the rim of the device. The black monoliths, the twisted and gnarled shapes, the ribbed surface that time had covered with wind-blown sand: It was all part of the AAnn-discovered transmitter. Or part of its upper regions, anyway. What more lay buried beneath his feet, under the sand and in the bedrock of the planet, he could only imagine. Maybe these two AAnn knew that as well. Xenologists, he wondered, or students of a more arcane specialty? Like a fisherman forced to cast with virtual bait, he chanced continuing the conversation. With luck, they wouldn't realize that his hook was empty.

"I've had the same problem with my superiors," he confessed, under no illusion that by expressing sympathy with their professional position he was establishing any sort of emotional rapport. "It's simply too big to be believed. And the age of the thing!" he concluded hopefully.

The garrulous, ingenuous couple did not disappoint. Flinx translated the hypothesized timeline they provided. If they were correct, it meant that the enormous mechanism atop which they were standing and conversing was between 485,000 and 500,000 years old.

To lavish so much time and effort on such an instrument, he concluded somberly, someone must have been in need of serious long-range conversation with somebody else. Or with something else.

"Still," he murmured, hoping to acquire a little more information before the AAnn grew suspicious, "its origin and purpose remain a mystery."

"*Ssssnt,*" the female whispered, "then you are no nearer the ansswerss than are we."

Too bad, Flinx mused. Too bad that their work thus far had not revealed that knowledge to them. As for himself, he now knew a great deal more than he had when they had begun, which had been less than nothing.

"You are alone," the male declared. When Flinx chose not to respond, the AAnn added, "Where iss your landing craft, your ssuppliess?"

"You know I can't tell you any of that." Let them wonder about the possible presence of other humans, he decided, and their unknown capabilities.

"It doess not matter." The female gestured with her weapon. "The ssoldierss will take charge of him, and find out. It need not concern uss." Her eyes were cold, her expression indifferent. "Thiss wasstess our time."

"I thought we were establishing some common ground." Flinx smiled encouragingly. "After all, we three are colleagues in science, something the military cares nothing about."

"We are not colleaguess," the male retorted. "We are competitorss. And all AAnn are ssoldierss together in the sservice of the Empire."

It was exactly the kind of dutiful, disappointing response he had been expecting, but there had been no harm in trying. The two researchers might be elderly, but they were not senile. They were still all AAnn.

"What sshall we do with him until ssomeone from Kyl Base can come to take him away?" The female gestured third-degree anxiety, coupled with a twist of lips and elongated jaws that suggested she wouldn't mind sampling a bite of soft mammalian flesh. Flinx tensed. On his shoulder, Pip's coils tightened, and he hastened to calm the minidrag by thinking only self-confident thoughts. Not yet, he told himself, and through empathetic consanguinity, her as well.

"Collar," the male declared briskly. Disappearing around a massive slab of solid black, he returned moments later carrying a length of silvery cord a couple of centimeters in diameter. Avoiding Pip's coils, he placed this around Flinx's neck. Stepping back, he fingered a pair of contacts on his instrument belt. A trio of tiny lights snapped to life deep within the cord as the two congruent ends proceeded to fuse seamlessly together.

"That cannot be removed without first entering the appropriate code," he announced to the accompaniment of second-degree satisfaction. "Try anything untoward, travel more than a tenth of a qadit from my sside, and the explosivess with which the loop iss impregnated will explode with enough force to ssever your head from your shoulderss. We use the material for making precission excavationss. It will ssuffice, I think, to keep a lone human from wandering."

Flinx indicated his understanding. "I know it is your responsibility to turn me over to the local authorities. I just didn't think there were any."

"It will take time for ssoldierss to get here from Kyl Base." The female sounded unhappy. "Meanwhile we musst, as you argued, tolerate your dissagreeable pressence. Do not think to take advantage of it."

"I don't see how I could. Not while I'm wearing this." Reaching up, he felt gingerly of the flexible collar impregnated with powdered explosive. Under the best of circumstances, he did not care to have anything around his neck except a certain flying snake. "Just make sure you don't fall asleep atop the control unit."

The AAnn responded with gestures to his attempt at humor. Among their kind, irony and sarcasm had always been appreciated.

"Do as you are told, and your life will be presserved. For as long as the military cadre conssiderss worthwhile, at leasst." Turning, the male indicated that the prisoner should walk in front of them. In tatters and battered boots, Flinx complied.

He had been given water. If they wished to keep him alive until the local command could take him off their hands, then food would likely be forthcoming. The deadly collar he could live with—for now. In spite of empty pockets and the absence of equipment belt or tool packet he still possessed the means for removing the device. That also would have to wait until the time was right, he knew. Everything usually did.

As they walked, he saw the black material around him and beneath his feet in an entirely new light. A transmitter of gargantuan size and incredible age, the AAnn insisted. Who had built it? Why was it situated on an empty, ovenlike, nowhere world like Pyrassis? Was this what the crew and complement of the *Crotase* had come all this distant, dangerous way hoping to find? If so, what possible connection could a prehistoric alien transmitting device have with the Meliorare Society, or with the sybfile of personal information he had tracked halfway across the galactic arm?

Through stealth and quick thinking he had acquired some answers, but in no wise were they keeping up with the rising flood of questions. Try as he might, he failed to link his purpose in being on distant Pyrassis with that of the crew from the *Crotase*, much less with the presence of an enormous antediluvian transmitter of alien design. It was entirely possible, he realized, that there *was* no link, and that the visitors from the Commonwealth vessel had come to this desert world driven by other reasons entirely. The revelation of the transmitter's existence was as unlikely as it was unexpected. While it engaged his interest and imagination, he knew he must not let it distract him from his purpose in journeying to this place. He was here to learn about and find out about himself, not to engage in xenoarcheology.

The elderly female AAnn gestured with the pistol, forcing his thoughts from confused contemplation back to inscrutable reality.

The weight of the explosive collar disturbing against his throat, he lengthened his stride.

Their neatly laid-out camp was a jumble of supplies, equipment, and laboriously acquired study material. In typical AAnn fashion, 90 percent of the living and working quarters were situated just beneath the sun-baked surface. A flattened dome with ground-level slits for viewing and ventilation marked the location of individual compartments designated for sleeping, eating, and research. His breathing skipped a beat at the sight of the lightweight two-person skimmer. Though the layout and controls were AAnn-designed and proportioned, he felt certain that given the chance he could divine enough of its functions to enable him to operate the vehicle. As they walked past, he tried hard not to stare at the tempting means of escape.

Whether he would be given that chance remained to be seen. Certainly he could do nothing while trapped beneath the watchful eyes of the two xenologists. What would they do with him when it was time for them to retire? AAnn required roughly as much sleep as humans. The explosive collar might keep him from fleeing, but it would not prevent him from prowling around the camp while they slept. Something as low-tech as a lock and chain would take care of any free-roaming notions their prisoner might have. Surely they had something like that in mind for him.

It was only slightly cooler below ground. The AAnn thrived in hot, dry climates. Flinx knew he could stand it, so long as they continued to provide him with water.

Taking the gun from his mate, the male kept watch on the young human while his companion disappeared into another chamber. "The military will not believe you are a fellow ressearcher, you know. They will assume you are a Commonwealth sspy and treat you accordingly."

Taking a seat against a blank section of wall, Flinx did his best to appear indifferent to his situation. "Then they are as stupid as they are unlucky, to be sent to a world as unimportant and out of the way as Pyrassis." He hesitated. "Unless, of course, there is something here worth spying on."

"You are trying to get me to provide military information." The muscular tail switched from side to side in a manner indicating mild amusement coupled with third-degree curiosity. "I have none to give. My mate and I are interessted in the passt, not the political pressent. Pyrassis intrigued uss for the very reasson that it interessted no one elsse." Accompanied by a high cheeping sound, teeth clacked together several times, denoting amusement. "I would be as ssurprissed as you if there exissted on thiss world anything of military value. There are mineralss in abundance, a condition of geology one cannot avoid noticing, but nothing that cannot be obtained more viably elssewhere. If there are large depossitss of ssomething sspecial or unique, we are unaware of it. My mate and I delight in our issolation. Even the location of thiss world is unimportant. Though such lore doess not fall within our areass of expertisse, I would be asstonisshed to learn that Pyrassis iss thought by the Imperial Board of Grand Sstrategy to have tactical importance." He settled into an AAnn lounge, a supportive puzzle of padded wires and posts that allowed his tail unrestricted range of movement.

"What iss your perssonal dessignation?"

"Flinx." A now relaxed Pip shifted against his shoulder.

"Only one naming? That iss unussual among humanss. Given the way you breed, the need for more than one sseemss a matter of necessity rather than choice." When Flinx did not respond, the xenologist added, "They will sstill treat you as a sspy. It iss procedure."

"You and your mate could vouch for my scientific interests," Flinx suggested helpfully. "As fellow researchers, we have a lot in common."

"We are not fellowss," the AAnn replied impassively. "As to whether we have anything in common, that would remain to be sseen. Though it matterss not." While not as flexible as a human face, that of the AAnn was capable of considerably more expression than, say, the insectoid thranx. "Your pressence here iss an unwanted intrussion and an unpleassant surprise. I find everything about you, from your physsical appearance to your body odor to the ssound of your voice, disspleassing. The ssooner the military hass taken you off our handss, the happier my mate and I will be."

Flinx rested his forearms on his knees. "That's not very hospitable of you."

"AAnn hosspitality is resserved for the Kind, and for itss friendss. Having allied yoursselvess with the loathessome hardshellss to resstrict the sspread of ssettlement that iss our right, you are neither."

The lanky redhead sighed. There was nothing to be gained by bandying politics with the elderly scientist. The AAnn believed they had the right to expand anywhere and dominate everyplace. No amount of argument would convince them otherwise. Where sophistry failed, however, the presence of numbers of large starships heavily manned by humans and thranx had proven more pragmatically compelling. That did not prevent the AAnn from continually probing, testing, and provoking Commonwealth resolve at every opportunity.

The female returned. No attempt was made by the pair to shield their conversation from the prisoner. They wanted him to hear.

The male's tone and gestures conveyed his annoyance. "There sshould alwayss be someone on contact at Kyl. What kind of outposst of the Empire iss thiss?"

"A very, very issolated one," his mate reminded him. "The information wass forwarded. As soon as it reachess the appropriate individual, I am certain that proper action will eventuate."

"*Isssspah*—I hope so. The human occupiess time and energiess far better sspent engaged in professional activitiess."

"You could just let me go," Flinx suggested amiably. "I'll walk away and you'll never see me again."

As he made the suggestion, he concentrated as hard as he could. You *have* to let me go, he thought. You *need* to let me go. There are a thousand reasons why you *should* let me go. So—let me go *now*. He had never tried projecting persuasion on a nonhuman. Whether his talent was functioning or not, he had no way of telling. The response from the AAnn, at least, was unequivocal. His mental straining had no effect on them whatsoever. Perhaps, he mused wryly, he would have had better luck if one of them had been searching for love.

More teeth-clicking as the female replied. "We may not be ssoldierss, but we know our duty. You thoughtfully reminded uss of it when we gave you water. You will remain here until the appropriate military repressentativess come to remove you from our pressence."

"And you will do sso quietly." The male brushed a clawed finger across the face of the unit that monitored the explosive collar. Flinx tried to hide his unease. The AAnn was elderly. If its hand accidentally stroked the wrong control the wrong way . . .

"I have no weapons," he lied. "I won't make any trouble."

"No." The male spoke with confidence as he turned to leave. "You will not."

They continued to give him water from what was evidently either a distiller or abundant storage, simultaneously curious about and repelled by his ability to process such copious amounts of the liquid. Following an exchange of questions and answers, food that was suitable for human ingestion was also found and provided. Though palatable, it was something less than tasty. The alien nutrients did serve to rapidly restore his physical strength, however. With renewed energy came renewed confidence.

He knew that he had to leave before the military arrived to claim him. Once in their custody his opportunities for maintaining his independence would be considerably diminished. Furthermore, someone might recognize the Alaspinian minidrag riding on his shoulder as something other than a thoroughly benign pet.

He would wait until they slept, free himself, appropriate the largest container of water he could easily carry together with some food, and go. The chaotic maze that was the anomalous surface of the ancient transmitter provided plenty of places in which to hide. While avoiding the attentions of a curious military, he could continue to seek the presumably well-camouflaged landing party from the *Crotase*.

Meanwhile, the blistering Pyrassisian sun was still high, and the two scientists were intent upon their daily tasks. Secured to a heavy supply container, unable to move, with the ever-present threat of the explosive collar rubbing against the back of his neck, he crossed his arms over his chest, closed his eyes, and tried to get some sleep.

# CHAPTER

# 11

When he finally awoke, it was dark save for the light from Pyrassis's two sizable moons. The wan, ethereal glow spilled into the room through a pair of slitted, ground-level observation ports. Neither the darkness nor the moonlight was what had awakened him, however. It was Pip. She was astir and fully alert, triangular emerald-green head held high, wings half unfurled ready to carry her aloft. Her small, bright eyes were focused on shadowed movement. Not AAnn, but something else with legs. Lots of legs. Too many legs.

No, they weren't legs, an unmoving Flinx decided as their serpentine owner continued to emerge from beneath the floor. More like fins, stiff paddlelike appendages that had evolved to propel the creature through sand instead of across it. Its long, narrow snout had no visible teeth. In their place writhed a quartet of questing, exploring tongues. Each slim protuberance was about a meter in length, or at least the portion that the creature chose to expose was that long. Every one of the four appendages tapered to a point. In contrast to the invader's mottled yellow-and-black epidermis, the internal appendages were tinted a striking crimson. They flicked rapidly in and out of the eyeless snout, sampling their surroundings. The hole or burrow from which it continued to emerge, he noted, had been bored through sand, avoiding the hard black ribbed material of which the suspect transmitter was composed.

Flinx remained calm, telling himself that this visitor from the cooler subterranean regions was only curious. Other than its size, it did not appear threatening. As he watched it slither across the floor, its multiple tongues nuzzling containers and packages, furniture and scientific supplies, his attention was drawn back to the hole in the ground. A low ridge of sandy soil had formed a ring around the opening from which the visitor was emerging. And emerging, and continuing to emerge.

How long *was* the creature, anyway?

The languidly rising cable of blood and flesh continued to issue from its eruptive burrow until the seated and much smaller inhabitant of the storage chamber decided that it might be time to put his carefully considered plans aside and get the hell out of there. Concentrating his thoughts, focusing his emotions, he launched Pip from his shoulder. Taking to the air, she hovered expectantly in front of him. Flinx was both relieved and pleased to note that the steady thrum of her wings did not distract the intruder from its ongoing inspection of the room's contents.

Caressing his explosive collar with the fingers of one hand, he gestured expressively with the other. As a child on Moth, he had often amused himself by teaching his slender winged companion to perform a number of simple tricks. What he was striving to have her do now might not be classed by others as a trick, and was not particularly simple. It was also potentially dangerous.

Pip recognized the tell-tale gesture as well as the position of her companion's fingers. Darting forward, she positioned herself carefully, took precise aim, and from the single forward-facing fleshy ridge that formed a narrowing tube on the underside of her upper jaw, dribbled a few drops of minidrag venom on the indicated place on the band that encircled Flinx's throat. Instantly the flexible, machine-woven alien material began to sizzle. Turning his head away from the rising wisp of toxic fumes, Flinx waited for several minutes. No stranger to the potent effects of the flying snake's poison, experience allowed him to estimate the speed of the advancing decay. Still, when he reached up to take hold of opposite sides of the collar with both hands, he was careful to keep his fingers away from the spot where Pip had drooled.

He did not have to pull very hard. In addition to being a powerful neurotoxin, the minidrag's venom was also highly corrosive. The collar broke apart easily in his fingers. Inspecting the remains, he saw that it had been eaten almost completely through. There had been some risk of the caustic liquid activating the powdered explosive that was integrated into the material, but he felt the odds to be in his favor. In order to render it safe and easy to handle, such lethal material was usually quite stable until precisely ignited—in this case by a remote electronic signal. Had he guessed wrong, he would not have had time to realize his mistake.

Shorn of the deadly neckpiece, he was free to leave. Or would be, as soon as the sinuous visitor from the Pyrassisian underworld finished its inspection of the storage room and returned to its hole. Trying to keep as much distance between himself and the probing, multitongued head as possible, and having finally freed himself, he rose and began to work his way around the back of the room. Bulky intruder notwithstanding, he would soon have a clear path to the doorway.

That portal promptly and unexpectedly popped open wide.

# REUNION

Light poured into the room, silhouetting a pair of AAnn figures. The opening of the door was punctuated by a florid hissing of syllables immediately recognizable as an AAnn curse of first-degree consternation.

The invading echinoderm's front end whipped around in response to the infringing illumination. A fifth appendage, narrow and tubular, emerged from the midst of the multiple tongues as the creature's entire upper length suddenly inflated. The pistol that flared in the intermittent darkness missed its target. The now frightened visitor did not.

From the central protuberance there issued a stream of gut-polished, fine-grained quartz sand no bigger in diameter than a pin. Sprayed at murderous velocity by air that was highly compressed within the whole of the intruder's unseen length, the slender stream of sand cut through polymer containers, a metal tank, and eventually, the right leg of Tenukac LLBYYLL. The AAnn xenologist hissed sharply at the searing pain. As he fell, he managed to fire his weapon again. His aim was no better the second time, and the shot struck only the ground, penetrating the ancient hard black material of the transmitter. As he struck the unyielding surface he lost his grip on the pistol. It flew from his fingers to bounce once before skidding out of sight beneath a massive ceramic container.

Faltering in the doorway, his mate Nennasu BDESSLL struggled to train her own gun on the writhing, convulsing intruder. A muscular coil whipped around her waist and knocked the weapon from her clawed fingers. While Tenukac struggled to stanch the flow of blood from the hole that went all the way through his leg, his now helpless mate was elevated into the air and brought slowly toward the head of the curious creature. A second set of tongues appeared inside the first layer. Smaller than the others, they were black instead of bright red, lined with tiny, backward-facing hooks, and framed a dark, efficient-looking gullet.

Between the agitated, frantic hisses of the two AAnn, the thrashing of the visitor's coils, and the hum of Pip's wings, the noise in the enclosed space was terrific. The female xenologist's weapon lay on the floor where she had dropped it. Hoping that the invader, its truly terrifying nature now fully revealed, could concentrate on only one potential prey at a time, Flinx dove forward, snatched up the fallen gun, rolled, took aim in the light pouring through the now vacant doorway, and fired. It was a very unpretentious weapon, and he was concerned even as he activated the firing mechanism if it would have much effect on so substantial an adversary. He needn't have worried.

Tongues and hook-lined tendrils flew in all directions as the head blew apart, splattering the floor, the stacked supplies, a good part of the room, and its remaining intact occupants with greenish red blood, Pyrassisian flesh, and bits of fractionated organs. A convulsing coil caught Flinx and knocked him to the ground, but he held onto the weapon. It would be another ten minutes before the rest of the attenuated organism would give a final, last twitch.

The female rushed to attend to her mate's injury. Neither of them paid much attention to their former prisoner, being wholly engaged in trying to stanch the flow of blood from the puncture in his leg. Flinx took the opportunity to examine the nearby metal container that had been pierced as cleanly as if with a laser by the fine stream of sand ejected by the now expired trespasser. Some kind of highly developed giant nematode or land-based echinoderm, he decided as he turned to examine the motionless carcass. Evolved into an efficient killer capable of slicing apart any enemy or prey by employing the most common component of its environment—common, everyday, ordinarily harmless sand.

By now the two AAnn had had enough time to realize that the human had not only saved their lives, but that the collar that had heretofore restrained his movements no longer hung around his neck. The female straightened.

"Truly, we are prepared to die. More than mosst, I believe, having sspent sso much time in thiss place. Allow uss if you will a few momentss to exchange our death chantss. We have been complementary for an honorable time, and our ancesstral liness require implementation of the formality before we die."

Offended as well as tired, Flinx gestured absently with the weapon. The AAnn were alien in more than shape—truly. "No death chants. I didn't shoot this thing just to end up killing you myself."

"You killed it to ssave yoursself." The female watched him intently out of slitted, reptilian eyes.

"That too," Flinx readily admitted. "If your conditioned natures simply can't countenance an act of altruism on the part of a human, then accept instead the excuse that I need your help."

His face contorted in pain, the male used his tail to lift himself into a shaky squatting position. "That we can believe. You have obviousslly sstrayed much too far from your camp, and it iss only through our good gracess that you are sstill alive." It was a pithy summation of the AAnn xenologist's perceived reality, coupled with an indirect plea for the human who was now in control of the situation to spare their lives. It also conveniently ignored the fact that they were in the process of turning him over to the local military authorities and had threatened to shoot him dead if he made the slightest wrong move.

Though their reasonable assumption that he had come from a camp was entirely wrong, Flinx chose not to enlighten them. Let them think that he had a real base of operations, shared perhaps with companions who were searching for him even now. As he considered how best to proceed, he noticed that the female's tail was probing beneath the edge of a massive container—where her mate's weapon had slid. The corners of his mouth turning up ever so slightly, he gestured with the gun he held and hissed a caution. The full length of the xenologist's tail immediately snapped back into view.

"It iss eassy to ssee why you were chossen to come and study here." Unable to divert the human's attention long enough to retrieve the second gun, the elderly female knelt to examine the new skin that was forming atop her mate's wound. "You sspeak the language of Empire almosst as if you had a proper tongue in your head." By way of emphasis, her own flicked in his direction. Pip reacted with a fluttering of wings, and Flinx had to calm her with several strokes of his free hand.

The AAnn lingua, so important in speech for lengthening syllables, was at once narrower and five times longer than that of any human, rendering Flinx's articulate approximation of the reptiloids' speech even more admirable. Over the years, he had learned to compensate for his shorter tongue by employing excellent breath control.

Glancing up from her work, the female gestured with third-degree interest at where the two halves of the bisected collar lay on the floor. "How did you get out of that?" Unaware that the explanation she sought was presently examining the dead body of the intruder worm, neither of his former captors paid any but cursory attention to Pip.

"Bit through it," Flinx responded without hesitation.

The AAnn exchanged a glance before the female replied. "Not with thosse pitiful calcified chipss you call teeth." She hissed disparagingly. The AAnn, Flinx knew, were famed for their skill at organization, their technical expertise, and their rigid, tightly knit society based on the structure of the extended family and a contemporary derivative of ancient reptilian nobility. They most assuredly were not noted for their tactfulness.

"I'll need water and a suitable container in which to carry it, some food, and new clothing. Then I'll leave you."

The female rendered a gesture of third-degree animosity. "We have little enough here to provide for oursselvess, and need all that we have to facilitate our work. We have toiled too long and too hard on thiss project to turn over our preciouss ssuppliess to a roving human!"

Flinx knew that such words and gestures were for show, part of the elaborate ritual of which the AAnn were so fond. The two scientists were in no position to bargain—or to object. But so long as it would facilitate his departure, he was content to play the role. He waved the gun, deliberately exaggerating the gesture.

"If you don't give me what I need, I'll shoot you both and take it anyway."

"Then as you are in possession of the only weapon, we have no choice but to acquiessce to your demandss." Both AAnn bowed and gestured ceremoniously.

They would have given him the supplies anyway, he knew, but having formally registered a semblance of defiance, they felt better about having to do so. The male abruptly straightened to his full height, causing Flinx's fingers to tighten on the pistol's double trigger. Between his injured leg and his age Tenukac did not pose much of a threat to the human and the flying snake, but Flinx was wary all the same.

The AAnn was not even looking at the liberated prisoner, however. His gaze had been caught by something on the floor behind Flinx. Realizing it might be a simple ruse, Flinx chanced only a quick glance back and down. What he saw nearly made him forget about the two AAnn.

A small section of sand-flecked black flooring where the male's second shot had gone astray was alive with flickering light. The white sparks raced through the material in utter silence, providing enough subdued illumination to read by.

"What's this?" he heard himself murmuring as he stared at the shifting fragment of entombed dazzle.

"*Vya-nar*—I do not know. With your permission, human." Helped by his mate, who braced his limping form with a supporting arm and tail, the male hobbled forward and crouched to examine the unexpected phenomenon. Reaching out and down, he tried to catch the scampering embers, but had to settle for gently stroking the black material with the scaly surface of his open palm. "Cold lightning. But what hass prompted it?"

"Your gun." The female had also knelt to investigate the twinkling radiance. "You fired at the ssand burrower and missed, sstriking the ssurface here insstead."

"I wonder," the male declared, "what would happen if the energy level could be increassed?"

"How do you mean?" Flinx was more intrigued by the imprisoned lights than he cared to admit. He ought to have been concentrating on gathering supplies and resuming his trek to the *Crotase* encampment. Instead, he found himself drawn by his assertive curiosity into sharing the pair of AAnn xenologists' budding excitement.

"Sshoot it again." Straightening with difficulty, the male stepped back, away from the place where the lights were rushing through the isolated corner of floor. "Sseveral timess. Full power."

Flinx gestured with the gun. "So that in doing so I'll fully discharge your weapon and thereby equalize the situation? I don't think so."

Tenukac indicated his leg with a gesture of second-degree assertion coupled with scrupulous regard. "I am barely able to sstand. We are not ssoldierss."

"All AAnn are trained in the arts of warfare," Flinx attested.

"Our training wass long ago, human. We are academicss, not fighterss." His tone was agitated. "We may inadvertently have made an important disscovery here. It sshould be purssued. Of coursse," he hissed diffidently, "nothing may happen."

"The energy bursst from the gun penetrated and entered the material of the floor without caussing any vissible damage," Nennasu pointed out. "We musst ssee what ressult the accretion of additional energy will yield."

"Probably a big hole in the floor." Flinx was worn out and hungry. But even as a child he had always been a sucker for logic, even if it originated from an alien source. Raising his hand and taking aim, he fired at the flickering spot on the ground. Pip immediately spread her wings, ready to take flight, but in the absence of any directly perceivable threat retained her perch on his shoulder. He fired a second time and a third in rapid succession.

The floor ought to have shattered, or melted, or been otherwise visibly marred. Instead, it reacted as if the power of the gun was irrelevant. The showy embedded discharges swiftly propagated, then exploded in all directions, spreading through the entire floor of the storage chamber and filling the enclosed space with sparkling, cold light.

"Outsside!" Ignoring the fact that he was ostensibly a prisoner in his own camp, Tenukac whirled and stumbled for the open doorway as fast as he could limp while continuing to rely on his mate for support.

The sun was not yet up. Would not be up for another few hours, Flinx knew. Nevertheless, outside it was almost as bright as day. Every ebony prominence, rim, jutting knob, disc, block, and arch was alive with swirling cold flame. Salvos of inborn lightning shot through every looming overhang and configuration as well as through the ribbed raven surface beneath their feet.

"Elevation," the female declared briskly as she turned, half hauling her mate with her. Lost in the fever of scientific discovery, they had all but forgotten Flinx and the weapon he held. He trailed behind them, Pip clinging to his shoulder.

A wide-beamed ladder designed to accommodate splayed AAnn feet stood propped against a tall black rectangle. Ignoring the glittering radiance that now cavorted beneath its pitted surface, the two AAnn started to climb, the injured male having to use his arms to pull himself upward.

A small observation platform from which an observer could look out over much of the surrounding synthetic terrain had been erected atop the sooty shaft. Surmounting the last step, Flinx found himself standing just behind the two xenologists. They were gazing wordlessly at the hitherto somber surface of the entombed transmitter.

As far as the eye could see, in every direction, it was resplendent with silent, eruptive light.

"All thosse repetitive energy bursstss from the weapon triggered ssomething." Tenukac's voice was hushed in the presence of discovery. "Woke ssomething up."

"Perhapss." Ever the conservative scientist, the AAnn Nennasu BDESSLL was not yet ready to concede sweeping pronouncements. "Certainly there iss ssome kind of activity being generated from an unknown ssource."

Her mate gestured second-degree impatience coupled with first-degree interest and underscored by an astute flick of uncertainty. At that point the entire exposed domain of the transmitter ignited in a storm of frozen pyrotechnics. It was as if every one of the millions of shimmering lights shooting through the dark surface had suddenly chosen to align themselves along the same axis and intensify at the same time. The turbulent, breathtakingly fierce burst actually lasted less than a second and was, like the display that had led up to it, resolved in total silence.

When a momentarily blinded Flinx could finally see again, he found himself gazing out across a barren blackness shadowed by hundreds of enigmatic ebony shapes, illuminated once more only by the light of the two bilious Pyrassisian moons.

"That wass . . . interessting." Nennasu's tail switched reflexively from side to side as she rubbed at her outraged eyes. "Ssomething happened, *assshusss,* but *what?*"

"Based on our ressearch to date, we have determined that thiss vasst field of blackness is the ssurface of ssome kind of transsmitter. Truly." Tenukac was already hobbling back toward the ladder. "I believe we may have jusst been witness to a transsmission."

"To where?" Flinx inquired sharply. It was as if he had not spoken. The AAnn ignored him, and likely would have continued to do so until he actually shot one of them. Although they did not know it, he had no intention of doing anything so radical except in desperate self-defense.

There was nothing, he reflected as he followed his excited former reptiloid captors down the wide ladder, to distract a person from their avowed purpose like a two thousand square kilometer effusion of cold, soundless energy from an unknown source. What the xenologists had not yet asked, and what was particularly beginning to interest him, was not whether the vision-numbing discharge had been some kind of transmission, but whether there was anyone or anything on the presumed other end to receive it . . .

All was quiet aboard the *Teacher.* Recycling elements kept the air clean and the water pure. The food preparator stood ready to deliver a variety of healthful, nutritious, and frequently tasty meals upon request. Thermosensitive paneling maintained the internal environment at a mean temperature suitable for a certain species of bipedal, binocular-sighted, somewhat fragile mammals. Other apparatus hummed softly, carrying out a multitude of essential functions, keeping the ship and its internal systems alert, primed, and ready for immediate activation.

In the main drop bay, a fully fueled and equipped second shuttle waited for instructions to leave its berth and go to the rescue of its owner. All that was needed for it to carry out this task efficiently and quickly was a succinct command coupled with the simplest of navigational coordinates. And even if those were less than wholly accurate, sophisticated instruments aboard the craft would enable it to locate the specific individual in question by means of visual keys, body signatures, and other telltales. All it had to do was be directed to do so and be provided with a minimum of guidance to the general vicinity of the person to be picked up.

But there was no one aboard authorized to issue the necessary order, including the controlling AI. So the shuttle sat in its bay and methodically performed its schedule of routine maintenance procedures, waiting in the same silence that had enveloped the entire vessel.

Yet in the near-total absence of sound and crew and active robotics, there was still movement.

What was striking was not that the half dozen or so leaves quivered; it was that they did so in unison, and in the utter absence of any detectable air movement. What was interesting was not that an entirely different plant had put forth multiple green-brown filaments over the sides of its container, but that at least one such filament had advanced across floor, dividers, and decorative barriers to enter the soil of every other recently transplanted growth. What was impressive about the several tendrils that thrust outward from the depths of half-meter-in-diameter pinkish blue blooms was their single-mindedness in extending themselves not to another planter rich with nutrients nor to a source of water, but to the access panel located clear across the lounge.

To an outsider wandering upon the scene it would have appeared that, too tightly confined to their planters, the resident growths had blossomed forth in search of more growing space. They would have chuckled at the prospect of simple decorative plants taking over, doubtless through neglect, the lounge chamber of a starship, and would have walked on. Had they lingered, and watched, and waited patiently, they would have been privy to several interesting and surprising developments, such as the increased flurry of floral activity that immediately followed a tiny eruption of light on the otherwise unremarkable surface of the planet below.

As there was no one present to make such observations, the uncommon activities that were taking place at an increasingly rapid pace on board the silent *Teacher* went unremarked upon.

# CHAPTER

# 12

If Soldier and Sustainer of the Empire Qiscep HHBGHLT appeared less than enthusiastic on duty that morning, it was with cause. Some might think it churlish for a trooper to belittle a posting to so beautiful a world, and indeed, Pyrassis boasted an amenable climate and pleasant surroundings. The trouble was that there was simply nothing to do. Where was the joyance to be had in congenial environs if it could not be shared?

When it came to such sharing, his fellow troopers did not count. What was missing was a real subsurface city like Oullac on Tyrton VI, or Ssness-ez-Veol on Blassusar itself. A place where a young soldier helping to propagate the spread of the Empire could properly honor his lineage, in celebration and in a sharing of accomplishment. There was none of that to be had on Pyrassis: only the scorching heat, which was much to his taste; the sere desert landscape, which was pleasing to the eye; and the absence of anything resembling AAnn civilization, which most mornings left him feeling mulish and out of sorts.

Woe bred brothers, however, and he at least had the satisfaction of knowing that his fellow troopers and officers partook equally of the same isolation and frustration. A distant and overlooked corner of the Empire, Pyrassis was bastion of little but the dreary hopes of those unlucky enough to be stationed there.

Qiscep did his best to conceal his true feelings, as did his companions. One could safely gesture dismay and ennui but could not voice it aloud. So while a trooper might respond crisply to command or interrogatory, he could simultaneously signify his disillusion with finger or hand, tail or teeth. In polite society such contrary conduct would not have been countenanced. But Pyrassis was a long way from Blassusar. The officers understood the need for those under their command, whose situation was even more forlorn than their own, to have some outlet for their frustration. There was not one among them who did not on the cusp of every major duty-tour rerequest transfer to another posting. If dangerous, there would be action and the chance for promotion. If safe, there would be civilization and the opportunity for interaction with others of their own kind. Anything would be an improvement over isolated, overlooked Pyrassis.

Aware of the adverse effects prolonged posting to isolated stations had on high-strung personnel, sector command was careful to rotate entire units on an accelerated schedule. As Pyrassis easily qualified for such special treatment, Qiscep had already seen two maintenance teams and one ballistics unit replaced in the past major timepart. His turn would come soon enough, he knew. Until that happy day arrived there was nothing he could do but keep up appearances, feed the chimera of fragile morale, and try not to run afoul of an officer in an especially sour mood. Because while the opportunities for advancement and promotion on Pyrassis were decidedly circumscribed, the demon of demotion was ever present and waiting to be fed.

Sitting in his cubicle, which a human would have found unbearably hot and a thranx insufferably dry, Qiscep apathetically scanned, noted, and where required, commented upon all incoming messages. Those that were routine, he ensured were transferred to the appropriate departments. He did not have to give his attention to anything else because every message and report that arrived at Pyrassis base was routine. Once in a while a trooper grew so bored that he neglected to correctly carry out his or her duties. That was when someone tended to get hurt. Like his compeers, the jaded Qiscep looked forward to such incidents—so long as they did not involve him. They constituted the only relief from the deadly dull lethargy of everyday procedure.

He hissed softly under his breath and leaned slightly forward. One of the several scanner satellites that monitored the surface of the planet as well as nearspace was reporting the eruption of a flare of light far off to the southwest, coordinates so-and-so, timing such-and-such. Probably a defect in the surveillance system, the bored Qiscep concluded. Especially given the stated parameters. Duration measured in nanoparts, intensity—the figure supplied for intensity was ridiculous, off scale, beyond validation. The only mechanism on Pyrassis capable of generating such a burst of activity was the deepspace communications unit that was sunk securely into the planetary crust, and it only procreated energy in space-minus. According to the report, the discharge in question had been propagated in space-normal.

He hissed softly and clacked his back incisors twice. It was a test, of course. In the absence of real work, the powers in charge attempted to maintain a semblance of efficiency through an endless series of tests, checks, and inspections. Positing an appropriate response through the neural headset that looped over his skull, he caused the report to be passed along to the proper division without comment. Let someone else deal with its maliciously cunning ramifications. In his capacity he was not required to test traps by sticking his tail into them: only to hurry them on their way.

More of the odious ordinary congealed and then dissipated in the space above his workspace projector. Another thirty tenth-timeparts or so of this rubbish and he could retire to the comparative balm of the communal sandroom, there to snuggle deep within the perfumed grains and dream of better tomorrows.

*Ess-uahh,* he murmured to himself as still more documentation formed in front of his eyes: another test. Unusual to encounter two such in the same morning. But not unprecedented. This one was more carefully crafted, more shrewdly conceived than its predecessor. Send the obvious first, then try to trip up a trooper with something more elegantly schemed than its transparent precursor. He was pleased with himself for having caught it so quickly. Prompt and confident detection should be worth a few shards of praise on his record.

So as not to miss anything or make a mistake, he studied the new document carefully, examining it for any hidden bureaucratic pitfalls. On the surface, it appeared perfectly straightforward. It would, he told himself as he scrupulously scrutinized each included formulation. It was the content that was perfectly outrageous. That was what made him hesitate. For a test designed to catch someone napping at their station, it lacked ingenuity.

He found himself vacillating. Would he get credit for taking a little initiative, or would his peers simply laugh at him for revealing hitherto unsuspected depths of gullibility? Furtively, he glanced around the workchamber. No one was watching him. At least, not in person. Should he follow through, or retire for a mealtime and contemplate his options while eating? The thought of something flavorful, heavily salted, and with the fur still on it tugged at his thoughts.

A check indicated that the message had indeed been relayed by satellite—not once, but twice. This squared with its distant professed site of origination. The language used, including the special annotations that substituted for the physical gestures that were so important a part of the AAnn language, did not suggest a military origin. If this was a test, it was far more cleverly constructed than its predecessor.

If he treated it as a test and was correct in his analysis, he would accrue commendation. If he was wrong, the consequences could be grave. If he did handle it as a legitimate communication and he was wrong, he would suffer little more than embarrassment and perhaps a small notation in his record. If he treated it as legitimate and was right, he would gain credit for carrying out his duties in a prompt, judicious, and opportune manner. Sitting silent before the projection, he juggled his options.

Mealtime could wait. Decision made—though not without second thoughts—he rose, set the automatics to operate in his absence, removed his headset, and exited the area, flowcopy in hand. No one in his cadre remarked on his departure. For this he was grateful, since it spared him the need to explain what he was doing.

The memorandum insisted that it be hand-delivered directly to the base commander. This put Qiscep in the awkward position of having to place not only his decision but his person before the commander. Much easier to accept censure via ceremonial directive than in person. Already he wondered if he had been too hasty, if there were factors he had not considered in making his decision. He could still change his mind, could still pivot on sandaled feet and turn back.

Then, all too soon, he was standing outside the entrance to the commander's office. Ruthless in the manner of machinery and callously indifferent to his unsettled state of mind, the door promptly asked him to identify himself and state his business. When he complied, it expressed misgivings, only to be overridden by the individual within. As it slid aside, Qiscep strode through resolutely, as if equivocation were as alien to him as the suppurating surface of Hivehom.

Relaxing on a sandlounge, Voocim DDHJ looked more the casual tourist than the commander of all military forces on the Imperial outpost world of Pyrassis. Neither her position, her posture, or her comparatively diminutive size caused Qiscep to relax for a tenth-timepart. With a couple of well-executed gestures and without a word, Voocim had been known to induce incisor-grinding shakes in the toughest trooper. Halting sharply, Qiscep reported in tones as crisp as if he were principal communications officer on a front line warship.

"Ssettle sself, ssoldier." Sliding clear of the tangerine-tinted sand, she slipped her feet onto the floor and extended a hand in the proper manner. "Herewith."

The flowcopy protruding from his longest claw, Qiscep passed the information and stepped back, awaiting the hoped-for speedy dismissal. It was not forthcoming. Instead, he had to stand and overheat while she perused the memorandum.

Silence thundered in the office, during which time the trooper forced himself to concentrate on the rotating three-dimensional projections of winsome foreign landscapes that filled the back wall of the chamber. Only when she had finished the last of the communication he had delivered did she look up, silent still, and appear to join him in examining the latest of the multiple decorative projections.

"Massterful, iss it not? The texture of the ssandfallss, the lugubriouss lope of the herd of *Umparss*, the prisstine clarity of the alien ssky."

"Very handssome," Qiscep agreed, since some sort of comment seemed to be in order.

"It iss a Bokapp rendering of a canyon on Tohtach. Not an original, of coursse. One doess not acquire Bokapp originalss through the Imperial recompensse of what the commander of a place like Pyrassis is granted." She eyed the trooper speculatively.

To his great credit, he elected to say nothing whatsoever. No response in this instance apparently being the correct response, she gestured fourth-degree satisfaction with one hand while holding the memorandum up to him with the other. Grains of colored sand trickled floorward from the lower hem of her uniform.

"What do you make of thiss, trooper Qiscep?"

It was what he had most feared: being asked for an opinion. With no escape route in sight, he plunged ahead.

"After due conssideration, Commander, I believe it to be a legitimate document."

"*Fssassh,*" she hissed. "I disslike dealing with sscientissts. For a cadre that purports to favor directness above all elsse, they can be detestably oblique." She fanned the air with the flowcopy. "Sso they have captured a 'sspy,' have they? And a human, at that! A sspy. On Pyrassis." She executed a complex gesture that simultaneously reflected disbelief, resignation, ire, and sarcasm. The undertaking was admirable to behold. Commander Voocim was justly noted for the eloquence of her limbs.

"Tell me, trooper: What make you of ssuch a claim?"

Though still nervous, Qiscep took comfort in his superior's palpable sardonicism. "It sseemss extraordinary, Commander. I am not a sstrategic analysst, of coursse, but if there truly iss an unauthorized human adventuring through thiss ssector of the Empire, I would not believe it to be a sspy."

"Why not?" Though her gaze was directed elsewhere, Qiscep knew that the commander's attention remained focused on him.

Not wishing to be forced into publicly demeaning his station but fearing to do anything but tell the truth as it was requested, Qiscep replied as firmly as he could under the circumstances.

"Becausse, having been possted to thiss world for several timepartss now, Commander, I have yet to ssee anything that iss, in my humble opinion, worth sspying on."

Voocim was silent for an uncomfortably long time. When she finally spoke, however, her reply was accompanied by a gesture of second-degree amusement. "Then we concur. There iss truly nothing on thiss comfortable but empty world that would sseem to me worthy of the attention of a ssophissticated Commonwealth operative. And it would have to be ssophissticated to have made it thiss far, landed without incident, and embarked upon itss work without attracting the notice of the planetary monitoring facilitiess."

"Then you do not think there iss a sspy?" Qiscep inquired reflexively.

"I did not ssay that, trooper." Rising, Voocim began to kick idly at the underlying sand, finding consolation in the ancient movement of innocent grains. The heated granules were balm beneath her unsandaled feet. "What I mean to indicate iss that I believe it to be possible." She held forth the flowcopy of the recently received message.

"Thiss communication iss genuine, but it doess not sspeak to the perceptive abilitiess of thosse who composed it. They are sscientists, trained obsserverss, but ssuch people have been known to make misstakes. They are xenologisstss, I believe, engaged in sstudying the hisstory of the planet."

"That iss sso, Commander. I ssaw them mysself once, when the male came to the base to pick up ssuppliess. I remember thinking that he did not sstrike me as in any way exceptional."

"Still, they are not foolss, thesse people. They have professional qualificationss. Perhapss they truly have found ssomething."

"It would be hard to misstake a human for anything elsse," Qiscep ventured to point out.

*"Heisssh?"* Perceptive, penetrating eyes bored into those of the trooper. He was immediately sorry he had vouchsafed an opinion. "How many humanss have you met, ssoldier?"

Qiscep's teeth clacked audibly despite a conscious effort on his part to forestall the reflexive reaction. "Actually, none, Commander. But I have read about them, and ssseen many insstructional visualss. They are bipedss, like uss, but tailless, ssoft-sskinned, and without sscales, physsically sslightly sstronger but sslower. They have average brain capacitiess of . . ."

"I too have sstudied them." Voocim cut off Qiscep's recitation of his decidedly minor accomplishments in the field of human study to tap the flowcopy with the tip of her tail. "But I alsso have never encountered one in the flessh. I am told by thosse in a possition to know that they are quite tassty."

This was an interesting zone of speculation into which Qiscep had never delved. "Sso if thiss iss an infiltrating human, we could perhapss eat it after concluding the formal interrogation?"

Voocim softly hissed second-degree disappointment. "Do you run your head againsst a wall to conssolidate your thoughtss? To capture and identify a human here, well insside Empire boundariess, would be a most worthy and notable achievement. Much honor would accrue to the liness involved. Furthermore, appropriate invesstigation of ssuch an important prissoner would not be carried out here, with the limited facilitiess we have at our disspossal, but on a fully developed world of the Empire, or at the very leasst aboard a capital vessel. Modern Imperials no longer think with their belliess, trooper!" For emphasis she tapped the back of her tattooed skull with the tip of her tail.

An abashed Qiscep conceded the logic of this. "I assk pardon for my foolissh reaction, Commander."

Settling herself into the dominion lounge, Voocim gestured to indicate that the soldier's gaffe was of no import. "At leasst you recognize one when you have committed it. I am afraid that many of your fellow trooperss would not ssee the inherent reassoning as quickly. One musst digesst information before consuming it." Almost absently she added, "For bringing thiss matter promptly to my attention when you could eassily have ignored it, I am promoting you one half-level in rank, change in sstatuss to be effective immediately."

Dizzy with delight and unexpected astonishment, Qiscep could think of nothing to say. Unbeknownst to him, that was exactly the right reaction. He had delivered the message in person hoping that in doing so he was not making a fool of himself. Now, instead of censure, he found himself advanced in rank. While he stood silently trying to control the twitching of his tail, Voocim called up the image of Officer Dysseen.

"Commander?" The flawless three-dimensional image responded swiftly. Qiscep tried not to snicker. He didn't much like Dysseen, and neither did his fellow troopers. The commander had roused the dozing officer from a nap, causing him to fall all over himself in his haste to both snap awake and present himself as a picture of readiness. To Qiscep's delight, the unpopular officer failed in both efforts.

Making no allowance for her subordinate's conspicuous drowsiness, Voocim snapped out orders. "Get a ssquad together. Light armss only. Get the coordinatess of that outposst camp where that mated pair of ssenior xenologisstss hass been working." She gestured in Qiscep's direction. "Thiss trooper can help you and explain what it iss you are to do there. Take him along as part of your complement."

Qiscep's spirits soared. If the improbable message was accurate as well as truthful and, unlikely as it seemed, the elderly researchers actually had come across a human spy, participating in its apprehension might mean yet another opportunity for promotion. He wondered who else would be on the squad with him. Regardless, they would have no idea of the significance of their afternoon flight. Should he enlighten them fully, or keep the most favored knowledge to himself? For any normal, lineage-respecting, suitably self-aggrandizing AAnn the answer was simple. Unless someone asked him a direct question, he would refrain from edifying his fellow troopers. Under such circumstances even Officer Dysseen might be persuaded to take note of recently promoted trooper Qiscep's long-overlooked abilities.

Commander Voocim took no further notice of him at all, however, until he hesitantly tapped his tail against the floor.

"*Wsssur?* You sstill here?" She gestured fifth-degree dismissal. "Go on; get out. Find Officer Dysseen. Coil him for me."

He was in, Qiscep knew. Like any sensible AAnn seeking advancement, Voocim knew that Dysseen, while never shirking his duty or jeopardizing his assignment, would also take every opportunity to appropriate any small triumphs for himself. Therefore Voocim needed a subordinate she could trust to keep watch on Dysseen's activities. Certainly Dysseen had someone watching Commander Voocim as well. With everyone constantly observing everyone else, it made for a very tight and flexible command structure in time of combat.

"I sshould not have to tell him," she was saying as Qiscep prepared to depart, "but remind Dysseen that we want thiss potential infiltrator alive. Dead alienss make poor ssources of information."

# REUNION

Unable to hide his excitement—something to break the deadly dull routine of everyday drudgery, at last!—Qiscep acknowledged the orders and genuflected a suitable exit.

Voocim was left with the synthetically introduced whisper of distant wind blowing lightly over the tops of pristine dunes, and with her own churning thoughts.

Was she doing the right thing? The dismissed trooper had plainly been understandably nervous about bringing her the flow of the recognizably eccentric communication. Was she risking too much in treating it as authentic? What if it was some kind of test?

The existence of a spy, and a human spy at that, on an AAnn world would be more than significant: It would be newsworthy. She had generously upranked the soldier because she expected this incident to serve as her own stepping-stone to promotion. Promotion all the way off this out-of-the-way, isolated, uninspiring world. Such practical matters aside, however, she was genuinely anxious to learn what a solitary mammal was doing on Pyrassis, violating an extensive catalog of Empire-Commonwealth treaties while simultaneously shitting on protocol. Her protocol.

A little righteous anger was agreeably refreshing. Much relaxed, she settled back to await the first word from Dysseen. Contrary to what she had told the trooper, they could at least carry out preliminary interrogation here at the base. They would simply have to be careful not to be clumsy in their efforts, thereby damaging the valuable property.

She wished she could have gone herself, to participate in the initial examination of whatever it was the xenologists were so adamant in reporting. But as base commander she could not do so. If anything untoward were to happen in her absence, the government's understanding of her actions would be exceeded only by its wrath.

So she remained behind when the two atmosphere planes emerged from their sand-colored underground haven to open their doors to the well-armed troopers who came pouring out of a natural tunnel in the side of the mountain. Urged along by their subofficers, they boarded the two waiting, whining craft with traditional Imperial speed and efficiency. Clearly, everyone at the outpost had been energized by the surprising change in routine. How much of a change they could not imagine.

Neither could Voocim, but she was hopeful.

Officer Dysseen was less enthusiastic about the possibilities. After being filled in on the details of the mission by the excessively eager Trooper Second Qiscep, he was more convinced than ever that he was embarking on nothing more than an elaborate exercise, Qiscep's energetic protestations to the contrary. He did not much like the newly promoted soldier, who strode about the interior of the transport proclaiming his perspicacity in recognizing the importance of the message he had personally, personally mind you, delivered to the commander. Dysseen didn't much like Commander Voocim either, but such was the fate of those condemned to service on isolated outposts of the Empire like Pyrassis. Since his posting he had attempted to make the best of an unpleasant situation. He would continue to do so; not out of a sense of duty or desire, but because until his allotted term was up he had no other choice.

The officer settled back in his seat. Even at the speeds of which the subatmospheric flyers were capable, it was a time-consuming journey to the place where the two senior xenologists had their camp. It would take most of the day to get there, and he had no in-

tention of spending it listening to the theories endlessly being propounded by the animated Qiscep. Feigning sleep would allow him to
shut the trooper out. The four subofficers could handle any unforeseen problems.

A spy indeed! And a human at that. True, Pyrassis was rich in
interesting minerals, but nothing of sufficiently overriding value to
tempt the Commonwealth into risking a serious diplomatic incident.
A thought occurred to him: What if the human was mentally unbalanced? It seemed incredible that it could be operating alone. There
must be others as well, even if the researchers had not encountered
them. Possible freelancers of a type unique to humankind, seeking
illegal riches. He smiled inwardly. If that was the case, and this was
not a test or exercise, then there might be something to be gained
from it after all. But he continued to discount the report, and would
believe otherwise only when he set eyes on a mammal or two in
person.

The electric splash of color that was the surface of Pyrassis rushed
past beneath the two speeding transports, a riot of copper-based minerals and their associated chemical relations. There seemed little to interest humans, Dysseen mused. But then, humans were known to not
always act in a sensible manner. It was a trait for which the higher
races, like the AAnn, had learned to both admire and pity them.

Pity any he encountered, the officer resolved. If he was lucky
and handled this correctly, that taciturn old egg-sitter Voocim might
even let him participate in the interrogation. That, at least, would be
diverting. He had never seen a human interrogated. In point of fact,
like Qiscep and everyone else on the two transports, he had never
seen a human in person. As he recalled from his training, they
tended to bleed easily.

He hissed softly and tried to snug deeper into the stiff, unyielding seat. There were worse postings than Pyrassis, especially for an

unmated male. Though he disliked Voocim, he supposed she was really no worse than any other midrange officer forced to accept such a remote command. Were their positions reversed he supposed he might be irritable much of the time himself. Opportunities for advancement, much less a chance at achieving the nobility, were nonexistent in a place like this. The line of thinking displeased him, and he closed it down.

Better to look forward to capturing rogue humans and putting questions to them. It might not result in advancement, but it would provide a distraction, an entertainment, some relief from the boredom of patrolling a place that needed no safeguarding.

Maybe, he thought, the human and any companions that might be traveling with it would resist capture. That would mean a fight. He felt his blood race. Something to look forward to indeed! He would just have to be careful not to kill the intruders. If he did not bring at least one back for questioning, Voocim would consign his gonads to the kitchen. He would have to remember to warn the members of his squad to shoot to cripple, not to kill.

A check of his personal chronometer revealed that they still had a number of timeparts to go before they arrived at the scientists' camp. Hearing the garrulous Qiscep advancing in his direction, he quickly settled his crossed arms behind his knees, lowered his head forward until it was resting on them, and resolutely closed his eyes.

# CHAPTER

# 13

If the two AAnn were concerned about the young human hovering over them, weapon in hand, they did not show it. Immediately after the vast, ragged acreage of the transmitter had released its wholly unexpected burst of energy, they had hurriedly climbed down from the observation lookout and descended to their living quarters and work area. Flinx had followed closely, keeping a careful eye on everything they touched, but had otherwise not interfered with their enthusiastic activity. He was as curious to know what had happened as they were.

They chattered so actively to one another, their swiftly moving hands and arms accentuating and adding to their conversation, that he had a hard time following what they were saying. Being adept only at conversational AAnn, there were a lot of scientific terms he didn't understand. He tried to get some sense of the debate by placing the blank spaces in the context of words and gestures that he did recognize.

To all intents and purposes, as far as the two scientists were concerned, he had ceased to exist. Their interest was now devoted solely and exclusively to analyzing and determining the nature of the emission. Had it been a random occurrence, or had it been prompted by the specific set of stimulations supplied by the weapon? And if the latter, could these be traced and a representative sequencing derived? If it was not random, then what had sparked the discharge? Was it purely electromagnetic in nature, or did it embody other properties? Was it precisely focused, or indifferently dispersed?

Unable to stand the uncertainty, he prodded the inspired pair for information. He had to do it twice before they heeded his presence.

"It iss mosst extraordinary." The female's vertical pupils flicked past him before settling on a set of readouts mounted on the wall nearby. "Who would have thought to try and animate a device by sshooting at it?"

"It always gets my attention," Flinx informed her. "What have you found out?" If required, he would threaten them with the weapon to get an answer. It was not necessary. Their excitement was too great to withhold, even from a transgressing human.

"Our insstrumentss recorded the outbursst in itss entirety." The male spoke without looking up from the instrumentation he was reviewing. "It originated from far below uss, where the heart of thiss device musst be located. Though of short duration, it wass quite powerful."

Flinx deliberated. "Subspace communicator?"

"The potential may be there. We do not know." The female kept shifting her attention between instruments and readouts, her manicured claws flicking nimbly across controls and contact points. "Thiss particular effusion was not directed outssysstem, but within. The apparent target iss as unexpected as wass the outbursst itsself."

Flinx moved a little closer so that he was almost standing between them. Locating the landing party from the *Crotase* was still his priority. Nothing could distract him from that. But his boundless curiosity would not let him leave. "What target?"

"As near as we can tell," the male informed him excitedly, "the emission wass directed to a point ssituated on the outsskirts of thiss ssysstem."

"There iss, of coursse, nothing there," the female added. "Although thiss ssector of the Empire iss little explored." Shifting her attention, she called forth a hovering, scaled-down image of the Pyrassisian system. Flinx saw ten worlds, ranging from one seared and scarred that orbited far too close to its parent sun, to a succession of gas giants situated farther out, and several stony-metal spheres of which Pyrassis prime was one. There was also the usual assortment of moons, subplanetary orbital objects, and a pair of dense, well-defined asteroid belts.

"If there's nothing there . . ." he began, only to be interrupted by the excited male.

"*Jssacch!* That iss the interessting quesstion, iss it not? Ssee thiss here?" With a clawed hand he indicated a small, rapidly oscillating graphic set high up on his instrumentation panel. "What do you think thiss ssignifiess?"

Leaning forward, Flinx tried to interpret the meaning of the vacillating abstract. "Some kind of fluctuating energy source?"

"No," the AAnn replied, "it meanss that you are not paying closse enough attention." Whereupon both he and his mate fell upon the instrument-gazing human from opposite sides.

Locked together in struggle, all three of them tumbled to the floor. Secondary devices went flying as Flinx fought to escape their grasp. The female had both hands on his right wrist, preventing him from aiming the pistol, while her mate was trying to put the AAnn equivalent of a hammerlock on Flinx's upper arms. An agitated Pip hovered anxiously above them, waiting for a clear line of sight into the skirmishing troika so that she could intervene. She would not do so unless she could be certain of not striking her companion.

For his part, despite an intense desire to avoid recapture, neither did the struggling Flinx want to have to kill the two senior researchers. His calculated benevolence was compromised by the fact that where *his* health was concerned, the two AAnn had no such compunctions. As he fought to escape their grasp, he found himself wondering why they did not bite him. Classic carnivores, the AAnn were well equipped with mouthfuls of sharp teeth. No grinding molars for them. He would have been appalled to learn that they refrained from doing so for fear of ingesting one of the poisons with which unclean humans were reputed to be saturated. Unbeknownst to him, he was spared some serious gnawing thanks to an unpleasant rumor. Having never encountered a human in person, and with their specialties focused elsewhere, the two desperate AAnn were taking no chances.

Consisting of one human and two AAnn, the ball of thrashing limbs spilled ungracefully across the floor. The indefatigable Pip tracked their every move. Nennasu would not relax her death grip on his wrist, and Flinx was having a harder and harder time keeping Tenukac from gaining control of his other arm. He concentrated as much as he could given the seriousness of the situation, trying to focus his feelings into a narrow, undiluted spike of suggestion. Pip kept darting in and out, searching for a clear line of fire, preparing as always to aim for the eyes.

Flinx felt he could grapple with their interlaced emotional states no more. He was tiring. Through their sheer weight if nothing else, the two AAnn were wearing him down. They would regain control of the weapon and, if they did not shoot him outright, reimprison him, doubtless in such a way that Pip could not free him as she had previously. He was twisting to try and make eye contact with the minidrag when he heard a familiar, subdued noise. He waited for the inevitable howl of agonized pain.

Instead, it was more like a hissing yelp. Even as he continued to fight, Flinx smiled to himself. Pip had divined what he wanted: to inhibit his assailants, to distract them, but not to kill. And that was what she had done.

She had spit little more than a drop, but even this minimal dab of caustic venom on the female's exposed thigh was enough to force the AAnn to release her double grip on the human's wrists in favor of flailing frantically at her leg. A tiny trail of vapor was rising from the gleaming scales. A second expectorated droplet struck the male on his bare shoulder. He immediately let go of Flinx and began rubbing wildly at the burning exterior of his scaly epidermis. The minidrag stood off and watched, hovering edgily near the ceiling, ready to deliver a more potent strike should it prove necessary.

It didn't. Both AAnn were now effectively indisposed. Climbing to his feet, Flinx ignored them as he searched for something with which to keep both out of his way. He found it in the form of a large perforated storage container equipped with a time seal. Herding both hissing, hurting, complaining scientists inside, he closed the lid and set the timer for its maximum number of fractional timeparts— approximately one day. They could handle being hungry for that long, and AAnn could go without water for several days. It would give them time to reflect on their perfidy.

"I save your lives from that worm thing, and this is how you show gratitude!"

"We are not bound to sshow gratitude to that which iss not AAnn." Peering out at Flinx through several of the perforations, the frazzled female looked as if she wanted to split him from orifice to orifice. "Esspecially uninvited repressentativess of the Commonwealth!"

"I am nobody's representative," he retorted, leaving them to ponder exactly what he meant by that. Let them continue to wonder if he was operating alone, or if others awaited his imminent return. "You'll be all right in there until the timer lets you out." He smiled thinly. "You can spend the time contemplating the wonder of your discovery. But before that, you need to tell me *exactly* where the outburst from the transmitter was directed. To satisfy my curiosity." He managed an appropriate gesture that was not too badly mishandled. "You owe me that much for saving your lives, and for continuing to spare them."

"We owe you nothing. Why sshould we tell you anything?" Tenukac hissed and gestured defiance.

Flinx raised the muzzle of the small weapon. "Because if you don't, I'll shoot one of you."

"Which one?" the male inquired. A human would have been horrified by Tenukac's response, but neither of the researchers blanched at the comment. It was a perfectly natural AAnn response.

"Both of you. A little at a time." He would never do any such thing, Flinx knew, but since they seemed ready to believe the worst of any human, he saw no reason to dissuade them from that opinion. Not while it might prove useful. In any event, he was acting exactly as an AAnn operative would have if placed in the same situation.

Having run through the formalities of capture, threat, and acquiescence, the female gestured first-degree assent underscored by third-degree reluctance. "The outermosst four planetss of thiss ssysstem are all gass giantss with atmosspheress of varying composssition and depth. The farthesst from the local ssun boasstss a ssingle moon, but it iss not a gass giant. It belongss to a class of sstellar objectss known as methane dwarvess. Bigger than a gass giant, but smaller than a normal brown dwarf. Interestingly, the attendant moon appearss to have a ssimilar atmossphere."

"That's interesting." Flinx's interest in astronomy reflected practical as well as aesthetic interests. "The average satellite would be much too small to retain that kind of gaseous amalgam."

"It could be drawn directly from the upper atmospheric reachess of the planet itsself. The moon orbitss exceedingly closse to the parent world. Inssofar as we are able to tell, the brief emission wass directed toward that moon."

"Any response?" The question was asked half in jest. Flinx knew he ought to be leaving, fast, but his insatiable curiosity demanded he take with him just one more crust of fact.

Teeth clacked amusedly. "From a gasseous moon orbiting an uninhabitable methane dwarf? You are imaginative, human."

"Alsso ignorant," the female added for good measure.

"I will assume that constitutes a 'no' in response to my query." The matter of the transmitter outburst settled to his satisfaction, he turned away from the container and began a search of his surroundings with an eye toward equipping himself for further travel.

The AAnn skinsuit he found hung in loose folds in several places and clung too tightly in others, but was still a considerable improvement over the rags that he had been wearing. The hole in the lower rear was equipped with a reflexive rictus that automatically tried to snap tight against the base of the tail he did not have. Instead, it continued closing until it was completely sealed, which was just what he was hoping it would do. There were no sunguards, the AAnn having no need of them. They could see without squinting or difficulty in the most intense sunlight. Other than that one omission, however, he felt more protected from the elements than he had in days. There was no cooling unit, of course, but at least the skinsuit would keep the sun's stinging rays from contact with his vulnerable flesh.

He had better luck adapting an AAnn field pack to his human frame, filling it with containers of water and dried reptiloid rations. In the absence of evaporated fruits and vegetables, he would have to survive on an all-meat diet for a little while longer. Taking his time, he also retrieved both of the scientists' hand weapons.

Thus equipped, he then demanded the activation code for the two-person skimmer parked outside.

"Thief," the male declared from within his perforated prison.

"Dirty mammal!" the female spat, then reluctantly recited the code.

Turning, he eyed them calmly. "You're both welcome. I wish you luck with your future research. It looks really interesting, but I'm actually searching for revelation of another kind." With a wave, he bade them farewell and started up the ramp that led out of the subterranean station. Their curses followed him until he was up top and out of earshot.

The weight of fresh supplies was reassuring against his back, while the sturdy skinsuit kept the ill-fitting pack from rubbing against his flesh. Once inside the skimmer, he unloaded them both. After spending several minutes deep in study, he tentatively entered the code the female had provided. The skimmer's engine stuttered to life, and the compact craft rose five meters off the ground. Though he experimented with the controls, he could not induce it to rise any higher. Still, it would clear the majority of obstacles in his path. While he could not travel in a perfectly straight line, neither would he have to deviate too often from his intended course.

Pausing near the base of the observation platform from which they had beheld the discharge of energy from the alien transmitter, he considered how best to proceed. Nothing for it but to assume that the *Crotase* encampment was still situated at the original coordinates. After his less-than-sociable encounter with the pair of AAnn scientists, he would be delighted to see fellow humans again: even potentially hostile ones, even from a distance. Settling on a bearing, he eased the accelerator equivalent forward. The skimmer headed off in a southeasterly direction, a reinvigorated Pip resting on the deck near his feet.

Less than an hour later, the engine died. He just did manage to wrestle the vehicle to a comparatively intact touchdown—his second crash landing on Pyrassis, he reflected ruefully. Though unfamiliar with the technical specifications of the alien craft, outwardly at least it appeared undamaged. The calculatingly deceitful AAnn had given him an incomplete activation code. No doubt intentionally, the skimmer had carried him far enough from their camp so that when it failed it would leave him with more than a day's walk to get back—by which time they would have emerged from their temporary detention to arm and barricade themselves against his possible return. Muttering an admiring curse, he shouldered his supplies and struck off on foot, Pip preceding him effortlessly through their sweltering black surroundings.

It was early evening when he spotted the approaching aircraft. There were two of them, still high but descending rapidly, and of unmistakably AAnn design. Though he could not be certain of their intended destination, based on his recent encounter he was pretty sure he knew where they were headed. While it was unlikely anyone aboard, even assuming they were looking for him, could spot a solitary figure far below wending its way among the ebon twists and curls of the inhumed transmitter, he took no chances, huddling beneath a sweeping overhang of black material until they were out of sight.

As he hurried onward, a rising roar overtook him from behind. They were landing at the scientific station, all right, descending sharply. He wished he had been able to put more distance between himself and the outpost before the borrowed skimmer had quit. Entering, they would soon find the penned-up pair of scientists. Glancing down at his feet he saw that he was not leaving much of a trail on the black, ribbed surface. Footsteps showed only where grains had accumulated in gaps or miniature dunes. Keeping that in mind, he did his best to avoid the softer, deeper piles of sand.

When they came after him, it would be with more sophisticated tracking methods than eyeballing the ground for footprints. Still, he had the impenetrable maze of the transmitter in which to hide, and a little bit of a head start. They might head off in the opposite direction, or decide to remain at the outpost until further instructions arrived. Variables were at work. He broke into a brisk jog and tried to lengthen his stride.

The AAnn craft set down alongside one another in the small flat area that was clearly marked a landing zone. A conventional navbeacon guided them in. Dysseen saw no reason to hesitate, and as expected, nothing materialized to challenge their arrival. On the other hand, his communicators were unable to raise the couple who had chosen to maroon themselves at this miserable place in the name of science.

"Probably busy at work, honored ssir," subofficer Hizzvuak declared. "Or out in the field. *Gussasst,* if they are not here, they would not know we were coming today, and would therefore not be expecting vissitorss."

Dysseen gestured third-degree concurrence. He liked Hizzvuak. The Subofficer was a straightforward and competent individual who never surprised. One half-squad stood ready awaiting the order to deploy. At least the long trip from HQ had silenced the insufferably talkative trooper Qiscep. That individual had finally run out of things to say regarding his own accomplishments.

It was getting late, he reflected as he glanced out the forward port. You would think that in a place as remote as this, individuals would take care to be back in their shelter by nightfall—an elder pair especially. He scratched under the base of a neck scale. One could never tell about scientists. He neither understood nor much liked them. But as with any AAnn, he recognized and acknowledged their vital contribution to the ongoing expansion of the Empire.

Hizzvuak was gazing intently out the port as the aircraft pilot finalized the transport's touchdown. "No ssign of alien intrussion, ssir. No vehicless, no aircraft." He indicated third-degree amusement. "How then would a ssusspected sspy make itss way to a place like thiss?"

"Musst have wandered away from itss own camp and out into the desert," Dysseen joked. "Come; we'll ssoon put an end to thiss. If nothing elsse, we can enjoy an evening meal away from the confiness of base and out from under the overlordsship of Commander Voocim."

Hizzvuak was more than amenable. "It will be a nice change, honored ssir. Dissimilar ssurroundingss." As he checked his gear he used the tip of his tail to indicate the view out the foreport. "What iss important about thiss place, anyway?"

Dysseen gestured ignorance. "I do not know. I do not follow the work of the outlying sscientific teamss." His pupils contracted. "The immediate terrain is composed of very sstrange sshapess, to ssay the leasst."

He ordered the lead half-squad to enter the shelter, leaving those from the other transport to set up a regulation secured perimeter. Not because he felt there was any danger, but because it was standard procedure, and because it would give the troopers something to do besides grumble about the long flight and the lateness of the hour. With himself in the lead, they entered the facility. It was unbarred and unlocked.

"Over here, Firsst Officer!"

Finding the two scientists confined in the storage container was enough of a surprise for one evening. Listening to them explain what had happened, Dysseen was jolted by the realization that their story was not the product of idle minds that had been too long away from burrowing company. Still, despite the rising excitement he felt, he was cautious.

"You decorate your remembrance with detailss, but that iss not enough to sspark full confidence."

Tenukac hissed his frustration. His quiet outrage had no effect on Dysseen and his attendant subofficers, but the recorded images that Nennasu recovered from the facility's security monitors did. They clearly showed the human, first as visitor, then as a prisoner of the couple, and finally as an armed escapee taking flight. Leaning forward, Hizzvuak pushed a finger into the three-dimensional image of a rapidly moving object.

"And thiss, honored intelligencess: What iss thiss?"

"Ssome kind of ssmall associated creature that travelss with the human. You know that they have a proclivity for sseeking the perssonalized company of thingss less intelligent than themsselves. I believe that ssuch attendant followerss are called 'petss.' "

"I have heard of that." Hizzvuak was captivated by the rapid movements of the tiny winged creature. "What other ssapience diss-playss ssuch a habit?"

# REUNION

"Perhapss it makess them feel more ssuperior to keep inferior beingss close around them," Dysseen commented thoughtfully.

"In thiss insstance it certainly makess thiss particular human feel ssafer. And with good reasson." Nennasu exhibited her leg. Dysseen's gaze traveled immediately to the conspicuous oval scar. "In defensse of itss masster, the flying creature ejectss under pressure a highly acidic fluid of whosse ultimate potential we remain in ignorance. When you run the human to ground, be careful to be wary of itss ssmall companion."

Dysseen was suitably impressed. "We will take care to eradicate it before we take the human into cusstody." He glanced at one of the traditional narrow ports that provided a view outside the station. "We will sstart after the intruder at firsst sunrisse."

Tenukac's agile fingers indicated second-degree confusion entwined with third-degree unease. "You would wait until morning? We took care to enssure that the skimmer it stole from uss would fail within the hour, but by delaying until ssunrisse you allow the creature that much more time to make disstance between uss."

"Do not tell me my job." Dysseen was polite but firm. "My ssoldierss have endured a long flight from Kyl Base. They are tired and hungry. Where iss thiss ssolitary human to go? A watch will be sset on both my craft. Any dissturbance, any energy manifesstation within a hundred *ogons* will automatically be recorded, and we will resspond accordingly. If we give them a little time, perhapss thiss human'ss associatess will appear and try to perform an extraction. That would allow uss to take all of them, or any automated craft that might be in usse.

"As for the ssolitary intruder itsself, it iss operating alone and in territory unfamiliar to it, itss ssole ssupport the ssuppliess it can carry on itss back. I have under me a full trained ssquad of Imperial trooperss with which to track the creature, and two aircraft to provide backup. I view the human'ss pressence as a fine opportunity for my ssoldierss to gain ssome field experience. It iss a welcome break in routine, for which we can only be grateful. Now—what can you tell me of the human'ss purposse in coming to Pyrassis?"

Nennasu gestured helplessness. "It wass not particularly forthcoming."

"That iss undersstandable." Dysseen was patient. Outside, the squad was busy establishing a night camp.

"We believe it came here for the ssame reasson we are here," the male explained. "To sstudy thiss ancient alien transsmitter upon which we are sstanding. But that iss only an assumption based on what it told uss. It might have been trying to conceal itss actual intentionss."

"We are atop ssome kind of transsmitter?" Dysseen glanced anew at the dark surface underfoot. "That iss very interessting. If that iss what the human told you, no doubt it iss what it will tell uss when we pick it up." He flourished sharp teeth. "If there iss another reasson, it will not take uss long to learn the detailss." Executing a gesture of second-degree thanks underscored by fifth-degree politeness, he stepped back. "If you will excusse me, I musst ssee to my ssquad."

Tenukac gestured for the officer to wait. "We have made an important disscovery here, honored ssir! The information musst be communicated as quickly as possible to the relevant authoritiess."

*"Vyessh, vyessh."* Dysseen made placating gestures. "Formulate your report, and I will ssee that it iss passed along as ssoon as iss feassible. There are alwayss demandss on the ssubsspace communicator." He turned toward the open exit.

"It really iss of the utmosst sscientific ssignificance," Nennasu called after him. "There are hypothetical ramificationss that . . ."

# REUNION

But Dysseen was already retreating from their enthusiasm, his sandaled feet and idly switching tail vanishing up the sloping walkway.

Sunrise brought the clarity of morning and a fresh resolve on the part of Dysseen to pick up the free-roaming human as quickly as possible. He had kept his evening report to base deliberately vague. If the peevish Voocim knew that there really was a human spy on Pyrassis, she was liable to show up to direct the search-and-seizure process in person. In quintessential AAnn fashion, Dysseen saw no reason why his superior officer should share any of the credit for the actual apprehension. There would be plenty of acclaim to go around once the intruder had been delivered safely to base.

The narrow, winding pathways between the arching black monoliths and buckled shapes of the alien surface precluded the use in the search of ground-based transport. Floaters were of no help either, since by traveling over the top of the irregular surface they might easily miss a single bipedal shape hiding beneath. That meant tracking the human on foot. It would be good practice for the troops. Of course, Dysseen had no intention of wandering around the vast rugged territory for days on end.

Once the stolen skimmer's beacon was located, half a dozen small seekers were sent to explore its vicinity. Expanding from a common axis, it took less than two hours for one searching the southeast quadrant to locate and identify activity commensurate with the movement of a human-sized object. Homing in on its target, it caught several fleeting glimpses of the designated quarry. Though it was doing an admirable job of trying to hide among the ruins, the human could not avoid forever the attentions of the persistent, tireless automated seekers.

Though the human had managed to cover an impressive amount of ground, Dysseen felt confident that his troopers would be able to overtake it by the end of the day. Their efforts would be helped in no small measure by the fact that the twin floaters stored within the two transport aircraft would land half of them in front of the fleeing human, and the other half behind.

"Remember," he warned his quartet of subofficers, "we want thiss individual alive. It iss imperative that we learn what it iss doing here, if it hass come alone or iss operating in conjunction with as-yet-undetected confederatess, and whether it iss doing sso rogue or in concert with Commonwealth approval. We cannot learn thesse thingss from a corpsse. Insstruct your trooperss accordingly." He gestured second-degree resolution. "If the human diess, ssomeone will be held accountable. The conssequencess will not be pleassant."

"What about the dangerouss ssmall flying creature that travelss with it?" subofficer Ulmussit inquired.

"Desstroy it on ssight. Jusst be careful not to harm the human." Gesturing dismissal coupled with a traditional third-degree supplication for good luck, he headed for the nearest floater.

Soon both of the compact craft were airborne, gliding smoothly over the highest prominences. Looking down, Dysseen wondered at the two scientists' classification of the eroded blackness as the surface of some ancient transmitter. It did not seem possible. But then, he was not here to reflect on the viability of work he was unqualified to judge. Picking up an actual live human intruder was far more important than some obscure archeological find, anyway.


Flinx heard the floaters and sensed the expectant emotions of their high-strung occupants approaching several minutes before he saw them. Taking shelter beneath the womblike bulge of two ebony towers, he watched as one of the low-flying vehicles swept past overhead. His hopes fell. Clearly, he had been spotted and his location ascertained. His movements were now circumscribed. Even so, he refused to concede his freedom. There were still things he could do, still a chance for escape.

But escape to where? If the landing party from the *Crotase* was still in the vicinity, they would surely have noted the recent surge of AAnn activity and, no matter how well camouflaged their camp, hastened to move elsewhere. That would eliminate any remaining chance he had of confronting or joining up with them. His choices seemed more desperate than ever: Evade the AAnn and die alone in the desert, or surrender to them and suffer whatever consequences they might choose to mete out.

His lips tightened. He had spent too many years avoiding the hostile attentions of others to relinquish his independence now. As soon as the floater was out of sight, he darted away from his hiding place and hurried off in the opposite direction.


Dysseen received word via his combat headpiece less than a tenth-timepart after setting down. They might actually have located the human faster had they employed all the resources at his disposal. But that would have made it too easy. He wanted to justify the time spent on the project, as well as give his troopers a chance to practice their field skills.

There was no way the human could escape their attention. With its route blocked in front and retreat eliminated behind, it could move without restriction only to left or right of its initially detected position. Those remaining options were speedily being cut off as troopers fanned out to encircle their quarry. It did not take long for a pair operating on the northern fringe of the closing southern group to identify a solitary figure, apparently dug in as best it could contrive, and waiting with weapon at the ready for whatever might come.

Admonishing everyone in the vicinity to continue to close the snare without alarming the prey, Dysseen rushed to the indicated location. The subofficer on site provided coordinates, which Dysseen promptly entered into his headpiece. Sensor lenses instantly pinpointed and zoomed in on the target.

It was too simple, but what else could one expect when modern battlefield gear was brought to bear on a single, poorly equipped fugitive? Without additional input or effort, Dysseen could clearly see two arms and a portion of shoulder clad in the skinsuit the two scientists had informed him had been appropriated by the human. The stubby, clawless fingers of the hand holding the stolen pistol were grimy with dust in a painfully obvious but nonetheless honorable attempt to camouflage the pale, soft flesh within. A lumpy shadow divulged the position of the head and neck. There was, as yet, no sign of the dangerous flying creature. No doubt its owner had it lurking in the background somewhere in a useless but admirable attempt to guard his rear.

A single shot with an explosive shell could have taken the human out. It would also simultaneously render it useless for purposes of interrogation. Everything would be much more simple and straightforward if the fugitive was a thranx. The insectoids responded readily to reason and logic. Dysseen knew from his academy studies that this was not always the case with humans. Though the mammal was overwhelmingly outnumbered and only lightly armed, Dysseen had no intention of risking even one of his troopers to capture it. It was completely surrounded, and they had plenty of time.

From his belt he took a voclo and clipped it to the pickup on his headpiece. As an officer of his class he was required to know a certain minimal amount of Terranglo. It was time to try it out.

"Human!" His voice echoed among the sharp projections and ropy coils of unidentifiable black material. The exclamation brought a satisfying response from the circle of concealed soldiers. Even the insufferable Qiscep was impressed. "You ssurrounded total now. You sshow sself, abandon weapon. Come uss. No danger you. Officer promisse. Come uss now. All assurancess given."

There was no response from the place of concealment. The stolen weapon remained pointed menacingly forward, and the human did not move. Irritated, Dysseen tried again.

"You come uss now, human! Come now, or die soon. No esscape more for you. Many Imperialss here. Big gunss."

The human must have heard. To be certain, Dysseen took the time to check with an unusually learned subofficer named Amuruun, who assured his superior that the particulars he had voiced in Terranglo had been adequate if not glib. Convinced that reasonable contact had been made, Dysseen reluctantly gave orders for his troopers to close in on the human simultaneously from all sides, and to be sure and shoot the flying creature the instant it was sighted. Having passed the directive along, he resumed his observations— and waited.

Worried, he stood alongside Hizzvuak. If necessary, the troopers were under instructions to fire to disable, but there was no guarantee some overzealous soldier might not inadvertently shoot the human in the head instead of a lower limb. Dysseen was not going to be able to rest easy until the intruder was safely in custody.

They kept waiting for shots to be fired; either from the human or his encircling captors. None echoed through the ghostly surroundings. Eventually, a voice whispered to the officer via his headpiece.

"You had better come and ssee thiss, honored ssir."

"What iss it? Iss the human ssafe?" Dysseen's tail switched uneasily. Something had gone wrong. He could hear it in the subofficer's voice.

*"Hassessh,* ssir, it certainly iss unharmed. Come and ssee for yoursself."

Vaulting over the low barrier behind which they had been waiting, Dysseen and Hizzvuak raced forward at an urgent lope, their long legs carrying them over anything but the most significant barriers. Approaching the human's hiding place, they slowed sharply. While Dysseen looked on in stupefied silence, his slightly laggard subofficer slowed to a halt alongside him.

The human's pistol remained up and aimed, ready to fire. The arrogated skinsuit glistened distinctively in the sun. Advancing, Hizzvuak gave the precisely poised bipedal figure a sharp kick, striking out with one of his powerful hind legs.

The carefully collected bits of broken transmitter material that filled the skinsuit collapsed into a pile of misshapen rubble, bringing down with them the longer, leaner fragments that had filled out the arms of the skinsuit. Supported by shards of rock that from a distance had passed for dust-camouflaged fingers, the pistol tumbled to the ground. Only the lump of carefully selected stone that had cast a skull-like shadow remained in place, now severed from the rest of its metamorphic mannequin.

Ulmussit's tone was dry. "As you ssee, ssir, the human iss unharmed."

"Very effective use of improvissed low-tech," Hizzvuak commented.

Dysseen was not amused. With nothing to work with but his alien surroundings, the lone human had made a fool of his pursuers.

"It could be anywhere behind uss now—but not far. Sspread out and find it. Use individual motion detectorss and all available ssenssoring equipment. I want it brought under control within the timepart!"

The order was passed. Once more the squad dispersed, this time fanning out instead of closing in. With both floaters searching from above, Dysseen felt confident they would locate and recover the human within the time space he had specified. This was merely a short-lived delay, one that would do the resourceful mammal no good. And if it happened to suffer some unpleasant but non-life-threatening injuries prior to being delivered to base commander Voocim, why, there would be no real harm done. A thoroughly annoyed Dysseen intended to inflict a portion of those himself.

Flinx was a lean, strong runner, but even in top condition he could not outrun a floater. One spotted his nearly naked outline less than half an hour after he had used his painstakingly fabricated decoy to buy enough time to slip through the net that the AAnn had been drawing tight around him. With nothing to be gained by looking in the floater's direction or following its flight path, he concentrated on maintaining his pace as he ran back toward the scientific outpost. If he could beat the AAnn troops there he might find material of use. Individual transport, perhaps, or the additional weapons the scientist couple was sure to have. He gave no thought to trying to hold either or both of the elderly researchers hostage. Following AAnn military convention, the soldiers would simply shoot at them to get at him, and then hold him responsible for their deaths.

Considering the distance he had to cover, his chances of improving his plight by trying to make it back to the outpost were slight to nonexistent, but anything was better than simply waiting around for the AAnn to pick him up. Even though checkmate seemed inevitable, he had resolved to continue the game until he was out of pieces. He still had Pip, who soared along above him, and perhaps another trick or two. At the very least, he would not make it easy for the AAnn.

A roar filled his ears, and sudden wind ruffled his long red hair from behind. Was the floater trying to run him down? If so, there was little he could do about it. The hand weapon remaining in his possession might be capable of damaging the military vehicle, but if he shot at them he risked being blasted in return. If they were going to attack him with a floater, he might as well surrender now and save himself an injury. Exhausted, breathing hard, he slowed and turned. Hovering dangerously close overhead while hot air danced in rippling waves around it was a large, highly mobile craft. It was not an AAnn military floater.

It was the other shuttlecraft from the *Teacher*.

A mellifluous voice broadcast down to him. "Good afternoon, Flinx. You are in need of transportation. Your ship misses you."

It was standard AI interfacing, interlaced according to his chosen program, but he could not have responded more gratefully had the words come from old Mother Mastiff herself.

"You could say that. Access, please."

Since the shuttle could not set down on the jagged black surface of the transmitter, a hoist was deployed. It was not an elegant means of embarkation, but it allowed Flinx to board. Pip accompanied him upward, having no need of such unwieldy devices.

Once within the familiar confines of the backup shuttle, Flinx threw himself into the pilot's seat and gave the order to return at speed to the *Teacher*. Further inquiry revealed that the shuttle's path had not been tracked, nor was it presently being monitored. As for the *Teacher*, it remained where he had left it, secluded in fixed orbit behind the outer moon. Within minutes they were accelerating out of Pyrassisian atmosphere. Only then did he begin to feel a little safe.

The distilled, recycled water the shuttle provided from its limited supply slid down his parched throat like refrigerated nectar. His fatigue fell away like dry skin as he contemplated the order he intended to put to the *Teacher*'s autochef, and the immersion shower he intended to take as soon as he could divest himself of his filthy remnant rags. It was plain what had happened. More than a reasonable amount of time having passed without any contact from its owner, the ship AI's intuitive programming had finally kicked in and sent the shuttle looking for him. Had he been marooned in a city, finding him would have taken forever. But on Pyrassis's barren surface, locating the only human on the planet had taken considerably less time.

He wanted to ask the *Teacher*, via the shuttle's instrumentation, about the present location of the presumed exploration party from the *Crotase*. He also wondered about the dried leaves that were lying on the deck close to the pilot's seat, but he was too tired to phrase the queries: too tired, and too consumed with anticipation of the decent food, water, and cleansing to come. There was nothing of such importance that it could not wait a little bit longer for examination.

When Dysseen reported what had transpired, Voocim was at once furious and pleased: furious that their empty-handed quarry had somehow managed to escape the attentions of an entire squad of presumably well-trained Imperial troopers, and pleased that her suppositions were confirmed. The human was a spy, all right, whose operations had been monitored all along by sophisticated instrumentation aboard an as-yet-undetected interstellar craft. It made the prize, when eventually it came to rest in her grasp, all the more attractive. A spy was definitely worth apprehending: a spy and its KK-drive ship considerably more so.

As a system of decidedly minor importance, Pyrassis was not

notably well defended against intrusion. But neither was it open and inviting. No claimed Imperial world was without protection. There were steps she could take, forces she could mobilize. The insidiously clever human had escaped the surface of Pyrassis. It would not escape the system. There was less room for improvisation in space than in atmosphere. Turning to her communicator, she began to issue the necessary directives.

# CHAPTER
# 14

Flinx had never had much of a real home, not in the traditional sense. Mother Mastiff had done her best to make one for him, but the rambunctious old lady had not really been the domestic type. As a result, and in the absence of true parents, he had spent most of his youth wandering about the streets and bazaars of Drallar, seeking diversion and enlightenment in place of familial comfort.

Many years and worlds later he was still wandering, but thanks to the adaptive skills of his whimsical, curious friends the Ulru-Ujurrians, he could now take a semblance of a home with him wherever he chose to go. The *Teacher* was a fully-equipped KK-drive ship capable of making the journey between star systems. Over the past couple of years it had become as much of a permanent home as he had ever known, one that could not only take him where he wished but respond to his needs and requests as he thought of them. As the shuttlecraft settled into place within the drop hold, he realized how much he had missed his ship's comforting, enveloping walls.

After days of wandering the arid desert of Pyrassis, the immersion shower was so satisfying, so relaxing, that it required a real effort of will on his part to step out and stand still while the system dried him. With his spirits revived, real food and sweet drink rapidly restored his spirits. Pip reveled in every one of the edible bits and pieces he passed her. Her dust-coated wings regained their stained-glass gloss, and a familiar luster returned to her green-eyed gaze.

None of this took very long. Though Flinx could gladly have done nothing but cleanse, eat, and sleep for days, he could not spare the time. Not if he wanted to stay on the track of the *Crotase*. Additionally, the AAnn responsible for the security of Pyrassis were now aware that at least one unauthorized human was prowling their vicinity. While Flinx did not know the limits of the locals' resources, he doubted they would allow him to roam free just because he had escaped the planetary surface. As long as he remained within Empire boundaries, his independence was at risk.

Did they have ships in-system that were capable of searching for him? He had to assume so since it could be fatal to assume otherwise. Accordingly, he directed the *Teacher* to monitor proximate space for suspect trajectories, to report any such to him immediately even if he was asleep, and to take whatever appropriate evasive action its tactical programming should deem necessary to ensure the continued safety of both itself and its sole human occupant.

None of which meant that he was giving up on his search: only that he was taking steps to ensure that he would be able to continue it.

Now that it was possible that his presence had been descried, and his escape from the surface via shuttlecraft reported, the AAnn would begin looking for him in orbit. Failing to find either the shuttlecraft or any other unidentified vessel nearby, they would invariably extend their search outward. Which meant that his time frame for tracking, observing, and making contact with the landing party from the *Crotase* was limited and getting smaller with every passing moment. Eschewing the comfort of the immersion chamber, he headed purposefully forward and settled himself in the owner's chair. Pip amused herself slithering in and out of the instrumentation, searching for vermin that weren't there.

It was not necessary to address himself specifically to the *Teacher*'s controlling AI. There was no one else on board capable of responding to his questions. "Has the position of the landing party under scrutiny changed from previous determinations?"

The ship did not hesitate. "It has."

That wasn't surprising, he knew. He called up the dimensional map of the region where he had spent the past difficult days. Interestingly, it identified the significant expanse of the buried alien transmitter as a geological feature.

"Show me the new location and refine the convergence."

"I cannot do that, Flinx."

He blinked. "Why not?"

"Because the landing party from the Commonwealth vessel in question is no longer on the surface of the world in question. Its members rejoined their ship several days prior to your recent return."

"Then they must be reconsidering the geographical location of whatever it was they came here to investigate."

"I surmise otherwise. Not only did they depart the surface, they have left the planetary vicinity."

Leaning back his head, Flinx closed his eyes. He was suddenly very tired. To have come all this way, to have risked intrusion into Empire space, only to have lost the trail of the one syb that might contain critical clues to his history, was almost too much to bear.

And the trail *was* lost. No ship could be tracked through space-plus. One had to know its destination, or at the very least its departure trajectory. Even then, and with the aid of sophisticated plotting and predicting instrumentation, trying to decide on a vessel's eventual destination without knowing where or when it planned to emerge from space-plus was an arcane art that bordered on the metaphysical.

Unless . . .

"You said they've left the planetary vicinity. Did they make changeover, or are they still in-system?"

"Their coordinates abide locally. I am presently receiving indications, and have been since they departed, that they have established an orbit around Pyrassis Ten, the outermost of this system's worlds."

A chance. There was still a chance. Excitement rose within him, tempered with confusion. What *did* the crew of a seemingly innocuous commercial vessel want with this unprepossessing AAnn system? Or were they simply moving until activity around Pyrassis quieted down, to avoid attention from the local authorities who had been stirred to unusual activity by the disclosure of Flinx's presence? Pyrassis at least presented certain credible commercial potential in the form of exotic mineral formations and possible other, as-yet-unknown resources. A cold methane dwarf accompanied by a single similarly gaseous moon would seem to offer no such potential.

Single moon. According to the venerable mated pair of contentious AAnn scientists, that was where the single abrupt discharge of energy from the alien transmitter had been directed. What was going on here? What possible connection could that unforeseen revelation have to do with the crew of the *Crotase*? Did it somehow suggest a connection between him and the missing sybfile? A myriad of musings rushed and crashed through his head, and none of them made any sense.

They *would*, he vowed as he gave directions to the *Teacher*. Sooner or later, somehow, they would.

It took longer to generate an approach to the edge of the Pyrassisian system by avoiding the plane of the ecliptic, but Flinx felt, and the *Teacher*'s AI agreed, that they were less likely that way to encounter any investigating AAnn craft, be they crewed or automated. It would also, if they were challenged, allow for a safer and more rapid insertion into space-plus, should flight to avoid confrontation become unavoidable.

Whether the forces stationed on Pyrassis were slow, or underequipped, or confused, or all those and more Flinx did not know, but he was greatly relieved when the *Teacher* commenced its final approach to Pyrassis Ten without having come upon anything more threatening than a robotic scientific satellite. Using techniques developed and adopted by the Ulru-Ujurrians and incorporated seamlessly into the *Teacher*'s design, he was able to circle the roiling, dirty brown mass of the enormous planet at cloud-top level. This allowed him to approach its solitary thickly clouded moon unobserved.

The *Crotase* was there, just as the AI had predicted. Shielded by advanced military technology that should not have been present on a private vessel, the *Teacher* ignored the other craft's rudimentary scanning devices and settled into an entirely separate orbit. While Flinx's ship could not be detected by the instrumentation on board the *Crotase*, that did not mean someone could not look out a port and detect with the naked eye the glint of another starship floating nearby. By stationing himself on the opposite side of Pyrassis Ten's single satellite, that most elementary possibility was avoided.

Arrival brought with it no revelation. In the elaborate and always growing catalog of substellar astronomical objects, neither the moon nor its parent world were especially impressive. Methane dwarves were among the most boring planetary types in the celestial lexicon. Pyrassis Ten boasted no psychedelically tinted cloud bands, no rings, and no volcanically swirling storms. Its atmosphere was brown, dull, and incredibly dense, even if it was seven times the size of Saturn. Its moon was similarly unmemorable.

Or was, until the *Teacher*, in addition to running standard approach scans, began to probe more deeply with its most sophisticated instrumentation.

"This orbiting object is not entirely of a gaseous nature. It has a solid core."

Gazing at the grimy brown sphere, Flinx was unable to descry any evidence of nonvaporous material. That wasn't surprising. Some methane dwarves had solid centers, others were effluvium all the way through, in still others certain gases had condensed to form entirely spherical oceans at their center. The same could easily be true of a companion satellite.

"Stony material, nickel-iron, what?" he inquired, only mildly interested.

"The core material is diverse in composition. Metals are present, though in atypical combinations. There are also stratified elements existing in deviant states. Metallic fluids, for example, and liquid metals. Altogether, a very anomalous affair."

"Core dimensions?" There was no sign of active weather among the lugubrious clouds of either planet or moon; no upward-spiraling tempests, no towering flashes of monumental lightning.

"Approximately four hundred and sixty-three kilometers by one hundred and thirty-nine."

Flinx frowned as Pip glided to a halt above his shoulder. "Approximately?"

"The core surface is very asymmetric, with many dips and rises discernible in all directions. This is not surprising when one considers its evident nature."

Curiouser and curiouser. "Which is?"

"The core is not natural. It is an artificial construct of unknown origin."

Flinx's interest in what had up to that moment been a remarkably drab satellite quickly blossomed. "Are you sure? That's an awfully big building project."

"I have been scanning and analyzing since contact was made. There is no question about it. The core of this 'moon' was not formed by natural processes. It was built."

Then why the gaseous methane-heavy envelope? Flinx found himself wondering. Camouflage? The result of some kind of leakage from within the inner phenomenon itself? An accident of celestial mechanics? What kind of object was he about to investigate? A relay station of some kind? A floating artificial colony, long abandoned? Deity help him, a ship? Whatever it was, it was four hundred and sixty-odd kilometers across. Even if he could gain entry to the interior, he was not going to be able to explore it in the few days likely to be available to him.

Most importantly, most intriguingly, if it was indeed the intended and not accidental destination of the brief burst of energy from the transmitter on Pyrassis, had it somehow or in some fashion acknowledged that transmission? In which case, what might happen next? He had almost forgotten that he was here to look for a sybfile containing information about his origins.

Of one thing he was reasonably certain: The local AAnn knew nothing of the existence of a massive, cloud-masked alien object on the fringes of this star system. If that were so, there would be a permanent research station out here dedicated to examining and exploring it.

If the intention was to disguise the object by giving it the appearance of a natural moon, its makers had done a superb job. Save for actual depth of atmosphere, there was no detectable difference, either chemical or visual, between the haze-shrouded satellite and the world it circled. Depending on how long the gravity-generating object had been in orbit, however, it might simply have drawn off enough material from the tenth planet to acquire the modest atmosphere of its own. The murky haze that enveloped it might easily have come about through natural processes and not via intelligent design.

"Can you hazard a guess as to the satellite core object's age?" he asked the *Teacher*.

"Without samples of actual material to break down and analyze, I cannot." The ship's tone was apologetic. "However, the methane-ammonia clouds surrounding it are of comparatively youthful inception."

Flinx rocked in his chair. "Then you've decided that they are as artificial in nature as the core material?"

"I did not say that. I cannot tell from their composition whether they are of natural or manufactured derivation. But I *can* estimate their age, which pertinent instrumentation places at between four hundred eighty thousand and five hundred thousand years."

Something about those dates prodded at Flinx's memory. Something more than the fact that they matched the AAnn researchers' estimate of the age of the great transmitter on Pyrassis. But he was too caught up in the excitement of the moment to stop and try to identify their significance. If any, it could wait until later.

"So you think the core object is of similar antiquity?"

"I did not say that." The *Teacher* had learned to be patient with its sometimes excitable owner. "Such a supposition, however, would not on the face of it be immoderate."

"Bring us in closer. And keep alert for activity on the part of the other Commonwealth vessel."

"I am already aware of this and continue to monitor its ongoing activities."

" 'Ongoing activities'?" Flinx was only momentarily taken aback. If there had been any danger, the *Teacher* would have taken appropriate action. At the very least, it would have notified him of any suspicions.

The synthesized voice was unruffled and beautifully modulated. "Since before we arrived in its vicinity, the other vessel has been running a general-purpose englobement scan. I have been deflecting it around us. Were my KK-drive functioning, our presence would of course be impossible to mask. On in-system power alone, however, I am well equipped to dissemble such attempts at detection."

"I thought so, but it's always nice to hear that everything's working. Will you be able to continue to do so?"

"Yes, unless the ship in question manifests abilities as yet unrevealed. Though unusually well equipped for a commercial vessel, its capabilities remain inferior to those of military craft. Or myself," it added, without a hint of boastfulness.

"Sensors detect the presence of ionized particles compatible with recent shuttlecraft emissions emanating from the vicinity of the Larnaca ship *Crotase*. Though dispersing rapidly, said particles remain concentrated in an arc suggesting that at least one transference from the base vessel to the surface of the satellite's synthetic core has taken place. I thought you would want to know."

The ship was right, as it usually was. "So they're trying to get inside and have a look around." Flinx rubbed his forehead, trying to decide whether to proceed as he should or as he wished to. "I don't blame them."

"Emissions continue beyond the external line of demarcation. It is my considered opinion that they are already inside."

Could he possibly corner someone and demand to know about the syb? If a segment of the crew had left the *Crotase* to go exploring, it might make his task of penetrating that vessel's security much easier. But if the people he wanted to talk to were now aboard the alien object, he might penetrate the other ship's security to no avail. So intent and preoccupied had he been with simply trying to track it down, he had never really thought through how to go about actually locating and accessing the missing sybfile once he came near enough to do so.

Now that he was forced to confront that ultimate possibility, he saw that it might come down to as unsophisticated a process as jamming a weapon in someone's face and demanding that they turn over what he had come for. The process might not be cultivated, but in Flinx's experience it was usually effective. While in the course of carrying it out, he could also have a look at the enormous inorganic fabrication.

"Can you take us in closer to the satellite without exposing us to electronic detection from the *Crotase*?"

"I believe so."

The *Teacher* began to descend. Very soon the view out the ports was obliterated by cloud, and Flinx was reduced to observing via monitors. On one, the *Crotase* appeared in perfect outline, her shape revealed by the *Teacher*'s probes. Though they continued to be scanned, his ship assured him that their presence remained unknown both to people and to instruments on board the other vessel.

Emerging from beneath the thick cloud cover, the vast scale of the alien artifact soon dominated the view on every monitor. As to the function or purpose of the arcane projections and protuberances that covered its surface, he could only imagine. Many were themselves larger than small cities. The complete structure itself far exceeded in size and volume anything built by humanxkind. The presence of the all-encompassing clouds prevented him from arriving at a true appreciation of its extent.

The hollow, or bay, or basin into which the shuttlecraft from the *Crotase* had descended was itself impressive. A docking port for many small ships, Flinx decided as he studied the steady stream of readouts—or for one mind-bogglingly huge one. Because of the intervening clouds, anyone aboard the shuttlecraft could not see the *Teacher* standing off just outside the bay, and its advanced masking electronics continued to conceal it from detection by other means.

"They are entering the object," the *Teacher* declared definitively. "I detect the cycling of a lock and the movement of small amounts of gas. Residual atmosphere is escaping from the artifact."

"Then this thing is pressurized?" Flinx remained skeptical. "After half a million years?"

"It is more likely that it is only responding to their presence, and pressurizing proximate internal partitions accordingly."

"Yes, that makes more sense. Can you analyze the leakage?"

A pause, then, "Oxy-nitro in breathable proportions. The collateral blend of trace gases I deem to be unusual but nonthreatening, at least if not inhaled over a long period of time."

That was not particularly significant, Flinx knew. The majority, though not all, sapient races thus far encountered depended with minor variations on essentially the same atmospheric cocktail to sustain life.

He had a decision to make. He could direct the *Teacher* to initiate an electronic assault on the *Crotase*'s cortex, or he could track those who had entered the artifact with an eye toward physically confronting one or more of them. The former course might be more productive, and promised less potential for sustaining bodily harm. The latter would allow him to have a look at this remarkable discovery. It took only a few moments for him to decide.

Not only did he want to know what was in that sybfile, he wanted to know why it had been taken and why the people who had absconded with it had gone to so much trouble to cover their tracks. That was information that could not be gleaned from hasty electronic perusal of molecular storage facilities.

"I need individual transport," he announced as he slid out of the command chair.

"There are three vehicles on board that fit the requirement. I have commenced prepping two for immediate use."

Flinx made his way back to the shuttle bay. In addition to simplex suits designed for inspecting and working on the exterior of the ship, there were three larger, more elaborate torpedo-shaped conveyances that would allow one person at a time to not only function and work in the harsh environment of the void, but to cover short distances without the need to utilize shuttle or ship. They could not operate at distance, but they did allow for extended periods of outside labor.

It was for the latter purpose that Flinx, after first taking water, some food concentrates, and a sidearm and firepak from ship's stores, slipped himself prone on his belly and chest into the first of the compact vehicles. He relaxed while the transparent, polarizing canopy slid shut above his back and the flight harness automatically fit itself to his body type. Pip snuggled down between his shoulders, her sinuous form light enough so as not to discomfort him, her tongue flicking occasionally against his ear or neck.

Rising on its braces, the solo craft was rotated and positioned for insertion into the main lock. Flinx let the *Teacher* program the transport's internal guidance system to deliver him to the place where the visitors from the *Crotase* had entered the artifact. All he had to do was breathe easy and hang on. There followed a brief final systems check, ignition of the small internal engine, a jolt, and then he was accelerating forward. As he exited the lock, the bulk of the *Teacher* shrank behind him and was quickly subsumed in swirls of methanic miasma. Soon he was enveloped in darkness.

A brief eternity later, the surface of the alien construct began to emerge from the gloomy brown mist. Though his restricted field of view prevented him from making visual confirmation, he correctly surmised that he was already deep within the approach bay that had previously been accessed by the *Crotase*'s shuttle. Studying the body of the artifact, he found he could not identify any of the material of which it was composed. It might be metal or glass or composite, or perhaps some kind of stasis-bound synthesis beyond his experience. The realization that he was soaring over a manufactured surface that had been fabricated when his ancestors were still hiding in trees was a sobering thought.

Though the *Teacher* informed him as his little vehicle began to slow that the shuttle from the *Crotase* was not far away, he never caught so much as a glimpse of the other craft, so obscuring were the clouds and so commodious the entry bay. He was, however, able to make out a ceiling and one wall as the *Teacher* gently inserted him into what it believed to be the access to the lock where it had earlier detected an internal atmospheric leak. How had the crew of the other ship activated the ancient apparatus?

The explanation presented itself shortly, as the *Teacher* informed him that a gravity seal of impressive proportions had sealed shut behind him. Personnel from the *Crotase* had not manually activated the alien device. It had detected their presence and responded accordingly. This supposition was confirmed by the *Teacher*, which assured Flinx that it had done nothing to stimulate any apparatus aboard the alien object.

An ancient welcome, Flinx reflected as his tiny craft, rocking slightly in the breathable atmosphere, settled to the deck. He felt he should respond somehow, though he had not the slightest notion of how to do so. As soon as the transport touched down and the engine cut off, he released and slid back the canopy. Rising from his prone, head-forward position, he stepped out of the vehicle and onto alien surface. A deep, low-pitched humming filled his ears as Pip rose above him, finding the unfamiliar air and gravity to her liking.

Walls rippling with incomprehensible prominences and eddies rose on all sides. Gravity and atmosphere were accompanied by slightly reddish internal illumination. Hoary though it might be, the artifact was nothing if not hospitable. So too, Flinx reminded himself warily, were cooks to querulous chickens.

With Pip settled securely on his shoulder, he closed his eyes and concentrated. Recent years had seen him gain more control over his talent, and maturation had also given him a deeper understanding of what he could and could not do. One thing had not changed, though: He remained at the mercy of its inconsistency. Sometimes emotions flowed from others to him as clear and sharp as words spoken in a vacuum. At other times they were blurred and indistinct. And for long, unpredictable periods, there was nothing; only a great emptiness in place of the sometimes overwhelming emotional chatter that often emanated from crowds of total strangers.

Here, aboard this unidentifiable alien object fabricated by an unknown race well before the beginning of recorded time, he was alone except for his minidrag companion and a small gathering of humans. In that place of utter isolation from other feeling intelligences, his abilities were more sharply focused. Right away he sensed a common emotional gumbo of hope, expectation, fear, envy, delight, and more: the usual flurry of feelings that signified the presence of an unremarkable, characteristic cluster of *Homo sapiens*. Distantly perceived emotions strengthened and then faded: His talent was not operating at full efficiency. But it was enough. Enough to denote the general location of those he wished to track down and, eventually, confront.

Relying on the mental bearing thus obtained, he started walking. Did those who had preceded him on board have an objective in mind, he found himself wondering, or were they just meandering? The former seemed unlikely, though based on what he had gone through and learned these past weeks, he was not ready to consign any possibility, however outrageous, to the realm of the impossible. For the life of him, though, he still had not a clue what a syb dealing with his personal history might have to do with a monstrous and previously unknown alien artifact lying hidden on the outskirts of a minor AAnn system. It seemed like every time he succeeded in acquiring a tiny new fragment of information about himself, he was destined to be confronted with some new, previously unsuspected, and ever greater mystery.

The corridor down which he found himself walking was illuminated by more of the same soft, diffuse, reddish light that had greeted him in the lock. Like the rehabilitated, inescapably stale atmosphere he was breathing, the lights had been activated in response to the arrival of the group from the *Crotase*. They remained on in his presence, acknowledging his progress without comment. Humidity was marked but moderate, damper than what he was used to on the *Teacher* but a welcome relief after the oven-baked air of Pyrassis. Pip basked in the moisture-steeped atmosphere that was so much closer to what she knew from her homeworld of Alaspin.

As he walked, he tried to make some sense of his surroundings, without much success. The artifact's internal design was fluid without being elastic, graceful but not delicate. Mysterious tubes and conduits split from solid walls to terminate inexplicably in midair. Gaps in the floor and ceiling revealed multiple levels beyond, but did not provide the means to access them. Imposing megaliths of metal and composite corporealities thrust upward from the floor but did not make contact with any other element of their environment. Devices of unknown purpose lay stacked loosely together in batches that shied away from him if he swerved to approach. There were exposed wires that were perfectly transparent, and what appeared to be opaque windows. Colors were generally but not exclusively muted: yellows, reds, orange, and tan, with splashes of vibrant purple and rose where one would least expect to see them.

Within bulges and protrusions, lights flickered and flashed, or ran and hid as he drew near. Patterns were rapidly forged and as quickly dispersed; some two-dimensional, others fully formed yet equally unrecognizable. Prominent in his hearing was the methodic dialog of slowly awakening mechanisms: clicks, hums, snaps, buzzes, rising and descending whines, trills, burbles, and a hundred unfamiliar auricular pulsations. He was surrounded and accompanied by a slowly swelling fanfare of light, sound, and sensation, much of it as understated as it was unignorable. The disciplined alien cacophony underscored his footsteps as he felt himself drawing slowly but steadily closer to the only other humans within range of his faculty.

He had already decided that he had no choice but to challenge them directly. At the mere anticipation of forthcoming confrontation, Pip stirred against his shoulder. The pistol he had brought from the *Teacher* hugged his duty belt. He would be outnumbered and very probably outgunned, but he had surprise on his side. A great deal of surprise. The last thing anyone from a trespassing vessel like the *Crotase* would expect to encounter deep within an AAnn system would be a fellow obtruding human.

With luck, the interlopers from the *Crotase* would split up to examine their surroundings. That would enable him to confront one or two of them apart from their colleagues. If that failed to produce the information he needed, he could use those he had questioned as hostages to compel the necessary data from their companions. Though no stranger to threat and violence himself, he was uncomfortable at the prospect of playing the role of enforcer instead of victim. The intruders from the *Crotase* wouldn't know that, however. He believed he had enough personal experience of individuals who positively delighted in the use of intimidation and violence to maintain an appropriately threatening facade until he had gained what he had come so far to acquire. As he walked, he tried out a few hopefully intimidating expressions, regretting the absence of a mirror. He knew that his youth would work against him. When you are twenty-one, even if you are taller than average, it is very difficult to terrify anyone on the basis of looks alone.

The exotic creations surrounding him had been constructed to a strapping but not cumbersome scale. Large arrays of cylindrical structures and their chaperoning conduits and connectors were at once majestic yet stylized in design. Passing through several wide portals as he tracked the continually fluctuating emotions of those ahead of him, he noted that the openings were designed to accommodate beings far larger than himself. Five full-grown terrestrial brown bears could have strode abreast through the narrowest of the doorways. Similarly, other components of the artifact's construction hinted that in the past, large, heavy bodies had once occupied and made use of the spaces through which he was presently roaming.

Who had built the artifact, and to what purpose? Was its obscuring cloud cover natural in origin or a deliberately acquired attempt at dissimulation? He drew no inspiration from what he saw. The artifact was imposing, sturdily built, and ancient beyond belief. Whether it was functional beyond its ability to react to the presence of and provide support for oxygen-breathing life-forms was not a question that interested him as much as did the location of the missing sybfile.

He continued to advance with heightened caution. From the strength of the feelings he was sensing, he knew he had closed the gap between himself and the exploration party from the *Crotase*. Unlike him, they were not tracking a particular target and so had advanced more slowly. With practiced hand he silently drew the pistol from his waist. A flick of one finger cleared the safety and powered up the weapon's coil. One or two crew members isolated from the rest was what he hoped to encounter. One or two he could keep separate for a few moments while he questioned them in peace.

But Fate dictates little in the way of serenity for those whose thoughts are encumbered by weighty questions. Pausing, he found himself staring in the direction of muted voices. Ever since he had begun shadowing the group, he had apperceived and discarded more than a hundred of their conflicting emotions. A lifetime spent surviving similar unavoidable encounters allowed him to sift through and ignore nearly all of them.

Now, suddenly, he had become aware of something else—something so unique, so extraordinary and unexpected, that Pip extended her upper body to peer anxiously into her companion's face. Flinx did not see her. He saw very little, being at the moment wholly occupied with newly perceived feelings that made no sense, no sense at all.

In his twenty-odd years of intuiting and analyzing the emotions of other people, he had sensed love, had sensed hate and joy, despair and triumph, gladness and dismay. Symphonies of suffering had washed over him in waves, and in crowded cities he had been forced to fight off the overwhelming feeling of ennui that so dominated the lives of most human beings. He had assimilated the exotic, out-landish, and sometimes grotesque emotions of intelligences that were not human, and the simple straightforward emotional utter-ances of the subsapient.

But only once before, he knew as his fingers tightened around the haft of the pistol, had he ever sensed anything that was so alarm-ingly like himself.

# CHAPTER

# 15

It changed everything. At first he thought he had imagined it. He had, after all, a very vivid imagination, prone to dreams of exceptional range and depth. Anyone seeing him at that moment could have been excused for thinking he was caught in the throes of some kind of mild paralysis—but he was merely concentrating.

There—there it was again! No dream, this. Insistent and unmistakable, pounding inside his head, demanding to be recognized. It was like viewing a cracked, badly distorted image of himself. While similar, it was also sharply different. He had never felt anything like it before.

Or—had he?

Visuals. He needed visual confirmation. The urgent need to isolate and question one or more members of the *Crotase*'s crew as to the whereabouts of the syb he sought had suddenly taken a backseat to identifying the source of the remarkable and disconcerting emotional projections he was now perceiving. Admonishing Pip with a gesture to remain on his shoulder, he advanced in the direction of the voices, keeping low and out of sight, utilizing the singular internal components of the artifact to conceal his rangy form. The voices grew louder. Discussion was in progress. By the time he had drawn near enough to see, peering out from behind a silvery sweep of metallic glass, it had progressed to argument.

There were nine of them, all human. Three women and six men; all custom-suited, all armed. No, he corrected himself. Six men, two women, and an adolescent girl. They were gazing at what appeared to be an enormous translucent membrane that stretched between two arching, tapering pillars of opaque electricity. The pillars hummed at the threshold of audibility while compliant streaks of gold-and-pink energy chased one another across the surface of the film. It looked like a razed segment of electrified soap bubble.

Two of the men standing side by side were carrying the bulk of the debate while their companions stood and listened, weapons at the ready. A couple of them kept glancing nervously about, as if they expected something fanged and ichorous to come leaping out at them from the depths of alien shadows, but for the most part their companions stayed relaxed. Competent professionals, Flinx concluded, hired for their skills and most probably a collateral talent for keeping their mouths shut. Uncommon feelings continued to press upon his mind even as he observed and analyzed. Eventually, his attention was drawn to the blossoming figure of the youngest member of the party. She stood off to one side, away from the ongoing argument, conversing quietly with two other members of the group. As she did so, she turned away from the glistening wall of anomalous light and came more fully into view.

The stab of recognition that pierced him could not have penetrated any deeper had it actually been fashioned of sharpened duralloy. Though changed, matured, and grown more beautiful than ever, he knew that face. No longer did it present the visage of an innocent child, though the mind behind it had never been innocent. It belonged now to an adolescent emerging into womanhood. She would be about fifteen, he decided. The only other Adept he had ever met. No wonder the distinctive, uncommon emotions he had picked up had sent a thrill of apperception through him.

Mahnahmi.

Abused ward of a wealthy merchant named Conda Challis, Flinx had first encountered her many years ago. Back then, he had just begun to try and seek out information about his parentage, only to find himself diverted into the matter of the ill-used Janus jewels. Eventually his searching had led him to a world under Church Edict, the remarkable home of the astonishingly ingenuous, childlike, and cerebrally advanced Ulru-Ujurrians. There, among others, he had been forced to deal with the unobtrusively precocious girl who had finally fled from them all: avaricious humans, rapacious AAnn, and curious Ulru-Ujurrians alike. The then nine-year-old had piloted her own escape in a fortuitously voice-responsive shuttlecraft—had fled shouting that she didn't know what she was, a cry Flinx had uttered aloud and in silence a thousand times himself in previous and subsequent years.

She had declared that she needed time to grow into herself. Corporeally, at least, she had certainly done that much. Flaxen of hair and ebon of eye, she stood on the cusp of stunning physical beauty. Her appearance was enough to disarm anyone unable to sense the cold, methodical, emotional depths beneath. The external shell was exquisite, glistening and pure—but the yolk was corrupt.

As he recalled, she had fled Ulru-Ujurr full of hatred at the way she had been treated while growing up, at the inability of others to appreciate her, and at a universe that had condemned her to such a life. He had watched the shuttle she had so unexpectedly commandeered shrink into the sky, and then he had turned his attention to other matters of more immediate import. Soon thereafter, she had been forgotten.

Now she was here, the only other unmindwiped Adept like himself that he knew about, on this colossal and cryptic alien artifact. The implied connection with the missing sybfile eliminated one, but hardly all, of the questions that had been bothering him since the file had vanished from Earth. By itself, that recognition did not explain what she was doing here.

Her talent, or talents, differed from his own in ways he had not been able to explore. To the best of his knowledge and as near as he could remember, whatever abilities she possessed were not nearly as developed as his own. They might be comparable, but were more marginal. Or they might merely be different. He had not come to know her well enough to be sure. He had not wanted to.

Now, it appeared, he might have to.

The first time she had set eyes on him she had asked her adoptive father, Conda Challis, to kill him. Challis had refused. She had sensed the depth of the anomaly that was Philip Lynx, and had been afraid. But her range of apperception had been more limited than his, and like him, her aptitude erratic. Certainly she was not aware of his presence now, whether because her own peculiarly individual skills were not functioning, because she was preoccupied, or because of something as simple as the physical distance between them.

Fascinated, he watched as she conversed with the other members of the crew from the *Crotase*. Having identified her, he now knew who was in charge of the expedition. Not the two burly men who continued to argue vociferously, gesturing and thrusting their hands at the pillars of energy and the coruscating transparency held in stasis in front of them, but the beautiful young woman standing off to one side. Oh, they might *think* they were in charge, but Flinx knew better. Completely unbeknownst to him until she had confessed to it, for years the child Mahnahmi had manipulated the merchant Conda Challis. It had served her purpose to pull strings from behind the scenes of life, to play the simple, trusting juvenile. Having perfected the game, he doubted she had abandoned it now.

What would he do if she sensed his presence? Once alerted to his proximity, he might not be able to hide from her. Had her talent matured, developed? If so, it might possibly have advanced in another direction, one he could not imagine. The Meliorares, the criminal gengineers who had meddled with his DNA before he was born, had been inconsistent in their experimentation. As far as Flinx knew, he and his abilities were unique. Because of that, the young woman standing before and slightly below him, chatting with her companions, was akin yet different.

While he stood watching, perceiving, and trying to decide how best to proceed, the others were not idle. Having apparently settled their argument, the larger of the two men who had been arguing addressed the others. Then he stepped forward, removed something from his service belt, and tossed it into the center of the glossy, glittering membrane that hung like a psychedelic spiderweb from between the two pillars of inscrutable energy. Flinx ducked down farther into his place of concealment, and a couple of the onlookers from the *Crotase* flinched, but all the blazing slice of transparency did was swallow the cast object whole. There was a soft crackle, a brief blaze of golden sparks to show where insertion had been made, and then nothing.

Triumphant in both debate and demonstration, the thrower turned to the others and took a few moments to harangue the man with whom he had been arguing. Flinx started to rise slightly from behind the ribbon of metallic glass to resume his earlier, clearer view. Mahnahmi had moved off to one side in the company of one of the men she had been talking to earlier.

Something impinged on the corner of Flinx's consciousness. It was not an emotion, but it was a feeling. He often experienced such sensations in the presence of other sapience. Usually they were a consequence of afterthought, random projections sloughed off by thinking minds without reflection on their meaning, the way dreams regularly disposed of frivolous material that collected like psychic garbage in the distant recesses of the subconscious mind.

This was different. He had felt something like it only once before, long, long ago, before he had encountered the pernicious entity known as Mahnahmi, so he knew it did not originate with or stem from her. He could not identify it. In any event he did not have time. His body and mind reacted, and he threw himself to the floor. As he did so, he caught the barest glimpse of Mahnahmi whirling around, unmistakable shock showing on her face, as she reacted to the same stimuli.

The shimmering, resplendent patch of bubblelike film imploded. The twin pillars of dusky energy were transposed from relatively benign towers of humming radiance into fiery lances of ferocious purple splendor. Shrieking and screaming, kicking frantically as they flailed and failed to find a grasp on something solid and immovable, one by one the crew members from the *Crotase* were sucked inexorably into the now feral translucent conflagration that filled the space between the wildly blazing pillars.

Screeching for help, one woman hung onto something that looked like a milky, semitransparent cable. Her body hung out behind her, feet kicking frantically, her hips and legs flapping up and down like a taut but tattered flag caught in a strong breeze. Ripped free from her torso by the power of the howling portal, or whatever the phenomenon was, first her duty belt, then her boots, and finally her coveralls were peeled from her body. Fingers bleeding from the effort of trying to hang on, she ululated a last cry of despair as her weakened fingers lost their grip and she, too, was sucked into the lethal maelstrom.

The raging, bellowing alien vortex showed no signs of losing strength. Flinx clung tightly to one of the supports of the silvery glass monolith whose bulk shielded him from much of the cataclysmic intensity. Her coils constricted around his upper arm, Pip was as firmly attached to her companion as he was to the immovable alien apparatus. Her eyes were shut tight as she kept her head turned away from the relentless pull. If her companion succumbed to it, she would, as always, go with him.

Hanging on for dear life, Flinx felt his feet rise slightly off the floor as the vortex tugged at him. Able to just peer beneath the convolute argent column, he saw Mahnahmi clinging with intractable determination to a dull metallic upright near where she had moments ago been standing and chatting easily. Clinging precariously to her right leg was the man she had been conversing with. The emotions that were chasing one another across the desperate crew member's face were manifold, but Flinx was able to read them as easily as words in a book. Or read *it*, because a primal fear utterly dominated everything else the doomed individual's psyche was experiencing.

He was a robust young man, and his grip was strong. He was doing as well as could be expected until Mahnahmi drew back her free leg and kicked him square in the face with the heel of her boot. It was enough. Grip lost, eyes glazed with the acquiescence that comes with approaching annihilation, he fell into the vortex and was swallowed up.

Then, as abruptly and indifferently as if someone had left the room, thereby activating the switch that turned off the lights, the eddying conflagration subsided. In slightly more than a minute it was once again a tranquil, innocuous membrane whose perfect transparency was broken only by the occasional transmuting golden discharge dancing across its surface.

Released from the maelstrom's pull, Flinx's feet dropped back to the floor. Breathing heavily, he took stock of himself and his surroundings. The terrible gravity that had been sucking at his lower body was gone. Though she eased the pressure of her coils, Pip remained firmly entwined around his arm. Slowly, he released his grip on the segment of glassine monolith that had kept him from being drawn into the vortex. His breathing slowed, steadied.

Except for the steady twin hum of the energy pillars, now restored to their original appearance, all was silent. Carefully, he rose and peered around the bulk of the glass mechanism. Everything was as before on the surface of the film. Of all those who had come adventuring from the *Crotase*, there was no sign of any of them save for the slim shape of a single survivor: nothing to indicate what had happened to the others, nothing to suggest where they had gone. The vortex might have been a transportation device of some kind that sent those who were drawn into it to another part of the artifact—or another part of the galaxy. Or it might be a storage device that was simply holding onto those it had inhaled for an indeterminate period of time. Or it might be a garbage disposal. Or something whose alien purpose he could not begin to envision.

Pip was up and off his shoulder the instant she sensed his reaction. He felt the rush of freshening animosity before he turned, but by then it was too late. Up and down, in and out, his talent had waned just long enough under the pressure of the preceding tragedy for the unseen individual to steal up behind him. The flying snake drew back her head sharply as she prepared to strike—and went down, enveloped in a mass of binding, sticky threads. As the fibers dried, her struggles grew feebler and feebler, until she lay motionless on the floor, wings stuck to her sides, her mouth sealed with pale white astringent matter. Only her slow, steady breathing showed that she was still alive.

Flinx found himself confronting someone as tall as himself, but differently built. The woman was clad in a jet-black jumpsuit whose legs were sealed, not tucked, into black boots that came up just over the ankles. On her head she wore a black skullcap foiled in crimson. A biting chill went through Flinx as he recognized the ensemble, which was complete to the singular belt buckle cut from a solid crystal of vanadium and inlaid with gold skull and crossbones.

A Qwarm.

The professional assassin was perversely attractive despite her hairlessness. Together with the intricately laden weapons belt that encircled her waist, total depilation was another hallmark of the members of the assassins guild. She held two firearms. One was the wide-muzzled pistol that had caught Pip with the glob of smothering restraint. The other, at once less imposing and more intimidating, was a phonic stiletto. A particular favorite of the Qwarm, it employed ultra-high-energy sound waves that could cut through almost anything. Eyeing it, Flinx was acutely aware of the vulnerability of his unarmored body.

Though Flinx was an experienced empathetic telepath, able to read the emotions of others, a very few humans were difficult to detect even when his talent was fully functional. Such uncommon individuals were hard to perceive because they functioned at a very low emotional level. The woman staring back at him was not emotionless: She had simply been trained to exercise exceptional control over her feelings. Only when she had been about to fire the semiliquid, congealing restraint at him had he been able to detect her presence. When Pip had risen to his defense, she had been forced to unload the weapon on the minidrag instead.

Stalk complete, her liberated emotions were now easier for him to read. He decided he preferred to think of the tall, muscular woman as an emotional blank.

"Move." Her voice was unalloyed ice, absolute zero, the nadir of compassion. She gestured with the stiletto. "That way."

"My companion . . ." He indicated Pip, who continued to struggle, albeit weakly, with the now hardened restraints.

"Forget your pet. It will not die. Only rest. You go forward, slowly. Go any other direction and I will cut the Achilles tendon of your right leg." She gestured meaningfully with the stiletto. The movement momentarily stirred air and sound together to produce an audible warning.

There was nothing he could do. With a last reassuring look and burst of empathy, he left the minidrag grappling with her bonds and started off in the indicated direction. He wanted to confront Mahnahmi anyway—though not like this.

The beautiful blonde had picked herself up and was staring thoughtfully at the flickering film that had swallowed all but one member of her escort. As she approached with her captive, the Qwarm spoke in a tone of voice that was slightly more respectful than the one she had used to address her prisoner.

"Madam Mahnahmi, I have found a male human intruder."

"Someone else is here? Maybe someone who's responsible for what happened to Jellicoat and the others." She started to turn. "Bring him over. By all the states of matter, if we've been preceded by a competitor in spite of all the precautions I've taken I'll—" She broke off as she caught sight of her bodyguard's charge. Years had passed, and time had wrought significant physical changes in them both, but the way her eyes widened showed that she recognized him instantly. Her emotional reaction, Flinx noted, was as unpleasant as could be expected.

"*You!* Here, now, in this place!" Her pert mouth, so adept at the childhood pouting he remembered well, contorted into a twisted grimace of hatred. "You spoiled everything for me years ago. I was some time recovering from your barging in then. Don't think I'm going to let it happen again!"

Unwavering pistol pointed at the exact center of her captive's back, the Qwarm was politely puzzled. Flinx sensed the phonic stiletto hovering dangerously close to his spine.

"You know this one?" the assassin asked.

Mahnahmi's flaxen hair shimmered in the internal illumination provided by the artifact, forming a lustrous, red-tinged nimbus around her head. Flinx knew it was no halo.

"Know him? Better than anyone else could." Walking over until she was within arm's length, she stared up into his face. "You meddling redheaded bastard. This is the second time you've intruded on my labors. *What did you do with the rest of my crew?*"

"Nothing," he replied calmly. "I was as taken by surprise by the device's activation as you were. Of course, it didn't take everyone. You squandered the life of one individual yourself."

"Kenboka?" His implied rebuke upset her not in the slightest. "He was starting to make it hard for me, hanging on my leg like that. Where the hell did *you* fall from?" A sudden thought made her look past him, past her bodyguard. "Briony, the last time I had the misfortune to encounter this one he had a pet with him. A dangerous aerial endotherm."

"Neutralized." The Qwarm gestured backward without shifting her eyes from her prisoner's shoulders.

Mahnahmi nodded once. Superficially, she was exquisite. Her emotions, however, plumbed the deepest depths of the disturbing. "Good. Do you remember, Flinx fellow, my last words to you before I was forced by your interference to flee Ulru-Ujurr and everything I had fought for years to bring about?"

"That was a long time ago." Could Pip gradually extricate herself from her bonds? It depended how resistant to her corrosive poison the polymers of the hardened restraints were.

"Not so very long ago, I think." Approaching closer still, she put a hand on his shirt and ran a finger up and down the center seal. " 'Some day, I'll even be strong enough to come back for you.' Remember that?" She uttered a short, unpleasant laugh. "I never expected you to come back for *me*."

"I didn't come here for that. Believe me, I never expected to see you again. Ever."

Cocking her head slightly to one side, she took a step back and regarded him with unwavering curiosity. "Then what *are* you doing here?"

"Maybe the same thing you are," he theorized tentatively. "Having a look around for my real self."

She hesitated, then laughed amusedly. "Really? If you don't know where it is, you must find the continuous absence of yourself very disconcerting. Fortunately, I don't have that problem. And soon, you won't either." Her expression darkened. "Since you don't remember the last thing I said in your presence I don't suppose you remember the first, either?"

He shook his head. "I was involved with the Janus jewels. You were a little girl."

*"I was never a little girl!"* Her mental blast of mingled fear and fury took him aback. "Never! Conda Challis saw to that, may his

bloated, arrogant, deviant carcass rot in whatever hell the theologically resourceful can invent for him!" Her voice fell, but her expression did not change. "What I said was, 'Kill him.' "

Flinx thought he felt the phonic stiletto make contact with his upper back, just beneath the left shoulder, aiming for his heart. The imminence of death struck him like a heavy hammer, obliterating all other thought, wiping his mind glassy clean. Several times before, he had found himself in such situations. Each time, something had happened. Each time, his mind blanked as something highly reactive that constituted a mysterious, unknown part of his brain responded to the threat.

This time, it seemed as if nothing could be done to prevent his impending demise. The Qwarm was too close, her reflexes too quick, the stiletto too lethal, the order too swiftly given. His hasty attempt to project disrupting feelings of fear and helplessness onto the assassin collapsed in a melange of mental chaos and confusion. A blackness descended over him, and he wondered if it was the duskiness of death drawing nigh. Only—there was no pain. Clean-killing as the phonic stiletto was, it still seemed as if there ought to be some pain.

When he opened his eyes, the Qwarm Briony lay crumpled on the ground four meters behind him, the stiletto still clutched tightly in her right hand, pistol in the other. Dazed and bemused, he stood swaying unsteadily, his vision more than slightly blurred. As it cleared, he saw a bewildered but not awed Mahnahmi gazing back at him.

"How did you do that?" She was staring straight into his eyes, as if trying to physically probe the mind beyond and the depths within. "You knocked her out. No—you knocked her out *and* off her feet. No hidden flashpak, no whirling martial arts high kick, nothing." Her gaze dropped to the simple, comfortable, everyday jumpsuit he favored when traveling aboard the *Teacher*. "I can sometimes do things like that, when I'm really, really angry. And I'm angry a lot of the time. But not right now. Right now I'm just curious. What did you use? Your inner, innate Talent? Or something more prosaic, some kind of charged repulsion field that automatically reacts to any attempt to inflict an unauthorized bodily infraction?"

"Yes, that's exactly it. You didn't think I'd come exploring into a place like this without some kind of defense, did you?" In point of fact he hadn't a clue to the specifics of what had happened. Something unknown and unrecognized had saved his life—and not for the first time, either. There had been a number of incidents, several times in his past when it seemed that his existence was about to be terminated, when something strange and unrevealed had intervened on his behalf. He was no wiser after this latest incident than he had been on previous occasions, no more enlightened as to the nature of whatever unknown self-defense mechanism continued to watch over him. That it had something to do with and was somehow related to his erratic, unpredictable abilities he had no doubt. It was immensely frustrating to possess such capabilities without having the vaguest notion of what they were or how they functioned.

Not that he was ungrateful. "Stay where you are," he warned her, "or the same thing will happen to you!" Would it, he wondered? Or would she, given her own singular, inexplicable abilities, be able to walk right up to him in spite of anything he could do and punch him in the mouth? Given the wildly variable nature of both their veiled aptitudes, anything was possible.

Now that he had gained a moment or two, he made a conscious effort to project fear and concern onto her, as he had once projected feelings of love and affection onto the mind of a security guard named Elena Carolles. She just stared back at him. Whether his failure meant that she was immune to his efforts or that his talent was simply not functioning at that moment, he had no way of telling.

He knew only that the imminence of death triggered something buried deep inside him, something designed to ensure his survival. It would be really nice, he mused, to know what the hell it was. For now, though, he would have to be satisfied with the knowledge that it existed. If it was by nature as variable as his other abilities, he knew he could not count on it to watch over him every time doom came courting.

His warning was enough to make her pause uncertainly, though she looked longingly in the direction of her motionless bodyguard. Her momentary hesitation provided all the time Flinx needed. Keeping his eyes on the indecisive younger woman, he retreated until he was standing next to the powerful but inert body of the professional assassin. Kneeling, he reached first for the phonic stiletto. Even while unconscious, the Qwarm's grip was so strong that he had to use both hands to pry first one and then the other weapon from her grasp. Searching her forbidding equipment belt, he found an assortment of restraints. Selecting one, he used it to secure her wrists and ankles. Mahnahmi looked on in silence, glowering at him as he worked, probably wondering if she ought to contest him for possession of the weapons. Even when sporting an immutable sulk, she was beautiful.

Carefully applied, the tip of the phonic stiletto made short work of Pip's adhesive bonds. Once freed, the flying snake began to clean herself, releasing minuscule amounts of toxin to dissolve away the last clinging bits of hobbling material. Leaving the minidrag to her toilet, Flinx deactivated the stiletto and attached it to his own duty belt. Then he returned to confront his pale, fair-haired nemesis. Habitually even-tempered, he was seething with exasperation and resentment.

# REUNION

Tracking him as he strode deliberately toward her, her gaze flicked from his face to the pistol gripped in one hand. She made no move to run or retreat. Was she, too, convinced that as a mutated Adept some inner mechanism would preserve her? Hadn't she just said as much? He remembered what she had done that last time he had seen her on Ulru-Ujurr, ripping up rugs and furniture with the power of her rage. Or was she simply the coldest, most self-confident individual he had ever met?

"I've been studying you," she murmured appraisingly. "If your suit contained an integrated defense mechanism, there would be indications. Understated, but discernible. I would have identified them by now. Whatever it was that overpowered Briony, it wasn't your churlish attire. It must have been something within you. Something very much like that which resides within me."

"So what?" he shot back defensively. "All you need to know is that it worked, and will work again if you try anything."

"Will it? Will it, Philip Lynx?"

Names, he thought. Random combinations of letters, signifying what? A person? A specific individual? Stars had names, and nebulae, but of what significance was the name of a single living being? Frustration surged within him. He had spent too long trying to cope with names.

She wasn't finished. "You really don't know what you did to Briony, do you? Or even how you did it?"

"Like I said, it doesn't matter."

"Oh, it matters, Flinx. It matters more than you can imagine. Not to me specifically, perhaps, but in the greater scheme of things. I know what you are about even if you don't, because you and I are about many of the same things. I knew you were dangerous the moment I set eyes on you, years ago when you came to visit Conda Challis. I knew you were the only one who could really know me.

And knowing me, I knew you would sooner or later present a problem if you weren't dealt with." She spread her hands and smiled engagingly. "This proves it."

"Maybe," he replied patiently, "if you wouldn't be in such a hurry to kill me, I wouldn't seem to pose such a threat to you."

"Adept with wit as well as with the Other, too." Her hands fell to her sides. "What now, Flinx? Are you going to try and shoot me? It will be an interesting experiment. What will you do if the inner me reacts to such a threat the same way the inner you does to threats against yourself?"

The pistol felt cold in his hand. "I ought to try. I have the right to."

"But you won't, will you?" Once again she flashed a smile sufficiently wicked to disarm all but the most decrepit of men, and most women. "First of all, you're not sure that you can, and second, the will to kill is not a dynamic constituent of your mental makeup."

"Don't be too sure. I've killed before." Flinx's expression tightened. A familiar weight settled on him, and he glanced over to see Pip, cleaned up and renewed, resting once more against his shoulder. "I don't enjoy it, but I can do it." His expression warped ever so slightly. "Dynamic constituent of my mental makeup or not."

"Yes." She was eyeing him thoughtfully. Fear remained absent as ever from her countenance. "I see that you can. But you won't try to kill me, Flinx." The corrupt smile returned, wrenched out of shape like a length of dirty scrap wire, no longer sensuous but debased. "Not because you can't. I have a feeling that you might be able to, in spite of everything I could do to prevent it. You won't do it, because you wouldn't kill your own sister."

# CHAPTER

# 16

Tight-lipped and tense, he met her unfathomable, dark-eyed gaze without lowering the pistol. On his shoulder, Pip stirred uneasily, confused by the emotions she was intuiting within her companion.

"You're crazy. Not just homicidal, but crazy. I can't kill my sister, because she's already dead. It happened years ago, after you fled Ulru-Ujurr. You knew her well. Her name was Teleen auz Rudenuaman." Memories came flooding back to him, unforced and unwanted. Of a confrontation on Ulru-Ujurr. Of revelations unsought. Of the memory of a terrible moment that could not be avoided. "Pip did it, defending me," he whispered. "She had no choice. Teleen would have killed me."

"Ah yes, the world of oversized furry freaks. I remember it all too well. I didn't like the place, and I didn't like the inhabitants." She turned away from him, and he gripped the gun a little tighter. On his shoulder, Pip tensed. But Mahnahmi was only looking for a place to sit down.

"You're so very much involved with yourself, Flinx. I sensed that years ago, and I see that it still dominates your life. Well, yours isn't the only reality demanding of attention. Try comprehending someone else's, for a few moments. Take a journey down a different avenue of life, Brother."

"Stop calling me that," he commanded her irritably.

She laughed. It was an uncommon laugh: inviting, musical, and yet foreboding. "Listen and I'll tell you a story, Flinx. Not quite a bedtime story; not really a daytime story, either. You were always so deeply interested in *your* history. Put yours on pause for a moment, and listen to mine.

"I am wealthy. I actually control a number of companies, under various umbrella organizations. There is an intentional focus on biochemicals, gengineering, pharmaceuticals, and related products. Larnaca Nutrition is the group whose resources I employ when I want to devote time to items of personal interest." The smile flattened slightly. "All tolerably innocuous, don't you think?"

At the sound of discordant mutterings from behind him, Flinx turned to see the bound Qwarm struggling with her bonds. Confident that she was adequately secured, he returned his attention to Mahnahmi. "That's hard to believe."

She pursed her lips. "Actually, I inherited quite a lot of it, so I had a firm financial base to build upon. As Conda Challis's 'adopted' daughter, I came into legal possession after his death." Unpleasantness danced in her eyes. "I'd been giving him advice and making many of his economic decisions for him for years without complaint. No one suspected that he was receiving monetary and commercial advice from a child. It's a sham that I continue to find useful. I have square-jawed, deep-chested, testosterone-saturated males 'running' many of my enterprises, alternating positions with piercing-eyed, svelte, cool-voiced women. Tools and division managers, all of them. They ultimately all report to me. Surreptitiously, so that the other great companies and trading houses never know where or how the really important decisions are being made. I've done well; well enough to allow me some leisure time to personally follow up on intermittent items of individual interest."

"Like Pyrassis," he stated.

"Yes, like Pyrassis."

"Conda Challis had no other relatives, no other heirs but you?"

"Oh, there were others." Now she was not smiling at all, and something considerably more sinister finessed her emotions. Flinx felt it as a suppurating malignancy, an utter absence of mitigating humanity. "All of them were eventually persuaded to drop their respective claims. Several received monetary recompense in return for abjuring any title to that miserable man's considerable holdings. Others had to be dealt with through legal channels. A couple," she added as impassively as if referencing the loss of a pair of earrings, "had to be morbidized." The smile returned, but this time there was no humor left in it whatsoever.

"You were of unexpected assistance, it seems. It was later that I learned that Teleen Rudenuaman had met a most welcome end on Ulru-Ujurr, but my sources could not tell me exactly how. Thank you for filling in that subsidiary but interesting detail. With her removed, the path to complete control of Challis's businesses became considerably less bumpy."

"That doesn't make you a relative of mine."

"Don't think I enjoy acknowledging it, or that I'm proud to admit to it. I don't *like* you, Philip Lynx. I didn't like you from the instant I set eyes on you. You pose a danger, a threat, a risk to me. I don't tolerate that."

"So much hatred." His voice was subdued, reassuring. "So much anger. It clings to you like a toxic cloud. If you're truly an

Adept like me, then you should be able to sense that I mean you no harm, that I'm no danger to you."

She looked at him and frowned. "I can't sense any such thing. It's true that we're both Adepts. But we're different, you and I. Similar and yet dissimilar." Her expression twisted into a sneer, and the bitterness that emanated from deep within her threatened to overwhelm him. "That's what happens when you're trying to develop and improve new kinds of 'tools,' isn't it? Too bad if the tools themselves, like you and I, aren't thrilled with the process. Nobody consults them, especially if it's all highly illegal. As was, and is, anything having to do with the work of the Meliorares."

There it was, at last. She had been leading him toward it from the beginning. Now there was no longer any need to question his original suppositions. If she was to be believed, the young woman standing before him was, like himself, a product of prohibited human gengineering. A eugenics offshoot propounded by a disgraced and outlawed society whose hope of giving humankind an artificial boost up the ladder of evolution had been met with outrage, approbation, and brutal censure. Anything having to do with the Meliorares lay buried under heavy Church Edict. Perusal of the Society's surviving records was forbidden to the public. Only authorized and meticulously screened researchers could gain access to the remaining material.

That was him, Flinx brooded. That was what *he* was—"remaining material." Nothing could change that fact. It was the same with Mahnahmi, if she was to be believed. Still, he reassured himself, that did not make this malformed, immoral, beautiful woman his sister. A distant genetic relation via an ongoing lab procedure perhaps, but not his sister. He said as much.

Smirking gravely, she shook her head slowly as she continued to stare at him. "You're brilliant enough in your own way, Flinx. But you drift through life encumbered by a clear conscience. Pockets of ignorance cling to you like barnacles to a sea ship. I labor under no such restrictions. Allow me to enlighten you."

Her intention raised no objection. Enlightenment was what he had spent his life seeking.

"And keep a mental hand on that little winged demon of yours. I don't want it in my face just because I happen to show some hostility. As you may have noticed, that's something I do quite frequently."

"So long as you don't threaten me directly, Pip won't attack."

"I'll remember that. You remember Conda Challis?"

Flinx thought back to his confrontations with the merchant in question. An unimpressive package of pulpy flesh and suspicion but possessing a sharp mind, Challis had been a successful merchant and trafficker in all manner of goods, both raw and manufactured. His hands were stained with conduct that skirted, and sometimes crept over, the line of law. An unpleasant, apprehensive, suspicious personality to whom Flinx would not have trusted the care of a potted plant.

Now that, he mused, given the alienness of his present situation and the exoticism of his current surroundings, was an odd analogy to use. He had no time to ponder on it.

"Yes, I remember him. And the business of the Janus jewels."

"Forget the Janus jewels. What is important in all this are people, not petty objects." As she looked away from him he could see her reflecting, remembering a past around which her emotions boiled with agitation. "Some memories are hard to resurrect. Some chronicles are difficult to reconstitute. Having the resources of large commercial concerns at one's disposal is a considerable help, but it does not guarantee success." She turned back to him, and for a brief moment she projected a little less undiluted rage, a little less fury at a historical narrative over which she had never had any control, and in which she had merely been one of many participants. "Pay attention now, Flinx, because it's a little hard to follow, and a lot harder to understand.

"The only emotions that deviant Conda Challis ever felt involved his own pleasure and preservation. To the best of my knowledge, he never married. That doesn't mean he lacked for female companionship. In addition to the usual sort of transient relationships, he bought and paid for a succession of mistresses. Objectively, I can understand why a woman might resort to such an occupation. Emotionally, I cannot." She made a gesture more difficult to interpret than those of the AAnn. "Maybe I'm not old enough. Intellect isn't everything.

"One of the women he leased in this fashion was a beautiful but impoverished fem named Rud Anasage. Terranglo slang is a fluid, constantly shifting medium of expression." She was watching him carefully. "You know that one of the things people call such a woman is a 'lynx,' after a particularly wild and slinky Terran feline."

"I know my mother's name," he informed her flatly. "I extracted it years ago from the main Denpasar archives."

She nodded tolerantly. "How adept of you. Did you also extract the knowledge that this destitute woman Anasage brought two daughters from a previous marriage into the business relationship she struck with Challis?"

"I know she gave birth to two children, but they were a boy and girl: Teleen and myself."

"How the hell would you know who is whom? You don't even know the numbers!" Mahnahmi's violence was all the more threatening for being held under tight restraint. "She had *three* children altogether: you, Teleen, and myself. I knew of your existence because when I was small she sometimes spoke of a middle child, a son, who had been taken away from her before I was born."

"That's quite a tale. You've built up an interesting mythology." He waited to hear what she had to say next.

"All myths have a basis in fact, Flinx. My mother—Anasage— also had an elder sister, Rashalleila by name, who had become a successful merchantwoman on her own thanks to a start given her by Anasage's since-deceased ex-husband. It was the husband's death that led directly to Anasage's impoverishment. There had apparently never been any love lost between the two sisters, despite the help and assistance Anasage's husband had provided to the elder sister. That was one of the things that compelled Anasage to strike her bargain with Conda Challis.

"Following Anasage's death, this Rashalleila was contacted. She was, after all, the only traceable next-of-kin. It amused Rashalleila to take charge of and assume partial responsibility for Anasage's eldest, the girl Teleen. Not only didn't Challis object to this arrangement, he was delighted with it. He had no use for the older girl." Once more a slightly deranged smirk consumed Mahnahmi's expression. "As you know from having met her, while not unattractive, Teleen was not exactly a fount of sensuousness, and Challis did have his pervert's standards.

"Teleen adopted a redaction of her aunt's name and threw herself into learning everything she could about her new guardian's various business enterprises. She was very good at it—though not quite good enough. Ultimately, all her accumulated knowledge and experience couldn't save her from the one thing she could never have expected to have to confront. You—her half-brother."

Flinx considered carefully before replying, simultaneously storing information while seeking the flaws in her assertions. "So if what you're telling me has any basis in fact, then we three were all related. If that's the case, how come I never detected anything out of the ordinary about Teleen?"

"Because her genesis had nothing to do with the work of the Meliorare Society. Her father was Anasage's first husband, the one who died young and left his wife insolvent. Our elder half-sibling was the obnoxious product of a natural union. Unlike you and me," she concluded relentlessly. "How do you think Anasage, our mother, survived after her husband died and left her with massive debts and no credit?" When Flinx could offer no reply, the fair, feral girl explained triumphantly.

"She went to work for the Meliorares! Since her jealous, hateful older sister Rashalleila refused to help her, she had few choices. Plus, she was angry. We can only theorize about the nature of her work with the Meliorares—and the options on offer aren't pleasant."

Horrified realization crept into Flinx's mind like invading parasites. "Then . . . the second child who was mentioned in the records I accessed years ago wasn't Teleen. It was . . . you."

The lissome girl-woman favored him with an ironic bow. "At your service, *Brother*."

He gestured with the pistol. "Proof. I need more proof than your words."

"You're an Adept, Flinx. I'm an Adept. You're special; I'm special. Tell me—how many 'special' others have you encountered in your searchings?"

"That's not enough. Congruity of aptitude doesn't establish an incontestable blood relationship."

With a sigh and a roll of her eyes upward, she proceeded to recite additional details of her personal history. "Lynx, Mahna . . . true name . . . born 539 A.A., 2939 Old Calendar in the suburb of Sarnath, Greater Urban Allahabad, India Province, Terra. Notes Additional: Mother aged 28 . . . Name: Anasage . . . Grandparents: unknown." Pausing, she eyed him intently. "There's more. Want to hear it?"

When he nodded slowly, she proceeded to repeat back to him the same information he had garnered years earlier from the files at Science Central, in distant Denpasar. "Infant normal—high R-wave readings—mother normal," and so on. Only, he knew that the infant did not turn out to be normal.

"I can see what you're thinking—and without employing any 'talent,' " she told him. "The Meliorares disguised their activities very thoroughly. Do you really think they would have allowed one of their 'experiments' to be accurately monitored by an independent, outside pediatrics authority? At the same time, they saw to it that you, and I, and others, were given a veneer of respectability."

"Our father. What about our father?"

"What?" Annoyed, she strained to hear him.

He hadn't realized he had lowered his voice. More forcefully he repeated, "Our father. Anasage's name was given. I couldn't find out anything about the father—although I have some ideas."

She responded with a snort of disgust. "You mean the sperm donor?" Seeing him wrought with tension, she grinned. "Well now, Brother. Maybe I have some ideas myself—and maybe I don't. It's a complex matter, this business of a ceremonial sire. Maybe I know something—and maybe I don't. If you kill me, you'll never find out."

"You're the one who keeps speaking of killing—not me." He peered deep into her eyes, trying to fathom the fury that emanated so palpably from the mind beyond. "All right. For the moment—just for the moment, mind—I accept that you *may* be another sister of mine. But in the absence of the recognized commonality of a correlative father, only a half-sister, like Teleen. Whether you're my full sister is still open to question. A few simple biological tests ought to answer that question."

"You think so?" she challenged him. "You really don't know very much about the Meliorares, do you?"

"As much as you or anyone else," he bluffed. "At least now I understand the antipathy you and Teleen showed for one another."

"Just because she was a selfish, uncaring bitch who didn't give a damn what happened to me, why would you think I showed any antipathy toward her?"

"If you're so much like me, what am I feeling right now?" he queried her.

"I don't need Meliorare gengineered abilities to tell me that, Brother dear. I can see it in your face, read it in your posture. And I don't need a mental 'lens' in the form of an Alaspinian minidrag to focus or amplify what abilities I do have."

He could not, did not try to hide his shock. "How did you know about that?" At the stir of emotion, Pip had stirred slightly on his shoulder.

"As I said, my abilities are different from yours. Stronger in some ways, in others weaker. *Different.* Isn't that a consequence typical of distinct experiments? With you, the Meliorares achieved one kind of result. With me, another. From what I have been able to discover, from the records that have been sealed and not destroyed, I get the impression our makers were not especially pleased and more than a little confused by both of us. Of course, we'll never really know what they had in mind, what particular paradigms you and I were supposed to fill." Her laughter was tinged with just a hint of hysteria.

"The experimenters are all gone—dead or selectively mind-wiped. Only a couple of the ongoing experiments remain." The smile vanished. "Even though I've done my best to terminate one of them."

He ignored the self-evident. She wasn't the first one who had tried to have him killed. "You knew our mother. I did not. What was Anasage like?" Did he really want to know? he found himself wondering even as he asked the question. What if the poor, dead woman turned out to be a disappointment, or worse? "I was sold on Moth, a hinterland world far from Earth. How did she lose custody of me?"

"I don't know anything about any of that." Mahnahmi's certitude was crushing. "The first I knew of you beyond vague mentions by her was when you showed up that day to speak to Conda Challis. If you recall, I was more than a little shocked. As for Anasage—" The young woman hesitated before resuming her reply in an entirely different tone of voice. "—I remember a strong, beautiful, intelligent, but deeply disturbed woman—with red hair, interestingly. You got her hair; I got everything else on that side of the genetic pool. She was caring—when she had the time. She was maternal enough— when she wasn't busy with something else. Insofar as I could tell, given my age, her relationship with Challis was strictly business. She had no feelings of warmth or affection for him whatsoever. To this day I don't know if that made me hate her more or less." She blinked, as if dragging herself back to the present. "She perished of a disease of many syllables. It was mercifully quick."

"Did she ever mention anything about your father—my father?"

Turning her exquisite profile to him, Mahnahmi deposited a gob of sputum on the floor. "Your father, my father, was an injection in a Meliorare laboratory. It's hard to develop feelings for tubes of glass and composite. Anasage never said anything about a biological begetter."

Another dead end. Flinx lurched onward. "Why did Conda Challis continue to look after you and not Teleen when Anasage died?"

"I don't know where you've been or what you've seen since the last time I tried to have you killed, Flinx, but despite your obvious intelligence it's clear that certain areas of your education have been neglected. I was a lot younger and a lot prettier than Teleen.

Challis . . . Conda Challis was a bipedal life-form raised up from primordial slime, with habits and vices to match his internal, intestinal, mental, and moral composition. He truly liked children, Brother dear. He especially liked little girls. And I . . . I had the ill luck to be his very favorite."

Rage poured out of her in a flood of ravaged emotion, an endless river of empathetic bruises. For the first time, Flinx understood a little of what prompted her to seethe at the entire universe. Years ago, he had not been experienced enough or knowledgeable enough to suspect the depths of Challis's depravity. Foulness that he was, the merchant was abusing the daughter of his own mistress while simultaneously claiming the child as his adopted own. Mahnahmi's developing years must have been a continuous and incomprehensible hell. At the same time, she had to look on while her older half-sister Teleen was taken in hand, taught, and patronized by their aunt Rashalleila.

"I'm sorry," was all he could think of to say. On his shoulder, Pip stirred.

"What for? You had nothing to do with it. Consider yourself fortunate. Challis liked little boys, too."

"I didn't exactly have an easy childhood myself." He proceeded to fill her in on selected fragments of his own personal history.

She responded to his revelations with a derisive laugh. "You had freedom, of a kind, and an adoptive parent who cared about you. While my innocence and my childhood were being treated like toilet paper, you were having adventures and exploring the worlds of the Arm." Her voice fell even as the intensity of her anger multiplied. "Don't speak to me of sufferings no greater than childish ineptitude. I could tell you stories that would knot your guts like a wet rag."

"Well then, at least I can say that I'm sorry I was forced, that day on Ulru-Ujurr, to watch Pip kill our half-sister."

"Teleen?" The young woman chuckled amusedly. "I was delighted to learn, when I once again reached civilization, of your unintended efforts on my behalf. Her death removed one more potential claimant to the patrimony of Challis's business interests."

He found he could not help himself. "You are one cold, calculating little bitch, aren't you, *Sister*?"

Again the mock bow put in an appearance. "I am immune to compliments, but coming from you, I appreciate the gravity of the specific designation." As she straightened, her gaze once more rose to meet his. "So—what are you going to do now?"

"Why are you so intent on seeing me dead?"

"Because as long as you're alive there's someone who can identify me as an Adept. Someone who can sense my moods, my emotions, and if they so desire, interfere with my intentions. Not to mention someone who could expose me to the authorities. I don't like sharing the spotlight, Flinx, even if we two constitute both the audience and the act. Your presence concerns me; your talent worries me. I would be more comfortable with you out of the way."

It was his turn to wax sardonic. "I'm sorry that my continued existence inconveniences you so."

"That's all right. It won't be forever. Are you going to try and kill me now? I'm still not entirely sure that you can." Hands on hips, she studied him out of bottomless black eyes, her voice a sinister purr. "You're not the only innocent zygote the accursed Meliorares imbued with curious talents, you know."

It was a direct challenge. Pip sensed it too. She rose from her resting position, wings outspread, eyes flashing, ready to strike. Flinx calmed her with commands as well as feelings.

"I don't want to fight you, Mahnahmi. I didn't come here for that. In case you haven't guessed by now, I came for the personal sybfile that was removed from Earth. You took it, didn't you?"

"Yes. Given its sensitive designation, it was safer to leave the original behind. Properly secured, of course. Like you, I have been researching my past—though not with such obsessive dedication. I found out about the work of the Meliorare Society and wanted to know more. My investigations told me nothing about a possible biological father. As I insinuated earlier, I'm not sure there ever was one."

"When I was on Earth recently and tried to access the original syb, it struck back at me."

Mahnahmi did not look surprised. "Information bomb. Once I had accessed, studied, and copied the syb, I thought it best to keep anyone in authority from tracking my work. None of that discouraged *you*, but then, you would have more reason than most to be persistent in trying to trace it. No one shadowed your progress and followed you here, I presume?"

"To an obscure AAnn world lying deep within Empire boundaries? Even if it was physically possible, why would anyone want to?"

"You underestimate our eminence, Brother dear. We may be the last surviving unreconstructed examples of the Meliorares' work. It would be worth a major promotion to the representative of any Commonwealth authority who brought us in, whether kicking and screaming or stiff and silent."

"They've closed the book on the Meliorare Society."

"You think so? Then for all your travels and experiences, you're still deathly naive, Brother mine."

He did not argue with her, did not debate the assertion. Though he felt otherwise, he could not be certain which of them was right. Commonwealth peaceforcers could be unnervingly persistent, and who knew what probes the United Church had placed on the work of the Meliorares? It distressed him to think he might still be an unofficial fugitive, with selective mindwipe awaiting him should he ever be confronted and identified by questioning authorities.

"There's one thing I still don't understand."

She shrugged diffidently. "If you're not going to kill me, then we have plenty of time to chat. What *are* you going to do with me?"

"I haven't decided yet." That was truthful enough he decided, as he spared another glance for the bound Qwarm. "There's something that's puzzled me ever since I located the sybfile in the bowels of Larnaca Nutrition storage and traced it to your ship." He watched her carefully, preparing to judge her response, trying to read her feelings even before she replied. "I've looked and looked, but try as I might I can't find any link between Pyrassis and the workings of the Meliorare Society."

As near as he could tell, both from her visible and emotional reactions, she was genuinely puzzled. "A link between Pyrassis and the Meliorares? It's not surprising you couldn't find one. There *is* no such link: no connection, not a damn thing."

If she was lying, he decided, it was with such skill that he was unable to detect it. "If that's so, then why did you go to the trouble of bringing the original syb containing the proscribed Meliorare data with you? If this dangerous journey into AAnn territory has nothing to do with the Meliorare Society and its work, then what *are* you doing here?"

She had laughed at him earlier, but those outbursts were nothing like the one that ensued now. She laughed until she cried, bitter tears mixed with genuine amusement. "You stupid boy! You really *don't* have a clue as to what I'm doing here, do you?"

He bridled but kept a rein on his temper. "Oh, I have a clue, all right." With a gesture he took in their highly advanced alien surroundings. "I just can't figure out how it ties in to the work of the Meliorares."

Her voice rose, echoing through the endless corridors. "That's because it doesn't *have* anything to do with the Meliorares, you empathic idiot!" Again her laughter rattled down through the vast empty spaces. "When you forced your way into the syb on Earth, it responded the same way it would to any unauthorized intruder. As for me keeping the data with me, whenever I travel off-world I always take a full complement of sensitive personal information along. Not because I think I'm necessarily going to need it, but because it's too valuable and too dangerous not to keep close at hand." Wiping her eyes with the back of her left wrist, she eyed him ruefully.

"You, of all people, should know that Church and Commonwealth are implacable when it comes to such matters. Not being able to risk the loss or discovery of such critical material pertaining to my history, I long ago took steps to make sure I would always have access to a copy, while at the same time ensuring that the original remaining on Earth was appropriately safeguarded. I wasn't taking along information having to do with you so much as I was protecting information dealing with me. The syb you're so desperate to see is safely locked up in my private annex on board the *Crotase*."

"Personal recorder DNP-466EX," he murmured.

"Armed and locked." Her expression contorted. "Unfortunately, what applies to one of us is inevitably applicable to the other. Don't flatter yourself that it's otherwise."

"All right." For the moment, he had decided to accept her explanation. "Then if it has nothing to do with the Meliorares, what are you doing here? Did you come in hopes of finding just the transmitter?"

Her countenance changed so quickly and she looked at him so sharply that he was momentarily taken aback. "So you know about that, too."

"It's pretty hard to miss a transmitter two thousand square kilometers in extent. Especially if you're standing right on top of it when it decides to transmit. It was no more than two or three days' hike from where you were camped. While I was there, it sent out a single signal. Very fleeting, very intense. I had neither the time nor the facilities to try and analyze it." He nodded at their softly humming surroundings. "But it was traced to this place."

"My people also caught it. As you say, it's hard to miss when you're camped on top of it." She nodded knowingly. "So you were that close to our camp? We couldn't linger long enough to run the kind of detailed analysis I wanted. There were indications of possible AAnn military activity in our general vicinity, and we had to leave faster than I would have liked. Like you, all we could do was trace and track the signal." She took a deep breath. "As to the rest of it, your supposition is partly correct: I came here looking for the transmitter. This artifact is the real bonus." She proceeded to concede the additional explanation he desired.

"Larnaca Nutrition does produce and market vitamin and other health supplements, and very profitably, too. But it's primarily a cover for far less traditional study, besides being my personal research arm. Like any influential commercial trading house or corporation, it's always on the lookout to purchase potentially lucrative scientific information. The hope is to acquire such knowledge before Commonwealth or Church scientists can get to it and do something asinine, like declare it freely available for the public good."

"Your company was engaged in unsanctioned xenology," he alleged.

She smiled thinly. "I prefer to think of it as extending the boundaries of human knowledge without wasting taxpayer credits. One of the company's agents procured some obscure intelligence about a diplomatically inaccessible, godforsaken desert orb the AAnn called Pyrassis. Buried among the stock generalities was a lot of rumor and very little fact. What there was of the latter was . . . intriguing. So was the challenge that investigating it further presented. It has nothing to do with the Meliorares, may every one of their misbegotten souls rot in an appropriate hell, and everything to do with making money. Beyond their historical value, which to institutes of higher learning, museums, and the like is considerable, ancient alien artifacts are often filled with exploitable curios." She indicated their surroundings.

"One this size is of incalculable commercial value. My people have been working on the Pyrassis project for over a year now, a project that they've had to keep secret from the authorities and our industrial competitors as well as the AAnn. Everything was going as well or better than anticipated. Then *you* show up. Of all people. You had to go pushing and shoving your trespassing way into a private, fortified storage facility and set off its security. That would have been bad enough, but no—you had to trace it to me. You've ruined everything." Frustration and anger spilled out of her in equal measure.

"I knew if Challis didn't dispose of you that day years ago that sooner or later you were going to cause me grief. Even so, I had managed to forget about you. What a fine forced recalling you've contrived!"

"If you'd stop trying to kill me," he informed her calmly, "you might find that we have things to talk about. To my knowledge, no one else who hasn't been mindwiped shares what you and I have in common."

"I don't *want* to have anything in common with you, Philip Lynx! I don't want to share anything with you. I don't want to have things to talk about. I want you to *die!*"

He felt for her. "You're expressing your hate for yourself, Mahnahmi. For what the Meliorares and Conda Challis made of you."

"Oh, now you're a therapist. I suppose that's a profession that would fit you, given your own peculiar abilities. Know that my thoughts, my mind, are not fodder for your infantile speculations, Flinx. I may be younger than you in years, but in other ways, I'm more mature, more developed."

"Yes, I can see that by how wisely and maturely you're acting." He gestured with the pistol. Behind him, the Qwarm Briony was starting to moan. "What *is* this place? Is it exactly what you were looking for? Besides the transmitter, I mean."

"We didn't know what we were looking for. There were no specifics. Only that there might be something in this system that was alien, and old. We thought that if we were going to find anything, it would be on Pyrassis. Instead, it's out here orbiting the outermost planet in the system, hiding close to a methane dwarf. Thoroughly cloaked against detection, too. If not for the signal that was sent out, that came from an alien transmitter, we never would have found it. Once we traced the signal's target, the rest was easy." She nodded at him. "As it obviously was for you, too. Where's the rest of your crew? On your ship?"

"Yes," he admitted readily. "On my ship." He did not add that it consisted entirely of mechanicals and a few recently acquired decorative plants.

"Liar." Her smile transmuted into a smirk. "I told you that in some ways I was more mature than you. My abilities are also erratic, but when they're functioning, like they are now, they speak to me of things you can't even dream about." Her tone turned momentarily wistful. "Sometimes I wish I couldn't dream. Mine usually are not very pleasant, and a lot of the time I wake up screaming. Conda Challis, and other . . . things." She sniffed derisively. "I can sense people coming toward us even as you try to convince me they're all back on your ship. I didn't notice you signal out. What did you do— make prearrangements for them to come looking for you if you didn't report back in by a certain time?"

Bewildered, Flinx tried to make sense of what she was saying. He fought to concentrate, struggled to detect whatever it was that had sparked her imputation. Crew? His crew could not be coming after him because there wasn't any beyond AIs and vegetable matter. He didn't think the latter could pilot a shuttlecraft. Even if existence had turned upside down and the flora decorating the *Teacher* suddenly acquired that ability, he doubted their fragile roots would allow them to march rapidly into the depths of the artifact.

Then something tickled that portion of his gengineered mind that was home to his unnamed, impenetrable talent, and he knew what she was talking about. She was not quite as adept, not quite as developed, as she would have led him to believe.

"You're right," he acknowledged. "There are people coming this way."

She was nodding knowingly to herself. "You see, Flinx. You can't delude your own sister. What you feel, I feel. What you sense, I sense."

"Not exactly," he murmured, even as he worked to isolate each approaching individual with an eye toward estimating their numbers. "There *are* people coming this way—but they aren't human."

# CHAPTER

# 17

The Imperial Pyrassisian task force closed on the moon of the tenth planet swiftly and without giving the limited-range sensors on board the *Crotase* adequate time to react. The fact that the Imperial Pyrassisian task force consisted of a single vessel, the *Sstakoun*, did not make its surprise or conquest any less complete. Though modest of dimension and slight of armament, the *Sstakoun* was a warship. However well-equipped she was for her class, the *Crotase*, registered to the company yclept Larnaca Nutrition, was not. As soon as the AAnn vessel was recognized, those on board the Commonwealth craft prepared to shift her outsystem the minimal number of planetary diameters necessary to safely activate her KK-drive.

These preparations were detected and reported to the captain of the *Sstakoun*, who promptly brought it to the attention of her operations superior Voocim, who immediately ordered that the Commonwealth vessel be disabled. Accordingly, a single small device was fired that in less than a minute did minimal damage to the other vessel's

KK-drive projection dish. Minimal damage was enough. Unable to generate the mathematically perfect pattern of a posigravity field, the *Crotase* was now unable to flee through anything other than space-normal. It could still escape the Pyrassisian system, however. At the speed of which it was now capable, in a few hundred years or so it might reach the nearest Commonwealth world. As this option was unanimously found by those on board to be singularly unattractive, they straightaway surrendered their vessel to the AAnn.

Having effortlessly incapacitated one intruder, the *Sstakoun* might well have done the same to the second ship in the vicinity—if not for the fact that the *Teacher* drifted unseen and undetected behind its highly advanced military masking screens. Nor was there any reason for those aboard the *Sstakoun* to suspect, much less infer, the presence of a second Commonwealth vessel. In the absence of further instructions from its master, the *Teacher* maintained power to its sophisticated deflectors, kept its silence, ignored the drama being played out nearby, and held its position just outside the roiling brown atmosphere of the alien satellite-artifact.

Had they initiated a more thorough scan of the immediate spatial vicinity, the AAnn might have detected the slight gravitational anomaly that ordinarily gave away the presence of a shrouded vessel, but they were too busy dealing with the one intruder that had not been able to conceal itself.

Captain Tradssij was speculating. "To intrude on Imperial sspace thesse particular humanss musst be either very confident or very foolissh. I would not think them foolissh."

The commander gestured second-degree astonishment mixed with third-degree outrage. "What are they doing here? Can they have come ssolely in hopess of discovering thiss extraordinary artifact?"

All eyes turned to the heretofore silent elder couple crouched at the far end of the sandy-floored conferencing chamber. Tenukac

# REUNION

LLBYYLL kicked free of the sterile, lightly scented, buff-toned granules on which he had been resting.

"My mate and I cannot sspeak to the military importance of the Pyrassisian ssysstem." Among the assembly, an officer or two guffawed, their soft hisses of amusement drawing the obligatory glares of disapproval from Voocim and Tradssij. "*Nssussa,* we are convinced that world iss not ssignificant enough to tempt humanss into transsgressing Imperial sspace." Several emphatic gestures of affirmation punctuated the xenologist's pithy observation.

"Converssely, thiss artifact, which iss of colossal dimenssionss and unknown origin, holdss the promisse of disscoveriess of ssufficient importance to entice the bold and the daring. Humanss too are known to possess such qualitiess, though they are ussually utilized in the sservice of base aimss. My mate and I are convinced that even as we sspeak to the matter, a team or two of individualss from the Commonwealth vessel are pressently engaged in exploration of the artifact'ss interior."

Voocim indicated understanding. "That iss my feeling alsso. However, now that we have dissabled their sship, we can deal with matterss of exploration and adminisstration at our leissure." She swung a dancing hand Dysseen's way. "Iss the boarding party assembled?" When the officer indicated in the affirmative, the commander rose. Warm particles trickled from her tail where it emerged from the soothing sand, as it did those of her staff.

"We will have the ansswerss to our quesstionss very ssoon. Thiss iss a great day for the Empire!" A loud, ascending hiss filled the room as the other officers joined her in saluting their achievement. At one swoop they had captured an intruding, spying vessel *and* made a scientific discovery of potentially enormous importance— and profit.

The two senior scientists would receive their due, of course, but no one doubted that every officer, subofficer, and general crew member would share in the approbation that was to come. Ancestors would be almighty honored, chapters of family would be elated, and the Commonwealth would be, at the very least, embarrassed. There was little more to do save assume formal possession of the challenged vessel and take into custody any humanx exploration party currently roaming the artifact.

The human crew of the *Crotase* was a surly lot. Voocim was not surprised: Anticipating discovery and jubilation, they now found themselves prisoners of the AAnn. Sidearms were collected, the ship's navigation-and-guidance system was secured, and individuals were assembled in the dining area under the watchful eye of armed troopers. Slitted eyes met round ones, and no love passed between them.

The intruders would have to face interrogation, but not here. Ample time for that back on Pyrassis, as official word of the unprecedented seizure was passed along to Sectorcav. Until then, there were more pressing matters to attend to. Voocim confronted the double line of disconsolate mammals, cleared her throat with an appropriate hiss, and ventured to test her somewhat rusty knowledge of Terranglo.

"I am Voocim DDHJ, commander of His Imperial Majessty's garrisson on Pyrassis. As ssuch, I am ressponssible for the ssecurity of thiss entire ssysstem, whosse integrity you have blatantly violated. Unless thiss is a remarkably undersstaffed craft, I surmisse that a number of your colleaguess are at pressent engaged in invesstigating the alien artifact that liess here with uss tail to tooth. We are quite familiar with crewing detailss for all the sstandard classess of Commonwealth vesselss, sso pleasse do not inssult my intelligence by claiming that all of you are pressently here aboard." She scanned the distastefully flexible faces that struggled to avoid hers.

"Who iss the ssenior officer, official, or dessignated repressenta-
tive extant, pleasse?"

A human of average size and pallid skin stepped forward. At
least, Voocim reflected as she made an effort to control her insides at
the proximity of the creature, the typical ruff of fur was absent from
its skull, giving that exposed portion of its anatomy a more tolerable
and almost AAnn-like appearance.

"I'm Mikola Bucevit. I'm in charge until the ship's owner
returns."

Ah, so the owner was part of the crew! Voocim was delighted at
the implied opportunity for ransom. Such undiplomatic maneuvers
would not be officially countenanced by the Imperial government,
of course, but upon payment of suitable fees to appropriate cadres,
they would not be countermanded, either. Events continued to un-
fold in an auspicious manner. Silently, she made obeisance to a benign fate.

"As you musst ssurmisse, we musst ssecure the remainder of
your crew. No one will be harmed, and you will all be treated in accordance with the relevant Imperial protocolss dealing with the
treatment of unauthorized intruderss. Eventually, if you cooperate,
you sshould all be ssuccessfully repatriated to your resspective
worldss." She started to gesture collaterally, then remembered that
humans only rarely used their limbs in conversation. "Firsst, you
will provide uss with the coordinatess utilized by your colleaguess
to enter the artifact."

"Why don't you figure 'em out yourself, snake-eyes?" The angry member of the engineering staff who had spoken shuffled his
feet while hovering behind Bucevit.

Voocim rendered a nonchalant gesture. A trooper took a step
forward, raised his weapon, and fired once. The few subsequent angry mutterings that rose from the pod of captured humans faded

rapidly. Voocim let the ensuing silence linger for a symbolic moment longer.

"Anyone elsse care to put forth ssimilarly disscourteouss ssuggesstionss? I attend with ssecond-degree avidity. No? Then, *rasshisst,* perhapss we can proceed in a civilized and orthodox manner."

The necessary coordinates acquired, Voocim took personal charge of the landing party. Dysseen remained on the human vessel to see to the preliminary debriefing of its remnant crew and to the changeover of its AI systems so that they would respond to AAnn control. Captain Tradssij returned to the *Sstakoun.*

With her, Voocim had two dozen heavily armed and fully equipped troopers under the supervision of Officer Yilhazz, a nononsense field officer. In addition, a pair of appropriately equipped techs drawn from the *Sstakoun*'s engineering team had been assigned to assist the two xenologists in documenting the initial exploration and evaluation of the artifact.

It was thus a well-prepared party that soon thereafter stepped out of their shuttlecraft into the artifact's lock. Marching past the silent, empty human shuttle, they were, like their predecessors, automatically and successfully cycled through by its ancient yet receptive instrumentation. A few moments later every member of the expedition was breathing the atmosphere of ancient corridors. At the first intersection, Voocim called a halt. The AAnn waited while their techs labored to divine the right path to follow.

Meanwhile, the xenologists hardly knew which way to turn. Everywhere they looked, there was something new, different, and of potentially startling import. The commander noted their antics with detached amusement. The elderly couple was going to be famous in domains of expertise that were closed to her. That did not mean she was uninterested in their work. The more she learned about this unprecedented discovery, the more knowledgeable a demeanor she could present when the matter was raised for discussion. Among those affianced to her own specialty, this would enhance her opportunities for advancement. Promotion to baron, she mused, and inevitably to lord would follow. Eventually, she envisioned herself becoming a participant in and an advisor to the Imperial Court itself. That which had for most of her life seemed beyond reach was now abruptly, providentially, at hand. All she had to do was let the scientists carry out their work and not interfere with that which had already been accomplished.

Had she known how few humans remained within the artifact, her spirits would have soared even higher.

The intruders could not escape, she knew. There was only one way out, via the shuttlecraft docked in the lock. Even so, she was taking no chances. As soon as the last of the troopers had disembarked and was safely inside the body of the artifact, the *Sstakoun*'s shuttle fired its engines to position itself directly alongside the Commonwealth craft. Thus, even if the humans who remained on the alien relic somehow succeeded in escaping, avoiding, or overpowering the AAnn who were about to go in after them, there was no way they could get back to their own starship. If they attempted to reboard the shuttle they had left behind, those on board the *Sstakoun*'s landing vessel waited to confront them with heavy weapons.

Furthermore, two armed techs from the *Sstakoun*'s crew were now on board the empty Commonwealth vessel. If any human renegades somehow succeeded in shooting or sneaking their way back onto their shuttle, they would find boarding an impossibility. The soft-skinned fugitives were trapped; albeit for an indeterminate time, but trapped they were.

The unpretentious, one-person transport vehicle tucked off in a far corner of the lock had been well hidden by its single passenger. Even if the insignificant, limited-range craft had been noticed, it would hardly have registered on the commander's consciousness. She was looking to detail a group, not an individual.

It took longer than Voocim would have liked, but the techs finally ferreted out the location of humaniform life-forms deeper within the artifact. She was surprised and pleased to see that their quarry had not penetrated nearly as far into the mammoth relic as she had feared. Either the humans had been remiss in their exploration or were simply making a thorough job of it. The newly arrived AAnn would be able to catch up to them sooner than anticipated. She was so pleased she could hardly contain herself. Only the energetic reflex movements of her tail made public her gratification. With the two techs in the lead and the senior scientists chafing at the enforced deferment of real work, the party started into the interior of the artifact.

"What do you mean, 'they aren't human'?" Mahnahmi regarded her brother, her adversary, with a wary eye.

"You're able to feel their approach, but you're not as sensitive as I am. They're definitely alien, most probably AAnn, and from the tenor of their emotions I sense that they're on the hunt—for us, I would imagine." Flinx glanced back the way he had come. Pip's head was up, and the flying snake, empathizing wordlessly with her companion, was now on full alert.

Mahnahmi did not need time to reflect on the import of her sibling's assessment. "If there are AAnn inside the artifact and they're coming toward us, then leaving is going to be bothersome. My guess would be that they're tracking us with the aid of standard life-form sensors." As Flinx nodded in agreement, she pulled a small communicator from her duty belt. "Then using this won't make us any worse off." She made no attempt to conceal her conversation from him.

"Bucevit, this is Owner speaking. Report your status. No nuances, please. I have some idea of what is going on."

The reply was delayed, and the signal itself weak from having to penetrate layers of alien fabrication. "Owner, this is Mikola. We have been taken into custody by AAnn troops based on and originating from Pyrassis." There was a pause during which Flinx could hear unctuous AAnn syllables in the background. "The *Crotase* is under control of the Imperial warship *Sstakoun* and is in the process of being reprogrammed to reflect her status as a captured vessel. We are accused of . . . There is a long list of infractions. I am informed that the shuttle that was used to convey you and the rest of the landing party to the artifact has already been seized and is presently occupied by their soldiers and technicians. An armed AAnn shuttle sits next to it in the artifact's lock."

Mahnahmi absorbed all this without a flicker of emotion crossing her face. "I see. And your personal situation, Mikola Bucevit?"

"I am well, save for the large hand weapon whose muzzle is presently resting against the back of my neck."

"Understood."

More distant AAnn conversation could be heard before the *Crotase*'s captain spoke again. "You are ordered to return to the lock forthwith and surrender yourself and the rest of our people to the soldiers now stationed there. If you do this, it is promised that your interrogation will proceed without incident. If you do not, the AAnn officer here says that he cannot give any assurances. They are impatient to conclude what they consider to be a meaningful policing matter."

"So they can take complete control of the artifact. Yes, I'm sure they're very impatient. Inform the senior AAnn officer present that I will consider his requests."

"They are not requests." The captain's voice rose slightly. "Honored Officer Dysseen declares that if you do not immediately . . ."

Mahnahmi switched off the communicator and reattached it to her belt. "Time to get moving. But first you need to help me with Briony." She started toward the still-bound assassin.

"Why?" Flinx didn't move. "So she can do now what she failed to do before?"

His sister eyed him sarcastically. "After what you did to her I think she'd hesitate before trying anything like that again. We need to free her so she can help us deal with our pursuers. If we can make it back to the lock without being cut off, we might at least have the opportunity to do something."

"Do what?" he challenged her. "You heard what your captain said. The AAnn have taken control of your shuttle, posted soldiers on board, have an armed vessel of their own standing ready in the lock, and have seized your ship."

She retorted as she knelt to free the Qwarm from her bonds. "Quite true. There remains unaddressed, however, the question of how *you* got here. Or in addition to everything else do you also have the ability to teleport yourself through open space?"

To his own surprise, he found himself hesitating briefly before replying. "Only in my dreams."

Briony's hands were free. Sitting up, she immediately set about helping her employer liberate her bound legs. "I sometimes have elaborate dreams. You wouldn't like them. Like I already said, I don't much like them myself." Rising and stepping back, Mahnahmi watched while the tall, black-clad woman used her long, dexterous fingers to massage sensation back into her cramped arms and calves.

The angelic adolescent met the mature woman's gaze. "I have to get back to the lock. AAnn soldiers will be trying to cut us off and capture us."

"I heard. I know what needs to be done." The woman's voice was devoid of inflection. "From which direction are they approaching?"

Mahnahmi pointed. "Now wait a minute," Flinx began. He had no love for the assassin, or for her employer, but the unspoken implications passing between them amounted to a vow of suicide on the part of the former. He said as much. His words did not give the taller woman pause. Before he could finish enumerating his points, she had vanished into the depths of the upper corridor.

"She hasn't got a chance," he murmured. "They'll kill her."

"Of course they will." The blonde's lithe loveliness did nothing to mute the chill in her voice. "She will die a true Qwarm, defending her employer. It is how they would all seek to die. All the better for us, hmm?" With that she headed off to their right. "There are at least two other corridors over this way that might lead us back to the lock while enabling us to avoid this annoying dilemma."

He would have argued further, but the Qwarm was out of sight and out of earshot, and he could feel the AAnn drawing steadily closer. Uncomfortable at the turn of events but unable to reverse them, he followed in his sister's wake.

"They were here, honored sir." The tech reading one of the life-form sensors was transiting the compact device slowly back and forth. "They're sstill moving, but in an oppossite direction." She looked up from the instrument. "I ssurmisse that ssome of them are trying to circle around behind uss in an attempt to reach the lock without interference, while one or more remain in the immediate vicinity in an attempt to engage our attention."

"*Dssasst*—it is what I would do." Voocim was not surprised. If the humans they were tracking were half-witted, they would never have made it this far into Imperial space. Pulling her communicator, she advised those on board the *Sstakoun*'s waiting shuttlecraft as well as those currently stationed on board the human's shuttle to be alert in case their quarry should succeed in their attempt. She did not think the warning necessary, but she was nothing if not thorough. They would run these humans to ground long before they could reach the lock.

That is what she believed, anyway, until the smaller signal they were closing on dropped from its place of concealment high up in the ceiling to land in the midst of the pursuit team, firing methodically as it fell. In the controlled chaos that ensued, two of Voocim's party perished in a flurry of destruction and one was badly wounded before the single human could be slain.

Breathing hard, Voocim knelt on powerful hind legs to examine one of several severed and badly damaged alien body parts. "Female. A very motile sspecimen." She added a gesture indicative of second-degree animosity underscored by third-level admiration. "Where iss the head?"

"Over here, Commander!" another trooper shouted.

Voocim took a moment to examine the skull, but it yielded no clues as to the nature or determination of their quarry. Hopefully, the remaining humans would not prove to be as dangerous. Leaving the bodies of the dead troopers to be recovered later, she ordered her party to accelerate the pursuit. Next time, they would be the ones to shoot first.

Briony's death having bought them precious minutes, Flinx and Mahnahmi succeeded in reaching the lock without incident.

"They're coming faster." Flinx stood concentrating, eyes half closed. "We've got five, maybe ten minutes before they arrive."

"I know that!" Perspiration plastered strands of his sibling's long golden hair to her neck and shoulders. "You're not the only one who can monitor the emotions of others." Crouching low behind a perfectly matched series of dully gleaming alien cylinders, she contemplated the spacious sweep of the air lock. Stars glittered invitingly beyond the transparent barrier. Parked side by side were the shuttle from the AAnn warship and the one from the *Crotase*. The armed reptilian figure standing in the open serviceway of the *Crotase*'s shuttle flourished a slender, deadly rifle and an actively twitching tail.

"Our options are restricted." She eyed him expectantly. "Where is your ship?"

"I didn't come in a shuttle," he told her. "Individual orbital service module."

Her eyebrows arched as she scanned his face. "Individual?"

"You're not too big. We can probably both fit inside. It'll be cramped, and will put a strain on the life-support system, but should suffice for a short, quick flight. The trick will be to avoid being blown up on the way out."

She nodded understandingly. "If these ancient alien automatics act with consistency, the lock will let us out as soon as it senses our approach. If that happens, even if our flight is detected the AAnn will need time to seal both shuttles. They can notify their warship of our actions, of course, but as you say, it's a short flight. By the time they decide on a course of action, we *might* be able to make it to your ship. It mounts defenses, I presume?"

"Some." His laconic response was deliberately uninformative. "Our chances for continued survival will certainly be infinitely better on board the *Teacher* than they are sitting here waiting for pursuit to arrive."

"Then let's not waste any more time. Where's the module?"

Keeping his head down, he began to scuttle sideways, the young woman following close on his heels. They were not seen by the AAnn, who were focused on the central and largest of the three portals that led into the depths of the artifact. The soldiers had been told that according to current life-form readings, the band of human fugitives was quite small. The idea that such a group might try to overpower and take control of one of the shuttles seemed absurd. Nevertheless, those guarding the two craft remained on active alert.

Not active enough to detect the two figures scurrying along the far wall of the expansive lock, however. Keeping to cover, of which there was plenty, Flinx and Mahnahmi made it to the cluster of tall, vaguely globular constructs where he had hidden the unpretentious but efficient transport. It was just as he had left it: nose pointed outward, canopy retracted.

Activating it via the remote on his belt, he watched as the interior telltales winked to life. "Get in," he told her. "Try to scrunch up in back as much as you can. Once I lie down facing the controls, you can uncurl and try to make a little more room for yourself."

"Sure, I can handle that." Climbing into the narrow, tight-fitting space, she crouched down against the rear of the small cargo area. It was intended to hold a few personal effects, not another person, and it just barely did accommodate her lissome form.

Flinx started to join her when a burst of intense dislike flooded his mind. At the same time, something struck his right knee hard enough to send flashes of pain up his leg and over his eyes. He stumbled backward, clutching at the injured knee. Even before he hit the ground, a soft hum indicated that the transport module's canopy was closing.

Her boot. With all the high-tech weapons he had avoided these past weeks, with all the death-dealing devices devised by the science of multiple species he had dodged, he had finally been undone by a swift kick from a sharp-toed boot. Had the blow been struck by anyone else he likely would have seen it coming and in his anticipation, avoided it. But he had forgotten that while Mahnahmi was not only skilled at sensing the emotions of others, she might also be adept at concealing her own. So used had he become to sensing animosity and therefore threats in others that he had grown careless. It was no comfort to realize that Pip had not sensed the danger either. When at last it had poured out of her in sheer, undiluted strength, it had done so simultaneously with the blow she had struck, giving him no time to prepare.

By the time he had struggled to his feet, limping slightly on his throbbing leg, the canopy was shut and sealed. Pip was aloft, darting and fluttering, seeking an enemy to strike. That enemy was protected behind a layer of transparent, photosensitive plexalloy not even the minidrag's venom could penetrate.

One hand resting just above his aching knee, he stared in at her. Her voice could not reach him, of course, but he could read her lips as she thoughtfully mouthed a few final words for his benefit.

"Sorry—I need this." And she added, by way of final, sardonic farewell, "Brother."

*"Why?"* he yelled at her. She could not hear him and, if she could read his lips, chose to give no reply. How terrible the fright, he thought. How horrific the suspicion and mistrust must be to drive her to fear everyone around her—especially the one person in the inhabited Arm who at least held out the possibility of empathy and understanding.

Purring softly, the transport module powered up, forcing him to retreat beyond reach of its drive. As soon as it rose from its temporary nest among the alien globes and oblongs, there was a noticeable increase in activity on both shuttles. Flinx had no time to stand and watch.

He made it back through the nearest inner portal before his presence was noted by the AAnn on either shuttle. If consternation and confusion combined to slow reaction time among the sentinels,

Mahnahmi might well make it clear of the artifact. What she would do then he could not predict, save that it surely would not be orthodox. She would be one young woman alone and unarmed, forced to confront a captured KK-drive vessel and an armed Imperial warship.

He almost felt sorry for the unsuspecting AAnn.

With all means of flight now denied him, and a party of irritated AAnn troops in close pursuit, he had no time to spare for contemplating anyone else's course of action. Of one thing he was certain: He could not stay where he was in the hope that some miracle would deliver him back to the waiting *Teacher*. Displeased at the one prospect remaining to him but having no other obvious options and no time to ponder possibilities, he turned away from the lock and retreated back into the unfamiliar depths of the inscrutable artifact.

# CHAPTER

# 18

Commander Voocim was not pleased. Already, she had lost two troopers and had had one put out of action because of the unexpected behavior of a suicidal human. Now at least one other remained at liberty within the artifact, while a third had somehow managed to escape the snare that had been set to trap the fugitives in the docking bay.

*Nissasst,* she told herself. It was only a temporary irritation. The human who remained on the artifact would soon be apprehended, while the one who had managed the remarkable feat of fleeing into space would shortly see that effort come to naught. Already, Voocim had been advised that the first human had taken flight in a small service module or capsule capable only of traveling between orbiting vessels. Its solitary passenger would soon fetch up alongside either the *Sstakoun* or the captured Commonwealth ship, where it would then easily be taken into custody.

If Voocim was impatient to terminate the foolish human

maneuvering, which after all could only have one conclusion, the two senior scientists accompanying her were even more vocal in their desire for it to come to an end.

"Thiss iss outrageouss, truly," Tenukac declared. "The mosst important sscientific disscovery of the lasst two Imperial agess, and here we are forced to delay our sstudiess until a few renegade, intruding humanss are taken into cusstody."

"Thiss delay will be included in our official report." The female Nennasu's chosen inflection was designed to indicate her displeasure.

"As you pleasse." Voocim added a gesture of second degree contempt—Tenukac sputtered when he saw it. "Thiss iss sstill a military expedition and will remain ssuch until I officially releasse you to practice your trade. Barring any more ssurprisess or noxiouss interruptionss, I promisse you that moment will arrive sshortly."

"I sshould hope sso!" With that, Nennasu and her exasperated mate subsided, for which Voocim was more than moderately grateful.

They continued to close ground on the remaining human. It could not run forever, the commander knew. She was looking forward to interrogating so energetic and elusive a specimen. By now most humans would have realized the hopelessness of their position and submitted to the inevitable. Active though it might be, the mammal could not get off the artifact or escape the efficient technicians' relentless tracking instrumentation. Very soon, Voocim believed, it would slow, turn, and hopefully capitulate without making any more trouble. The AAnn commander had no need to remind her soldiers to be wary of a potential suicidal reprise by yet another disgruntled target. She still very much hoped to take it alive.

On board the occupied *Crotase*, Officer Dysseen was apprised by a subofficer of the impending arrival of the tiny craft.

"We have hailed the module and received no ressponsse." The AAnn's eyes flexed expectantly. "Itss approach iss being monitored by the *Sstakoun*'s predictorss. The interior iss generating a life-form ssignal conssisstent with the pressence of a ssingle human occupant, though the ssignal iss exceptionally weak and givess indication of fading. There iss no indication the craft iss armed or carrying hazardouss or explossive material. The *Sstakoun* wisshes to know if it sshould be desstroyed."

Dysseen considered. "There iss nothing ssupiciouss or evassive about itss approach arc?"

"No, honored ssir," the subofficer reported. "It iss converging on a sstraight heading for thiss vessel'ss lock."

The senior officer gestured third-degree understanding. "Allow it to arrive and dock. Monitor it clossely at all timess. We now have control of thiss sship'ss limited weaponss' ssysstemss. If thiss vehicle beginss to exhibit deviant behavior, eliminate it. If not, access itss interior immediately ssubssequent to itss arrival and bring the occupant to me."

The subofficer saluted, adding an extra fifth-degree gesture of respect, and left, leaving Dysseen to meditate on the unanticipated arrival. Guidance confirmed that the solo vehicle had recently departed the surface of the alien artifact. Clearly, it contained one of the fugitive spies who had been pursued by Commander Voocim. Its fleeing occupant would not find a sympathetic welcome waiting for it on the Commonwealth vessel. Apprehension of the single fugitive would be a routine matter. He turned his mind to other business.

The subofficer in charge of the capture party waited impatiently for the air in the lock to cycle through. Immediately following the all-clear and the separation of seals, he led his trio of troopers quickly toward the tiny vehicle. Everyone held their weapons at the ready, alert for any deceptions or tricks. Following the subofficer's directions, they spread out to flank the slim craft and waited for its occupant to emerge.

When the canopy slid back, the subofficer advanced cautiously, preceded by the muzzle of his rifle. Within the craft's cockpit lay a single human. Female, and based on the subofficer's limited knowledge of humankind, recently entered into maturity. Carefully, he prodded the prone figure with the tip of his weapon. It did not stir.

One of the troopers was equipped with a field medical pack. Hurrying forward in response to the subofficer's gesture, she ran a basal prognosticator over the motionless shape.

"No heartbeat, no resspiration in progress. There iss ssome ssuggesstion of E-pattern activity, but brain functionss appear to be virtually nonexisstent."

"Paralyssiss." The subofficer grunted noncommittally as he slung his rifle across his back. "Bring it."

"If it iss dead, or nearly sso," the soldier observed, "why not ssimply dump it into sspace?"

"Even a dead sspy iss proof of sspying. In any event, the decission is not ourss to make. Bring it, and I will conssult with Supervissing Officer Dysseen."

Hissing their displeasure, but not sharply enough to incur the subofficer's wrath, two of the troopers lifted the limp, unresisting figure out of the transport. It was not heavy. Deciding how best to proceed, each slipped a limp human arm over their shoulders, thus supporting it in an upright position. The apparently defunct organism hung slackly between them. Its head, enveloped in unfettered strands of gold-colored keratin, hung toward the floor from the flexible neck while each of its soft, pulpy arms dangled on either side of a scaly, uniformed shoulder.

They were halfway to the bridge, having passed a number of their colleagues in the corridors, when the two soldiers supporting the corpse decided to adjust its position. As one arm sprawled limply across the back of one trooper, the drooping five-fingered hand clutched convulsively around the shank of a pendant rifle. Fingers slid through the trigger guard to cover the activator. Since the weapon was slung muzzle upward, the resulting shot when two of those fingers contracted messily removed the back of the weapon owner's skull.

As the trooper collapsed, dead before he struck the deck, the human spun away from her other startled supporter while ripping the weapon that had just been fired from his deceased companion's back. A second shot blew a gaping hole in the other soldier. Meanwhile, both the subofficer and the surviving trooper were just sufficiently stunned by the speed of the "dead" human's reaction that their responses were slightly slower than usual. Two more salvos, aimed and fired with unhuman dexterity and swiftness, completed the hasty trashing of the reptilian escort.

Without pausing to see if they were dead, a startlingly revivified Mahnahmi raced in the direction of the *Crotase*'s brig. Confirmed in her assumption that arriving AAnn would first take control of her ship before landing soldiers on the artifact, she had taken the precaution of playing dead as a precondition of returning to her vessel. Subsequent developments had confirmed the wisdom of her decision. That she was possessed of certain unique abilities that enabled her to play dead better than perhaps any other member of her species had greatly facilitated the headway she had made thus far.

The last thing the sluggish solo guard posted outside the *Crotase*'s brig expected to encounter was a reason for his posting. That he realized this too late gained him no respite from Mahnahmi's unswerving attack. Within minutes she had freed the rest of her surviving crew, whose consolidated presence she had sensed from several decks below. All were present save one unfortunate engineer who had previously given rash voice to his sentiments in the presence of the AAnn commander.

Mahnahmi had moved so rapidly that the stunned escort she had coldly and efficiently liquidated still lay where they had fallen in the corridor. Arming themselves with the assortment of available AAnn weapons, the competent crew of the *Crotase* proceeded to quietly eliminate one unsuspecting trooper after another. By the time the AAnn were alerted to the unexpected insurrection in their midst, it was too late. Two more of Mahnahmi's crew died in the ensuing battle for control of the *Crotase*. Their loss saddened her because it meant the ship would not be run as efficiently on the journey homeward.

When one of the crew pointed out the wounded Dysseen as the overseer of the occupying force, Mahnahmi took care to see that he was preserved. They found him trying to transmit details of the uprising to the *Sstakoun*. Though Mahnahmi could speak passable AAnn, for the benefit of her crew she addressed the officer in Terranglo.

"Your efforts are futile. I had my engineering staff insert a cycling static pattern in the communications system before we came up here. Anyone on your ship trying to contact you would assume you were experiencing a simple malfunction and wait for it to clear before considering the possibility that something more serious had occurred. Any further attempts to report on the resurgence of my crew will meet with a quick end."

Tottering slightly from the wound beneath his fourteenth rib, Dysseen rose. "Who are you, and where did you come from? I have not sseen you before. Were you hiding ssomewhere on thiss sship?"

Her expression did not change, nor did the tenor of her voice. "This is *my* ship. I am the owner, and I just arrived back."

"Jusst arrived . . . ?" Dysseen gawked at the young human female. "You came on the transsport module! But it wass reported to me that the ssingle occupant wass dead!"

"I was. It's a little skill I've refined over the past couple of years. I find that with time and practice I can perform progressively more interesting parlor tricks. Some of them, like playing dead, really dead, turn out to have unforeseen uses. Here's another trick."

An appalling pain struck Dysseen's skull, as if someone had taken his brain in a giant fist and squeezed. When the lights of torment had begun to fade from in front of his eyes, he was able to stare at the unprepossessing female in horror.

"How—how did you accomplissh that?"

"You mean, it worked?" Mahnahmi was delighted. "That's only the second time I've tried that. The other time it was on another human, and nothing happened. How about if I try it again?"

"No, *psshassta,* no!" A frantic Dysseen executed a desperate gesture of first-degree supplication underscored by first-degree anxiety. "I beg the death of an honorable sservant of the Emperor."

"Why beg for death? Cooperate, and I'll see you put off in the same service module that brought me here. Once we're safely on our way outsystem, your people can pick you up."

Dysseen's tail flicked uneasily from side to side. "I can trusst you to do that?"

Mahnahmi shrugged. "You're welcome to choose any of your other options." She nodded meaningfully to a grim-faced crew member, who responded by raising the muzzle of the AAnn rifle he was carrying. "If it's death you prefer, I promise that you won't have to beg for it."

It took less than a minute for the suffering officer to weigh his choices. If picked up by the *Sstakoun,* he could commend himself to the mercy of the appropriate Imperial court. Rank might be degraded, but he would still be alive.

"What iss it you want from me?"

"As you know, we'll need to move several planetary diameters out before we can initiate changeover. In order for us to have the time we require, you'll have to explain our movements to your counterparts on the warship. Once we're far enough out to activate the KK-drive, I'll kick you out of the lock in the module. If you're unfamiliar with human instrumentation I'll even have one of my techs show you how to set and activate its homing beacon."

Dysseen did not need to ponder any longer on the offer. "I am agreed. But your triumph will be ssmall. You will be detected trying to leave Imperial sspace, and confronted before you can enter changeover."

"I don't think so—not if you do your job well. And, of course, no one's going to hunt us down once we're in space-plus." Her cool countenance loomed resolute before him. "Not only will we decamp safely to the Commonwealth, we'll find a way to return and take control of our rightful discovery before squabbling Imperial bureaucrats can decide what to do about it. In any case, I guarantee that you won't have to worry about it." Stepping forward, she and the *Crotase*'s chief communications tech positioned themselves before the relevant ship's systems.

"Pay attention to what I want you to say." The sidearm she held rose symbolically. "And don't try to so much as improperly inflect a syllable. I speak excellent AAnn." She proceeded to demonstrate the pertinent skill to a degree where Dysseen was suitably impressed. "Your people will wonder why you are contacting them with audio only. Explain that it is a collateral problem with the preceding static cycle that your techs are working to resolve."

Dysseen was calm, effective, and quietly eloquent. Mahnahmi was quite pleased. The *Sstakoun*'s position remained fixed as the human vessel began to adjust and modify its own, nor did the warship's weapons veer to track the *Crotase*'s movements. Despite the crew's anxieties, all maneuvers were executed progressively and without haste so as not to raise suspicions on the AAnn craft.

Mahnahmi was as good as her word. As soon as her ship had moved the requisite five planetary diameters out from the methane dwarf around which the artificial, gas-shrouded moon orbited, the AAnn officer was assisted into the compact transport module and its distress beacon activated. While he drifted clear of the *Crotase*, Dysseen was able to watch as a deep purplish red radiance took shape in front of the Commonwealth vessel's KK-drive projection dish. As the posigravity field deepened and intensified, the former prize ship slowly but with rapidly increasing speed began to move outsystem. By the time the *Sstakoun*, homing in on the module's electronic lament, began to fill his field of view, the humans' craft had long since vanished into the impenetrable depths of space-plus.

Dysseen hissed in relief. It took him a moment to realize that though his hissing had ceased, the sound itself had not. A quick glance at the vehicle's minimal instrumentation revealed the onset of an alarmingly rapid fall in atmospheric pressure. Frantically, he attempted to decipher the humanoid readouts in a frenzied attempt to discover the source of the problem. When he finally isolated it, the explanation was as elegant as the realization of what had taken place.

The outflow had not been programmed to activate until the *Sstakoun* acknowledged his position.

As he raged in silent desperation, trapped in the coffinlike transport module, a number of words the remorseless human female had spoken came back to him. She was right—he would not have to worry about what happened to the Commonwealth vessel, just as he would not have to beg for death. As a species with a highly developed sense of irony, the AAnn officer could appreciate the situation better than many others. His appreciation would have been even greater had he not been the focus of it.

He was probably still alive when those aboard the *Sstakoun*, getting no reply from the module, used grapplers to draw the tiny craft into the air lock. By the time the compartment had been properly pressurized and medical personnel were able to reach and force an opening into the vehicle, however, the honored officer was no longer able to respond. Unlike the human female, he did not possess the ability to feign his own death.

He could only limn it for real.

Moving as fast as he could, a weary Flinx penetrated farther and farther into the artifact. It did not seem to matter which way he turned or what twists he deigned to take: The proximity of pitiless AAnn emotions remained constant in his mind. The well-trained, well-conditioned soldiers recently relieved from boredom were not going to give up until they ran their quarry down. Plainly, their detection and tracking equipment was as efficient and relentless as the technicians operating it.

His heart threatened to thump a hole through his chest. Weak from fatigue, he halted and bent over, resting his hands on his knees as he fought to catch his breath. Pip fluttered solicitously in front of his face, doggedly trying to encourage her friend and companion to resume his headlong flight. He found himself wishing he could somehow borrow a portion of the minidrag's seemingly inexhaustible energy. Sensing that the AAnn closing in on him were not resting, unable to see any other course of action but refusing to yield either to them or to his fatigued body, he straightened and staggered onward.

Worst of all was the realization that he could no longer sense the emotional presence of his deceitful sister. Somehow, Mahnahmi had managed to flee from his ken. As he stumbled ever deeper into the limitless relic, he found himself wondering how much to believe of what she had told him. Without access to the sybfile she possessed, how could he really know what was true and what she had invented about his history? Was she really his legitimate sister, as seemed to be the case? Or was she just a clever adapter of information gleaned from the syb she had appropriated? Mockery seemed to be the order of the day.

Of all the people in the galaxy, *she* was the only one in possession of the erudition that could validate or invalidate her claims. *She* was the only one with access to the information he wanted and needed, the irreplaceable personal knowledge that had been explosively excised from the Terran Shell. There were others—others who were interested in him, others who were curious about his origins and abilities, perhaps even a few who knew enough to fear him. But among them one and all, as far as he knew, only she was consumed with hatred.

What he would do when his spent body would not carry him any farther he did not know. Perhaps the same mysterious, inexplicable aptitude that had previously rescued him in desperate situations would once more manifest itself. He was not comforted by the idea. A sufficiency of inscrutability seemed an inadequate recourse to rely upon.

He had been tottering down a comparatively narrow corridor when he suddenly emerged into a large room. An explosion of conduits and conductors radiated from its center. There were thin panels of self-supporting reflective material, several ornate laceworks of spun metallic glass whose functions dwelled in a land beyond elusive, and a number of free-floating geometric shapes that appeared to pulse steadily in and out of existence. In the approximate center of this farrago of strange devices a single horizontal slab that appeared to have been poured from a cauldron of molten ceramic or plastic protruded from the floor. It lodged beneath a transparent dome containing a second smaller dome that was too large to be a helmet, too small to be a body capsule.

Gaping, Flinx stumbled to a halt, his lower jaw hanging slack. Pip hovered about his head, her agitation unabated. He sensed that the pursuing AAnn were very close now. What was startling, even shocking, about the deceptively simple-looking slab-and-dome creation was neither its appearance nor its design nor its location.

It was the fact that he recognized it.

# CHAPTER

# 19

Bewildered, the strength in his legs gone, he approached the gleaming dome-covered slab as if in a waking dream. Everything was as he remembered it: the color of the slab, the sleekness of its slightly concave surface, the faint luminosity of the outer dome, the beckoning arc of the curving interior transparency that was neither glass nor plastic nor any material known to Commonwealth science. Even as he recognized it, he knew it was not the one he had seen before, some six years ago. That would have constituted an even graver, greater impossibility. This was a different one, perhaps slightly larger, but of almost identical design and construction. In identifying it, he also knew what it was. Because he had, those selfsame six years earlier, activated one just like it—or nearly so.

It was a Tar-Aiym control platform.

Memories came flooding in unbidden: Of a jovial but resolute merchant named Malaika. Of his pilot Atha Moon, who was well-nigh as comely as her name. Of two longtime acquaintances who became his friends and mentors; one human, one thranx. Of a towering monolith on a world far, far away in a place of sterility and mystery humans called the Blight. Of himself, concerned for an unexpectedly cataleptic Pip, entering a dome identical to the one that now rose before him. Dizziness ensuing, followed by pain, confusion, resistance. Then acquiescence, an overwhelming brightness, and a kind of numbing enlightenment, as if a smothering had been cleared from his mind. Since that time, that moment, he had never been quite the same.

Alien phrases reached his ears: rising, sibilating voices fraught with anticipation, coming closer. He had felt the deaths of at least two AAnn together with that of the self-sacrificing Qwarm Briony. As was the case with any feeling sentients, the reptiloids did not take kindly to those who killed while fleeing. Under such circumstances it was reasonable to assume that his interrogation would be harsh and his future unpromising.

If he entered into the dome, there was an excellent chance nothing whatsoever would happen. Should that be the case, then he would lose nothing by the trying. If, on the other hand, anything transpired, however unobtrusive, it might be enough to cause the AAnn to pause and reconsider, or even to decide that the apprehension of a single human was not worth challenging the unknown. He remembered the seemingly innocuous iridescent film that had forcefully assimilated nearly all the members of Mahnahmi's exploration party. The same fate or worse might await him beneath the glistening dome. Could it be worse than being taken prisoner by the AAnn? If nothing else, it was certain to be quicker.

Poised on the brink of discovery was not a bad place to perish. As shouts of expectation reached him, he came to a final decision and strode forward. Reaching the dome, he took a deep breath as if preparing to duck underwater, stepped inside, and lay down flat on the slab. It was cool against his back and designed to accommodate a body far more massive than that of any human. Above him, the partial inner and more complete outer domes displayed a confusion of incomprehensible schematics sculpted solid and multidimensional from alien materials. Puzzled and a little disconcerted, Pip folded her wings and landed on his shoulder.

Nothing happened. The domes remained as he had first seen them from a distance, the lighting in the chamber ample but subdued. He could hear clearly the voices of the pursuing AAnn as they entered the room. This was a waste of time, a useless exercise, he decided. His legs felt a little better. He determined to make an attempt to resume running, to delay his capture until the last possible moment. Grimacing slightly at a mild cramp in one thigh, he started to rise from the slab. As he did so, something moved against him.

Curled into a tight, fetal ball of coiled muscle, Pip was twitching to an unheard rhythm. Her trembling was steadfast and regular, as if something more than her breathing pattern had changed. As he stared, something danced past his face less than a meter in front of his eyes. It was a ball of red-gold energy that pulsed like a live thing. Captivated by its silent beauty, he watched it drift sideways until it made contact with the wall of the outer dome. There it was promptly absorbed, its light and substance dissipating into the photoporous material like water into a sponge. Tilting back his head, his gaze fell on the interior surface of the inner dome.

Like lavender fireflies, a thousand lights were dancing within the curving transparency.

Shivering slightly, he closed his eyes and lay back down. The coiled weight of Pip, his companion since childhood, was unreasonably reassuring against his neck and shoulder. An inner peace slipped over him like a blanket. He was entering a place he had been before, related yet different. And this time, unlike the first, there was no pain.

Weapons at the ready, Voocim and her soldiers rounded a bend in the corridor along which they had been racing. Leading the way, the techs operating the life-form sensors were the first to enter the chamber. So sharply did they pull up, their sandaled feet catching against the slightly ribbed decking, that they were nearly run over by those soldiers following close behind. Like her troops, the commander was forced to raise a clawed hand to shield her eyes.

Dominating the center of the chamber they had entered was a slightly elevated dais upon which rested a kind of couch or bench. This was covered with an outer dome of some glassy material that presently was ablaze with integrated green-and-gold fire. Occasional upheavals of coruscating cobalt blue detonated in the depths of the prismatic tempest like thunderbolts within a storm cloud. From the surface of the profound turbulence, globes and streaks of dynamic energy leaped in all directions, as if escaping from the concentrated inner uproar.

Subofficer Amuruun raised a hand and pointed. "The human iss there, Honored Commander!"

"I ssee it!" Voocim hesitated. "It appearss to have activated ssome kind of localized energy field."

"But how. . . ?" The subofficer gestured fifth-degree uncertainty while his expression revealed the first inkling of fear.

Voocim saw she would have to act quickly. "An automatic reaction on the part of the artifact, no different from the activating of lightss along the corridorss we have been ussing or the operation of the large air lock when confronted by an arriving sship. The human iss operating nothing, becausse there iss nothing here a human can operate. Or an AAnn, or anyone elsse. It iss a dessperation act on the part of the fugitive. It iss also an inssufficient one." Casually raising a hand, she executed the appropriate gesture.

"As you know, I would prefer to have the human alive. Corpssess are notorioussly unressponsive to quesstioning." The attempt at humor had a calming effect on Amuruun and the rest of the troopers. "Fire a warning sshot at the lower end of the sstructure. That sshould rouse the human and alsso put an end to thiss dramatic but harmless dissplay."

Obediently, the subofficer stepped forward and took careful aim with his own rifle. A graceful weapon designed to be carried easily, it threw a shell whose diminutive size belied its striking power. The almost imperceptible flash that was lost in the glare from the domes was accompanied by a brief but violent exhalation from the side of the weapon.

The shell struck the dome where it disappeared into the opaque dais. A momentary flare was visible at the point of impact—and that was all. The structure of the dome was not breached, and the explosion did nothing to quell the colorful conflagration that continued to rage in and about its surface. Voocim expressed irritation.

"Again," she ordered. Gesturing acknowledgment, the subofficer took another step forward and raised the muzzle of his weapon anew. This time he aimed beneath the outer dome at the base of the slab that was supporting the recumbent human.


Something unimaginably profound within the inorganic bowels of the artifact had just concluded an extensive review and analysis of preponderant reality. Among several thousand other factors newly apprised, it had determined that a single A-class mind was present and functioning. This exhibited an aberrant structure, but one that was at least ascertainable. Other minds were present that were not

A-class. Furthermore, these were engaged in irritant activities. ETTA energies responded. Dismissing the observed proximate beings as a negligible distraction to be briskly dealt with, that which had sluggishly begun to stir moved on to more consequential activities.

A skull-sized globe of flickering azure incandescence burst forth from the apex of the outer dome and flew straight toward Amuruun. Uttering a startled oath, he tried to duck away from the onrushing ball of blue fire. He did not succeed. The globe touched him on the upper arm. There was a momentary flash of sapphire light, a faint smell of ozone, and a lingering but rapidly dissipating coil of pale blue vapor corkscrewing its way upward into nonexistence where an instant before the subofficer had been standing. Voocim gaped at the hovering sphere of animated effulgence. Darting to its right, it made contact with another horrified soldier. As he threw up his clawed hands in a futile attempt at defense, another flash was replaced by a second wisp of evaporating bluish haze. At this, the rest of the troop broke and ran.

Their commander ran too, her legs pumping, powerful thigh muscles propelling her back up the corridor. Screams and hissing howls of desperation followed close behind. The two senior scientists were shouting also, trying to communicate something instead of simply shrieking in fear. From time to time there was an occasional flash and smell. Gradually, the outcries became fewer, the blue flashes more infrequent.

Gasping for breath, Voocim threw herself behind a massive bulwark of somber gray polycarbide. The corridor was silent, the illumination balanced and restrained. She huddled like that, alone and hunched over, her scaly epidermis squeezed tight against the protective palisade. Would the cerulean specter grow tired and return to the luminous chamber? The *Sstakoun*'s shuttle waited in the lock. It was still an appreciable distance away, but like all her kind she was a strong, powerful runner. Given even a momentary respite from pursuit, she felt she would be able to make it safely back to the ship.

Slowly, cautiously, she rose, straightening a little at a time to peer over the edge of the bulwark. The exotic material was warm to the touch, almost ductile despite its apparent solidity. Her eyes widened.

The silent sphere of indigo energy that hung motionless in the air less than an arm's length from her face had no eyes, but it saw her anyway.

Lambent orbs of refulgent energy drifted lazily back toward the blazing dome, to be reabsorbed into its energetic essence. Green-and-gold phlogistons grew intermittent, then scarce. Sequentially, full transparency returned to the structure. The volume of light in the chamber dropped from overpowering, to bright, to a pastel normalcy.

Flinx blinked. He was still tired, but otherwise unhurt. Sitting up, his first thought was for Pip. She was already aloft, fluttering outside the domes, waiting for him to join her.

He rubbed the back of his neck. Something had happened after he had entered the dome. He had gone to sleep, for how long he did not know. A glance at one of the compact instruments attached to his service belt provided the answer. Strange—his period of unconsciousness had seemed longer.

Remembering his pursuers, he looked up sharply. The chamber, as well as the corridors beyond, were deserted. Had they changed their minds, or at the last minute decided to take another route? His good fortune was hard to believe. Could dome and distance have kept them from noticing him? Tentatively, he slid off the slab. It was still cool on contact. Entering the corridor, he searched for signs of his stalkers. Finding none, unable to perceive any emotions save his own, he started forward at a hesitant trot, trying to maintain a steady pace in the event he suddenly had to change direction. Though he felt confident his talent was still working, he was puzzled by his inability to detect even the faintest twinge of emotion from so much as a single AAnn.

Tradssij was standing before an impressive array of readouts, idly scanning and committing to memory mundane ship data while wondering if something more might have been done to save the unfortunate Officer Dysseen from the perfidy of the escaped humans, when technician Osilleel approached.

"Honored Captain, there iss ssomething you musst look at."

Amenable, Tradssij followed the tech to her station. Above the projector lens, a full three-dimensional depiction of the tenth planet of Pyrassis, its moon, and its immediate spatial surroundings hovered in stasis. Taking her seat, the technician slipped her induction headset back over her scales. Immediately, the image transposed, the view zooming in to resolve on a reduced area. It showed the artifact, still partially cloaked in its dissimulating synthetic atmosphere. The confiscated human starship continued to occupy concordant coordinates.

The same, however, could not be said for the artifact.

Tradssij leaned forward, his prominent snout almost piercing the projection. "What iss happening here, technician?"

Osilleel replied in an awed tone of voice that showed she too was being affected by what they were seeing. Every other tech and officer in the vicinity had also turned to stare.

"The artifact iss dropping toward the ssurface of the planet,

Honored Captain. It hass not entered into a declining orbit. The descent is vertical, in contravention of normal gravitational preceptss."

*"Barrisshsst."* Tradssij snarled softly. Without hesitation, he proceeded to give orders. "Inform our people aboard the sshuttle to evacuate their possition immediately and return to the *Sstakoun.* We will come forward to meet them, dock, and bring them back aboard as quickly as possible."

Behind him, a subofficer voiced what everyone was thinking. "Captain—Commander Voocim, the sscientific complement that iss traveling with her, and the resst of the exploration-and-capture team are sstill insside the artifact."

"Truly," Tradssij replied in the clipped tones of command, adding an especially brusque gesture of second-degree concern coupled with first-degree comprehension. "However, until we are able to asscertain exactly what iss happening, I will rissk no more of my crew than iss necessary. In the abssence of communication or explanation from the landing party, I musst do what I believe to be mosst efficaciouss under the circumsstancess. When the ssituation hass sstablized, the sshuttle will be ssent back to the artifact to remove Commander Voocim and her group."

No argument arose from those AAnn on station. All felt the captain's ratiocination of the situation to be accurate as well as succinct. Adjusting course, the *Sstakoun* began to move toward the regressing artifact and away from the place where it had recovered the transport module containing the body of Officer Dysseen.

Flinx arrived outside the lock less out of breath than he had expected. The continuing dearth of any AAnn emotions found him puzzled but relieved. Here, at least, he had expected to perceive something, only to be confronted with no evidence of feeling sentience but his own.

The reason for the absence of any significant reptilian emotion was immediately apparent: Only one vessel remained within the lock, and it was not AAnn. As near as he could detect, there were no longer any guards aboard the craft from the *Crotase*, either. Having escaped in Flinx's transport module, Mahnahmi had left her own shuttlecraft behind.

But why had all the AAnn gone? Had their starship fled orbit as well? Too many events of the past hour were inexplicable. Still, comprehensible or not, the indisputable fact was that he was alive and free.

Nothing and no one challenged him as he entered the lock and cautiously made his way toward and eventually into the unsealed shuttlecraft. The internal layout was relatively typical, the majority of shuttles being built along certain fundamental, common lines. Like all such craft, it was designed to be operated with little effort or training. As he studied the readouts, Flinx felt increasingly confident it would respond to his simple, straightforward instructions.

He felt even more sure of himself when the ship's systems activated in response to his first verbal command. Given the most generalized coordinates and description, the shuttle's automatics would be able to lock onto the *Teacher* and home in on her. Barring surprises, within a short while he would finally be back on board his own ship, surrounded by its familiar confines. He found he could barely contain his anticipation. Pip darted contentedly around the bridge, reveling in her companion's first upbeat emotions in some time. And still he could not sense the menacing presence of any potentially contentious AAnn.

Now that it was almost over, his only regret was that after all he had been through and everything he had suffered, beginning with his sojourn on Earth and ending in this abject outback corner of the AAnn Empire, he had failed to recover the sybfile containing the precious information about his ancestry. It remained with Mahnahmi. As the shuttle cleanly exited the cavernous lock, he found himself once more contemplating the panoply of unfamiliar stars. The syb was out there, she was out there with it, and he did not doubt that he would encounter both of them again.

That was when the shuttle's automatics announced, in a clear and emotionless male voice, that a starship other than the one he had chosen as a destination was approaching swiftly from several planetary diameters out.

The *Sstakoun*'s weapons master hovered close to his captain, his intricate induction headset a triple metallic band that traversed the upper portion of his golden-scaled skull. Together the two AAnn studied the dimensional projection that showed the Commonwealth shuttle departing the massive, rapidly descending artifact.

"Report," Tradssij hissed.

A technician responded without looking up. "Detection iss weak at thiss range, Honored Captain, but preliminary sscans indicate only two organic life-forms aboard the fleeing vessel."

"Mark itss coursse," Tradssij spoke sharply. "Highesst ressolution quadrant sscan."

Sounding surprised, another technician reported in a moment later. "Gravitational dissturbance collateral with a massked vessel exisstss at point two-four-five, hypothessizing forward from vissible smaller craft'ss pressent trajectory."

Tradssij was quietly furious. "We have been indolent. That sshall be corrected." He gestured appropriately to weapons master Haurcchep. "Extirpate."

The senior officer responded accordingly, relaying the command together with the necessary ancillary instructions to the fire control team situated elsewhere on the ship. A component of the *Sstakoun*'s limited but deadly arsenal was activated.

Aboard the shuttle, Flinx scrutinized the projection that showed the AAnn vessel rapidly closing on his coordinates. There was nothing he could do. The shuttle was not designed to execute elaborate evasive maneuvers, and the light armament it carried would not penetrate a warship's minimum defensive field. Maybe they were just coming in for a closer look. If only they held off long enough for him to board the *Teacher*, he felt he would be able to hold his own. The Ulru-Ujurrians had equipped it with more than adequate defenses. But as long as he was stuck on the slow-moving shuttle, he was helpless.

The shuttlecraft's voice directed his attention to the other tridimensional display. Intending only to glance in its direction, he ended up staring at it for a very long time. Then, realizing he had no need of onboard technology to perceive what was being manifested, he turned and walked to the unpretentious viewport that curved around the forepart of the ship. Everything that had been delineated in the tridee display was as apparent to the naked eye as it had been to the shuttle's monitors. There was no need for magnifying devices or vision-enhancing instrumentation. Whether he altogether believed what he was seeing was another matter entirely.

Thousands upon thousands of square kilometers of dense cloud cover, dull brown and bronze tinged with orange, faded yellow, and red, had begun to shrink from the periphery of the methane dwarf. Not by means of simple evaporation or from being blown out into space due to some inexplicable internal cataclysm, but in response to a powerful unknown force that was sucking clouds, upwellings, and entire storm systems inexorably downward. As the thick, abyssal atmosphere was thinned, the inner core of the swirling planet began to reveal itself. Like a few other methane dwarves, Pyrassis Ten boasted a solid center. Unlike the heart of similar celestial bodies, the tenth planet of the Pyrassisian system brought to light an albedo that was off the charts.

Perhaps because it had been polished.

As the enshrouding atmosphere of the gigantic globe was drawn forcibly downward into a complex of gargantuan vents and intakes, the serrated surface of the inner planetary core was exposed. Billions of lights, intensely brilliant and of multiple hues, began to wink to life within the crust of synthetic structures the size of small continents. From a rather dull orb of ordinary aspect, the tenth planet of Pyrassis's sun was metamorphosing rapidly into the most dazzling sight in the immediate heavens.

As torrents of cloaking atmosphere the size of whole mountain ranges continued to flow into unfathomable depths, they threw off continual salvos of lightning tens of kilometers high. The towering electrical discharges struck the shimmering surface of the newly exposed core without visible effect. As Flinx looked on in awestruck silence with Pip cuddled close to his neck, the artifact he had first thought to be a moon continued to approach the core's solid surface. Only when it seemed as if a devastating impact was inevitable did a portion of the planetary crust retract ponderously inward. Descending gradually and under flawless control, the artifact concluded a stately entrance into a holding bay capacious enough to admit a real moon.

Big enough to boast its own atmosphere, the artifact, whose size had stunned him when the inorganic nature of its origin had first been revealed, was nothing more than a lifeboat. It was the tenth planet of the Pyrassisian system that was the actual *ship*. Staring hard at the gleaming surface and the manifold diverse projections with which it was studded, a chill traveled through Flinx unlike any other he had ever experienced—because he recognized at least a few of those lofty, monumental shapes. Subsequent magnification on the dimensional display only confirmed identification of an image he had resurrected from memory.

Clearly visible on the curving, burnished exterior of the artificial globe were no less than a dozen krangs, the ancient Tar-Aiym weapon that was capable of dynamically generating and projecting forth a Schwarzchild discontinuity. It was a device, a weapon, against which nothing could stand. If symmetry held, still more of them were likely to be found on the other side of the exposed surface. As to the multitudinous other revealed protrusions and concavities, the intent behind their ominous contours and configurations could barely begin to be inferred.

Half a million or more years old, the tenth planet of the Pyrassisian system was a Tar-Aiym warship twice the size of Earth.

And it was waking up.

Aboard the *Sstakoun*, surprise and astonishment at the planetary transformation they had been observing turned to fright underscored by second-degree panic. As Tradssij and his officers shouted and argued over what to do next, it did not occur to anyone to countermand the just-given order to fire at the evacuating Commonwealth shuttlecraft. A few seconds too late, it struck the captain of the AAnn ship with appalling realization that dispatching explosive devices in the general direction of the newly revealed colossus might be interpreted by an unknown sentience as something other than a benevolent gesture. Stammering excitedly into the tiny voice pickup that hovered alongside his snout, he frantically tried to rescind the order.

Deep within ancient factitious profundities impenetrable to human or AAnn thought, the synthetic sentience that was the sequentially awakening Tar-Aiym vessel detected a threat directed at the only A-class mind in the immediate astral vicinity. Though the ship was far, far from fully operational, it determined that it was capable of taking certain unassuming measures to countermand the impending danger. As concentric rings of turbulent light expanding to the diameter of a small sea erupted from its summit, a single imposing device of Himalayan dimensions discharged a blinding fork of lightninglike energy so intensely purple it was almost black. When this intercepted the pair of individually powered incoming explosive devices, they vaporized in twin puffs of scattered particles.

His glistening, scale-covered throat suddenly drier than even a desert-loving AAnn would have experienced, a solemn and oddly distracted Tradssij XXKKW pensively voiced the order for the *Sstakoun* to power up its posigravity drive despite the fact that they were too close in-system for reliable activation. It did not matter. A drive field had barely begun to form within the nexus of the ship's KK-drive projector when the *Sstakoun* was struck by a second compacted helix of furious energy emitted by the azoic planetary core. The result was that the space hitherto occupied by the AAnn warship was forthwith filled with a somewhat larger volume of rapidly dissipating particles from whose constituent atoms every last electron had been forcibly stripped.

Flinx watched the implausible awful transpire. Not unreasonably, he wondered if he might be next. But nothing happened. There was no follow-up, no third eruption of desolating energy. Except for the stable, progressive emergence of thousands and thousands of additional lights on the uneven surface of the planet-sized alien warship, no new or startling class of resplendent power revealed itself.

He thought back to his brief, enigmatic slumber atop the Tar-Aiym control platform. For whatever reason, the majestic and incomprehensibly ancient vessel below had resolved not to look upon him as an enemy. Whether that apparent decision constituted a permanent or temporary state of affairs he had no way of knowing—and he was not about to tarry in the vicinity to find out.

Several excited exchanges with the *Teacher* served to clarify the status of the approaching shuttlecraft. Flinx was not displeased to note that he had acquired a replacement for the one he had crashed on Pyrassis, though he wished the method of acquisition could have been otherwise. He genuinely regretted the premature death of any sentient being, even an AAnn.

His relief upon exiting the interior air lock to find himself once more within the comforting, familiar confines of his own ship was immense. Even the smell of it was exhilarating. Without pausing, he headed directly for the bridge. As he passed through the lounge where he tended to spend the majority of his time while traveling in space-plus, he noted absently that the decorative flora that had been presented to him by the considerate citizens of the distant planet its inhabitants called Midworld appeared to have held up exceptionally well in his absence. Oddly, there were even a few fragments of soil scattered across the otherwise spotless deck; moist terrestrial blemishes occupying locations unexpectedly far from their planters. No doubt a consequence of sluggish, limited movement by the burgeoning alien growths with whose intimate characteristics he was not yet wholly familiar. He made a mental note to see to it that the ship's hygienics system was careful to recycle the scraps. In space, dirt was a precious commodity.

The bridge greeted his arrival contentedly, as if he had never been away, as if nothing untoward had occurred in his absence. As if the vapor-shrouded planet-sized body outside the port had not been unexpectedly transformed from an apparently ordinary methane dwarf orbiting an unremarkable star in a notably undistinguished star system to the most inconceivable and improbable discovery since the revelation that humans shared the galaxy with other intelligent species.

In addition to being the most unbelievable and improbable of its kind, the discovery was also, potentially, the most dangerous.

What would happen when he left? Abandoned once more to its isolated orbit, would the artifact regenerate its mantle of dense, artificially spawned methane atmosphere, resuming once again the appearance of a dreary, mundane world? And what of the effortlessly annihilated AAnn? Had they managed before their abrupt and absolute demise to communicate the true nature of their find to others of their kind? What about the departed Mahnahmi? If he was capable of activating a Tar-Aiym control platform, could she not do the same? The thought of a tool of true ultimate destruction the size and power of the artifact falling into the hands of his hate-filled sister raised possibilities too dreadful to contemplate. What could he do to prevent her return? If he warned the AAnn against her, they would uncover the nature of the artifact for themselves. He seemed to have few choices—all of them bad.

As it turned out, resolution and solution were provided by the artifact itself. Very soon following his return to the succoring confines of his ship, the alien orb began to move. Because of its unnatural proportions he did not notice the initial activity, and had to be alerted to the change by the *Teacher*.

"You're sure it's moving?" Gazing out the port at the immense, now internally illuminated sphere, it was difficult to ascertain any motion by sight alone.

"Yes, Flinx." The ship's AI was quietly emphatic. "Velocity is increasing exponentially and will shortly become salient to the unassisted human eye. There is evidence of the activation of a posigravity field of unparalleled dimensions evolving in the vicinity of what might freely be designated as the northern pole."

As always, the AI's analysis was correct. It was not long before Flinx could perceive not only movement but the blossoming of the space-distorting drive field as well.

"It's going to have to move a lot farther than an orbit or two out-system if it's going to safely initiate any kind of changeover," he murmured, as much to himself as to the ship.

"Though in the absence of sufficient data I am unable to accurately compute mass, I would estimate the minimum secure distance for safe activation at not less than three-quarters of a local AU. Given no suspension of the speed at which the artifact continues to accelerate, it should reach that point in approximately two hours and thirty-four minutes."

"Then," Flinx declared with some alacrity, "we had better get moving ourselves." Reacting to her companion's surge of anxiety, Pip rose from his shoulder to hover solicitously above and behind him.

The *Teacher* replied to the assumption without remarking on its owner's lack of specifics. "Shall I enter coordinates and initiate preparations for entry into space-plus?"

"Yes. Take us out and stand ready for changeover. I'll supply a destination, but I want to remain in normal space until I see what happens. So long as we keep at a safe distance, we shouldn't have any problems."

The field being generated by the artifact continued to amplify to an extent that would have astonished Alex Kurita and Sumako Kinoshita, the architects of the first KK-drive. Two hours and thirty-six minutes after it had first begun to move, the artifact blurred briefly, was engulfed in an intense burst of celestial radiance, and vanished. A deeply contemplative Flinx spent a long time gazing at the empty space the evanesced world-ship had occupied. At what point in time would the AAnn notice that the system of Pyrassis now encompassed nine and not ten worlds? To what incomprehensible phenomena would they ascribe the inconceivable anomaly? People lost track of credits and diminutive personal effects and small items of clothing—not planets.

The important thing was that it was gone from where it had been, had taken itself elsewhere, was no longer where it had been known to be. Perhaps, he reflected thoughtfully, having been reanimated after a slumber of half a million years only to find itself with no traditional enemy to fight, it had gone in search of updated orders. If that was the case, it would go looking for them in the Blight. There it could wander harmlessly forever, in the vast stellar region of systems rendered sterile by the prehistoric war between the Tar-Aiym and the Hur'rikku, unmolested by bellicose AAnn or Hatharc, Quillp or Branner, human or thranx.

Most important of all, it would be far from Mahnahmi's grasp. Some day, he knew, he would have to deal decisively with his sister. Or she with him.

But for now, he was free of such onerous concerns. Free to roam again in search of enlightenment and wisdom. It did not occur to him to travel in search of amusement, or simply for diversion. He did not have the mind-set. Pensive but no longer apprehensive, he absently began to caress the back of Pip's head as she settled down again onto his shoulder. Soothed by the steady motion of his fingertips and the warmth of his body, she closed her eyes and went to sleep, her coils taut against him.

As he provided the *Teacher* with a destination and the ship obediently set about making preparations for changeover, he found himself wishing he had been more fully cognizant of what had taken place while he had been lying semiconscious on the Tar-Aiym control platform. While grateful for the outcome, it would have been nice to know how he had done what he had done: how much of it had been a consequence of his and Pip's actions, and how much that of the artifact acting on its own. Perhaps it was just as well that he did not. He would have been both dumfounded and stunned by an explanation that was at once simplistic, incredibly convoluted, and pregnant with measureless meaning for far more than his own, singular future.

Everything that had happened from the moment he had lain down on the platform had occurred because the planet had been talking to a plant.

# A NOTE ON THE HISTORY OF INTERSTELLAR TRAVEL

Those with a taste for history know that the modern KK-drive that powers Commonwealth ships swiftly across vast interstellar distances was invented in 2280 A.D. by the husband and wife team of post-graduate students Alex Kurita and Sumako Kinoshita, of the technologically advanced Namerican tribe.

Working in the field of applied high-energy physics, the couple was initially drawn to the pioneering work of the German mathematicians Theodor Kaluza and Oskar Klein not because of their theories, but because, by one of those wonderful bits of serendipity that inform the entire history of science, the two men happened to have the same last initials as the married students.

With Einstein having previously shown that gravity arises from the four-dimensional curvature of space-time, the two Germans worked to demonstrate how the electromagnetic force arose from a fifth dimension, an unheard-of concept in 1919 A.D. According to the Kaluza-Klein theory, each point in normal space is actually a loop in the fifth dimension. Studying higher energy KK echoes of Z and Y bosons at the Winnipeg greater particle accelerator, Kurita and Kinoshita were able to develop a practical means for generating quantum gravity. Engineering designs based on their equations resulted in the construction of the first Caplis generator, variations of which power all interstellar vessels by accelerating them to speeds that allow them to slip into the fifth dimension, more commonly known today by its colloquial designation, space-plus. Later work by others building upon the work of Kaluza-Klein and Kurita-Kinoshita led to the discovery of a practical means for sending communications as resonating loops through the sixth dimension, or space-minus.

—*Excerpted from* A Technological History of the Commonwealth, *supervising ed. Repinski & Mutombu; Heidelberg University Press, Europe, Terra; volume 446. All rights reserved, known space and multiple dimensions.*

# ABOUT THE AUTHOR

ALAN DEAN FOSTER has written in a variety of genres, including hard science fiction, fantasy, horror, detective, western, historical, and contemporary fiction. He is also the author of numerous nonfiction articles on film, science, and scuba diving, as well as novel versions of several films including *Star Wars*, the first three *Alien* films, and *Alien Nation*. His novel *Cyber Way* won the Southwest Book Award for Fiction in 1990, the first science fiction work ever to do so.

Foster's love of the far-away and exotic has led him to travel extensively. He's lived in Tahiti and French Polynesia, traveled to Europe, Asia, and throughout the Pacific, and has explored the back roads of Tanzania and Kenya. He has rappelled into New Mexico's fabled Lechugilla Cave, panfried pirhana (lots of bones, tastes a lot like trout) in Peru, white-water rafted the length of the Zambezi's Batoka Gorge, and driven solo the length and breadth of Namibia.

Foster and his wife, JoAnn Oxley, reside in Prescott, Arizona, in a house built of brick that was salvaged from a turn-of-the-century miners' brothel. He is presently at work on several new novels and media projects.

For further information on the Commonwealth and other worlds of Alan Dean Foster, try this Web site: alandeanfoster.com